Crumpets And Cowpies

by
SHANNA HATFIELD

Crumpets and Cowpies

Copyright © 2015 by Shanna Hatfield

All rights reserved.

ISBN-13: 978-1505403213
ISBN-10: 1505403219

Shanna Hatfield
shanna@shannahatfield.com
shannahatfield.com

Special thanks to Hardway for sharing his great photos of Eastern Oregon!

To Jemma -
You've been such an inspiration to me
and I'm grateful every single day
for the privilege of knowing you...

Books by Shanna Hatfield

FICTION

CONTEMPORARY

Love at the 20-Yard Line
The Coffee Girl
The Christmas Crusade
Learnin' the Ropes
QR Code Killer

Holiday Bride Series
Valentine Bride

Rodeo Romance Series
The Christmas Cowboy
Wrestlin' Christmas
Capturing Christmas

Grass Valley Cowboys Series
The Cowboy's Christmas Plan
The Cowboy's Spring Romance
The Cowboy's Summer Love
The Cowboy's Autumn Fall
The Cowboy's New Heart
The Cowboy's Last Goodbye

Women of Tenacity Series
Heart of Clay
Country Boy vs. City Girl
Not His Type

HISTORICAL

Baker City Brides
Crumpets and Cowpies
Thimbles and Thistles
Corsets and Cuffs

Pendleton Petticoats Series
Dacey
Aundy
Caterina
Ilsa
Marnie
Lacy
Bertie

Hardman Holidays
The Christmas Bargain
The Christmas Token
The Christmas Calamity
The Christmas Vow

NON-FICTION

Farm Girl
Fifty Dates with Captain Cavedweller

Savvy Entertaining Series
Savvy Holiday Entertaining
Savvy Spring Entertaining
Savvy Summer Entertaining
Savvy Autumn Entertaining

Chapter One

Liverpool, England
September 1890

"I could ravish you with kisses."

The urge to press his lips to the firm, unmoving surface beneath his feet nearly overcame Thane Jordan. Gratitude filled him as he placed his cowboy boots on solid ground and glanced back at the ship that had served as his floating home for the past thirteen days.

"Merciful heavens!" A feminine voice, gasping in shock, drew his attention to his immediate right. A matronly woman with an attractive girl at her side gaped at him. "Well, I never, sir!"

Thane tipped his hat to the young woman, winking roguishly. Slowly turning to her affronted chaperone, he gave her a thorough once-over. "Maybe you should, ma'am. Your bloomers might not be in such a tight bunch if you did."

"Oh!" Insulted, the woman spun around, grabbing her young charge by the arm and marching away from the pier where passengers continued to disembark. The girl smiled coyly at him before disappearing into the crowd.

Thane chuckled at their hasty retreat. He could have simply explained he aimed his comment at the ground he stood on, not either of them, but he found inordinate satisfaction in irking the uptight woman. He held little regard for propriety and bucked it every opportunity he could.

Removing his hat, he raked a hand through his dark blond hair, grown long from his continued procrastination of visiting a barber. After replacing the Stetson on his head, he rubbed at the scruff growing on his face and frowned at the ship behind him.

If a desperate need to return to his ranch in eastern Oregon didn't force his impending journey back across the ocean, he'd refuse to leave dry land again. No wonder his brother, Henry, chose to stay in England instead of sailing back to New York when he left fourteen years earlier.

Thoughts of his brother made his chest constrict with unwarranted pain. He picked up his leather traveling bag in one hand and propelled his feet forward, still a little wobbly on his legs as he adjusted to being on land again.

He'd spent most of the time aboard ship seasick. Every movement up and down with the waves sent his stomach churning.

Determined to wipe the misery from his mind, he wanted to find somewhere he could soak in a hot bath, eat a decent meal, and sleep through the night.

Instead, he walked along the pier, taking in the stacks and stacks of cotton bales. Most of the world's raw cotton traveled through Liverpool's ports. Cotton was the reason Henry left America and Thane moved to Oregon.

Once he reached the street, Thane hailed a hansom cab and handed the driver the address of Henry's solicitor, a man named Arthur Weston.

A month ago, Thane looked up from fixing fence on his sprawling cattle ranch to see his friend Tully Barrett racing across the pasture toward him. The telegram he delivered, from Mr. Weston, informed Thane that Henry passed away from injuries sustained when he took a fall from his horse.

Named as Henry's sole beneficiary, the missive from Weston asked that Thane make immediate arrangements to travel to England to settle his brother's estate. A flurry of telegram messages passed between the two men as Thane demanded to know why he needed to make the journey. Weston provided vague responses, continuing to insist he come.

Finally giving in to the solicitor's unyielding request he attend to matters in person, Thane tied up loose ends on the ranch. He left with Tully's promise to keep watch over the place until his return.

The train carried him from Baker City, Oregon, across the country to New York City. He booked passage on the first boat headed to Liverpool and regretted leaving the peaceful sagebrush-dotted hills of his ranch with every mile the ship crossed on the open sea.

As he settled himself against the smooth leather seat of the cab, Thane took a deep breath, inhaling the scents of saltwater, fish, coal, and roasting meat. Hungry after days of illness with little more to eat than hardtack and soda crackers, the rich aroma of the meat made his stomach rumble.

"Solicitor, bath, then food," he muttered as the cab rolled along cobblestone-paved streets, lined with lamps and neat brick buildings standing three and four stories high.

Men in top hats strolled beside women dressed in the latest styles, enjoying an afternoon outing in the warmth of the sun.

Since he spent the majority of his time alone or with his hired hands, Thane possessed limited knowledge about women's fashions, other than what his friend Maggie tried to teach him. He held no interest in seeking an education on the matter. As long as his female counterparts appeared pleasing to the eye, he didn't care what they wore.

However, the finely dressed women drew his gaze while the passing scenery captured his admiration.

While the cab traversed down the busy street, he took in a store with a cutlery sign in the window just a few doors down from a café. A hotel sign hung high overhead, welcoming guests. Making note of the location of both the hotel and café, Thane decided he might soon be able to find a filling meal and a comfortable bed.

The cab finally pulled to a stop in front of a red brick building with ornate gold lettering painted on the shiny glass windows.

"'Ere we are, good chap. Mr. Weston's office is up on the second floor, it 'tis." The cabby grinned at Thane as he stepped out of the conveyance and paid him. Thane tipped his hat to the cabby and started toward the door.

"Do ye need me to wait for ye, sir? 'Appy to wait for ye." The cabby gave him a hopeful glance, grateful for the generous tip Thane included with his fare.

"You best move along. I don't know how long I'll be here or where I'm going when I leave." Thane nodded to him again and turned the knob on the door, stepping inside the building and staring at a broad set of wooden stairs.

Resolute, he jogged up the steps and read a large brass sign hanging on the wall, finding Mr. Weston's name among those listed. A few paces down a corridor, he knocked on a door bearing the man's name and opened it.

A pale, slight young man glanced up from a desk covered in papers and files, pushing a pair of round spectacles up the bridge of his nose.

"May I assist you, sir?"

Thane neither frowned nor smiled, keeping his face impassive as he spoke. "I'm here to see Arthur Weston. He's expecting me."

"I see." The young man rose to his feet and looked up at Thane. He stood with his feet slightly apart, towering above the clerk on the opposite side of the desk. "And your name sir?"

"Thane Jordan. Brother to the late Henry James Jordan."

"Just a moment, sir."

The young man quietly walked to a door behind him, tapped lightly, then stepped inside.

He reappeared within a moment and motioned for Thane to have a seat on a straight-backed chair beneath a window.

"Mr. Weston is indisposed at the moment. If you'll please be seated, he'll attend to you directly."

Thane nodded his head and took a seat on the hard chair. He set the traveling bag on the floor before crossing a foot over the opposite knee, leaning back, and waiting.

The young man picked up a pen, dipping it in a well of ink, and continued writing on a thick piece of stationery.

As the pen scratched across the paper, it grated on Thane's tightly strung nerves. Mindlessly drumming his fingers on his thigh, he fastened his steely blue gaze on Mr. Weston's door, willing the man to appear.

Patience had never been his strong suit. Tired and hungry after traveling more than twenty-five hundred miles across America and that far again on the ocean, he just wanted to sign whatever necessary papers Mr. Weston needed and be on his way home. In fact, if they completed business immediately, he could be on a ship headed home by the following afternoon.

The sound of voices carried across the open space as two men exited Mr. Weston's office. A tall, white-haired man with a tan face and athletic build walked out accompanied by a short, portly man nervously twirling the end of his walrus mustache between his fingers.

The two shook hands at the door then the portly man touched a finger to his top hat and exited.

Thane uncrossed his foot from his knee and stood, pleased Arthur Weston appeared to be of sound mind and body.

"Mr. Jordan, I offer my sincere apologies for the wait. I received your telegram, but held no certainty as to the day of your expected arrival. Welcome to Liverpool, sir. Arthur Weston at your service."

"Mr. Weston, nice to meet you. I appreciate you meeting with me since I don't have an appointment." Thane shook the man's proffered hand then picked up his bag and followed the solicitor into his private office.

Anxious to settle Henry's affairs, he took a seat in a leather-upholstered armchair. Thane dropped the bag at his feet, waiting for Weston to get to the point of why he had to travel thousands of miles to sign a few papers.

"I trust you had an uneventful journey?" Weston asked as he opened a drawer and removed a file stuffed with papers.

"Most people would consider it so," Thane answered vaguely. "I don't particularly enjoy the water."

"Were you seasick on the crossing, sir?" Weston glanced at him as he riffled through papers.

"You could say that."

"Nasty bit of business, what? I must say, I try to avoid the need to sail myself. These legs much prefer solid ground beneath them."

Thane nodded his head. "I'm curious, Mr. Weston, why I had to travel all this way to sign a few papers for Henry's estate. Couldn't you have mailed them to me?"

"No, sir. I assure you, settling your brother's estate entails much more than signing a few papers, as you so aptly put it."

Weston slid a thick stack of papers across his desk to Thane. "These are the legal documents regarding Henry's business holdings."

Thane sat up a little straighter and leaned forward as Weston slid another handful of papers toward him.

"These papers detail his personal holdings."

Thane felt the muscle in his jaw tighten. So much for signing a few papers and heading home tomorrow. "Anything else?"

"Yes, sir. This includes the terms of his will."

Thane stared at the third stack of papers the solicitor slid his direction, holding back a discouraged sigh.

Weston sat back in his chair and studied Thane Jordan. He'd known Henry since the day he arrived in Liverpool until his death. His mind worked to associate the tough, rugged man in front of him to the jovial, smiling friend he'd known. Henry was a gentleman in every sense of the word, maintaining a meticulous appearance as a successful and prosperous businessman.

The cowboy sitting across the desk from Weston needed an appointment with the barber and a set of respectable clothes. Although he didn't arrive dressed in buckskins, like Weston rather imagined a man living in the western wilds of America might appear, his woolen jacket and corded front chambray shirt were not of the quality he'd expect someone related to Henry to wear. He absently wondered if Thane Jordan even owned a decent suit.

From what information Henry had shared when he engaged Weston to prepare the details of his will, he knew Thane disappeared from Henry's life when the lad turned sixteen and moved from his last known location without sending his brother any forwarding address. Henry engaged any number of men of questionable character over the years to track down Thane, finally locating his whereabouts in late spring.

Upon finding his residence in Oregon, Henry debated sending Thane a letter. In the meantime, he bequeathed everything he owned to his brother, surprising Weston. It certainly came as a shock to those in Henry's household when he read the will to them upon the man's death more than a month ago.

"Do you have any questions, Mr. Jordan?" Weston asked, resting his arms on the top of the desk as Henry's brother continued to stare at the papers without touching them. Curious if the man could read, he contemplated how best to broach the question. "Would it provide assistance to you if I read the documents aloud?"

Careworn, Thane sat back in the chair with a sigh. "My belly's as empty as a forgotten post hole and I can't sit here for a couple of hours listening to you read all that legal mumbo jumbo. I'll take the papers with me and review them this evening, but why don't you tell me the important points right now."

Weston's eyebrows rose toward his snowy white hairline, but he nodded his head.

"It is my understanding that you and your brother have not communicated in a dozen years. Henry was beside himself when he realized you left South Carolina and moved on. He managed to hire someone who finally located your whereabouts in the spring. At that time, he came to me and changed his will, leaving you everything."

"What, exactly, does everything include?" Thane leaned forward with his elbows propped on his knees, staring inquiringly at his brother's lawyer.

"Your brother owned, both outright and as a partner, more than a dozen successful cotton mills in Bolton, where he resided. In addition to his home there, he owned a lovely vacation home in Bath. He also recently engaged in a partnership with several shipping business here in Liverpool."

"I thought he lived here, in Liverpool."

"No. He moved to Bolton after he became a partner in his first cotton mill. He stayed with me when he had business to attend to here in the city and I hope you'll do the same."

Intently gazing at the man across the desk from him, Thane slowly nodded his head. "I appreciate the offer, Mr. Weston. It's very kind of you."

Weston rose to his feet, gathered the papers he'd set on the desk and placed them in a file then enclosed it in a leather satchel similar to the school bags many children carried. After handing the bag to Thane, the solicitor motioned toward the door.

"Shall we proceed to my home? I'd like to think my cook might be able to provide a filling meal for that fence post hole you mentioned."

A smile worked at the corners of Thane's mouth and he again nodded his head. "Thank you, sir."

"Please, call me Weston. Now, I'd like to hear all about your life in the west. Is it as untamed and wild as the stories I've read, that sort of rot?"

Thane grinned, cocking an eyebrow. "Depends on what you've read."

"Rightly so, my good man."

After a hot bath and a good meal, Thane spent the evening visiting with Weston and his wife, Margaret, at their well-appointed home. The next morning, Mrs. Weston handed a basket of food to her husband as he climbed into a comfortable coach, taking a seat opposite their guest.

"I must say, I think it best if you spend a few days acquainting yourself with Henry's holdings in Bolton before you make any decisions," Weston said when Thane questioned the need for making the day-long trip to the northeast.

"Can't I read the papers and sign them here?"

"There are matters there that require your personal attention, sir. I'm happy to provide assistance and of the details last evening, but I believe it would behoove us to discuss the details of your brother's will whilst we journey to his home today." Weston waved to his wife as the coach pulled onto the street.

"If it's all the same to you, I'd rather wait. I'm still trying to resign myself to Henry's death. You say he fell off his horse while he was riding home from his office?" Henry was the one who taught Thane to ride. He had a hard time believing his brother could take a spill for no reason and break his neck.

"From what I know, Henry left his office, riding fast and hard, as he so often did on his way home. It was raining that night, already dark. No one knows if the horse slipped, stepped in a hole, or spooked, but the end result was the same. The doctor said Henry didn't suffer, that the end came quickly."

Thane barely nodded his head in acknowledgement of the statement and focused his gaze out the coach window. He'd suggested riding to Bolton horseback but Weston quickly assured him they needed to travel by coach. At least it was a private coach and Thane had one side all to himself. It gave him the ability to stretch out his long legs. He still felt cramped from the days of confinement on the ship due to his illness.

The few times he'd felt well enough to venture from his room on the ship, he'd joined a group of men who conversed about everything from the first electric chair execution that took place a few weeks prior in New York to the admittance of Idaho and Wyoming to the union earlier that summer.

Discussion of a new ship in the popular White Star Line, reputed for its speed and attention to detail, stirred his interest. Unfortunately, it wasn't due to sail out of Liverpool for three weeks. By then, Thane planned to be home at his ranch.

"May I inquire, sir, have you ever met any Indians?" Weston asked from his seat across the coach, hungry for more news from the American West. The previous evening, his guest had offered several stories appropriate for genteel ears since Margaret sat with them, enraptured by the tales Thane shared.

"A few. We don't have too many in the Baker City area, but there's a reservation near Pendleton, north of where I live. The Indians are just trying to survive, like a lot of the rest of us."

"Have you witnessed any of them performing something called the ghost dance? I read in the newspaper that many of the tribes are engaging in the ritual at the urging of a man named Wovoka."

"No, I haven't seen any ghost dancers. While many of the tribes believe it will bring a return of their old ways, the dance mostly has a bunch of white folks in a panic, worried about uprisings."

"Surely you jest."

Thane glanced at his traveling companion and shook his head. "Nope. Personally, I think they ought to leave the Indians alone and let them do their dances. It's bad enough we've shoved them off their lands onto reservations; we shouldn't forbid them from honoring their traditions."

Weston continued asking questions about life in the West and on a ranch. While working through the basket of food Mrs. Weston provided, the men maintained a lively conversation that stayed far away from discussions of Henry or his passing.

The afternoon moved toward evening as the coach slowed and turned down a lane, rolling to a stop in front of a large stone home resembling a miniature castle with gables, turrets, and multiple chimneys gracing the roofline. Ivy and climbing roses trailed over the arch around the doorway while a profusion of blooming flowers and green lawn completed the pastoral scene.

"We made jolly good time," Weston said, smiling at the coachman as he opened the door to the conveyance. "Welcome to Breckenridge Cottage."

Henry's cottage looked nothing like Thane imagined. It was vastly different from the small, humble cabin he called home.

Curious, he followed Weston down the cobblestone walk to the front door. Thane took a deep breath, inhaling the cloying aroma of the flowers.

Rain began to fall as they stepped beneath the overhang covering the door. Between the dreary skies and perpetual dampness, he couldn't wait to return to the somewhat arid conditions of eastern Oregon.

Though he expected Weston to produce a key and open the door, Thane hid his surprise when the man knocked and turned to him with a smile.

"I thought this was Henry's place?" Thane asked, confused.

"Indeed, it is."

"And someone lives here?"

"They most certainly do. I planned to discuss further those details with you today on our journey, but you made your preference clear on that topic. I rather enjoyed our conversations about your life in the West. Regardless, by deferring to your wishes, you shall meet the occupants without forewarning."

"Forewarning? Now, wait just a dang minute, Weston. I've got…"

The door opening forced Thane to clamp his mouth shut, although he continued to glare at his traveling companion.

"Weston! How nice to see you."

The feminine voice floating out to Thane caused him to shift his gaze from the solicitor to the beautiful woman standing in the doorway, smiling in greeting. Light from inside the house highlighted her auburn hair and created a soft glow around her shoulders. Ladylike and elegant in appearance, Thane wondered if she had royal blood pumping through her delicate veins.

"My dear, I do so hope you received my correspondence explaining our arrival."

"Indeed, I did, kind sir. Please come in." She stepped back to allow her guests entry. "You're just in time for a spot of tea."

"Wonderful. I'm glad we arrived when we did," Weston said, removing his hat and coat and hanging them on the mahogany hall tree in the entry.

Thane removed his Stetson and jacket, leaving them beside Weston's things before turning to the woman.

Weston thumped him on the back as he made introductions. "Thane Jordan, I'd very much like you to meet Jemma Bryan, Henry's sister-in-law."

Thane clenched his jaw and curtly tipped his head to the woman. Her smile slowly melted as his annoyance pounded between them with a palpable force.

Weston stood rooted in place when Thane pinned him with an angry glare. "Henry was married?"

Chapter Two

Confused, Jemma gazed between Henry's solicitor and his brother. In all the years she'd known Henry Jordan, he'd never once mentioned a brother.

The first knowledge she possessed that one existed occurred the day Mr. Weston had read Henry's will. The terms he set forth left her speechless and in a state of shock. Hopeful that Henry's brother would choose to forfeit his inheritance and stay in America, her optimism soon faded.

Keen disappointment settled over her when she received a letter from Weston earlier in the week, advising her that Thane Jordan traveled to England to make the necessary arrangements to settle Henry's estate.

Furtively studying the man who looked as if he could rip Weston apart with his bare hands, she took in his thick hair, desperately in need of a good trim. He had a strong, commanding presence, along with a handsome face, at least what she could see of it, covered as it was by a layer of scruffy blond stubble. She wondered if he misplaced his razor on the ship's crossing and hadn't been able to replace it.

The clothing he wore looked every bit as rugged as the man they covered. Although not shabby, his attire lacked the quality she would have expected from Henry's kin. The shirt and pants seemed a bit large for him, but not overly so.

Comparisons of the man to her sweet brother-in-law failed to reveal many similarities. Thane Jordan was taller and broader than Henry had been, but he lacked the kindly warmth her brother-in-law always exuded. The only definable resemblance came from his eyes. The color was the same shade of blue as Henry's although while his often twinkled with humor, this man's looked cold and hard.

Taken aback by the unrefined westerner, she placed a hand to her throat and tried to tamp down her fear of what havoc he would wreak in her life before he returned to America.

Thane glared threateningly Weston's direction. "I think you better start talking, Weston."

Jemma took a step away from the two men, bumping into the family dog as he stood behind her, eyeing the stranger.

As she reached out a hand to the pet, Weston grinned and patted the animal's head, making the canine's tail wag with pleasure as it fanned back and forth across the spotless floor.

"No need to fret, Jemma, dear. Everything is quite all right."

"Is she a swooner?" Thane noticed the woman next to him turned unusually pale as she worried a cameo pinned to the thick lace covering her long, graceful neck.

"I assure you, Mr. Jordan, I am not a swooner. I've never fainted in my life and I most certainly don't plan to begin at this most unfortunate instance." Jemma found it impossible to look into the man's face and instead glanced at the plain cotton shirt he wore. No suit jacket, no waistcoat, just a shirt any working class man might own.

Unsettled by the crude interloper, she turned and tripped over the dog when he pushed against her legs.

Thane grabbed her arms to keep her from falling and she hurriedly pushed herself away from him.

"What is that thing? It looks like a lab climbed under the fence and got friendly with a poodle." Thane studied the large curly-haired black dog with interest. The animal neither growled nor acted friendly, staring at him with cool disinterest.

"This is Sir Rigsly. He's a curly-coated retriever. Henry got him to hunt birds, but he's definitely been more of a pet than a hunter. He won't bite, but he's not fond of strangers." Jemma trailed a hand across the dog's tall back as she walked down the hall to the drawing room.

"I've never heard of his breed before." Thane studied the dog's sturdy form, admiring his straight back and intelligent eyes.

"The breed is fairly new, introduced here a few decades ago. Most people use them for upland bird and waterfowl hunting," Jemma explained as she stepped past the dog into the drawing room.

"Where is Greenfield?" Weston inquired of the butler's whereabouts as he motioned Thane to follow their hostess.

"He's running a few errands and should be back soon." Jemma walked over to where a tea tray rested on a low table near a grouping of chairs and a settee.

"I say, where's the rest of the help, Miss Bryan?" Weston fixed her with a probing look, compelling her to respond.

"Everyone has left except for Cook and Greenfield," Jemma blurted, rubbing the cameo with trembling fingers while her other hand wrapped across her middle. "With the state of things in such a sticky-wicket since the reading of Henry's will, the staff began seeking posts elsewhere."

"Why did you not send word?" Weston looked imploringly at Jemma. "How are you managing?"

"Quite well, truthfully. We're learning to do things for ourselves and making do."

"Bosh! You should have made me aware the situation here so rapidly deteriorated. Henry would want you well provided for and given the care to which you are accustomed."

She frowned at Weston. "If that's what Henry wanted, he wouldn't have left things in such a fretful condition." Jemma snapped her mouth shut before she said something she'd regret. Thanks to Henry's bequeathment solely to his brother, he'd left those residing in his household scrambling to make sense of his wishes.

Annoyed, Jemma took a seat on the settee and poured tea into the two cups on the tray, realizing she'd need a third. Weston and Mr. Jordan had just taken seats and both hurried to stand as she rose to her feet.

"I'll fetch another cup and be back momentarily. Please excuse me."

Thane waited until she left the room to focus his angry glare on Weston. "Answers, man. I want answers. Now."

"I tried to tell you, Thane. Your brother was married to a beautiful girl named Jane Bryan. She passed away three years ago and Henry was beside himself with grief. Jemma stepped in, taking over the management of the household and the…"

Jemma returned, forcing Weston to refrain from finishing his comment. She poured herself a cup of tea, motioning for the men to help themselves to a tray with sandwiches and sweets.

Thane ate two sandwiches and began working on his third when the front door opened and the patter of childish footsteps echoed down the hall. A cherubic face peeped around the doorway. Glossy eyes snapped with lively interest beneath a mop of strawberry blond curls.

Thane assumed the girl must belong to someone in the house. She bore a resemblance to Miss Bryan, but if the uptight woman was her mother, he assumed Weston would have introduced her as a missus instead of a miss.

The dog lifted his gaze to the child and wagged his tail in a friendly greeting as he lounged in front of the fire.

"Hello, there, Miss Lily." Weston beckoned the child to join them. She continued to hover in the doorway swishing her skirts back and forth before releasing a giggle and running across the room to the elderly man.

As he lifted her up in a hug, he kissed her rosy cheek and bounced her on his knee. "How does this day find you, sweetheart?"

"I'm great, Mr. Weston. How are you?"

"Very well, my dear." Weston placed a comforting hand on the child's back and grinned. "Would you like to meet your uncle from America?"

"Yes, please."

Thane choked on the tea he'd just swallowed and clanged the cup into the saucer. Afraid he'd break the expensive china, he set it down on the table in front of him and coughed loudly into a napkin Jemma thrust into his hand.

"Uncle?" he croaked, glaring at Weston. "I'm an uncle?"

"Indeed, you are. Thane, I'm most pleased to present your niece, Lillian Jane Jordan, better known as Lily. She's three."

Thane had no more idea what to do with a three-year-old than he did with the unnecessary assortment of silverware he'd worked his way through at dinner the previous evening. When he fastened his gaze on the child, she shyly ducked her head against Weston, hiding her face.

"He's scary, Mr. Weston." Lily whispered loud enough for Thane to hear.

Bothered by her words, he took a calming breath. After schooling his features into a less intimidating expression, he held out a hand to the child. Although he didn't know Henry had wed much less produced a child, he wanted to meet the little person who was his last living connection to his brother.

"It's nice to meet you Lily. Would you mind coming closer?"

The child turned her head far enough she could see him with one shiny copper eye, warily observing him.

Thane forced an amiable smile to his face and extended his hand her direction again. Determined to win her over, he held his breath, waiting to see what she'd do.

Lily slowly slid off Weston's knee and sedately moved within his reach. She placed her tiny hand on his big palm. The contrast of her milky smooth skin to his tan, work-roughened hand caught his attention. He felt warmth spread from her little fingers straight to his heart.

He'd never been around kids, wasn't even sure he liked them, but this daughter of Henry's made a lump lodge in his throat as she gazed at him with open interest.

"Are you my uncle?"

Thane cleared his throat, afraid if he moved, Lily would run from him. "I guess I am."

"Are you mean?"

Jemma tamped down the spontaneous desire to assure her niece the big man was definitely mean, undoubtedly uncivilized, and about to throw their entire existence into turmoil. Wisely, she held her tongue and sipped her tea.

"No, Lily. I'm not mean," Thane assured the child. "If I seem that way, I'm not trying to be."

Lily studied him for a long moment. "Did you know my papa?"

"Yes, I did. Your papa was my brother."

"Are you going to visit him in heaven?"

"Someday, I hope to see him there, but I'd like to stay here a while longer."

Lily tipped her head and tentatively reached out a finger, touching the bearded scruff on Thane's face. He forced himself not to jerk away from her innocent exploration. He wasn't accustomed to anyone touching him or being in such close proximity.

As the little girl pressed against his leg, he breathed in her scent. She smelled of sunshine, flowers, and something sweet he associated with babyhood. He remained quiet as she poked a thumb into an indentation in his cheek and traced her fingers across his chin.

Concluding her uncle meant her no harm, Lily climbed on his lap, leaned against his chest, and sighed contentedly. "Are you going to live here with us?"

"No, Lily. I have to take care of some business then I'll sail on a big ship back to America and ride a train to my ranch."

"Why?" Lily wiggled her feet with energetic enthusiasm as they hung over Thane's solid thigh.

"Because that's where I live and I have to go back. My cattle and horses will miss me."

"You have horseys? My papa rode horseys." Lily stared up at him with bright eyes.

"Your papa taught me how to ride. Did he teach you?" Thane counted the smattering of freckles across her button nose and found himself thoroughly charmed by the way she pursed her little rosebud lips before she spoke. "I'll take you for a ride before I leave."

"Absolutely not!" Jemma interjected, thumping her teacup and saucer onto the table while shooting livid glances at Thane. "She's much too young and besides, considering how... well, with that... there will be no riding in Lily's immediate future. I forbid it!"

Thane ignored her outburst, keeping his focus on the engaging child on his lap, full of life and questions.

"Every Jordan knows how to ride." His tone held a degree of coolness, but he continued smiling warmly at Lily.

"I know how."

Thane whipped his gaze around, connecting with a boy who so closely resembled Henry, he nearly dropped Lily on the floor. No one mentioned his brother also had a son. Although the lad shared the same copper eye color of his sister and aunt, he was the spitting image of Henry from his straight brown hair and the tilt of his chin to the way he carried himself as he walked.

"And who might you be?" Thane finally found his voice, although it sounded strained when he spoke. Inundated with so many conflicting emotions in such a brief period, he began to fear he'd soon be overwhelmed with them.

"Henry James Jordan III, sir." The boy bowed to him before taking a seat beside Jemma on the settee.

"That's my brother, Jack." Lily giggled, pointing to her sibling. "He's nine and thinks he knows everything."

"Lily," Jack warned, staring at his sister. "You better…"

"That's enough." Jemma placed a gentle hand on Jack's shoulder and the boy snapped his mouth closed.

Stunned to discover Henry had a wife and offspring, Thane glanced back at the doorway to see if any more children emerged from the depths of the house.

"It's just these two," Weston said quietly, hiding his grin behind his teacup. "I assure you, they're more than a handful."

"I reckon they probably are if they've got Henry's blood flowing in their veins."

Lily yanked on his shirt, directing his attention back to her before he could further observe Jack. "Did you know there's a dragon that lives in the tree outside my window? He's purple with a big tail and he eats daisies and frogs for dinner."

"Is that so?" Thane furrowed his brow to keep from laughing at the child. Apparently, she had an active imagination along with an expansive vocabulary.

"Yes. Jack doesn't believe me, but the dragon is there. We could ride him to your ship. Have you ridden a dragon before? May I go with you to America? May I visit your ranch? What's a ranch, Uncle Thane? Is it a fun place to live? Do you have a little girl? Do you like me?"

Scrambling to formulate an answer to even one of Lily's rapid-fire questions, Thane had no idea how to respond. He wanted to get to know both children, yet feared what that would do to his ability to keep his distance from them.

Conscious of his obvious discomfort, Jemma intervened.

"Why don't you two run off to the kitchen and see if you can be of help to Cook or Greenfield for a while?" Jemma suggested, wanting to curtail Lily's stories as well as get down to the business of settling Henry's estate. She intended to find out exactly what Thane Jordan planned to do with his brother's holdings, including Breckinridge Cottage and the children.

"I want to stay with Uncle Thane, Auntie Jemma. Please?" Lily turned to her aunt with a becoming pout.

"No, poppet. Now, my darlings, off with you both. Take Rigsly with you." Jemma motioned for Lily to follow her brother as he walked toward the door and patted his leg. The dog lumbered to his feet and moved close to Jack but Lily remained on Thane's lap.

She wrapped both arms around his neck and squeezed before kissing his cheek. "You smell like my papa. I think I'll keep you." Lily jumped off his lap and skipped after her brother.

Childish chatter drifted back to them as the siblings made their way down the hall to the kitchen with the large canine.

Thane slumped back in his chair and forked a hand through his hair, still at a loss for words. Until he set foot in Weston's office, he'd somehow hoped that Henry wasn't truly gone, that it was some elaborate plan or scheme on his brother's behalf to see him again.

Losing track of Henry hadn't been intentional. Thane left their South Carolina home abruptly and sent his brother a hastily penned note telling him of his plans to head west. He promised to write when he was settled, which he did. But after that, he never heard from Henry again.

He'd often wondered why his brother shut him out of his life. Henry must have moved from Liverpool to Bolton about the time he moved to Oregon. It appeared his last letter never reached his brother.

Regret filled him that he let pride stand in the way of keeping in touch with a brother he'd loved deeply.

Now, Henry was gone, leaving behind two children, a huffy sister-in-law, an aloof dog, and a tangle of affairs that needed immediate attention. No wonder Weston insisted he attend to matters in person.

He would have appreciated the man letting him know about Henry's family, though. Thoroughly disturbed by their unexpected introduction, Thane's thoughts tumbled over each other until he sat forward and grabbed his head in his hands. If he were at his ranch, he'd have saddled his horse and ridden out across the range until he could make sense of things.

Although he longed to go for a horseback ride and work through his problems, it seemed impossible. He was stuck in the house as the rain dripped with dreary steadiness outside. With effort, he held back a sigh and glanced at Miss Bryan.

Despite her immediate dislike of the man, Jemma experienced a moment of compassion for Henry's brother. It had to come as a shock to discover Henry had not only married, but also left behind a family. Then again, if the man hadn't disappeared into the wilds of Oregon and shut his brother out of his life, the details wouldn't come as a surprise.

Upset again on Henry's behalf, she'd heard from Weston how desperately her brother-in-law searched to find his only living relative. She had a most unreasonable desire to pour what was left of the now-cold tea over Mr. Jordan's dark blond head.

Knotting her hands on her lap, she lifted her gaze to discover Weston shaking his head at her, giving her a knowing smile. The man had always been unbelievably astute at reading both her and Jane's moods.

"Perhaps Mr. Jordan would like a few moments to himself to gather his thoughts. I'm sure meeting all of us has been something of a surprise," Jemma said, rising to her feet and lifting the tea tray as she stood. "Weston, would you mind showing him to the guest room next to yours?"

"I'd be happy to, my dear. I think it best to wait until after the children are in bed to discuss Henry's will," Weston suggested.

Jemma nodded in agreement while Thane stared at the thick rug beneath his feet. It looked imported and costly, like so many of the furnishings he'd noticed in the house.

He had much to learn about his brother.

After Jemma breezed out of the room with the tea tray, Weston escorted Thane up a set of impressive mahogany stairs to the second floor bedrooms. He opened the door to a room decorated in shades of dark blue and green and motioned for Thane to step inside.

"Will this be satisfactory?"

"It's fine, Weston. Thanks." Thane didn't bother to look around the room, walking directly to the window and leaning against the frame, staring out at the rain-laden sky.

"Are you well, sir?"

"Not particularly. This is worse than the time I got bushwhacked and stampeded. I never expected all of this." Thane waved his hand around, encompassing the room but meaning the entirety of the situation.

"I tried to impart the necessary details, sir, but you..." Weston stopped speaking when Thane turned a cold glare his direction.

"You don't need to keep repeating it. I told you I wasn't ready to hear what you had to say so I can't toss the blame anywhere else. I just had no idea..." Thane swallowed down the lump that once again formed in his throat. "I didn't realize Henry had a family. A lovely family, from the looks of it."

"He doted on Jane and the children. After Jack, they'd nearly given up on having another. By some miracle, they found themselves anxiously awaiting the arrival of little Lily."

"Is that what happened to Jane?" Thane asked in a moment of comprehension. "She died in childbirth, didn't she?"

"Yes. Henry blamed himself. She nearly died when Jack was born but eventually gained back her strength. No one expected to lose her when Lily was born, least of all Henry. Jemma has been a blessing. In all forthrightness, she has been the one raising both children. Jane spent so much time abed after Jack was born, then with subsequent illnesses. Jemma filled the role of both aunt and mother. She's the only mother Lily has known."

Thane nodded his head, feeling an even greater need for some fresh air and the opportunity to gain control of his thoughts. "I'm going for a walk. What time do I need to be back?"

"Jemma mentioned dinner service at seven. You might want to dress for the occasion."

Weston left Thane alone in the room, staring down at his Levi's and work shirt. He didn't own a bunch of fancy clothes because he had no use for them on the ranch. He had a suit he wore on Sundays when he made it to church, but beyond that, his wardrobe consisted of denims and flannel or chambray shirts. If Miss Bryan didn't care for his mode of dress, she could keep her appealing coppery eyes fastened elsewhere.

Quietly walking down the stairs to the front entry, Thane shrugged into his coat and settled his hat on his head. After turning up his collar, he opened the door and stepped outside into the bitter drizzle.

Jemma stood in the front parlor and watched him trudge down the lane with his hands shoved into his pockets, shoulders rounded against the weather.

Although he provoked her temper, pity for the man softened her heart. It had to be difficult and trying to align his thoughts to all he'd discovered since arriving in England.

With a sigh, she let the lace panel covering the window fall back into place. If he was upset with what he'd already learned, she dreaded his reaction when Weston reviewed the full terms of the will with him. She'd heard them a month ago and thoughts of fulfilling Henry's requests still made bitterness churn in her stomach and anxiety plague her thoughts.

Chapter Three

With a muscled forearm braced against the fireplace mantle, Thane stared over his shoulder at Weston.

"That can't be right, Weston. Did Henry have a mental abnormality that obscured his ability to think rationally?"

"Henry had all has faculties about him when he made his will." Weston frowned and glanced at Jemma for support. She failed to notice his unspoken request, lost in the loathing glares she continued to cast toward Thane.

"I can't take those children. I don't care what his will states, I can't take them." Thane paced from the fireplace to the window and back again, visibly agitated. "Even if I wanted to take them, which I don't, my ranch is no place for a couple of kids, especially two who are accustomed to a way of life vastly different from a modest cabin in the American West."

"Please, Weston, isn't there anything we can do?" Jemma looked at the solicitor with pleading eyes. They'd had this conversation many times before, but Henry's will made his desire for Thane to raise the children perfectly clear. "I can't bear the thought of them growing up in America while I'm here."

"That's another thing." Thane continued pacing while he spoke, stopping briefly to incline his head toward Jemma. "Why didn't Henry at least leave Miss Bryan this house? According to the terms of the will, he's left her penniless and homeless. Why would he do such a thing, considering the circumstances?"

Surprised by Thane's question as well as his concern on her behalf, Jemma snapped her head his direction. He shrugged his shoulders and shoved his hands into his pockets then resumed his post leaning over the mantle, staring into the flames.

When he returned from his walk soaked to the skin, she'd asked Greenfield to draw him a hot bath. The man looked like he had yet to warm up, the way he continued to linger close to the fire.

"Henry didn't intend for her to be penniless or homeless." Weston spoke to Thane then nodded to the woman fidgeting in the small side chair next to him. "I assure you, my dear, Henry meant no slight. When he asked me to record his will, he seemed quite convinced Mr. Jordan would make sure you received proper provision for the future."

Thane snorted and stabbed at the fire with a poker, making sparks fly out and land on the hearthrug. The dog raised his head from his bed on the floor nearby and sniffed the air.

Frustrated, Thane stamped out one lingering ember, battling the urge to kick a hole through the floor.

Jemma scowled at Thane, biting her tongue. If Henry had any idea what an uncouth cavedweller his brother had grown into, he would never have left her or the children at his mercy.

"Let's go over this again, shall we?" Weston feathered the papers in his hand.

"No." Thane glowered at Weston. "Reading it again won't change anything. Henry provided a sizeable inheritance for the children, accessible when they turn eighteen. He left everything else, down to the last blasted teacup in this house to me. I'm to either stay here in England or take the children with me to America, but they are officially mine. It's up to me to decide what to do with his business holdings, this house, and make provision for Miss Bryan…" Thane thrust his hand Jemma's direction, "and the remaining servants. Correct?"

"That sums it up precisely." Weston set the papers on the table beside him and leaned back in his chair. "Very well, indeed."

Jemma's teacup clattered against the saucer as she set it on the table. "That does not sum it up very well. Not at all." Perturbed and fighting feelings of betrayal that Henry left her in such a predicament, Jemma kept her posture impossibly straight and lifted her chin with a touch of defiance. "As a matter of fact, the teacups are mine. They belonged to my mother, hence they aren't Henry's to give away, as are many of the household goods, including the rug you seem intent on destroying with embers from the fire. The children belonged to Jane as much as they belonged to Henry. Therefore, they should have the opportunity to be cared for by her last remaining relative."

Thane stared at her, censure filling his features. "They aren't a rug or a painting to be bartered over, Miss Bryan."

Unsettled by Thane's icy tone, his cool gaze pierced her composure. "Good heavens!" Jemma rose to her feet as tremors of anger rushed through her. Oh, how she wanted to slap the smirk from the American's face. "I am well aware of the children, Mr. Jordan, as well as their needs, their likes, their dreams, and wishes. I'm the one who nurses them through illnesses, kisses scraped knees, wipes away their tears, and listens to their prayers. How dare you insinuate I think those two precious babies are mere possessions!"

Hastily turning on her heel, Jemma started to storm from the room but Thane grabbed her arm and pulled her to an abrupt halt.

"I didn't mean it that way, you mule-headed woman. Henry, for whatever misguided or crazy reason, wanted the kids to be with me." Thane couldn't ignore Jemma's trembling limbs or the fury sparking from her eyes. He'd never seen a woman so infuriated and fully anticipated the moment when she'd break down into hysterical sobs.

When she continued to glare at him, pressing her kissable lips together, he persisted. "Look, I'm no happier about this than you are, but I want to do right by Henry and those kids. I don't want this house and I certainly don't want his money. I just want to get things settled and go home."

"I'll thank you to keep your hands to yourself, sir." Yanking her arm from his grasp, Jemma took a step back, away from his domineering presence. "I'd be happy to pack your things and send you on your way. You couldn't make me any happier this very moment if you'd take your leave and never return."

Weston guided her back to the seat she'd occupied minutes earlier. "Jemma, my dear, please calm yourself. I'm certain we can work through an agreeable solution to this problem." He motioned for Thane to take the chair opposite of her. The man begrudgingly sat without making further comment.

Before speaking, Weston spent a moment gathering his thoughts as he sat in the chair next to Jemma. "So far, you two have discussed only two options: Thane staying here with the children or taking them to America. It's not feasible for Mr. Jordan to uproot his life in Oregon and move here permanently. He's made that abundantly clear. However, Mr. Jordan readily admits he is not equipped for, nor accustomed to children, presenting quite a dilemma. On the other hand, Miss Bryan and the children share a special bond and it would be a tragedy to separate them. Nonetheless, Miss Bryan will soon be left without a home or a source of income and has no way to support two children."

Thane drummed his fingers on the arm of his chair, narrowing his gaze at the solicitor. Weston led the conversation in an obscure direction and he wished the man would hurry up and reach the destination. They'd spent the last three hours discussing Henry's will, as well as how unsatisfactorily the terms suited both he and Miss Bryan.

Out of patience, he leaned forward and braced his elbows on his knees. "Your point, Weston. Get to the point."

"Righty ho, my good man. The only reasonable recourse is for Miss Bryan to accompany you to America. You'll have someone to help you with the children, someone who already loves them, and she'll have the security, protection, and provision of a home you can provide."

Jemma sucked in a gulp of air and sat with her mouth slightly open, gaping at Weston as though he'd committed blasphemy. She started to speak, only to have Thane interrupt her.

"Are you insane, Weston?" Thane jumped to his feet, towering over both Jemma and the solicitor. "I've got no use for a woman in my life, especially one who detests me as much as Miss Bryan."

"I never stated my feelings for you, even if your assumption is profoundly accurate." Jemma glared at Mr. Jordan, wishing he'd sit down. It was hard to collect her thoughts when he stood over her, looking so formidable and indisputably handsome. "Weston, your suggestion is utterly ridiculous and completely inappropriate. You know as well as I do it would be untoward for me to travel with Mr. Jordan, regardless of the children's presence. It simply isn't done. My reputation would be in tatters. Where would that leave me or the children?"

Weston smiled at them both, unbothered by their hostile looks or heated words.

"I quite agree, Miss Bryan. It is unacceptable for you to travel as a single woman with Mr. Jordan, which is why you two should wed immediately."

"What?" Jemma squawked, rising from her chair, thoroughly disconcerted by Weston's suggestion. "No, Weston. I'm afraid that is out of the question."

"You darn sure got that right." Thane glared at Weston then Jemma. If he ever took a wife, which he had no plans of doing, he wanted a docile, compliant woman who wouldn't cause him any grief. He would only wed a female willing to yield to his guidance and direction.

Beautiful as she might be, Jemma Bryan was the farthest thing he could imagine from a biddable spouse. Strong-willed, determined, and independent, she held no qualms of speaking her mind or putting him in his place. She'd admonished him like one of the children when he tracked mud into the foyer after his walk. Throughout dinner, she'd frowned when he rested an elbow on the table or committed some other etiquette blunder. After she'd tucked the children into bed, she'd politely hinted at his lack of social graces as they gathered in the parlor.

No, a lifetime listening to the woman harp on him definitely wasn't worth a kiss or two from her soft, inviting lips.

Desperate to dislodge the thoughts attempting to take root in his mind, he resumed his pacing.

"She wouldn't last two days on the ranch, Weston. Miss Bryan is not suited to western life, not at all." Satisfaction filled Thane at the look on the woman's face, daring him to evaluate further her inability to embrace a new lifestyle. "A woman like her wouldn't do at all."

"You needn't speak as though I'm not standing right here, Mr. Jordan. A woman like me, you say, is ill suited for your lifestyle. You don't know a thing about me, but I'm quite capable of adapting to whatever situation may arise. However, considering your barbaric tendencies, the last person I'd willingly wed is you."

Thane strode across the room until he stood toe to toe with the woman then bent down so their noses nearly touched. "Tell me, Miss Bryan, what on earth would a barbaric man like me do with a sharp-tongued, pampered princess like you?"

Flustered and intimidated by the man's size and strength, Jemma leaned away from him. The raw, physical power he possessed bore evidence in the way his shirt stretched across his broad shoulders and chest.

At such inappropriate proximity, she could see a mole on his cheek and the way his thick eyelashes rimmed penetrating blue eyes. His enticing masculine scent enveloped her, making her head swim and leaving her ill at ease.

Reviled yet fascinated by Henry's brother, she fought an inner battle to draw closer or run away from the brute. She stood her ground and returned his unwavering gaze with a determined glare of her own.

"I'll have you know I'm neither pampered nor a princess, although my mother's cousins have ties to the throne. As for what you would do with me, sir, the answer is positively nothing because I won't have a thing to do with you. You are insufferable, arrogant, and nothing like Henry or his associates. They were gentlemen in every sense of the word."

"I never claimed to be a gentleman, Miss Bryan. If you want to bandy about names, I can think of a few choice selections for you. Let's start with spinster. I can see why no man has succumbed to your beauty because only a weak-minded dolt would get tangled up with a woman so full of sass and stubbornness."

A gasp escaped Jemma as she raised her hand to slap Thane. He grasped her wrist and held it in his hand while wild currents raced up both their arms at the contact.

Tension crackled between them with such force, it left a charged atmosphere looming over the occupants of the room. Even Rigsly seemed aware of the electric mood and lumbered to his feet. Shoving between the humans casting each other cold, intolerable glares, he growled low in his throat as he lifted his head to the stranger holding Jemma's wrist.

Thane glanced down at the dog, wondering if the canine would really bite him if he felt his mistress was threatened. Not willing to find out, he dropped her hand and took a step back.

Weston rose from his seat and held his hands out in a placating motion. "Please, both of you. There is no need for insults or accusations. Let's be civil about this, shall we?"

"Lest I say anything else to injure Miss Bryan's delicate sensibilities, I believe I'll retire for the evening. Good night."

Thane walked out of the room and up the stairs before he could further insult the stimulating and infuriating woman Weston had inanely suggested he marry.

Yanking off his clothes and sliding between the cool sheets, Thane bent one arm beneath his head and stared at the ceiling through the darkness.

The last time he'd seen his brother, he'd told him he'd be gone six months at the most. Full of plans to become wealthy with something he'd invented that would help revolutionize the cotton mill industry, Henry promised he wouldn't be gone long. He tried to get numerous investors in the South interested in his creation, but no one was willing to test it on their equipment. After scraping together enough money to purchase a ticket to Liverpool, Henry set off to seek his fortune.

Thane knew Henry had found an investor willing to not only back him, but also make him a partner in a mill. From letters they exchanged before they lost touch, he even knew Henry decided to stay in England for an indefinite period. What he didn't know was that Henry had fallen in love, taken a wife, and had a family, or that he'd become so wealthy.

Curious if Henry had any idea of the mayhem he'd created with his last wishes, in the stillness surrounding him Thane thought he could hear his brother chuckling.

Chapter Four

"Shall we begin without Mr. Jordan?" Jemma turned an inquisitive glance to Weston.

The solicitor took a seat at the table and nodded to Greenfield as he set a plate before him filled with tempting selections to begin the day. The children sat on either side of their aunt, quietly waiting to eat their breakfast. They lifted their heads at her question.

"Is Uncle Thane here?" Lily asked, leaning against Jemma's arm. "He didn't go away like my papa, did he?"

"No, poppet. Your uncle is here." At least Jemma assumed the horrid man was still in residence. She hadn't seen him that morning although she'd been up for hours. In fact, she'd barely slept at all. Upset by their exchange before Thane stormed out of the room, she stewed with fury in the wake of his words.

At twenty-eight, she was long past the age to marry. Instead of having her own home, husband, and children, she'd given up her dreams to help her sister. Jane and Henry tried many times to introduce her to potential suitors, but none ever interested her. As the years trickled by, they finally ceased in their matchmaking efforts when she ran off one suitor or another due to her intelligence, obstinacy, and independence.

The only man to pique her interest since she was seventeen happened to be the one who stoked her ire to an irrational level. Thane Jordan was rough, horrible, and utterly lacking any form of sophistication.

Why, then, had she stayed awake most of the night? The deep timbre of his voice and the way his eyes sparkled when he held Lily danced through her mind. An unbidden desire to know what it would be like to be held close to that powerful chest in his strong arms kept her tossing and turning.

In the pre-dawn hours, she climbed from her bed even more distraught than when she'd entered it. She had to work to sound pleasant and keep from frowning as she greeted the children and accompanied them to the breakfast table. Braced to deal with their intimidating uncle, relief washed over her to discover the dining room empty.

Weston soon joined them, but Mr. Jordan failed to put in an appearance. Curiosity as to his whereabouts finally got the best of her.

"Where is Mr. Jordan?"

"I don't know, my dear. I tapped on his door on my way down, but received no answer. Perhaps the long voyage and all that transpired yesterday left him weary." Weston draped his napkin across his lap and smiled at Jemma.

She couldn't picture Thane Jordan as one who would laze the day away in bed, even if exhaustion overtook him.

"I'll go see if he's in his room," Jack offered, jumping to his feet and racing away from the table before Jemma could call him back. The boy soon reappeared, clearly troubled by the way he shuffled his feet and stared at the floor as he returned to his seat next to her. "He's not there and his bed is already made. Do you suppose he left?"

"Who left?" Thane asked, striding into the dining room, grinning as Lily squealed and ran to him with open arms. He picked her up and tossed her in the air, making her giggle, before reaching out a hand to ruffle Jack's hair as the boy approached him.

"We thought you left, Uncle Thane. I checked your room and you were gone." Jack studied the tall man who looked like his father, yet didn't.

With Lily still balanced on his arm, Thane squatted down so he could look the boy in the eye. He placed a hand on Jack's shoulder, giving it a gentle squeeze. "I promise I won't leave without giving you a proper goodbye, son. You've got my word on it."

Jack nodded his head then once again returned to his seat next to Jemma. Thane carried Lily to her chair and set her down as he eyed the children's aunt. With a roguish quirk of an eyebrow, he offered her a curt nod then walked around the table, taking a seat next to Weston.

"Did you sleep well?" Weston asked as Greenfield brought in a plate of steaming food for Thane.

"Like a baby," Thane lied. If he'd gotten more than an hour of sleep, he would have been surprised. Mulling over Weston's outrageous suggestion, the terms of the will, and his introduction to Henry's two children provided worry enough to steal his sleep. Thoughts of Jemma's porcelain skin, auburn hair, and copper eyes snapping with fire kept him wide-awake. The few times he did slumber, he dreamed of what it would be like to kiss the exasperating woman's lips. He awakened annoyed and disgruntled.

Thane heard Jemma utter something beneath her breath and turned his gaze to her. Under his scrutiny, her cheeks glowed bright pink so she set her focus on helping Lily butter her toast, cutting it into smaller pieces.

"Where were you, Uncle Thane?" Jack asked after Weston offered a blessing on their meal.

"I went for a ride this morning. Henry has some fine horseflesh in the stable." In two bites, Thane consumed one of the three sausages on his plate before cutting into an egg. The traditional breakfast of bacon, sausages, eggs, toast, beans, tomatoes, mushrooms, and black pudding proved more than adequate to conquer his appetite. "I'd like to spend some time riding each of his horses before I decide what to do with them."

"Jolly good, sir. That's a grand idea." Weston sipped his tea and ate his breakfast in good humor while Jemma pushed hers around on her plate. "Perhaps Miss Bryan would care to join you for a ride."

Jemma glared at Weston. "I wouldn't want to intrude on Mr. Jordan's time spent with those much more akin to his class and temperament. In fact, were he to ride in a northern direction, I believe he'd find a striking resemblance to himself if he viewed the southern-most quarters of his mount."

Offended yet amused that she'd refer to him as a horse's hind end, Thane couldn't help but admire her wit and ability to insult him while smiling decorously. A smirk lifted the corners of his mouth as he held his teacup up in mock salute before returning to his breakfast.

When the children finished their meal, Jemma asked them to carry their plates to the kitchen then run upstairs to make their beds and tidy their rooms. They obediently complied, although Lily chattered non-stop as she followed her brother out of the room.

"It is imperative we resume our conversation from last evening and come to a satisfactory resolution of this conundrum posthaste." Weston wiped his mouth on his napkin then glanced from Thane to Jemma.

She set her fork on her plate and folded her hands primly on her lap, waiting for Weston to elaborate on his plans.

The two men exchanged a look beyond her comprehension before Thane slowly nodded his head.

Early that morning, riding out across the fields beyond the cottage, Thane considered all the available options. The further he rode the more clarity he gained. He wanted to get to know Jack and Lily, to keep his last ties to Henry close.

In addition, after watching the way Miss Bryan mollycoddled his nephew, he wanted him to grow up to be a man's man, not some pasty-faced weakling afraid of his own shadow. The best place to do that was on his ranch.

As Weston stated, he needed someone familiar with caring for the children. Miss Bryan seemed the best candidate for the position. He knew she loved the kids as her own and it would devastate her if he separated them.

Despite his inclination to give her a hefty payment for her trouble and send her on her way, he decided to explore the possibility of Miss Bryan joining him in America.

He would have no problem taking her along as the children's nanny, but Miss Bryan was correct in that it would ruin her reputation for her to stay with him without a proper chaperone. Concerns over propriety mattered little to him, but he wouldn't damage her reputation.

Marriage to the beautiful, wasp-tongued Miss Bryan would at least put an end to all the unwed women in Baker City setting their caps for him. Trips into town left him infuriated when the single females wouldn't leave him alone, plying him with invitations to dinner, to join them for picnics, and go for walks.

Women were nothing but heartbreak and trouble. He learned that from an early age. It was the reason he never intended to wed.

If he married a woman he didn't even like, and it was in name only, it would provide him with a degree of protection from husband-hunting females while assuring his heart remained safe.

By the time he returned to the stable, brushed down the horse, and fed the rest of the animals, the idea of taking Miss Bryan as his bride no longer struck him as appalling.

Convinced Miss Bryan would wrinkle her nose if he walked in smelling of horses, he took time to wash and change before hurrying to the dining room, only to find everyone seated.

Miss Bryan looked lovely in a gown the color of summer peaches as she sat flanked by Jack and Lily. Too bad such an attractive female had to be so thorny and outspoken.

Throughout breakfast, he wondered how to broach the subject of marriage then Weston provided a prime opportunity with his suggestion they resolve matters.

"I agree, Weston. The longer we wrangle with this won't make it any easier." Thane looked to Jemma and she gave an almost imperceptible nod for him to continue. "I've taken into consideration Henry's wishes, the needs of the children, and what would be most beneficial to all parties involved."

When Thane paused, Jemma leaned forward, waiting. "And...?"

"I think Weston's idea holds merit. In the vein of doing what is best for the children, I'm requesting the honor of your hand in marriage, Miss Bryan."

"You are what?" Jemma rocked back so hard in her chair, it nearly tipped over. A most unladylike grab for the edge of the table is all that kept her upright. "How could I possibly marry you? I don't love you. I can't even claim to like you, Mr. Jordan. You are quite possibly the most maddening man I've ever met."

"Don't flatter yourself, honey. I sure didn't take one gander at you and fall madly in love. You're the most opinionated, obstinate, razor-tongued woman I've had the misfortune of encountering." Thane held up a hand to silence her when she opened her mouth in rebuttal. "However, you love my brother's children with a fierce devotion and I don't want to take them away from you. What I propose is a marriage of convenience, in name only. Your sterling reputation will remain untarnished. As my wife, I'd provide for you, protect you, and share whatever I have with you. Everything except my bed."

Jemma drew a deep breath, prepared to lambast him, but Thane's stony glare held a warning.

"Before you insult me further or push my patience beyond endurance, I encourage you to think over your next words very carefully. If you need time to consider my offer, I plan to spend the day at Henry's office, going over his accounts. You can give me your answer this evening."

Without waiting for her response, Thane rose from the table and strode from the room.

Weston stood and reached across the table, patting Jemma's hand. "I think you would do well to at least consider the possibilities Mr. Jordan has offered. We'll return this evening in time for dinner."

Left alone after Weston's departure, Jemma let out the breath she'd been holding and sat in a state of shock until the children ran into the room, ready to begin the day's lessons.

Grateful for the routine of her day, Jemma went through the motions of helping the children with their lessons and consulting with Cook over the menu for dinner. She worked in the kitchen garden and among the flowers when the sun shone brightly in the early afternoon.

Dirt covered her hands and the knees of an old dress she'd slipped on before she went outside. Upon her return to the house, she decided to take tea in the kitchen with the children and save Cook the bother of setting out tea in the drawing room.

Rigsly slept at their feet, near the kitchen's hearth, as they enjoyed hot tea and warm crumpets.

"Have you met Uncle Thane, Cook?" Jack asked as he spread jam on his crumpet.

"Indeed, Master Jack. I meet him this morning when he passed through the kitchen." The round-faced cook smiled at the boy then cast a covert glance at Jemma. "He's a very handsome and polite gentleman. Any woman would be lucky to snag him for a husband."

Jemma choked on her tea and slapped a napkin to her mouth as she coughed and wheezed.

"Is he looking for a wife?" Confused, Jack glanced between his aunt and the cook.

"I don't know. What do you think, Jemma, dear? Is Mr. Jordan in need of a wife?"

A heated glare met the cook's impertinent grin. "Mr. Jordan is in need of a great many things, but I don't believe a wife is the first that comes to mind."

Greenfield, who happened to walk inside in time to hear Jemma's statement, hid his smile. He set a basket full of produce on the counter then kissed his wife's cheek as she stirred a pot on the stove.

"Mister Jordan seems like a fine chap, Miss Bryan. A fine one, indeed. Our dear Henry would have been quite proud of him, I do believe."

Lily hopped down from her chair and began dancing around the room singing, "Uncle Thane is a fine chap. A fine chap. He's a fine chap, indeed."

Unable to endure hearing any more of Thane's praises, Jemma excused herself and rushed outside. A quick glance up at the sky confirmed she wasn't in danger of getting soaked from a rainstorm.

Troubled, she hurried to the barn and saddled her mare, a dappled-gray thoroughbred named Jael. She'd owned the spirited, though good-tempered horse since Jack was a baby.

In need of fresh air and a few quiet moments, she climbed on the horse, riding slowly as her mind wandered over all that had transpired since tea the previous afternoon.

As she contemplated her options, she pulled the pins from her hair and stuffed them into her pocket.

Alone and single all these years, she didn't have any hope of a husband. Now that the offer of marriage loomed before her, she didn't eagerly reach out to grasp it. Too much of a romantic to settle for anything less than love, she didn't have any idea how she could endure years married to a man she didn't love, much less like.

Although he was handsome enough, despite his shaggy hair and beard, Thane Jordan was not a man to open up his heart and let a woman inside, let a woman truly know him.

No, if she married the overbearing boar, it would be for the sake of the children and them only. Visions of Jack and Lily growing up overseas in some forsaken little cabin with only Thane's uncivilized guidance made her urge the horse into a gallop as she tried to decide her best course of action.

Conflicted and uncertain, she finally returned to the cottage. She tried to hide her surprise when Thane stepped out of the stable and watched her approach. After reining Jael to a stop, she accepted the hand he held out to her as she dismounted.

"That's a fine horse," he said, rubbing a hand along Jael's neck. The horse tossed her head then appeared to study him. Jemma wanted to stamp her foot when Jael nuzzled Thane's chest and let out what sounded like a contented sigh as he rubbed a big hand over her head and along her neck. "What a beauty. What's her name?"

"Jael. It's from the…"

"Bible story. I know it." Thane glanced at her. "I reckon you chose it because it's a name of strength and determination."

"Something like that." Jemma's tone was clipped as she led Jael into the stable. She removed the saddle then brushed down the horse's shiny coat. She didn't expect Thane to recognize the name and certainly not the reason she chose it. His astuteness left her ill at ease.

Thane leaned against the door of the horse's stall. Quietly observing her skilled movements, he decided there might be more to Miss Jemma Bryan than an uptight, haughty female who annoyed him to no end.

She no longer wore the expensive gown she had on at breakfast. Instead, the worn cotton dress covering her trim figure had dried mud on the knees and streaks of dirt along the front. It looked as though she'd wiped her hands on it several times as she worked in the garden.

Although pinned up in the latest fashionable style that morning, her hair currently flowed freely around her face and down her shoulders. The sunlight trickling through the open stable door danced in bright beams among the silky tresses, highlighting the deep, warm shades of red among the rich brown locks.

His fingers fairly trembled with the desire to run through the strands so he shoved his hands into his pockets, hoping to find something to distract his attention.

"You ride very well. Have you ever tried a western saddle?"

The brush Jemma ran along the horse's side stilled as she turned to glare at Thane. "Absolutely not! It wouldn't be proper. Not at all."

"Bet you've wondered what it would be like, though." He prodded her, grinning when her shoulders stiffened at his words.

"Regardless, it isn't acceptable. I don't know what the women are like where you come from, but such questionable behavior most certainly isn't tolerated here. It simply isn't done."

"I see. What type of behavior is deemed acceptable by those such as you?"

"It would be a waste of breath to explain it to you." Jemma put away the brush, removed Jael's bridle, and gave the horse her evening portion of feed before closing the stall door and hanging the bridle with the rest of the tack.

Thane followed her as she left the stables and started toward the house. With every step she took, the swish of her skirts and bounce in her hair left him with an unreasonable longing to haul her into his arms and kiss her smart mouth until it turned pliable beneath his lips. Confident of his ability to draw a response from her, he briefly considered exploring how much effort it would take.

Angry at the wayward direction of his thoughts, he pulled her to a stop with a hand to her arm. "Look, lady, you've got to get over everything I say making you mad. I'm just funnin' you."

"It's Lady Jemma Bryan to you, sir, and I don't find your words, tone, or behavior amusing in the least."

Jemma yanked her arm from his grasp and marched into the house, slamming the door behind her.

Thane watched her walk off, surprised by her title. If she was The Lady Jemma Bryan, that meant her father held a title. Unsuccessful in his attempts at remembering his peerage lessons from school, he gave up and decided to question Weston about the matter later.

The man could have introduced her that way yesterday. Title or not, he still would have done his best to ruffle her feathers. Something about her provoked him and he had yet to decipher what it was.

Casually strolling into the kitchen, he found Cook and Greenfield busy with dinner preparations. "Mrs. Greenfield, might I trouble you for a glass of milk and one or two of those tasty little cookies you served yesterday?"

Entranced by his charm and good looks, the woman poured his milk and set the sweet pastries on a plate at the table. Thane removed his Stetson, washed his hands at the sink, and took a seat at the table.

"I'm glad you enjoyed them, Mr. Jordan. We call them biscuits, we do." Mrs. Greenfield, better known as Cook, smiled at him favorably while Greenfield began gathering the necessary dinnerware for the upcoming meal.

"Back home, biscuits are like bread, made with baking powder. They're right tasty smothered in gravy or served with butter and jam. Where I grew up in the south, biscuits were a staple and my mama often made them with buttermilk. Mmm, mmm, but they were good."

"Buttermilk, you say?" Cook glanced at him as she washed and sliced carrots.

"Yes, ma'am." Thane helped himself to another cookie. He liked the jolly cook and her husband. They assured him they had located new positions and could start within a month. Glad they wouldn't be left without work, he planned to leave them a generous bonus in their final pay envelopes.

"Pardon my asking, sir, but your accent seems to vary considerably. Does that come from living in the west?" Greenfield asked as he counted out the appropriate number of napkins.

"I reckon so." Thane grinned, inflecting more of the southern accent he grew up with into his voice. When he left South Carolina, he tried to rid himself of his accent. For the most part, he had. Nonetheless, on occasion certain words or phrases brought it back.

When he finished his glass of milk, he set the glass and the plate from his cookies in the sink and bowed to Cook. She tittered and smiled, shooing him out of her kitchen.

Thane wandered down the hall, following the sound of a piano played quite enthusiastically without any real musical ability.

At the parlor door, he watched as Jack and Lily banged out a song on a beautiful piano he hadn't noticed before. Weston read a newspaper while Rigsly lounged on the floor near the children.

"Do you sing, too?" Thane asked as Lily spun around on the piano bench and lifted her arms to him with a smile wreathing her sweet little face.

"Uncle Thane! Did you see me play? Jack and I like to play the piano." Lily bounced in his arms and patted his cheeks.

"I did see you play, Lily. Have you been taking lessons?" Thane asked, enchanted with the impish child.

"Yes. Auntie Jemma is teaching me and Jack." Lily wrapped her arms around his neck and leaned close, whispering in his ear. "Jack doesn't want to play because it's for girls, but he doesn't want to hurt Auntie Jemma's feelings."

"Is that right?" Thane asked when Lily leaned back and stared at him. "What would Jack enjoy doing?"

"Playing outside in the mud or riding a pony or playing knights with the sword Papa gave him."

Thane quirked an eyebrow at Jack and the boy nodded his head.

"May I see your sword, Jack?"

"Yes. It's in my room. I'll go fetch it." Jack jumped up and started out of the room, but Thane put a hand to his shoulder to stop him. "Why don't you show it to me after dinner? If you two don't mind the company, let's go outside for a while since it's still warm and not raining."

"I think that's a splendid idea, Mr. Jordan," Weston encouraged, giving Thane an approving nod. "A little fresh air would be just the ticket."

Thirty minutes later, Weston lifted his head from the newspaper he read and gazed out to a side lawn. Convinced his eyes deceived him, he hurried to the window and stared out at the mud-covered trio laughing and playing in a puddle left from yesterday's rain. Thane held a filthy child in each arm and all three of them laughed unabashedly.

Unable to recall the last time he'd seen such happy smiles on Jack and Lily's faces, he experienced concern over what their aunt would say upon discovering their disheveled and dirty state.

In a rush to get out the door, Weston came to a halt when Jemma called out to him from the bottom of the stairs.

"Weston, it's been awfully quiet in the house. Are the children still with you?"

"No, madam, they are not. Their uncle took them for a walk. I was just going to step outside and see if they'd returned." Weston edged toward the door, hoping to keep Jemma inside and somehow sneak the children upstairs to the bath before she discovered them.

"I'll accompany you outside, then." Jemma looped her arm around his and waited as he opened the door and escorted her outside. "It's lovely out today, isn't it?" She glanced over the green grass toward an arbor where fragrant flowers blossomed despite autumn's approach.

"Quite." Weston attempted to direct her around the opposite corner of the house, but Jemma tugged on his arm when she heard Lily and Jack's laughter.

"The children sound most happy about something. I wonder what Mr. Jordan has found to entertain them so."

Pleased with the children's uplifted spirits, Jemma gasped in horror as she rounded the corner of the house and took in the children, covered from head to toe in mud. It even plastered Lily's curls to her head.

"My heavens! What have you done to the children?" In the short time it took her to bathe and change after leaving Thane at the kitchen door, he'd turned the children into filthy urchins.

"Auntie Jemma! See me! I'm a mud princess. Uncle Thane said so. Don't I look bee-you-tee-ful?" Lily struck a pose with one hand in the air and the other fisted at her waist. Thane laughed while Weston hid his chuckle behind a cough.

"Oh, poppet, you, um… you definitely appear, well…" Jemma focused her fiery gaze on the instigator of the trouble. "I hope your uncle realizes what a mess this will make in the house for someone to clean up."

"I'll take care of it," Thane said, piercing Jemma with his stare, daring her to dash Jack and Lily's fun. "Sometimes a boy just needs to get dirty and Lily couldn't be left out."

Jack nodded his head at Jemma in agreement, eyes sparkling with something that had been lacking since his father passed away.

Weston wisely backed away from the group, watching from a distance that guaranteed he would remain clean.

"Come play with us, Auntie Jemma. Please?" Lily grabbed for her hand, smearing mud along Jemma's sleeve and skirt.

"Oh, Lily. I don't think that's a good idea. It's nearly time for dinner and it will surely take an hour to scrub all the mud from your hair."

"Please, please?" Lily begged, yanking on Jemma's hand again.

"No, poppet. Let's get you inside." Jemma tugged on Lily's hand, but the little girl set her feet and stuck out a quivering lip while tears filled her big eyes.

"No. I want to play more. No, no, no!"

Jemma narrowed her eyes at Thane, blaming him for Lily's bad temper. If it wasn't soon averted, she had no doubt a full-fledged tantrum awaited them.

Thane knelt next to Lily and gently lifted her chin so she looked into his face. "Lily, your aunt is right. It's almost time for dinner. Maybe we could eat outside since it's still warm and the sun hasn't yet set. I noticed a table in the kitchen garden behind the house." Thane turned his gaze to Jemma. "Do you think we could have a picnic there and worry about cleaning up later? They can eat if we wash their hands and faces."

"It's completely barbaric and without a bit of..." Jemma stopped herself and let out a long, exasperated sigh. "Yes, I suppose that would be fine." She reached for Lily's hand again, but Thane scooped the child up in one arm. He bent and lifted Jack in the other and let him climb up onto his broad shoulder. Although Jack was old enough he didn't like hugs and kisses, he didn't mind the attention from his newly introduced uncle.

"I'll see to the kids. We'll meet you outside the kitchen in a few minutes." Thane walked off in the direction of the stables with the children, both jabbering away while Jemma gaped at his retreating figure. Weston disappeared inside to warn cook they'd be dining in the garden.

A glance down at her soiled dress and muddy hand did nothing to cool her temper. Jemma marched inside the house to change — again.

The pump at the stables provided an acceptable place to wash the children's hands and faces before Thane herded them to the house. Weston lounged in a chair, absorbing the sunshine and reading his earlier discarded paper.

Broadly grinning as they approached, Weston set the paper aside and motioned for Thane to take the wooden chair next to him while the children flopped down on the grass with Rigsly. "I thought for sure you'd caught the wrong end of the stick when Miss Bryan discovered what you and the children had done."

Thane chuckled and rubbed a hand across his beard. "I don't know about catching the wrong end of the stick, but I'm pretty sure she would have liked to beat me with one."

Weston laughed and slapped Thane on the shoulder. "Right you are, my good man. It does the children good to enjoy the sunshine, laugh and play. Henry didn't have much time for them with all his business endeavors and Miss Bryan focuses her training on indoor activities."

"There's nothing wrong with a little mud squishing between their toes once in a while." Thane grinned when Lily ran over and climbed onto his lap leaning her muddy head against his chest.

The more time he spent with the children, the more he warmed to the idea of taking them to America and making a life for them on his ranch. He had no experience dealing with children, but he already felt something pricking his heart every time he looked at Jack and Lily.

"Did you two have fun?" Thane asked, looking at Jack as he spoke.

"Oh, yes, Uncle Thane. It was grand." Jack rolled onto his back and threw his arms open wide as he stared up at the blue sky.

"Just remember that this was a special treat and you can't play in the mud without your aunt's permission. Okay?"

"We 'member, Uncle Thane." Lily plucked at one of the buttons on his shirt as she jiggled her feet. "Can we please do it again now?"

"No, Lily." Thane's voice was firm but kind as he glanced up at the kitchen door when it opened. "See, here comes Cook and Greenfield with our dinner. I'm so hungry, I could eat a mud pie."

Lily giggled. "You can't eat mud."

"How about a muddy little girl named Lily?" Thane made a growling noise. Lily leaped from his lap and raced over to Jemma as she walked outside carrying a tray.

Burying her face in her aunt's skirts, she started to cry. "Don't let him eat me, Auntie Jemma. Don't let him eat me!"

Hands full of the heavy tray, Jemma struggled to move close enough to the table to set it down with Lily clinging to her legs. Weston hurried to take the tray so Jemma could pick up Lily and cuddle her close.

"Sweetheart, your uncle is only teasing. He wouldn't eat you or Jack or any of us."

"Promise?" Lily asked, raising her tear-streaked face from Jemma's shoulder.

"I promise, Lily. I'm sorry I scared you. I only meant to tease." Thane stood close to Jemma, wanting to reach out to Lily but concerned he'd make her cry again. In light of how much he had to learn about children, he certainly hoped Miss Bryan would accept his proposal. "I would never hurt you or Jack."

"Why?" Lily turned her head so she could study him.

"Because I wouldn't." Thane didn't feel the need to admit he cared for the children more than he'd thought possible in just the day he'd known them.

"Why?" The little girl held his gaze.

"Lily…" Jack's tone carried a warning his younger sister ignored.

"Why, Uncle Thane?"

Thane released a sigh, hesitant to voice his feelings, but wanting to reassure the children. "Because I love you, that's why."

"Okay." Lily wiggled for Jemma to set her down and ran over to the table where Greenfield and Cook set out their meal.

Cook's eyebrows nearly touched her hairline as she took in Lily and Jack's muddy appearances, as well as Thane. As she turned back to the kitchen door, she gave Jemma a glance and shook her head.

Until she rid Lily of her mud coating, the folly of putting on a clean dress forced Jemma to don the dress she'd worn to work in the garden. Scandalized by the upheaval Thane Jordan had wrought in such a short time, she hoped the escapade in the mud would be the last such uncivilized adventure.

Dinner was lively, with Weston carrying much of the conversation. When they finished eating, the solicitor, Greenfield, and Cook carted everything back inside. Thane helped Jack bathe in a tub set up in the laundry room near the kitchen while Jemma carted Lily to the upstairs bath.

After she tucked the children into bed, washed herself and dressed again, she went to her room to spend a few moments gathering her composure before meeting with Weston and Mr. Jordan in the formal parlor.

Still uncertain what decision she should make, Jemma knew she needed to make one soon. Lost in her thoughts, she opened her bedroom door, stepped into the hall, and bumped into Thane. He exited the bath, wearing nothing but a pair of clean trousers made of a fabric she'd learned was denim.

Shocked at the sight of his shirtless chest, firm with muscles and covered in tan skin, her gaze dropped down to his snug pants then traveled back up to his head. Water droplets clung to his hair and a smile played about the corners of his mouth.

"Merciful heavens, Mr. Jordan! You most certainly should not traipse about the house in such a state." Jemma turned her back to him and stared at the wall while heat seared her cheeks. The sight of his broad chest, dusted with golden hair, filled her vision, even when she squeezed her eyes shut.

"I'm out of clean shirts. I was going to see if I could rustle up one of Henry's old shirts to wear until I can get some laundry done."

"Leave your soiled things in the laundry room. Cook will see to them tomorrow. In the meantime, Henry's clothes are still in his room. If you care to accompany me, I'll see if we can find something."

Swiftly walking down the hall, Jemma opened the door to a large bedroom decorated in shades of navy and cream. She opened the door to a closet and pulled out a shirt, holding it behind her. "Try this on."

Thane worked his arms into the too-tight sleeves but couldn't get the buttons to meet over his chest.

"Guess I'm a little bigger than Henry." Thane's attempts at extricating himself from the shirt proved fruitless. Unable to slide the sleeves off his muscular upper arms, a grunt escaped as he worked to free himself.

Intrigued by the rustling noises he made, Jemma cast a glance over her shoulder. The sight of him ensnared by the ill-fitting garment tipped her mouth up into a smile.

Slowly turning around, she folded her arms across her chest and stared at him. "Perhaps I should leave you in such a state. You don't seem nearly as menacing or daunting when you spin around in circles like that."

Thane narrowed his gaze and glared at her. "If you're just going to stand there gawking, you might as well help get this thing off me."

Every social grace instilled in Jemma from the time she was Lily's age urged her to leave the room and not look back. However, she ignored the impropriety of being in a bedroom with a half-dressed man she'd known only twenty-four hours and stepped behind Thane, tugging on the shirt.

The more he struggled, the more she fought down her giggles until they burst forth like bubbles, popping around him in a delightful sound.

"Are you even trying to help?" He smirked at her over his shoulder.

"Yes, but you remind me of Lily. She is forever trying to yank off her dresses and getting them stuck halfway then she runs screaming through the house, sure it's trying to smother her to death."

Thane chuckled. "I know how she feels."

Jemma gave one sleeve a vigorous tug and the force of the motion knocked her backward onto the bed. Since the sleeve still encased Thane's arm, he tumbled down on top of her, causing her to suck in a gulp of air.

His warmth seeped into her while his masculine, enticing scent flooded her senses, making her take another deep breath. In mesmerized fascination, she watched as a muscle bunched in his jaw and his eyes went from cool to molten.

Her gaze roved past his chin and down his neck as she took in his taut, tan muscles. A swarm of butterflies burst into a frenzied flight in her stomach and she felt slightly lightheaded.

Accustomed to being around men who dressed properly, with jackets and waistcoats over their shirts, she'd only ever seen Henry or her father in shirtsleeves a few times. She'd never seen a grown man shirtless before and admired the awe-inspiring form of Thane. Desperately wanting to touch one of his impressive muscles, to discover what it felt like beneath her hands, Jemma clenched her fingers together.

As she lifted her gaze to his face again, she wondered what it would feel like to have his bearded cheek pressed to hers. Jemma battled the urge to pull his face down and satisfy her curiosity.

Aware of her perusal of his upper anatomy, Thane held still, rapturously rooted to the spot. Jemma's soft form fit so well against his angular planes as he breathed in her feminine, alluring fragrance.

He stared down into the warm coppery depths of her eyes and took note of the amber flames flickering there. What little sense he had left dissipated when she parted her lips and he began to lower his head to hers.

"Might I assume you two have resolved matters?" Weston asked from the door. Jemma squeaked with surprise while Thane rolled off the bed and to his feet.

"No, you may not assume such a thing." Jemma scrambled to stand and almost fell to the floor as her skirts twisted around her legs. Thane reached out a hand to steady her but she jerked her arm away. "Mr. Jordan was at a loss for a clean garment to wear and we were simply trying to find something of Henry's. Apparently, they are not the same size."

"Apparently." Weston struggled to hide his grin. "I've got a shirt you can borrow, my good man. I think I'm probably closer to your size than your brother."

"Thank you, sir." Thane ripped the sleeves from Henry's shirt and handed the ruined garment to Jemma before following Weston from the room.

Staring at the fabric balled in her hand, Jemma fought the need to fan her face and cool her heated cheeks. She had no idea men looked so… virile beneath their clothes. Or perhaps it was just Thane Jordan.

After tossing the shirt on the rumpled bed, Jemma rushed from the room and down the stairs, even less certain what her decision should be.

Chapter Five

Jemma carried a tea tray into the parlor and set it on a low table in front of the settee. Rigsly followed her, plunking down on the floor next to her as she took a seat and settled her skirts.

"Whatever shall I do, Risgly? What do you want to do?" The dog lifted his head and blinked his dark brown eyes at her, woofing softly.

"What does that mean, boy? I still have not fine-tuned my ability to speak canine." Jemma smiled and rubbed the dog's head.

Male voices preceded Weston and Thane into the room, giving Jemma time to neatly fold her hands on her lap and straighten her spine.

The men appeared to be in good spirits as they strode in, both smiling. Thane wore one of Weston's shirts. It appeared too small, but at least he could button it across his chest.

Averting her gaze from his chest to the tea in front of her, she poured three cups and handed one to Weston then Thane before taking a cup and saucer in her hand.

"Now, then, shall we discuss the proposal Mr. Jordan made this morning and resolve all this uncertainty?" Weston asked after taking a drink from his cup and returning it and the saucer to the table beside him.

"Have you given our conversation any consideration, Miss Bryan?" Thane asked, watching her closely.

Although she maintained her perfect posture, he detected a slight squirm as she sat on one end of the settee. Rigsly must have sensed her discomfort, because the dog rose to his feet and plopped his big head on her lap, whimpering.

She lifted one hand and absently stroked his head while setting down her tea with the other.

Lady Jemma Bryan might be a freethinking nuisance, but she was one of the most graceful and polished women Thane had ever met. As he admired the curve of her cheek, the length of her neck, the elegant form of her fingers, he unexpectedly wished he could be the dog.

Aggravated by his thoughts, he returned his gaze to her face, looking at her expectantly as he awaited her response. "Would you consider marrying me and moving to my ranch in America, for the sake of the children?"

"I've done little else but consider it today." She dropped her gaze to her lap, realizing she'd examined every alternative.

Her biggest dilemma didn't stem from leaving everything she'd ever known, including her friends and heritage. She had no fear of crossing the ocean or traveling across the vast country of America to a remote ranch in Oregon. Grave concerns about living somewhere that was no doubt primitive with a lack of civilized accoutrements didn't bother her.

The one thing that gave her pause, made her stomach roil with nervous energy and her thoughts whirl like a feather in a windstorm, was the man sitting across from her with his unyielding gaze fastened on her face.

Thane Jordan made her uncomfortable, infuriated, and entirely fascinated.

Would he treat her with respect as his wife? Would he continue to goad her until her anger sparked and she lost control of her ability to bite her tongue as she'd already done repeatedly since they'd met the previous afternoon?

Would he keep his promise their marriage would be in name only? Would he attempt to enforce his husbandly rights?

Would he, indeed, provide for her and the children? She knew Henry left him a wealthy man. Would he hoard the money or waste it on gambling, drinking, and lasciviousness?

Would he fill the role of a father to Lily and Jack or continue to behave as the indulgent uncle who spoiled them? After spending thirty minutes on her knees next to the bathtub scrubbing mud off Lily, she hoped he didn't plan to do such irresponsible things often. An occasional frivolous moment without regard to the consequences could be accepted, but she couldn't deal with such behavior daily. It would spoil the children and leave them completely unmanageable.

There was also the matter of Thane's physical presence. He commanded attention, even in his working clothes with unkempt hair and that scruffy beard. Thoughts of seeing him without his shirt, of feeling his weight against hers on the bed, filled her face with heat and infused her cheeks with color.

"Come now, Miss Bryan, with those pink cheeks you look as though you're indulging in inappropriate thoughts." Thane's tone was teasing but his words made her even more ill at ease.

Jemma opened her mouth to speak, snapped it closed, and tried again but failed to produce a sound beyond a sigh.

Much to her dismay, Thane rose from his chair and sat next to her. He took the hand not resting on Rigsly's head into his and looked down at her face.

The smile he gave her held compassion and care, unlike the smug smirks she had quickly grown to expect.

"Miss Bryan, perhaps it would set your mind at ease if you voice your concerns and we discuss them before you make a decision."

She nodded her head, but found it impossible to vocalize even one of her questions with him sitting at her side.

"Why?" she finally asked, lifting her gaze to Thane's.

"Why?" he asked, confused. "Why did I ask you to marry me?"

"Yes."

"Because of the children." Thane continued to hold her hand but his eyes focused on a spot in the distance, something only he could see. "Coming here and finding Henry really and truly gone made me realize I don't want to lose my last connection to him, to my family. Henry was all I thought I had left and now there are Jack and Lily. I want to help them grow up to be good people."

Jemma remained silent so Thane continued speaking. "I don't know a thing about raising kids or having a wife, but I'm willing to learn, for their sakes. It won't be easy, and my ranch is nothing like this cottage, but I promise you'll never go hungry and life there will be busy and fulfilling." He looked at her again as he finished speaking.

As she considered his words, Jemma slowly nodded her head. "What do you expect of me?"

"To help raise the kids, keep up the house, prepare meals. I wouldn't expect you to help outside on the ranch. You can plant flowers or a garden in the spring, if you're of a mind to. If I failed to make it clear this morning, I don't expect our marriage to be anything except a business arrangement of sorts. I give you my word it would be in name only, unless you decide otherwise."

She took a moment to study him, to make sure he was sincere. "What will I be allowed to bring with me?"

Thane glanced around the room, at the dog with his head contentedly nestled on her lap, and released a sigh.

He would probably regret it later, but he smiled at her with an open expression.

"What do you want to bring?"

"A few of the household items that belonged to my family. My wardrobe, of course, and the children's things. It would be prudent to pack some of Jane and Henry's things the children might like to have when they are grown."

"That sounds reasonable," Thane said, anticipating a much longer list. "Anything else?"

She gave him an imploring glance. "If it isn't too much to ask, I'd also like to take Rigsly and my horse."

"You may have your dog and horse, although getting that dog to the ranch is going to be interesting. Will he do well in an arid climate?"

"His breed hunts both waterfowl and upland game. Rigsly should do fine and I thank you for agreeing to take him along. He is part of the family to the children and it would break their hearts to leave him behind."

Thane nodded in agreement and glanced at Weston. The man winked encouragingly before taking another sip of his tea. "Any other questions that you'd like answered, Miss Bryan?"

"How would you treat me?" Jemma asked. The question and her voice held an almost child-like tone.

"Treat you? What do you mean?" Thane's brows furrowed together, creating twin vertical lines down the center of his forehead.

"Will you continue to insult me, call me names, and test my patience?"

Thane laughed and leaned back against the cushions of the settee. "Most likely. You and I get along about like two cats with their tails tied together and stuffed in a gunnysack. Have no fear, I will treat you as a woman I respect and admire. It's in my nature to tease and prod, and

I've always been able to provoke people past the limit of their patience. Call it a gift."

Jemma's mouth turned upward, but she shook her head. "How am I to know you wouldn't insult me in front of others, as you've done here?"

"It's all family here, isn't it? At least I would consider Weston part of your family. Rest assured, I will treat you with the utmost consideration around others. At home, though, you'll just have to get used to me ruffling your bloomers."

Weston howled with laughter while Jemma drew in a shocked gasp. "Sir! That is no way to speak to a lady."

"To any lady, perhaps not, but I think it'll do for you Lady Jemma." Thane lifted the back of her hand to his lips and pressed a soft kiss to her delicate skin. "Will you please marry me?"

Despite her head telling her to run up to her room and lock the door, Jemma lifted her gaze to Thane's and offered him a small smile. "Yes, I believe I shall marry you." The feel of his hand holding hers made her skin tingle. However, the touch of his warm lips and soft beard on the back of her hand made feelings she'd never experienced course through her veins and settle in the pit of her stomach.

Afraid of what she had just agreed to do, she pulled her hand away and lifted her cup of lukewarm tea. She hoped Thane Jordan proved to be a man of his word.

"What do you mean by 'read the banns at church Sunday,' Weston? I have no idea what you're talking about." Thane plunked down his cup of tea at breakfast the next morning and stared at the solicitor. At least Weston waited until the children left the table to bring up a topic that would no doubt result in he and Jemma butting heads once again.

"The pastor of the parish will read the banns for the next three Sundays. I assure you it is quite necessary for your marriage. Since you aren't British, I think we should also procure a common license, but it is tradition for banns to be read."

"But I planned to wrap up business and head for home as quickly as possible. I thought we could see a justice of the peace and be on our way." Thane glanced over at his intended as Jemma's teacup clanged against the saucer in her hand. She set down the cup with a look of horror on her face.

Irritated by what he viewed as a pointless delay, he leaned back in his chair and ran a hand over his head. "Might I presume to be wrong in that assumption?"

"Indeed," Jemma said, glancing to Weston for confirmation. Rattled at the prospect of a hasty wedding as it was, she couldn't imagine not holding it in the church she'd always attended. In addition, she wanted her friends around her as she pledged her troth to the insufferable, intriguing, handsome Mr. Jordan.

"Please tell me this isn't going to be a full-blown shindig. Can't it be a quiet, small ceremony? We need to leave as soon as possible. I've got a ranch to run and can't be gone any longer than absolutely necessary." Thane ignored Jemma's cool glare and turned his attention to Weston.

"I believe the shindig, as you call it, is up to the lady to decide. Of course, with only a few weeks to plan, it will be a scaled down version of anything she may have hoped to carry out." Weston smiled encouragingly at Jemma. "Do you have any specific ideas in mind, my dear?"

"I started a list this morning, but I do think it proper to have a small celebration after the ceremony. I'm sure

Catherine and Charles would be more than happy to host it at their home."

"Splendid idea, my dear." Weston enthusiastically slapped his hand on the table. "Good show. Will you speak to them right away?"

"I thought to call on them today and share the news."

"Who are Catherine and Charles?" Thane asked, dreading the social calls he'd be forced to endure until he could set foot on a boat bound for America.

"Catherine is my dearest and oldest friend. She and her husband, Charles, also own several prosperous mills here in Bolton. His father is the Duke of Winterbury. Perhaps you noticed their home on the way to Henry's office yesterday. It's the stone manor just before you enter town." Jemma tipped her head and gave Thane a smile that put him in mind of a cat waiting to pounce on a bird.

"You mean the castle? Your friend lives at the castle?"

"It's not a castle, per se, but a very fine manor. Don't you think, Weston?"

Weston nodded in agreement. "Very fine, what? And such a lovely place for a gathering after your wedding. Yes, my dear, you should visit Catherine today. What will you do for a gown?"

"I'm going to contact Madame Beauchene in London. She used to do all my gowns, before…" Jemma's voice cracked as tears welled in her eyes. "Please excuse me, sirs. I have much to attend today."

Thane and Weston both rose from the table as Jemma made a hasty exit. Once she left the room, Thane sank into his chair and rubbed a hand over his face.

"I think we better skip going over Henry's accounts today. You are going to tell me everything I need to know about this wedding and any other particulars that I need to wrangle with between now and the time we leave."

"Yes, yes, of course, Thane. Shall we venture into town? We have a multitude of details to cover in a very limited time." Weston set down his napkin, motioning for Thane to precede him down the hall and out the door.

Chapter Six

"Lily, love, please do try to sit still." Jemma bent down and whispered in the little girl's ear. The child nodded and held perfectly still for almost a minute before she began squirming again.

Jemma couldn't blame the child. She wanted to squirm in her seat as well, but kept her back straight, posture impeccable, as they sat on the wooden pew at church.

When Mr. Jordan appeared at the table that morning wearing a new suit as fine as any Henry possessed, it left her stunned and speechless. She had yet to recover from the shock of seeing him so well dressed. The cut of the suit emphasized his wide shoulders and muscled form while the gray color brought out smoky flecks in his blue eyes.

Admiration filled her as she studied the gray topcoat with covered buttons and matching waistcoat, dark gray trousers, and starched short-collar shirt with tie. However, he hadn't altogether abandoned his western manner, wearing his cowboy boots rather than dress shoes. At least he'd polished them.

Even with his hair in need of a good cutting and his beard in need of a trim, he still looked handsome and quite dashing.

As they walked into church that morning, Jemma put on a friendly smile and worked her way to their pew, ignoring all the whispers about the man who trailed behind her carrying Lily. Once they settled into their seats, Jemma made certain Lily sat between them while Jack insisted on sitting between Thane and Weston.

The pastor began the service and Jemma tried to focus her attention on the sermon but found her thoughts and gaze drifting to Thane. Although he took great pleasure in upsetting her, she admitted he was good with the children. As Lily continued to fidget, he lifted the child and held her on his lap.

Lily released a contented sigh and nestled against his chest. Within moments, she closed her eyes and fell asleep. The sight of the darling girl held so tenderly by the big man made Jemma smile and filled her with hope that she'd made the right decision.

When the pastor read the banns at the closing of the service, she knew it was too late to change her mind.

People she'd known for years rushed to her, offering their words of congratulations and surprise at not having met her intended. Most of the well-wishers realized the reason for the marriage when she introduced him as Henry's brother.

Some of the joy fled from the day for Jemma when a few of the women gave her sympathetic glances and softly spoken words of encouragement.

Thane took one of her hands in his and carried Lily while Jack clung to Jemma's other hand, making their way outside.

As they strolled across the lawn toward the carriage, he leaned down and his warm breath stirred the tendrils of hair around her ear.

"Buck up, ol' girl. It could be worse. I could be a drunken, toothless degenerate, intent on having my way with you."

Offended by his words, she tugged Jack forward and climbed into the carriage with Weston's assistance.

Coolly glaring at Thane as he sat down, still cradling Lily, she wondered if she could find some way of putting him in his place. No doubt, it would only serve to encourage him to insult her further. She pressed her lips together and turned her focus to Charles and Catherine as they hurried their direction.

"You almost left before we could say hello," Catherine said, leaning into the carriage and smiling at Thane. "I'm Catherine. We're so pleased to meet you. Henry and Jane were so dear to us and we look forward to having you take a meal or two with us before your wedding. I'm so excited you and our beloved Jemma are allowing us to host the ball after the ceremony."

Thane managed an appropriate response then shook Charles' hand as he introduced himself.

"We won't keep you, my good man, but perhaps we could go riding or out on a hunt one day soon." Charles offered him a friendly grin.

"I look forward to it," Thane said, finding the idea of a hunt appealing. "Maybe next week?"

"Certainly, sir. I'll send word with a date and time."

Charles escorted Catherine back to their waiting coach. Thane watched the couple depart as their carriage began the drive home. Lily awoke and chattered about the trolls that lived under the bridge, the fairies who danced in the daisies alongside the road, and the magician who lived in the gatehouse at Catherine and Charles' manor.

"He's not a magician, Lily," Jack said, tired of listening to his sister's stories.

"He is. He made a coin fall out of my ear last time we visited Catherine. So there." Lily stuck out her tongue at her brother and he reached out to grab it, making her squeal.

"Hey, now. You two settle down." Thane gave them a warning glance and they both quieted without question.

He turned his gaze from the children to the expensive pants covering his legs. It was bad enough Weston had dragged him to a tailor and forced him to buy a new suit, two pairs of trousers, and half a dozen shirts along with a ridiculous top hat, he'd had to endure shaking hands and acting like the doting husband-to-be in front of everyone at church.

Condemned by his own morals, he felt like a fraud and a hypocrite. He needed to go for a long ride to sort out his thoughts.

The vicious yank he gave his tie loosened it as they walked inside the house. Jemma raised an eyebrow, informing him the pastor and his family would soon join them for lunch.

Annoyed, Thane rolled his eyes then stood in front of the mirror in the hall, attempting to fix his tie. Not doing more than jumbling it into a knot, he turned around to find Jemma staring at him, shaking her head.

"That will never do." A step forward brought her so close Thane could see copper and amber sparks in her eyes as she tugged out the knot he created and set about tying it properly.

Thick eyelashes fluttered against her smooth cheeks while she worked. Her soft, womanly fragrance filled his nose and he glanced down, admiring the curved shape of her figure, covered by a peacock blue dress with intricately embroidered panels running down the length of the skirt. A matching hat covered her shiny auburn hair. A plume on the side of it batted his cheek with every movement of her head.

"That is the proper way to wear your tie," she said, patting his chest as she finished, then jerking her hand back as if she'd touched open flames.

She started to walk down the hall toward the kitchen, but he grabbed her hand and gave it a squeeze. Her eyes shot up in surprise and she gazed at him uncertainly.

"Thank you, Lady Jemma. If I didn't mention it before, you look lovely today. That's a very nice color on you."

Cheeks fused with hot color, she nodded her head. "Thank you, sir." Gently pulling her hand away, she rushed down the hall and disappeared into the kitchen.

Thane hung his Stetson on the hall tree, having refused Weston's urging to wear the top hat. He decided to save it for his wedding to wear with the unbelievably expensive suit the tailor worked on altering. According to Weston, the wedding would be quite an affair, even if Jemma didn't have much time to plan it.

They agreed to wed the Monday after the final reading of the banns. The ceremony would take place in the late afternoon at the church with a dinner celebration planned at Catherine and Charles' home following the ceremony. The next morning, they would travel to Liverpool and the following day board a boat for America.

If he could get through the next three weeks, a boat ride across the ocean, a train trip across America, and an hour-long wagon ride to his ranch, life could return to normal.

"I think perhaps I imagined the whole thing," Jemma said, sipping a cup of tea as she and Catherine sat in the sunny drawing room.

Catherine laughed and laid a hand on Jemma's leg, patting it reassuringly. "I assure you even my active imagination couldn't conjure up Thane Jordan."

Jemma frowned at her friend then both of them laughed.

Since the reading of the banns the first Sunday in church, Jemma had hardly seen Weston or Thane. The two of them returned to Liverpool after the banns were read the second Sunday and had been gone all week. With the wedding just days away, Jemma grew more nervous and apprehensive with every passing moment.

As though she could read her mind, Catherine put an arm around her shoulders and gave her a comforting hug. "You're doing the right thing, Jem. The children need to know their uncle, but they also need you with them. It's a brave thing for you to leave behind your life here and venture off to America with a man you've barely met."

"And not entirely sure I like." Jemma recalled the times she'd conversed with Thane since his arrival at the cottage. He never failed to irk her, insult her, or leave her perplexed and disconcerted.

"Are you blind, my friend? What's not to like about the American? He's tall, handsome, strong, and rugged. Half the girls at the parish are hoping he'll take a fancy to them before you two wed."

"They are not!" Jemma glared at Catherine, noticing her friend's teasing smile.

Catherine took a dainty bite of a lemon tart and a sip of tea before answering. "Perhaps not, but he has caught the attention of most of the women. Charles and I are both impressed with him."

"That's because he treats you both with respect and courtesy." Jemma refreshed her tea and furiously stirred in a dollop of cream. "I find him to be boorish, crass, and most often obnoxious."

Instead of responding, Catherine continued sipping her tea, trying to hide her grin.

Irritated, Jemma set her teacup and saucer on the table, knotted her napkin between her hands, and released a worried sigh. "What if he turns out to be a fraud? What if he's a womanizing drunkard who hates children and leaves us with nothing?"

Catherine laughed again then took note of Jemma's serious expression. "My darling girl, I do believe in the time he's been here, if he was any of those things, someone would have noticed. Weston speaks quite highly of him and they've spent most every day together. Moreover, didn't you sell some of your paintings and statuary so you'd have your own money, in the event something untoward happened?"

"Yes, I did. Fortunately, Weston and Mr. Jordan have been gone so much they haven't noticed anything missing from the house. Besides, I've been busy packing. I hope if they do find something amiss, they'll think I'm planning to take it along."

Catherine's gaze fell to a trio of trunks Jemma had filled with various things from the drawing room she just couldn't bear to leave behind. "Did Mr. Jordan give you a limit on the number of trunks you can take?"

"I asked in generic terms what I could take and received his approval for my request." Jemma stared at her lap, aware that she'd been somewhat vague and misleading with Thane. If she gave him a detailed list of everything she planned to take, he'd refuse the majority of it.

"Jem, you do realize everything you pack will have to be freighted to Liverpool, put on a ship, then freighted to a train, then somehow taken out to his ranch. From what I heard he and Charles discussing, his cabin, as he called it, is quite small. Where do you think you'll put everything?" Catherine gave her friend a concerned glance.

"I don't know, but there are some things I just can't leave behind. I just can't." Jemma dabbed at the tears threatening to spill down her cheeks. After inhaling a calming breath, she straightened her shoulders. "Perhaps I got carried away, but I don't know what else to do."

"Come on, Jem." Catherine rose to her feet and held out a hand to her friend. "Let's review what you've already packed and what else you plan to take. I'm sure we can narrow it down a bit while still making sure you have everything you need. There's still time to sell a few things if you continue to refuse to take the funds I offered."

"Of course I refuse to take any money from you and Charles. You've already done far too much, especially hosting the dinner for our wedding. I won't take anything else from you except your friendship, advice, and a promise to write to me in America."

Catherine sniffled and wrapped a hand around Jemma's waist as they strolled down the hall to the front parlor where Greenfield left the packed trunks. "I'm going to miss you, my dear friend, but Thane has already provided me with his address, so at least I'm assured of a means of staying in touch with you. It will take such a dreadfully long time for a letter to reach you, though. I understand there is a telegraph office in Baker City so if an emergency arises, we at least have that as a faster mode of communication."

"When did you find out so much about Baker City? Thane's hardly spoken a dozen words about the place I'm soon to call home."

"He and Charles went for a ride last week then he stayed for luncheon. That's when I decided you could do far worse than marrying Henry's brother. He has the most marvelous eyes, don't you think?"

Jemma grinned at her friend's teasing and opened a trunk so they could sort through the contents.

Nervously standing beside Weston, Jemma jumped when he patted her hand as it rested on his arm.

He bent down to whisper in her ear. "You're a beautiful bride, Lady Jemma. It's a true honor to walk you down the aisle."

Jemma took in a tight, frightened breath. "Thank you, Weston, for this, and for always being so helpful. I appreciate all you've done for us and will miss you greatly."

"Now, now, my dear. Let's get you married to Mr. Jordan and we'll worry about maudlin goodbyes another day." Weston gave her a lopsided grin, making her smile.

Jemma reached up and adjusted her veil then fluffed the train behind her before nodding to Weston. The two of them walked up the aisle. She raised her gaze to the man waiting to become her husband and almost tripped as she took in his appearance.

Dressed in a black tailcoat of the finest fabric with matching trousers, the fitted jacket accented Thane's muscular form. A white silk brocade waistcoat topped a white shirt with a stand-up collar accented by a white silk bow tie. Despite his formal dress, Thane wore his cowboy boots.

Although surprised by his finely made and exact-fitting suit, his hair and face gave her a moment of pause. He'd finally gone to a barber. Gone were the long, shaggy locks she'd grown accustomed to seeing. He'd carefully combed his short, thick hair into place.

Even more shocking were his freshly shaved cheeks, revealing a face more handsome than she could have imagined. He smirked at her and twin brackets framed his mouth, calling her attention to his generous lips.

Fortified with a deep breath, she finished her walk to Thane's side. She kept her gaze demurely averted as Weston placed her hand on Thane's arm before taking a seat beside his wife in the front pew, next to Lily and Jack.

Thane glanced down at Jemma's delicate hand resting on his arm and noticed the slight tremble in her fingers.

As she floated down the aisle in a gown that made her appear regal and elegant, the sight of her made his mouth go dry while his heart thumped in a rapid beat. He could easily picture her as a princess at court with the proud way she held her head and carried herself.

No matter how much he tried to convince himself it was of no importance, his bride was a beautiful woman. One he found himself attracted to, despite the fact she tested his patience and often left him perturbed.

Purposely focusing his attention back on the pastor, the man soon asked for the ring and Thane removed it from his pocket. Sliding it on Jemma's finger through the slit in her glove, he repeated his vows in a strong, determined voice.

He listened as Jemma recited her vows, her tone steady although her hand trembled in his. When she settled her copper gaze on his face, he gave her fingers a reassuring squeeze. Mindful of the fear mingling with apprehension in her eyes, he wondered what upset her most — marrying someone she didn't particularly like, leaving behind her home, or surrendering her independence to a man.

"You may kiss your bride." The pastor grinned at him over his spectacles. Thane thought he saw the man wink and smiled back at him.

"With pleasure," Thane whispered, lifting the filmy veil from Jemma's face and lowering his head so his lips were close to her ear. "I don't know how you English seal your vows, but I intend to do a good job of it."

Jemma's eyes widened at his comment, but she didn't have an opportunity to move away from him. As he wrapped his arms around her impossibly tiny waist, he drew her closer and pressed his mouth to hers, gently at first, then with a hungry ardor that took even him by surprise.

Slowly raising his head, he took in her flushed cheeks and the fire burning in her eyes. For a moment, he regretted his decision the marriage would be in name only. From her reaction to his kiss, he thought there might be one area of married life in which they'd be completely compatible.

Abruptly pulling his thoughts back in line, he placed a hand to the small of her back and walked her down the aisle amid cheers from the guests in the packed church. Although Jemma assured him most people would be too busy to attend a ceremony on a Monday afternoon, it appeared her status as a well-loved member of the church and community drew a large crowd.

Ushered into a coach, they were driven to Charles and Catherine's stately home. Upon reaching the manor, the butler escorted them into the library where a photographer had a camera set up, ready to capture their images.

"Oh, this is a lovely surprise." Jemma said as the man positioned Thane in a chair and had her stand beside it.

Thane remained quiet as the man fussed with the abominable top hat Weston demanded he wear. Beyond endurance, Thane yanked it off his head and tossed it aside, glaring at the photographer.

"I think the gentleman is ready. Shall I adjust your skirt, madam?"

Jemma turned to fluff her train and accepted his assistance in draping it artfully for the photograph.

Satisfied with their positions, the man prepared to take the photo. Thane glanced over at the two feet of space separating him and his new bride. "Just a moment," he said, wrapping a hand around Jemma's waist and drawing her close against the side of the chair. Her hands settled on his shoulder and the photographer took the picture before she could pull away.

"Please, stay perfectly still and I'll take another."

Disturbed and simultaneously thrilled by Thane's familiarity with her person as his hand rested around her waist, Jemma stood motionless.

The photographer prepared to take a third photograph. "Would you care to smile for this photograph? You are just wed, after all."

While the photographer prepared to take another photo, Thane whispered a comment to Jemma about the photographer resembling a bowlegged monkey, with his overly long arms and protruding lips. She found his words completely inappropriate, but entirely funny.

Plagued by a desire to laugh, she smiled in amusement while Thane looked at her with a smirk on his face as the photographer took the photo.

By then, Jack and Lily appeared and Jemma insisted they all pose together for a photograph, then she had a photo taken that included Charles and Catherine, Mr. and Mrs. Weston, and Mr. and Mrs. Greenfield.

Once they finished with the photographs, Thane took the children with him while Catherine ushered Jemma upstairs to change.

As Catherine helped her out of her wedding dress and into an elaborate peach-colored gown accented with brocade roses and airy lace trim, Jemma thanked her for providing the photographer.

"Thane made arrangements for that, Jem. He asked if I thought it would be a good idea, and I knew how much it would mean to you to have photos. He's the one you need to thank. Thane asked him to bring his equipment to make prints of the photos tonight and we'll each have copies. Isn't that wonderful?"

Surprised by Thane's kindness and generosity, Jemma didn't know what to think. The more she discovered about Thane Jordan, the less confident she felt around him.

"I know you think he's a crude and arrogant beast, but mercy, Jem. He looks quite acceptable in a fine suit with a haircut and a shave. Don't you agree?"

He appeared far beyond acceptable and much more along the lines of utterly spellbinding. However, Jemma kept her opinion of how appealing she found her husband to herself.

"I suppose he looks suitable."

Catherine stepped in front of her and took her by the shoulders, giving her a teasing shake. "Could you not see through your veil, Jem? Was it clouding your vision?"

Jemma laughed and shook her head. "Of course, not."

Catherine gave her another pointed stare and Jemma released a sigh. "I will concede that despite being a brute, he's quite a handsome one. I thought he appeared dashing and debonair."

"See, that wasn't so hard," Catherine teased, adjusting the short train on Jemma's gown. "Now, let's join your party."

A few hours later, after they'd eaten a delicious meal, those attending the celebration gathered in the ballroom. Uncertain if Thane possessed any dancing skills, Jemma started to look around for him. Before she took a step, she breathed in his familiar scent as his warmth enveloped her.

"I suppose it's expected for the bride and groom to begin the dancing," Thane said quietly as he bent near her ear.

"Yes, that's correct. Do you know how to waltz?" she asked, turning to gaze at him.

With a smirk, he took her hand and led her onto the dance floor. "You're about to find out."

Surprised by his agility as he waltzed her flawlessly across the floor, Jemma relaxed a little. So far, Thane had filled her day with unexpected, yet pleasant moments. If their marriage proved as harmonious as this day had been, maybe she'd been dreading it without reason. As she cast a subtle glance at the attractive man who held her in his arms, a tingle of excitement raced through her. She was his bride, at least in name.

While they danced, Thane rubbed his fingers along the pale skin of her arm, exposed by the short sleeve of her dress. He knew it would bother her, but couldn't seem to help himself.

He wondered where she and Catherine disappeared after the photographs. He'd glanced up as she made her way down the stairs in a beautiful evening gown the same shade as the peaches he used to snitch off their neighbor's tree when he was a boy. The taste of her lips was every bit as sweet. Now that he'd had a sample, he wanted more and pondered how soft her skin might feel to his callused hands.

A compulsion to reach out and touch her skin worried him all through dinner. As they danced, the desire to rub his fingers down the expanse of her arm left him distracted. Finally surrendering to the urge, her skin felt as soft and smooth as he imagined, only warmer.

When he turned his gaze to her face, warning sparks shot from her eyes, although she continued smiling. Witness to any number of her smiles during the last few weeks, he recognized this one as a smile letting him know he tread perilously close to invoking her wrath.

It was not the time or place to provoke her, so he tipped his head slightly and led her in another dance.

Once the guests began to disperse, the newly married couple made their way to the foyer where Jemma and Catherine engaged in a series of tear-filled hugs with promises to write and stay in touch. Thane shook Charles' hand and thanked him for his hospitality and help, inviting him and Catherine to visit his ranch, if they ever found themselves venturing to America.

"We might just take you up on that, ol' chap, and see what all the fuss over the Wild West is about."

Thane grinned and slapped him on the back. "You do that. I'll make sure you get the full western experience, complete with branding cattle and riding broncs."

Greenfield and Cook took Lily and Jack to the cottage, tucking them into bed after giving them a few minutes to enjoy the ball. The devoted servants would close up the house before moving on to their next position.

Thane made sure they received adequate compensation for their years of dedicated work. He also extended an invitation for them to come to America if they ever tired of the English weather.

Weston and his wife, Margaret, who were also staying at the cottage, departed earlier in the evening, leaving Jemma and Thane the opportunity to have a private moment or two on their ride home together.

After settling the top hat on his head at a cocky angle, Thane walked Jemma out to the waiting coach and helped her inside.

He sprawled on the seat across from her, studying her flushed cheeks and the tense set of her shoulders.

"You can relax, Lady Jemma. I'm not planning to ravage you."

"Good heavens!" Her glance went from the window of the coach to his face. His mocking grin caused her to shake her head. She didn't know how he accomplished it, but he seemed to grow more handsome as the evening wore on. The hat, set at a rakish tilt on his head, made him appear even more charming than he had before.

It was a pity she knew it was all a façade. Beneath his fine suit and natty hat lurked a man bent on teasing her without mercy and stirring her temper at every opportunity.

As she recalled the kiss he'd given her to seal their wedding vows, she felt her cheeks flush. At least the gathering darkness kept him from seeing the spots of telltale pink.

She'd been kissed a few times as a much younger girl, but nothing prepared her for the sensations created by the touch of Thane's mouth to hers. Just thinking of the exchange made her lips tingle with the desire to experience his kiss again.

Harshly berating herself for her ridiculous, romantic notions, relief flowed over her when the coach stopped in front of the cottage. Thane stepped out then reached in a hand to help her down.

They strolled up the walk together and she started to go in the door, but Thane put a hand to her arm, stopping her.

"For the sake of tradition," he said, then swept her into his arms and carried her inside.

Nearly undone by the feel of his strong arms carrying her, his eyes gazing into hers with warmth, something she couldn't quite describe drew her into the moment.

Inside the foyer, Thane set her on her feet and closed the door.

Befuddled and overcome by the experiences of the day, Jemma decided she needed to go to bed before she said or did something she'd later regret.

She started up the stairs, then stopped and looked back at him. "Thank you for today, Mr. Jordan. I appreciate all you did to make our wedding a happy memory."

"You're welcome, Lady Jemma." Thane removed his hat and bowed to her with a flourish. "Since we're married, though, I'd prefer you call me Thane."

"Very well, Thane. Thank you, again, and good night."

Jemma hastened up the steps to her room, changed into her nightgown and took down her hair. After pulling on a wrapper, she hurried down the hall to check on the children. She stopped by Jack's room and found the boy spread across his bed with his covers half off, one arm flung above his head.

He looked so much like his father and uncle.

Jemma righted his covers, tucking them in around him and gazed at him a moment, hoping Henry and Jane would be pleased that the children would be in the care of their only two living relatives.

After she ran light fingers through the boy's hair, brushing it away from his face, she kissed his forehead and quietly left the room.

When she stepped into the hall, she heard a deep, masculine voice and followed it to Lily's door. A peek inside the room revealed Thane rocking the child in the chair by the window.

"Yes, Lily, you looked just like a fairy princess today in your pretty dress. Did you have a good time?"

"Oh, yes, Uncle Thane. It was the bestest day. Did you see me dance, Uncle Thane? I danced and danced."

Thane chuckled. "I did see you dance, honey. Do you like to dance?"

"Yes. I'm the bestest dancer and I sing, too. Want to hear me sing?"

"Maybe tomorrow. Right now, it's past your bedtime. Don't you think you ought to go to sleep?"

"I'm too excited to sleep," Lily said, then yawned as Thane continued to rock her slowly back and forth in the chair. "Did you see Auntie Jemma? She was so pretty in her gown."

"She is lovely," Thane agreed. "Your aunt is a very beautiful woman and I'm sure you'll grow up to look like her."

"Oh, goodie. I want to grow up like Auntie Jemma and marry a pretty boy like you."

Jemma could see Thane's smile in the light of the lamp sitting on a nearby table. "You don't call boys pretty, Lily. You should call them handsome."

"Then you're the most handsome boy in the world. My papa was handsome. You won't leave me like papa, will you?"

Thane held her a little tighter and kissed the top of her head. "No, sweetheart. I won't leave you."

Lily's voice grew sleepier and she nestled closer against Thane. "Are you and Auntie Jemma my papa and mummy now?"

"I suppose so, Lily. Your aunt and I promise to take good care of you. Now close your eyes and go to sleep. We have a big adventure awaiting us tomorrow."

"Okay, Uncle Thane. I love you."

Jemma watched as Thane carried their niece to her bed and tucked her in, gently brushing the curls away from her face before pressing a soft kiss to her tiny cheek. "I love you too, honey. Sweet dreams."

Thane blew out the light and backed out of the room, almost bumping into Jemma as she lingered in the hall, brushing at the tears on her cheeks.

He pulled Lily's door mostly closed then gripped Jemma's arms in his hands, looking into her face. "What's wrong?"

"Nothing," Jemma said, trying to swallow back her tears. She knew Thane cared for Jack and Lily, but his tender attention to the little girl touched something in her heart.

All the excitement of the day made her weepy, or so she told herself as she lifted moist eyes to Thane. "Thank you for seeing to Lily. She sometimes has trouble falling asleep."

"I didn't mind. She's a sweet little thing when she isn't throwing a tantrum or demanding attention."

"Welcome to the world of a three-year-old child." Jemma grinned as Thane released his grip and walked with her down the hall toward her room. "Jack was the same way at her age, but by the time he was four, he settled down quite a bit."

"I have a feeling Lily won't be as quiet or solemn as Jack."

Jemma nodded. "I agree with your assessment. She's a spirited little thing full of grand ideas and a wild imagination."

Thane leaned against her doorframe as she stepped inside her bedroom. "I bet you were a lot like her as a child."

"Possibly, but I refuse to admit anything."

She started to close her door, but Thane held out a hand, stopping its progress. "Thank you."

Uncertain what she could have done to earn his thanks, she glanced up at him and studied his face, searching for a clue. She'd more or less been a thorn in his side since the day he set foot in the cottage. "For what?"

"For marrying me. I think we'll do fine." He bent down and pressed a brief kiss to her cheek then walked off in the direction of his room.

Chapter Seven

The sound of Thane calling Jemma's name echoed through the house as she helped Cook pack a basket of food to eat on the way to Liverpool.

"You better go see what the kerfuffle is about, dear." Cook tipped her head toward the door. "I don't think you should keep your husband waiting."

"Impatience is not a virtue. He can wait until I'm finished helping you. Besides, it is abominable for him to raise his voice in such a disgraceful manner. Mr. Jordan needs to learn respectable comportment." Jemma finished wrapping sandwiches in brown paper and carefully set them inside the basket. The sound of boots clomping down the hall at a brisk pace made her heart beat faster.

Thane strode into the kitchen, tipped his hat to Cook, then turned the force of his cool glare on Jemma.

"I've been calling for you? Didn't you hear me?"

"Indeed. Bellowing about the house like a caged bull, I'm sure everyone from here to Bolton has heard you. Is it too much to ask to be addressed in a civil tone, sir?"

"It is when you've lied to me, you conniving little wench." Thane cupped her elbow in his hand then propelled her down the hall and out the front door. Marched to where wagons waited to be loaded with their belongings, Thane motioned to the stacks of trunks she'd packed and directed out to the front lawn.

A glance over the piles of trunks assured her nothing had been missed. "What is the problem? How dare you call me a wench or a liar! Why I ought to…"

"Explain yourself!" Thane ordered, glaring at her. "You told me you wanted to take a few things that belonged to your mother and a few things for Jack and Lily to remember Jane and Henry, along with your clothes, the dog, and your horse. This, my dear Lady Jemma, is more than a few things. There are thirty-two trunks out here. Thirty-two! You better decide what you absolutely can't live without and what you'll leave behind, because I'm telling you right now, you can take sixteen of them and not one more!"

Jemma's mouth opened, but Thane clapped a hand over it before she had a chance to speak.

"Let me warn you, I meant what I said. You have thirty minutes to decide what goes and what stays. If, at that time, you still haven't chosen, I'll decide for you. Am I clear?"

Angry, she narrowed her gaze and wished she weren't a lady so she could tell Thane Jordan what she thought of him. Brusquely nodding her head, she turned to the men Thane hired to transport the trunks to the ship in Liverpool.

"Gentlemen, if you please, I'd like…"

Thane stalked off in the direction of the stables, incensed that Jemma thought he'd allow her to take that many trunks. He had in mind she might have a dozen but when he discovered thirty-two trunks waiting to be loaded, he'd seen red.

The woman was crazy. No one needed that much stuff. Once they reached his ranch, he had nowhere to put any of it. She'd find out soon enough his small cabin would barely have room for the four of them, let alone all her fripperies.

This was why he'd avoided women all these years. They were nothing but trouble, and irritation and… soft curves and alluring fragrances.

Infuriated with himself for the direction of his thoughts, he took several calming breaths before opening the stable door and readying the horses for transport. Rather than spend the day trapped in the coach, he planned to ride Henry's stallion, a beautiful black horse named Shadow.

In addition to Jemma's mare, he wanted to take two of the other thoroughbreds along. When he ventured to England at Weston's request, he never pictured himself returning to America with a new bride who loathed him, two orphaned children, four horses, a dog that still hadn't decided if he was friend or foe, sixteen trunks, several traveling bags, and more money than he could possibly spend in a lifetime.

After Jemma agreed to marry him, he sent a wire to his friend Tully, begging him to have the hired hands at the ranch add on two bedrooms to the cabin and half a dozen stalls to the barn. He hoped by the time they reached Baker City, the additions would be complete.

If they weren't, he didn't think it would bode well for tranquility in his home.

Saddling Shadow, he led him, along with the other horses to the wagons waiting in front of the house. Weston and his wife joined Jemma as she directed which trunks to keep and which to return inside the house. Jack and Lily played with Rigsly as Greenfield and Cook tried to keep the children from getting dirty.

Thane left the horses tied to a hitching post then picked up Lily and tossed her in the air. "Did you get your dolly, honey?"

"No, she's in my room." Lily wiggled for him to set her down then ran inside the house.

Jemma followed her inside as the men carried the last of the trunks back to the parlor. Thane walked behind her and stopped as she stared at the empty room. Most of the rugs, paintings, and décor had disappeared over the course of the last few days, leaving the house barren, except for the furniture.

"I know this is hard for you, Jemma, but it's for the best." Thane rested a gentle hand on her shoulder and, to his surprise, she didn't shrug it off.

"It's quite difficult to say goodbye to somewhere that has been my home for so long. Part of me feels like I'm abandoning Jane and Henry and the rest of my family by leaving." A fortifying breath didn't bring the sense of calm she needed so Jemma turned to face her new husband. "I didn't think it would be so hard to go."

A lone tear rolled down her cheek, causing Thane's heart to soften toward his wife. The glistening drop disappeared beneath his thumb as he brushed it across her cheek. He pulled her to his chest and gave her a comforting hug. "You can take the memories with you wherever you go and that's what counts. No matter where you are, you'll always have those you love with you in your heart."

Jemma nodded against his chest and took another restorative breath. "I'd like to walk through each room before we leave, to make sure we haven't forgotten anything."

Thane dropped his hands and stepped back then followed her from room to room. The chipped corner of a doorframe marked evidence of Jack tripping on the rug and hitting it with his chin when he was four. A spot on the wallpaper in the hall bore testament to where Lily spilled an inkwell she wasn't supposed to have back in the spring.

Jemma ran her fingers along the banister of the stairs, lingered at the doorway to her bedroom, then fought back tears as she stood in Lily's room, clutching the little girl's favorite blanket to her chest.

"Jemma, we've got to leave. Everything will be fine, you'll see." Thane grabbed Lily's pillow off her bed and another blanket he'd seen her dragging around the house, then took his wife's elbow and walked her to her room.

"I'll give you five minutes to collect yourself, and then we have to leave." After taking the blanket from her hands, Thane left her in her room and walked down the hall. She heard his boots treading down the stairs followed by the front door opening.

Resigned, Jemma walked into the bath down the hall, splashed her face with water, and tidied her hair before returning to her room. She slipped her arms into a light duster, buttoned it over her dress then pinned on a hat, and pulled on her gloves. She picked up her reticule and traveling bag. With a final glance around the room that had been hers since she was fourteen, she stepped out and shut the door. One final check of the children's rooms assured her everything was packed. Sedately, she walked down the stairs and into Cook's arms.

"No more tears, dearie. You have a grand adventure ahead, so don't waste your time looking behind you. Greenfield and I will miss you and we promise to write. You let us know as soon as you are settled at the ranch. By then, we should have a new address to send to you." Cook patted her back as they walked to the door where Greenfield executed a deep bow then pulled Jemma into a fatherly embrace.

"Oh, Greenfield, how will we ever get along without you?" she cried, hugging the dear man she'd known all her life.

"You'll do quite well, I'm certain. Mr. Jordan will take good care of you and the children. I'm sure of it."

"I'll miss you both terribly. Don't forget to write."

Cook smiled through her tears. "We won't, Jemma, dear. Now, off with you before the children see me crying again."

Jemma hurried to the coach where Thane stood talking to Weston. He lifted Lily inside and watched as Jack scrambled in. Weston helped his wife in then took the seat beside her.

Thane gave Jemma his hand. "All will be well, Lady Jemma. You'll see."

Blinded by her tears, Jemma nodded her head and took a seat inside, grateful she wouldn't have to spend the day in close quarters with Thane. Jack and Lily settled on one side of her, leaning out the window and waving as the coach started down the road.

"I shall miss this beautiful, wonderful place every single day," she said, craning her neck to see the cottage until the coach went around a bend in the road.

Aware she needed to put on a brave face for the children, she settled back against her seat and smiled at Jack then Lily. "Are you children excited to go to Liverpool?"

"Yes, but I wish I could ride with Uncle Thane." Jack looked longingly out the window to where his uncle rode Shadow beside one of the wagons and talked to the driver.

"We'll have a jolly good time here in the coach," Jemma said, tickling Lily and making her giggle.

"I say, dear, it's a shame you had to turn back so many of your trunks. I do hope you were able to keep those you needed most." Margaret Weston leaned across the space and patted Jemma's hand reassuringly. "These men don't always understand what a woman's heart holds dear."

"No woman's heart holds thirty-two trunks worth of special treasures." Weston observed, earning a glare from both his wife and Jemma.

"I shall make do, quite well, in fact." Jemma smiled at Margaret then turned her gaze out the window.

Fully anticipating Thane refusing to take some if not most of the things she truly needed, Jemma rounded up every trunk she could find, including borrowing several from Catherine and a few from some of her other friends.

Although she filled less than half of them, she hoped when he saw such an overwhelming number of trunks waiting to be loaded, he'd allow her to take all of those she packed, which totaled fourteen.

Pleased with her foresight and her accurate assessment of her husband, she had everything with her she originally intended to take. Greenfield and Cook would return the empty trunks to the proper owners and Thane would be none the wiser.

The accusation he tossed at her of being conniving wasn't far off the mark. Smug with the success of her scheme, she smiled at Lily as the little girl clutched her doll to her chest and began telling an imaginative tale about a prince, a pony, and a magical flower.

At noon, they stopped beneath a clump of trees near the road. The children ran off some of their energy while Jemma and Margaret spread a cloth on the grass and set out the picnic lunch.

Thane engaged the two youngsters in a game of tag. Rigsly joined in, barking and woofing as Lily tried to catch her uncle. At one point, Jemma wasn't sure the dog wouldn't take a bite out of the man in his excitement, but when he barked and wagged his tail, she decided their faithful canine was starting to warm up to Thane.

The children ran around after they'd eaten while the lunch things were packed and put away in the coach.

Jemma turned from brushing the wrinkles out of her skirt to find her nose pressed against Thane's chest. The children's laughter and Rigsly's barking drowned out his approach.

"Gracious! I didn't hear you." In her haste to step away from him, she caught her heel in the hem of her skirt. Thane grabbed her arms to keep her upright then bent down and lifted her skirt just enough to free her shoe.

Embarrassed, heat rushed into her cheeks and she tucked her head, hoping Thane wouldn't notice.

"No need to blush, wife," Thane said, grinning down at her with an odd light in his eyes. "I'd like Jack to ride with me for a while and wanted to make sure you didn't mind."

Surprised that he thought to seek her opinion on the matter rather than telling her what to do, Jemma gave him a pleased smile. "Jack would love that. He mentioned this morning that he wished he could ride with you instead of inside the coach."

"I'm glad to hear that." Thane removed his hat and ran a hand over his cropped hair. After letting it grow long, he hadn't yet become accustomed to the short length, or his exposed chin. Daily shaving was a bothersome nuisance he didn't particularly enjoy, but the look of adoration and interest on Jemma's face was worth the nick he'd suffered that morning.

As he settled his Stetson back on his head, he glanced down at his wife and caught her staring at him.

Flustered, her hand went to the cameo pinned at her throat, rubbing it with nervous fingers. He noticed she did that anytime something caused her concern.

Curious as to what currently bothered her, he didn't have time to decipher it. When he started to step away from her, she reached out a hand and gently touched his arm.

"It looks nice." She spoke in a low, quiet whisper.

"What looks nice?" he whispered in return.

"Your um... your hair and your... face."

Unsuccessful at subduing a smirk, Thane gave her a roguish wink and turned away, walking toward Shadow with a swagger in his step. Pleased she liked the changes in his appearance, he didn't take time to examine why he cared.

Hours later, they stopped in front of Weston and Margaret's home where they'd spend the night. Jack trailed behind Jemma as she carried a sleeping Lily inside the house and up to bed. The boy rode with Thane for a few hours that afternoon until one of the horses tied to the back of a wagon began acting up. Thane settled the boy in the coach then went to take care of the horse.

While Jemma and Jack joined Weston and Margaret for a simple meal, Thane accompanied their trunks and the horses to the dock where they'd be loaded directly on the *S.S. Teutonic*, one of the White Star Line's newest steamships.

Impressed with tales of the ship's speed, Thane hoped the crossing to America would pass quickly. It was one reason he chose to leave so soon after the wedding. Weston received word the ship was due to sail and Thane insisted they be aboard when she left Liverpool bound for New York City.

Satisfied the animals were well cared for and Jemma's multitude of trunks were properly loaded, he paid the wagon drivers, giving each a generous bonus, then hailed a cab and returned to Weston's home.

While Thane ate his dinner, he and Weston sat in the library and went over final details.

The majority of Henry's holdings had been sold, although Thane kept the partnership Henry had in a shipping enterprise with their friend Charles, as well as two partnerships in mills located in Bolton.

Everything else he'd sold, including the cottage Jemma so loved. He hated to make her leave somewhere she'd clearly established strong roots, but there was no help for it. If she wanted to be with the children, she had to go to America.

Since she'd claimed most of the belongings in the house were hers, Thane never questioned what she'd done with them. He assumed many of the household goods were contained in her multitude of trunks.

Thane felt only marginally guilty about refusing to take half of what she packed. He could have squeezed in a few more, but a man had to draw the line somewhere. He'd noticed she only brought fourteen trunks and wondered if she miscounted. Either that or she'd taken his words to heart and had pared down her selections to the most essential items. Even then, nothing he considered necessary amounted to more than one trunk, possibly two if he included all the children's trappings. Evidently, he had much to learn about necessities from a woman's point of view.

Once he finished his business with Weston, the two men trudged wearily up the stairs. The solicitor showed Thane to a room down the hall from where he'd stayed on previous visits. "Sleep well, my friend, tomorrow will no doubt be a tiring day."

Thane accepted the hand Weston held out to him and shook it warmly. "I appreciate all you've done, Weston. You've not only been a great help and advisor, but a good friend."

"It was my pleasure, Thane. I must say, you managed to wrap things up much more quickly than I expected and quite profitably, too. I do hope you and Jemma will consider your marriage as more than a business venture, mutually beneficial for the children. At any rate, my good man, you'll find your wife's room connected to yours. Jack and Lily are across the hall. Good night."

Weston disappeared around the corner and Thane took a deep breath before checking on Jack and then Lily. Both children slept soundly so he shut their doors and opened his bedroom door. Drained, he removed his clothes and started to climb between the cool, crisp sheets when a noise drew his attention to the door across from his bed, granting entry to Jemma's room.

Briefly debating what to do as he stood at the portal, he listened to her sobbing. Unsure if he should ignore her cries or offer some form of comfort, his first inclination was to climb in bed, put a pillow over his head and give in to his exhaustion.

The compassion that had been steadily growing in his heart for the woman dictated he see if there was anything he could do to help. He pulled on his trousers and knocked on her door before turning the knob and pushing it open.

Curled on her side in the bed, quiet sobs wracked through his wife.

Uncertain what to do, Thane strode across the room and scooped her from the bed into his arms before sitting down on the edge of the mattress and cuddling her as he'd done with Lily on numerous occasions.

So overwrought with emotions, Jemma lacked the strength or the will to struggle against him and instead let herself cry, held comfortingly in his strong arms.

Soothingly, his big hand rubbed along her back while he murmured words of comfort and gently kissed her temple.

"Are you injured somewhere?" He finally asked, wanting to know what could cause such heart-wrenching despair in a woman who, just hours earlier, had laughed and smiled with the children.

"No…" Jemma stammered between sobs.

"Are you about to die from some fatal diagnosis you failed to mention?"

"No…"

"Did Margaret refuse to let you have dessert? Or did Weston send you to your room for being cheeky?"

The corners of her mouth twitched with a suppressed grin as her tears subsided. "Of course not."

"Then why are you sobbing like Lily during one of her tantrums? Unless you're about to die or the world is ending and someone forgot to tell me, I can't think of anything to cause such a storm of tears." Thane dug a handkerchief out of his pocket and placed it in her hand.

She dabbed at her red eyes and swiped at her nose before releasing a shaky breath. "What a sight I must make." As she raised herself from his chest, she pushed the hair back from her face, noticing Thane wore nothing more than his trousers and they weren't even properly fastened. Streaks of salty tears trailed down his muscled chest and she mopped at them with the soggy handkerchief.

Thane caught her hand and held it in his, gazing at her imploringly. "What made you cry, Jemma? It's not like you to dissolve into hysterics. Something upset you."

"I feel quite silly, truthfully." Shamed he discovered her in a fit of self-pity, she hated to admit the reason behind her tears.

"Silly or not, what caused you to be so upset?"

"Leaving my home. I've never lived anywhere other than Bolton and I shall greatly miss my friends, the church, the cottage, Greenfield and Cook, even Weston and Margaret. I shall miss it all so dearly." Her voice caught and tears stung her eyes again. To her surprise, Thane pulled her against his chest and rocked her back and forth until she had control of herself again.

A choppy laugh escaped her as she dabbed the tears from her face again. "I assure you, Mr. Jordan, I'm not usually given to displays of this sort. My sincere apologies for interrupting you."

"I wasn't asleep so don't worry about it. And I thought we agreed you would call me Thane. Mr. Jordan sounds quite formal for someone who's sitting on your bed holding you while you're wearing little more than a scrap of cotton."

Fury danced in her coppery eyes as she sucked in a gulp, causing him to grin. "Must you always be so vulgar? My nightwear is perfectly respectable."

"For an old woman or a nun, perhaps." Thane set her on her feet and stood, letting his gaze slowly travel from her unbound hair to the tips of her bare toes peeking from the hem of her prim gown.

Heat seared through his veins as he trailed his finger along her jaw and gently pushed up her chin, forcing her to look at him. "I know this is difficult for you, Jemma, but the hurt will ease and you'll set down roots in Baker City. I'm proud of you for doing this. It takes a brave, strong woman to venture into the unknown with a dashing man she's not all that fond of at her side."

His teasing made her smile and she nodded her head. Thane leaned down and softly kissed her cheek then turned and strode across the room. "If you need anything, you know where to find me. Sleep well, wife."

After closing the door behind him, Thane lit the lamp on the table near the bed and opened his traveling bag. He removed a square wrapped in soft leather, folded back the covering, and stared at the photo of him and Jemma smiling at each other on their wedding day. The photographer said he didn't care for the pose, since it looked too informal. Nevertheless, it was Thane's favorite of all the images the man had captured.

His thumb caressed the edge of the photograph, admiring the beautiful gown Jemma wore. Catherine said some woman in London rushed to make it for Jemma. He had no idea how much something like that cost, but the way she looked in the perfect-fitting gown was worth every cent.

Only moments ago, it had felt so good, so right to hold Jemma in his arms, he had to leave the room before he decided to act on the husbandly rights he promised her he'd not pursue.

The sinuous feel of her through her cotton gown combined with her alluring fragrance floating around him nearly pushed him beyond the edge of reason. Glorious waves of auburn tresses tumbling around her shoulders and down her back hadn't done anything to ease his wanting.

When he rashly promised she'd not share his bed, they were still complete strangers.

After the past weeks of watching her with the children, of seeing her care and compassion for others, of hearing her laughter and invoking her anger, he no longer thought of her as a stranger.

He didn't necessarily think they were friends, yet, but he no longer disliked her. She still infuriated him more than any other human alive, but she also fascinated and intrigued him.

When he was with her, strange, new emotions filled him. He felt the need to protect her, keep her safe, and tease a smile out of her. Desire for the woman he'd wed filled him with an intensity he'd never experienced. It went beyond her lovely form and beautiful face, right down to her tender heart.

With a frustrated sigh, Thane wrapped the photograph and returned it to his bag then blew out the lamp. His trousers dropped to the floor then he climbed into bed and tried to relax. As sleep eluded him, he listened but no sound came from the room next door. He wondered if Jemma finally slept. Heavy eyelids drifted closed and he let himself dream of holding her in his arms, kissing her with all the passionate longing she stirred in him.

Chapter Eight

"Goodness gracious."

The awe resonating in Jemma's tone caused Thane to glance down at her as they followed a white-coated sailor to their stateroom aboard the *Teutonic*. The grand staircase, constructed from tempered and mellowed English oak, loomed before them as an impressive sight.

"It's quite something, isn't it?" Thane bent slightly and whispered in her ear as the sailor led them down a hall to their room. When Thane asked Weston to make their travel arrangements, he assumed their friend would book second-class staterooms, since the *Teutonic* was the first ship in the White Star Lines fleet to offer an option between first class and steerage. Much to his surprise, the man reserved them one of the best staterooms on the ship, or so their guide proclaimed.

The sailor opened the door to a large sitting room, complete with windows overlooking the promenade around the deckhouse, causing Thane to believe his assessment.

"It's pretty!" Lily exclaimed as she bounced in Thane's arms. The child had been so full of excitement, darting hither and fro as they tried to walk onto the ship, Thane feared she'd end up in the water or completely lost if he didn't carry her.

Jack held tightly to Jemma's hand, although his eyes lit in wonder as they made their way to their room.

"Will this serve your needs adequately, sir?" The sailor stood just inside the main door and swept his hand in a grand gesture across the comfortable parlor with three closed doors surrounding it.

"I'm sure it will be fine. How many bedrooms are there?" Thane asked, stepping inside, but keeping his hold on Lily. Jack let go of Jemma's hand and ran to the window where he could watch people coming and going.

"Two, sir." A tall young man appeared and the sailor took his leave. "Sir, I'm Tipton, your room steward. I'm here to make sure you and your family are comfortable during the voyage." He walked across the parlor and opened a door revealing two individual brass beds with rails on the sides to keep the occupant from falling out, should they hit stormy weather on the open sea. The room's furnishings included plush chairs, a dresser, a desk between the beds, and a small closet.

The steward crossed the parlor to a door located close to the windows where Jack continued to watch passersby with rapt fascination. When the man opened it, Thane took note of the large brass bed, meant for two, along with other furnishings similar to the first bedroom.

The third door opened to reveal a private bath, a welcome and unexpected convenience.

"Should you need anything during the voyage, this panel connects you to the necessary departments within our great floating city. You'll not find finer accommodations on any ship on the ocean than we offer." The steward stood straight and tall as he delivered this information, clearly proud of the ship he called home.

"Thank you, Mr. Tipton." Thane looked around the room, glad for the private bath, although he hated to share the space with Jemma and the children. With his inclination to be overwhelmed with seasickness, he'd rather do it alone than where the others could witness his misery.

Determined to worry about it later, he turned toward the hall as their luggage arrived.

Glad he'd packed his suits in an accessible trunk instead of one of the many down in the cargo hold, he knew as first class passengers they would be required to dress for dinner each evening as they dined in the ship's main saloon.

Jemma started to ask for her trunk to go into the room with the small beds but Thane directed it be placed in the room with the large bed.

She frowned at him but snapped her mouth shut, taking Lily from his arms and going to stand at the window with Jack.

"I'd be happy to help unpack your luggage straightaway, sir," Tipton offered, taking a step in the direction of the children's room.

"That won't be necessary, but thank you for the offer." Thane slipped the steward a coin. The man grinned broadly as he stood at the door. "The dining room is open from five this evening until eight. You'll find it on the main deck, mid-ship. For you sir, you'll find a barber's shop, smoking saloon and library. Many of the men like to gather there for the bon voyage. Your dog is on Deck F, where we keep the kennels. He'll be walked three times a day, but you're welcome to find him there anytime. However, we do not allow pets in the rooms. If you'd like, I can have tea and crumpets brought up immediately."

"That would be fine. Will the ship leave port on time?" Thane asked as the steward moved into the hall.

"To my best knowledge we will, sir. We should be underway in about an hour." Tipton tipped his cap and hurried down the hall.

"I should like to speak with you a moment." Thane glanced down as Jemma walked beside him on the promenade deck. She wore a copper silk evening gown the same striking shade as her eyes and put him in mind of an autumn nymph as they strolled along in the fading sunlight.

After partaking of the tea Tipton delivered to their room, they went out on deck and watched as the ship departed in a great gusty billow of steam.

Jack and Lily were convinced Rigsly needed attention, so they checked on the dog. Jemma and Thane allowed the children to play with him for a while before they all returned to the stateroom and changed for dinner.

Thane caught his breath when Jemma emerged from the bedroom with her hair caught up in a loose chignon at the back of her head, wearing the shimmering gown.

As they ventured to the grand dining room, shallow niches along the way containing figures carved in wood drew their interest. Impressed with the grandeur of the ship, the four of them took seats in the dining room.

Thane admired the plaster pattern overhead, highlighted by finely molded rosettes set at intervals around the domed ceiling. Done in tones of subdued ivory, the dining space looked elegant and refined, rather like his new bride.

Once their meal arrived, Lily, who'd endured more excitement than any three-year-old could be expected to handle with grace, burst into tears when Jemma insisted on cutting her meat.

"I'll do it myself! I do it!" Lily shrieked, jerking her head forward and banging it on the edge of table. Tears began to fall in earnest, so Thane picked her up and rubbed her back, telling her to settle down and stop crying. She quieted soon enough.

He used his napkin to wipe her tears, kissed her forehead, and set her back in her chair. She took a few bites of food before she slumped wearily against his arm. Pity for the child had him picking her up again, settling her on one solid thigh. While he finished eating with one hand, the other kept Lily upright. Concerned the child feel safe and loved, he had no care for the number of etiquette rules he broke as he ate his meal.

Jack showed signs of fatigue as he finished his dinner, although he kept pulling his head up and gazing around, trying to stay alert.

"There will be plenty of time for exploring tomorrow," Thane assured the boy as Jemma set down her napkin, rose to her feet, and offered to take Lily. He shook his head and put his hand to the small of her back, guiding her from the main saloon. Jack trailed along behind them.

With Lily settled into the curve of one arm and Jemma's hand resting on his other, they strolled in companionable silence until she mentioned wanting to speak to him.

"Later?" Thane didn't want to get into whatever discussion she planned until the children were asleep.

She nodded her head and stepped behind him, resting her hands on Jack's shoulders. "How do you like the *Teutonic*, Jack?"

"It's a grand ship, isn't it, Auntie Jemma?"

"Indeed. I heard Mr. Tipton say he'd be happy to take your uncle on a tour tomorrow. Perhaps you could go along." Jemma glanced at Thane as he turned around and smiled at his nephew.

"That's a fine idea. Would you like to go with me, Jack?"

"Yes, sir." Jack's eyes spoke of his excitement although he offered only a small smile.

"Great. We'll plan on it. Now, how about we see what color the sun paints the water from that spot over there." Thane led them to a section of the deck where they could watch the setting sun.

Jemma stood with Jack in front of her, both her hands on his shoulders as Thane stood beside her holding a sleeping Lily. The lower the sun drooped, the cooler the air seemed until Jemma felt thoroughly chilled.

Sudden warmth made her glance over her shoulder as Thane moved close behind her, blocking the breeze. He placed the hand not holding Lily around her waist and drew her, along with Jack, back against him.

Trying to ignore the sensations his proximity created, she focused her gaze on the golden orb sending streaks of pink and orange brilliance across the water. "It's spectacular, Thane. Thank you for thinking of this."

"It does seem like a nice way to end the day," Thane rumbled from behind her, pleased she'd called him by his given name instead of sir or Mr. Jordan.

They watched until the sun almost disappeared. The electric lights on the ship flickered to life and stewards hurried to close the shutters over the stateroom windows, to ensure the privacy of their guests.

"I think we better head in before I have to carry two sleepy kids." Thane smiled down at Jack who could barely keep his eyes open. "Can you make it, son?"

"Yes, sir." Jack leaned against Jemma as they turned to go inside and made their way down the hall to their room.

Tipton met them at the door and asked if they needed anything. Thane assured him they had everything they needed for the evening and thanked him for his offer of assistance.

Inside the room, Thane carried Lily to one of the small beds in the second bedroom and left her for Jemma to undress while he helped Jack get ready for bed. After tucking in the boy, Thane bid him sweet dreams while Jemma settled a limp and still sleeping Lily beneath the covers. She kissed the little one's rosy cheek and brushed curls away from her face then turned to Jack, kissing his forehead and hiding a smile as he struggled to keep his eyes open.

Thane walked out of the room after placing a kiss to Lily's forehead and waited for Jemma to join him in the parlor.

Once she settled her skirts around her on the settee, he sat beside her, much to her dismay. She hoped he'd stay on the other side of the room in one of the four chairs surrounding a mahogany table.

"What did you want to talk about?" Thane asked as he relaxed against the comfortable upholstery of his seat.

"Our room arrangements." Unable to force herself to say sleeping arrangements, heat burned across her cheeks. If she had to share a room with Thane, she wouldn't be able to sleep a wink.

"I figured you'd set up a fuss about me putting the kids together, but it makes sense for three reasons."

Jemma glared at him, waiting for him to explain himself. When he continued to sit quietly, she smacked his leg lightly with the reticule still hanging from her wrist. "By all means, explain them to me."

"I assumed the kids would need to go to bed earlier than either of us plan to, so it works for them to share a room."

"I concede that is reasonable." Jemma tipped her head toward Thane. The children were exhausted and it would have been silly to put them in separate rooms, possibly waking them both when she and Thane retired for the evening.

"The second reason is because I'm not going to have the whole ship blathering about you and me sleeping in different rooms. With Tipton spending so much time in here, it wouldn't take him long to figure out you and Lily shared a room while Jack and I took the other. I don't give a flying fritter what people have to say about me, but you do. I won't stand for people whispering behind your back."

Surprised by his concern for her reputation, she didn't know what to say. Struggling to form an appropriate response, she finally settled on a simple, "thank you."

Thane nodded his head then swiped a hand down his face before leaning forward and resting his hands on his knees. "There's something you don't know about me, but I reckon you'll find out sooner rather than later."

Jemma couldn't imagine what information he deemed necessary to share, and braced herself for the worst. Maybe he was a drunkard or a gambler like she and Catherine had teasingly discussed. "Please continue."

Thane sighed and cast a sideways glance at her. "I snore when I sleep and I'm an early riser, so I don't want to disturb either of the children. If Jack roomed with me, he'd likely be kept awake by my snoring and as I rose each morning. The kids need all the rest they can get."

"Of course, that is practical." Jemma hid her amusement that the mighty Thane Jordan admitted to a fault such as snoring. Regardless, she hoped he didn't plan to share the bed with her. The concerned glance she cast his direction earned a roguish grin from him.

"As for our sleeping arrangements, I thought I'd sleep out here. Since I get up early, I can have everything set to rights before Tipton arrives in the morning with our breakfast."

Jemma looked around the parlor. Although finely appointed, the settee wasn't long enough to accommodate Thane's frame nor was there any other piece of furniture large enough for him to rest comfortably. "But where would you sleep?"

"I can make a bed on the floor. I've slept on a lot worse and it won't bother me at all, as long as you're willing to share a pillow and a blanket."

A relieved sigh escaped her and her good humor returned. "I may even give you two pillows."

Thane chuckled and she decided she quite liked the sound of it, rumbling deep in his chest.

He leaned over and pecked her cheek then squeezed her hand. "I'm glad you're feeling so generous. If you want to get ready for bed, I'll take another walk around outside before settling in for the night. Just leave the pillow and blanket out here and I won't bother you."

"Are you sure you'll be comfortable?"

"I'll be fine, Jemma. Don't give it another thought." He stood and helped her rise then walked to the door, glancing back to watch the sway of her skirts as she entered their bedroom. Even if the woman had insisted he share the bed, he would have refused.

The amorous thoughts swirling around in his head would have made it impossible to be in the same bed with her and keep his hands to himself. It would be akin to leaving a delicious piece of candy in front of Lily and expecting her not to eat it.

Firmly closing the stateroom door behind him, he decided a stroll in the night air might help clear his thoughts if not cool his interest in his very alluring wife.

Chapter Nine

Jack raced across the deck to where Jemma and Lily sat on a deck chair reading a storybook, enjoying the fresh air and sunshine.

"Guess what, Auntie Jemma?" The boy leaned against her leg, more excited than she'd seen him in a long time.

"I'll never guess, so you must tell me immediately," she said, giving him a loving smile.

"Mr. Tipton took Uncle Thane and me to see our horses and he showed us where the men shovel in the coal that makes the ship run. Did you know the ship uses more than two hundred tons of coal a day?" The boy leaned closer and she put the arm not steadying Lily on her lap around his waist and kissed his cheek.

"I did not know that. What a fascinating bit of information. What else did you learn?" Jemma waited for his response, thrilled he seemed engrossed in the workings of the ship. All too often of late, little held his attention as he quietly went through one day followed by the next. She knew he missed his father terribly and was pleased Thane took such an interest in both of the children. He spent time with them individually as well as together and she could see how his presence influenced Jack in a positive manner.

"The *Teutonic* was built in Belfast and its one of the fastest ships on the ocean. Its maiden voyage was last year, and Mr. Tipton said it was the first armed merchant cruiser."

"My gracious, you learned any number of intriguing details. Did you check on the horses?"

"Yes. They were happy to see us," Jack said, glancing back at his uncle as he approached. "Weren't they, Uncle Thane?"

"I believe they were, but that could have been from the carrots Tipton provided for you to feed to them."

Jemma laughed as Jack shrugged. "That was very kind of him."

"We'll be docking at Queenstown soon to allow more passengers to board. Tipton said it usually takes about two hours then we'll head out for the open sea." Thane picked up Lily and tossed her in the air, making her giggle.

"Again, Uncle Thane! Do it again!"

He tossed her a few more times then she wrapped her little arms around his neck and kissed his cheek. "I want to see Shadow. Can we walk Rigsly again? When do we get a snack? I'm hungry. Can I swim in the water?"

"How about we go back to the stateroom and have some lunch?" Thane suggested, holding out a hand to help Jemma to her feet, playing the role of the attentive husband. "Or would you rather dine in the main saloon?"

"Our room would be fine. It's easier for Lily there." Jemma took Jack's hand and the four of them progressed to their room. Tipton stopped by shortly after their arrival and took their orders for lunch, promising to return soon.

"What do you think of the ship, Thane?" Jemma asked after they'd eaten. The children sat at the window watching people board the ship from the dock in Ireland. "Does it compare to the one you traveled on last month?"

"The *Teutonic* is far and above superior to the ship I traveled on in every sense. I had no idea a ship could be so dandy."

"It is a lovely ship, and from what I heard, a fast one." Jemma sipped her tea and gazed at him over her cup, unaware of how appealing he found that particular pose.

"It is fast, which is one reason I insisted Weston secure our tickets for it. The less time spent on the ocean, the happier I'll be." Reaching across the table, he gently lifted her hand in his and brought it to his lips, kissing her palm. "I think it best if the children stay inside while the passengers board, but I'd like to talk to a few of the men. Will you be fine if I'm gone for an hour or so?"

"Perfectly."

Jemma kept the children busy for the next hour then Thane appeared, taking them all out to the deck so they could watch as the ship left the port and headed out to the open sea.

When Lily and Jack got tired of waving to the gathered crowds, Thane suggested they take Rigsly for a walk and went to the kennels to get him. Jack wanted to hold the dog's leash so Thane kept close beside him, ready to grab it at a moment's notice. Jemma held Lily's hand as the little girl dawdled along, chattering about fairies that lived in the water, the monsters that hid under her bed, and what she wanted to eat for dinner.

Determined to head off a tantrum when Lily began to pucker her lip and rub her eyes, Jemma declared it time for her nap. She took the child back to the stateroom while Jack and Thane continued to walk the dog, letting him wear off a little of his caged energy.

The rest of the day passed quickly. After a pleasant evening and tucking the children into bed, Jemma and Thane both settled in for the night — her alone in the big bed and Thane on the hard floor.

The next morning, they ventured out on the deck to see nothing but blue sky and water in every direction.

"The ship seems to move right along," Jemma said as she and Thane sat in chairs watching Jack and Lily play nearby with a few other children.

"Tipton said the captain plans the trip to take seven days. I'm all for anything that gets us off the water and onto solid ground as quickly as possible." Thane felt fine when he awoke, but seeing nothing but water made him queasy. He wished he'd skipped breakfast instead of eating so heartily from the selection Tipton delivered to their room.

Movement off the side of the ship drew Thane's attention. He rose to his feet and glimpsed a school of dolphins playing in the water.

Swiftly stepping back to where Jemma sat in a chair looking at him, he took her arms in his hands and lifted her to her feet then pulled her to his side. "See, look out there." He pointed in the direction of the dolphins.

"Oh, dolphins!" She clapped her hands together then turned to where the children played. "Jack, Lily, come here, please."

The two children ran to her and she lifted Lily while Thane settled Jack on his shoulder.

"Those are big fishies," Lily observed, watching the dolphins jump out of the water.

"They're dolphins, honey. They're nice fish," Thane explained to his niece.

"Technically, they're mammals," Jemma said, looking at Jack. "We read that they're quite intelligent. Do you remember studying about them last year, Jack?"

"Yes, Auntie Jemma. They can talk to each other, can't they?"

"That's right. I'm so glad you remembered. What else do you know about dolphins?"

"They have a remarkable sense of sight and a group of them is called a pod." Jack beamed at his aunt, pleased he remembered the lessons she'd taught him.

"Excellent, Jack. You're such a bright student."

Jack soaked up her praise while Lily patted her cheek to get her attention. "I'm bright, too, Auntie Jemma. See me. I'm a dolphin princess!"

"Yes, you are, poppet."

The four of them watched until the dolphins disappeared from sight then the children scampered off to play with their new friends. Jemma returned to her seat and picked up the needlework she'd begun the previous afternoon. Fully expecting Thane to sit beside her, she glanced up as he disappeared toward the other end of the ship.

Somewhat miffed he didn't say anything before striding off, her anger increased with every hour that passed. She didn't see him again all day. After dining in the stateroom with the children, she made them take baths then tucked them into bed, listening to their favorite adventures of the day. She read them a story from one of her favorite childhood books, kissed them good night, and assured them their uncle spent the day attending to business matters.

Furious, she fumed at his sudden disappearance, waiting for him to return to the room. Fatigue forced her to give up her vigil in the parlor and she climbed into bed, planning to lecture him in the morning.

The sound of the door banging open and male voices roused her from her slumber. Quickly jumping out of bed, she stuffed her arms into the sleeves of her wrapper. She whipped open the bedroom door and glared into the face of Tipton, expecting him to be Thane. Two other stewards held her husband upright as they half-dragged him into the room.

"Sorry to wake you, Mrs. Jordan, but your husband needed some assistance back to the room." Tipton motioned for the men to help Thane into the bedroom.

Jemma stepped aside as they positioned him next to the bed and helped him fall back.

"Good heavens! Has he been imbibing in spirits? Is he inebriated?" Jemma asked, appalled at such behavior.

"I'm plastered, Lady Jemma." Thane's slurred voice did nothing to help her growing rage. "Snockered and rip roarin' roostered."

Tipton motioned for her to step away from the bedroom as the other stewards positioned Thane so he wouldn't fall off the bed. She followed him to the far side of the parlor where he lowered his voice, ensuring Thane couldn't hear.

"No, madam. Mr. Jordan hasn't touched a drop of liquor, but he is quite ill. Your husband's been heaving over the side of the ship for hours." Tipton motioned for the other stewards to leave as they exited the bedroom. "He refused to return to your stateroom, planning to spend the night in the library near the gentlemen's lavatory. The ship's surgeon insisted we bring him back here and put him to bed. Doc said to give him plenty of water and tea to drink and dry toast if he'll take it until this passes. Mr. Jordan seemed quite insistent you not see him in his current state."

"Thank you, Tipton. I'll see to his care. Have a good evening." Jemma smiled at the helpful young man.

"Thank you, Mrs. Jordan. You as well." Tipton strode across the parlor then closed the stateroom door as he left.

Jemma took a fortifying breath then marched into the bedroom and flipped on the electric light. Relieved Thane wasn't drunk and only sick, she shook her head. "You, sir, are a foolhardy cabbagehead."

"Insults will get you everywhere, sweetheart," Thane mumbled although he didn't lift his head or open his eyes.

"I ought to toss you out on your ear, Mr. Jordan, but my Christian duty compels me to offer my assistance." Grateful Tipton told her the truth, Jemma decided to let

Thane carry on his charade for now. "Don't you ever again come home in such a state! Do you hear me?"

Too sick to argue, or even speak, Thane opened his eyes and tried to glare at her. It made the room spin around so he squeezed them shut again. He refused to be sick in front of his wife.

"Let's get you settled and see if you can't get a bit of rest, shall we?" Jemma moved Thane's hat from where one of the stewards set it on the edge of the bed to the dresser. She lifted one of her husband's long legs and attempted to pull off his boot but her gentle tugs didn't budge them. Wrapping her arms around one, she gave it a firm yank and found herself sitting on the floor holding his boot.

She rolled her eyes, got to her feet and repeated the process until both boots rested on the floor. After removing his socks, she dropped them next to the boots. She worked his topcoat over his broad shoulders followed by his waistcoat and left them in a pile by his boots.

With his face a shade of greenish-gray, Thane provided no help to her efforts, although he did attempt to hold himself upright as she removed his outerwear. He slumped back against the pillows once she removed the waistcoat and moaned.

"I'm fine like this," he whispered, catching her hand in his as she pulled the tails of his shirt from his trousers.

"No, you aren't. Besides, your clothes are filthy and you stink."

Determined, she unbuttoned his shirt and helped him rise enough she could slip it off. Her hands hovered in the air when she got to his trousers. Although he'd be more comfortable without them on, she hated to think about the intimate familiarity involved in removing them. By pretending he was Jack, she unfastened them and worked them over his hips and down his strong legs, tossing them onto the pile of his clothes.

In vain, Jemma tried not to stare at his muscular form. The cotton drawers he wore barely covered his thighs. With an averted gaze, she pushed on him until he rolled to one side and she could pull the covers over him.

"Where is your nightshirt?" she asked, stepping toward the dresser drawer where he'd unpacked his things.

"I don't own one."

Jemma's mouth rounded into an "O" and she spun around, wondering what Thane normally slept in. Heat rushed into her cheeks as his bare chest and finely formed legs filled her vision. In need of a moment to gather her thoughts, she hurried from the room to their bath. She dampened a towel then filled a glass with water.

Upon her return to the bedroom, she held the glass for him to drink. After he took a few sips, she set it on the bedside table then gently sponged his face and hands, working her way over his chest and stomach. Thane opened one eye and stared at her as she went through her ministrations.

"Thank you," he whispered.

Curtly, she nodded her head. "You're welcome." She took the cloth back to the bath and rinsed it before entering the bedroom again.

A search through a storage cupboard in the closet unearthed a chamber pot she set next to the bed, in the event Thane felt ill during the night. With the refreshed cloth, she wiped his face again and forced him to take a few more sips of water before turning off the light, removing her wrapper, and climbing into bed exhausted.

Curling up on the side of the bed far away from Thane, she fell into a fitful sleep. Each time he was ill during the night it awakened her. He grumbled and fussed at her attending to him and by morning, they were both worn and weary.

As sunlight sneaked around the edges of the window covering, Jemma took a refreshing bath and dressed for the day then checked on the children to make sure they were sleeping. She requested Tipton deliver a breakfast tray and bring anything the ship had on hand with mint.

When she returned to the bedroom, Thane rested on his side, pale and wan, with the muscles in his jaw clenched into a tight bunch.

Since the first day they'd met, he'd appeared larger than life, fearsome, and tough. Now, he looked quite vulnerable and helpless, tugging at something in her heart. She thought, perhaps, she could come to like him with some effort. At least if he stopped acting like such a ninny.

"There's stubbornness, Thane Jordan, then there's plain stupidity. I do believe you have undoubtedly crossed the line."

He opened his eyes and gave her a weak smile as she stood at the foot of the bed. "I apologize for coming in drunk and for being sick."

"In that case, you won't mind if I have your rasher of bacon this morning and bring it in here, just so you can watch me eat it."

Thane turned an even sicklier shade of green at the thought of bacon and clenched his jaw so tightly, she thought he might rupture a muscle or crack a tooth.

A long-suffering sigh escaped her as she moved to his side. The full force of her coppery gaze settled on his as she bent down and shook her head in displeasure.

"I know for a fact you didn't have a drop, not a single drop, of liquor yesterday. Furthermore, I don't believe you're the kind of man to waste time or money on drunkenness. You're seasick, aren't you?"

Surprised she'd seen through his ruse, Thane slowly nodded his head. "Unfortunately, I am. It would have been less humiliating if you'd thought I'm a worthless drunk."

Jemma snapped upright and fisted her hands on her hips. "That is the most ridiculous thing you've yet uttered, sir. Why would any woman want a drunk for a spouse? I much prefer to know the sea makes you ill than to worry about you being besieged with tendencies to disappear and return home in an inebriated state."

Thane closed his eyes and swallowed hard. Jemma hurried to give him a sip of water and wipe his forehead again.

"I'm truly sorry, Jemma. I spent the whole blasted trip to England sick. Since I was fine the first few days, I'd hoped I wouldn't be ill this trip."

"Don't give it another thought, Thane. It's not something you can help or control. We'll just make the best of it." Her fingers brushed across his forehead in a soothing motion and she smiled at him. "It must have been miserable for you."

"It wasn't fun."

She'd noticed when they first met Thane's clothes appeared loose on him. His illness onboard must have been the reason. He had filled them out quite nicely in the last few weeks. Jemma hoped he wouldn't suffer too greatly from his current illness on their way to America.

"Certainly not. I will do my best to nurse you back to health quickly so you can enjoy what is left of our trip. Tipton said the ship is progressing right on schedule and we should be in New York on Wednesday, as planned."

"Please, Jemma, I don't want you staying in here. Go spend the day on deck or in the ladies' reading room but not here." Thane grasped her hand with a surprising amount of strength while his eyes pleaded with her to agree.

"I'm used to nursing sick ones, although Jack and Lily are much easier to coax into doing my wishes." Jemma gave him a coy smile as Tipton knocked on the stateroom door and entered, carrying a large tray.

Quickly closing the bedroom door behind her, Jemma thanked Tipton and accepted the packet of peppermints he gave her along with a few stems of fresh mint.

"It's not much, madam, but it's the best I could do. Will the mint settle Mr. Jordan's illness?" Tipton asked as he stood at the door.

"That is my hope. Thank you so much for your assistance, Tipton. It is most appreciated."

"You are quite welcome, Mrs. Jordan. Please ring if you need anything further. I'll stop by in about an hour to pick up the tray."

Jemma nodded and set about steeping a few leaves of the fresh mint in the pot of hot tea. After pouring a cupful and adding a generous spoon of sugar, she carried it to the bedroom where Thane rested.

Hesitant, she attempted to discern if he slept or merely had his eyes closed. He finally opened them and stared at her.

"I brought you a cup of hot tea."

"I can smell it. What's in it?" Thane wrinkled his nose as he pushed himself back against the pillows until he sat upright in bed.

"Mint and sugar." Jemma held the cup out to him. "Take a sip. The mint should help settle your stomach."

"I don't think so." Thane clenched his jaw and pressed his lips together as his stomach gurgled.

"Don't act so childish. Just take a sip." Jemma held the cup to his mouth and refused to budge until he parted his lips and took a drink.

Surprised by the pleasant flavor of the tea, Thane took the cup along with another long swallow. "That's good."

Jemma waggled a finger at him, filled with smug satisfaction. "You should mind me. I know what's best for you and I intend to see that you get it."

"Are you sure about that?" Thane asked. Although the words sounded innocent, the look in his eyes and his intended meaning made her blush.

The happy chatter of Jack and Lily saved her from making a comment as she rose to her feet and hurried from the room, shutting the door behind her.

"Good morning, darlings. Did you sleep well?" she asked, dropping to her knees so Lily could give her a hug. Jack wrapped one arm around her shoulder and kissed her cheek.

"I dreamed I rode on a dolphin, Auntie Jemma. It was such fun." Jack's face beamed with excitement as he pulled out a chair at the table and waited for her to take a seat. Pleased her nephew remembered his manners, she nodded at him encouragingly as she sat down and settled her skirts.

Lily climbed into the chair next to her and Jack took the chair on her other side.

After asking a blessing on the meal, the children ate with hearty enthusiasm. Jack wanted to check on Rigsly and take him for a walk while Lily chatted about playing with her new friend in the ladies' reading room.

"Is Uncle Thane still gone?" Jack asked, remembering the disappearance of his uncle the previous day.

"No, love. He's here, but you children will have to leave him be today. I know, Jack, you hoped to spend time with your uncle exploring the ship, but perhaps Mr. Tipton will find someone to help you walk Sir Rigsly."

Disappointed, Jack dipped his head and silently finished his breakfast. Lily wiggled incessantly as she ate, humming her own little tune and intermittently tossing her curly head from one side to the other.

Since she was eating and not causing a fuss, Jemma let her be. After setting aside two pieces of dry toast, Jemma finished her breakfast and made herself another cup of tea. She enjoyed the strong mint flavor and hoped it would help settle Thane's stomach.

Once the children finished their meal, she asked them to wash their hands and faces, brush their teeth then get dressed. In their shared bedroom, she got out Lily's garments and made her bed, waiting for the morning tussle with the strong-willed child to ensue.

Jack hurried into the room, dressed, made his bed, and tidied his things before taking one of his lesson books and going to sit by the window in the parlor.

Lily skipped into the room and climbed onto the bed next to where Jemma sat. "Time to get dressed, Lily."

"I'll do it myself!" Lily stated, as she did every morning. She tugged at her nightdress, getting it halfway off and stuck on her head. The child began to whimper so Jemma gently removed it then handed Lily her undergarments.

Lily insisted she put on each piece herself. Too tired to worry about whether Lily's chemise was on inside out or backwards, Jemma let her do as she wished.

"Hold up your arms, lovey, and I'll drop the dress over your head." Jemma gathered the pale yellow gown in her hands.

Lily crossed her arms and shoved her hands into her armpits while her lower lip came out in a pout. "No. I'll do it myself."

"Lily, lift your arms up, please. Auntie needs to go see how your Uncle Thane is faring and we need to get you ready to go out for the day."

"No."

"Please, Lily. Just lift your arms up, poppet."

"No."

Playfully poking a finger into Lily's side, Jemma made her giggle. The little girl lifted her arms into the air and Jemma dropped the dress over her head. Quickly settling it into place, Jemma fastened the buttons up the back, tied the sash then set Lily on the bed so she could put on her shoes.

"I want to do my shoes," Lily insisted, holding out both hands.

Jemma handed her one of the soft, black leather shoes and pointed to her left foot. "Put that one on your left foot."

Lily began tugging it on her right foot and Jemma tapped her other foot. "This is your left foot. Put it on this one."

"Why?"

Vexed, she held back a sigh and the desire to take the shoes, stuff Lily's feet in them and move along with her day. Instead, Jemma gave the little girl a tender smile.

"If you put your shoes on the wrong feet, they will hurt. You don't want to spend all day with hurting toes do you?"

Lily shook her head with such enthusiasm, her curls danced in a tangled mess.

Jemma clenched her hands as Lily put on her shoes. The child threw herself back and lifted a foot so fast in the air, she kicked Jemma's nose. "Can I button them?"

Gently rubbing at her nose, stinging from Lily's unintended abuse, Jemma picked up the buttonhook and took the little foot in her hand. Expertly fastening the buttons on one shoe, she quickly finished the other.

"When you get older you can button them, but not yet, Lily." Jemma stood and picked up a hairbrush as Lily attempted to run out the bedroom door. She snatched the child in one arm and sat back down on the bed, brushing the wild tendrils into some form of order. She pulled them back from Lily's face and fastened a yellow bow in the downy locks then kissed the wiggly child on her nose.

"Why don't you take a picture book and sit with Jack for a while then we'll go out for a stroll."

"Okay." Lily grabbed one of her books and skipped out the door to join her brother.

Relieved, Jemma straightened the bed, put away Lily's things, and stepped into the parlor just in time to see Lily open the door to the other bedroom.

"Lily, come back here, please." Concerned what the little girl would do or say, Jemma stopped in the doorway just in time to see Thane leaning over the side of the bed with his head buried in the chamber pot and Lily patting his bare back.

With a groan, Thane lifted his head and gave her a look that let her know he didn't appreciate an audience to his suffering.

Lily scrambled onto the bed next to him and leaned her head against his arm. "Uncle Thane has an owie, Auntie Jemma. Fix it. Fix Uncle Thane's owie. Please?"

"I'm trying to, poppet, but you need to leave your uncle alone right now. Okay?"

Lily's lip protruded in a pout and tears shimmered in her eyes, but she slid off the bed and shuffled across the floor, burying her face against Jemma's skirts.

"I appreciate you coming to check on me, Lily. You do as your aunt says." Thane lifted himself enough to smile at the little girl before flopping back against his pillows.

Lily sniffled and left the room, running over to Jack and sitting close to him as he gazed at Jemma with a concerned glance.

"Your uncle is seasick, Jack. Nothing to worry about. He'll be perfectly fine soon."

Thane muttered something she couldn't hear. She gave him a warning glance and closed the door to the bedroom, leaving him to wallow in his misery alone.

Tipton chose that moment to tap at the door and enter, ready to pick up the breakfast tray. Lily ran over to him and tugged on his hand.

"Mr. Tipton, my uncle's sick and Auntie Jemma said we can't play with him today."

Tipton squatted down and gave Lily a serious look. "Is that right? I must say, that sounds like a terrible bit of business for your uncle. Perhaps you and your brother would like to go with me to take the tray back to the kitchen then I could escort you to Mr. Johnson. He'll be walking your dog soon and wouldn't mind the company, if your aunt approves, of course."

Jemma nodded her head in grateful appreciation. It would be hard to keep the children entertained and provide the care Thane needed. If she could get them out from underfoot for even an hour or two, it would give both Thane and her time to rest and regroup.

Lily squealed and did an excited little dance while Jack calmly closed his book and picked up his cap.

Tipton picked up the tray in one hand and held out the other to Lily, who grasped it excitedly.

Jemma hurried to the door and glanced down at Lily before she stepped into the hall. "Be on your best behavior, both of you, and mind your manners."

"Yes, Auntie Jemma." Jack nodded solemnly, although a spark of adventure twinkled in his eyes. Lily grinned and blew her a kiss before skipping down the hall with Tipton.

As soon as they disappeared around the corner, Jemma closed the door and hurried to the bedroom.

Focused on caring for the sick man, she emptied the chamber pot then rinsed out the towel she'd used to sponge Thane's face. She wiped it soothingly across his brow, down his cheeks, and along his chin. "I take it the tea didn't set well?"

"Not particularly, then again, water doesn't set well either."

"We must keep you drinking liquids. I'll have Tipton send for the doctor. He took the children with him, so we have a small reprieve before they return. Would you like to take a bath? It might help you feel better?"

"Are you offering to help with that, too?" Thane opened his eyes and gave her a cocky smile. At least she assumed that was his intention although it looked more like a grimace in his current state.

"Certainly not. I'd be utterly offended by your implied suggestions if you weren't so thoroughly incapacitated." Jemma pulled back his covers and helped him gain his feet. He swayed slightly as he leaned against her and they made their way to the bath.

She began running water into the tub while Thane leaned against the doorframe for support. "In fact, in your current condition, you hold no threat to me at all, so I shall ignore your comments and pretend you've grown delirious in your weakened state."

Thane chuckled and moved aside as she tried to step past him in the narrow space. He inhaled a whiff of her fragrance. Instead of making him sick, he found the aroma pleasant. In the tight quarters, her arm rubbed against his stomach as she squeezed out the door and color heightened her cheeks.

"I'll be here if you need anything. Take your time," she said, not looking at him as she stepped across the parlor, putting distance between them.

"Thanks."

After closing the bathroom door, Thane took off his cotton drawers and slid into the tub, sinking into the warm water. Mortified Jemma had not only discovered his tendency toward seasickness, but that she'd cared for him like a child, he felt somewhat emasculated. It wasn't a feeling he liked or wanted to know with any degree of familiarity.

If he could keep himself steady enough to dress and make it to the gentlemen's lounge, he'd spend the day there, so she wouldn't be witness to his weakness or feel compelled to care for him.

The tender feel of her cool fingers on his brow, the way she'd brushed against him numerous times as she cared for him during the night, the slight weight of her on the mattress next to him made him realize how much he wanted his wife.

Although her tongue was no less sharp, the more he got to know her, the more he witnessed a gentle, giving spirit that truly cared for others.

Reluctant to embarrass himself further, Thane finished his bath, brushed his teeth, and realized he'd have to make a dash for the bedroom in a towel because he refused to put on his drawers from the previous day.

With the towel secured around his waist, he cracked open the door and didn't see Jemma in the parlor.

Swiftly covering the few steps to the bedroom, he rushed inside and closed the door. In the moment it took him to steady his spinning head, a startled gasp sounded across the room. Jemma leaned over the bed as she put a fresh pillowcase on his pillow, gaping at his nearly naked form.

"Whatever are you doing?" she asked, staring at him, unable to take her eyes away or turn her back to the fine masculine form hovering in front of the door, wearing nothing but a towel about his waist. Muscles she had no idea existed bunched as he crossed his arms in front of him and took a sidelong step toward the dresser.

His fingers grasped the knob of a drawer and he jerked it open, pulling out a wad of white cotton. "Getting dressed. Unless you plan to help with that, too, I suggest you turn your back or leave the room. However, I'm more than willing for you to stay if you like." A devilish smile rode his generous mouth as he pretended to loosen the towel around his waist.

"Mercy!" Jemma tossed down the pillow in her hand and made a hasty exit out the door before slamming it behind her.

Thane chuckled as he pulled on his drawers. A wave of sickness forced him to rest against the fresh sheets and his next coherent thought was of Jemma carefully tucking the sheet around him, murmuring something about him being an insufferable brute.

Content, he let himself rest in slumber.

Chapter Ten

The next two days passed in a blur of illness for Thane, but he finally began to feel better. He didn't know if it was Jemma's thoughtful attention, the peppermints she insisted he suck, or the calmer waters they traveled on, but he awoke that morning hungry and ready to be out of bed.

A quick glance offered assurance that Jemma slept soundly beside him. He took advantage of the opportunity to study her. Although she'd braided her hair before she climbed into bed the previous evening, the lively tresses worked free of the confines and fell in a tumble around her. Not wanting to chance waking her, he resisted the itch in his fingers to brush tendrils back from her face and caress the silky, fragrant strands.

Creamy skin and pink cheeks looked like fine porcelain. From the few times he touched her, he knew it felt every bit as soft and smooth as it looked.

Slightly parted lips drew his attention and he longed, quite desperately, to kiss them. Kiss them repeatedly until she surrendered to the passion that sizzled between them. She'd never acknowledge or admit it existed, no matter how obvious it might be.

Rashly, he'd assured her theirs would be a marriage in name only. Not a man to go back on his word, he'd honor his vow. How he wished he'd never made that promise because he could think of little else beyond making Jemma truly his.

The fact that she was just a few feet away with only the cotton of her nightdress separating him from her luscious curves forced him out of bed before he did something that would shock or anger her.

As he pushed himself up, his hand bumped something and he picked up Lily's beloved doll. Thoughts of the little imp sneaking in and tucking her doll into bed with him, hoping to make him feel better, made him smile. Gently, he set it on his pillow.

Quietly gathering a change of clothes, he adjourned to the bathroom and took a leisurely bath, shaved, and combed his hair then brushed his teeth. Satisfied with his proper grooming, he opened the door and almost tripped over Jack.

"Hello, son. How are you today?" he asked, reaching out a hand and patting the boy's shoulder.

"Fine, sir. Are you well?" Jack asked with a hopeful glimmer in his eye.

"I'm feeling much better." Thane glanced at the clock on the wall, noting the time. "What are you doing up so early?"

"I just needed to use the facilities," Jack said, pointing to the bathroom behind Thane.

"Of course. If you aren't sleepy, why don't you get dressed and the two of us can take a little stroll while the girls sleep."

"Yes, sir!" Jack excitedly responded by rushing in the bathroom and shutting the door. Thane chuckled and carried his dirty clothes back to the bedroom. After slipping on a waistcoat and coat, he picked up his boots and walked into the parlor, closing the bedroom door behind him.

Quietly opening the window, he breathed in the fresh air and watched as the sun stretched golden fingers across the morning sky.

Jack rushed out of the bathroom to his room and soon emerged half-dressed, carrying his shoes in one hand and his shirt in the other.

Thane motioned him over to his chair and helped him finish dressing. He ruffled the boy's hair before Jack settled a cap on his head. Concerned Jemma would worry if she awoke and discovered him gone, Thane found a piece of paper in the small corner desk and penned a hasty note.

He left the note on the table in the center of the room then he and Jack went for a walk around the deck, taking Rigsly for a morning stroll before returning to the room. Tipton met them in the hall and his face lit as he noticed Thane up and about.

"It is a fine thing to see you out this morning, sir. Indeed, are you well upon this day?"

"Reckon I am, Tipton. Thank you so much for your assistance while I was ill. It's appreciated."

"You are most welcome, sir. I'll be back in an hour to collect the breakfast dishes, unless you and Mrs. Jordan would like to dine in the main saloon this morning."

"No. Whatever you brought is fine."

Tipton tipped his head and hurried down the hall while Jack and Thane walked into the room to find Jemma and Lily sitting at the table, waiting for them. Jemma bent her auburn head over Lily's strawberry blond curls and the sight of the two together made Thane's heart skip a beat.

The woman who haunted his dreams glanced up at him with a warm smile. "You appear much improved today."

"I feel better. Thanks for taking care of me."

"My pleasure. I'm accustomed to caring for whiny little ones." The teasing grin she gave him made him smirk. He raised an eyebrow at her, deciding she no longer seemed quite as aloof as she had when they boarded the ship just a few days earlier.

After breakfast, Tipton offered to take Lily and Jack with him, as had become the routine while Thane was ill. Grateful for an hour of quiet, Jemma sent them on their way, turning from the door to find Thane watching her.

Flustered by his intense gaze, she touched her chignon to make sure it was in place then glanced down to confirm she hadn't spilled something on her dress during breakfast.

"What are your plans for the day?" she asked, brushing at non-existent crumbs on the table. Tipton had made sure none remained when he carried out the breakfast tray.

"I thought I'd take care of some paperwork that needs my attention before we arrive in New York and then probably go see what news I missed while I made a fool of myself in here."

"A fool of yourself? From being sick?" Jemma walked over to where he sat by the window and shook her head. "You've made a fool of yourself any number of times since we met, but not because you were ill. That just let me know you are indeed human and fallible."

Before he could respond, Jemma turned and disappeared inside their bedroom. Taken aback by her words, he sat for a few minutes lost in his thoughts before retrieving a leather satchel with all the legal papers from Weston. Pulling out a folder and a few sheets of writing paper, he spread them out on the table and began jotting down notes.

Jemma carried a book out to the settee and sat down on one end, looking as relaxed as he'd seen her since they left Bolton.

Companionable silence filled the room until the door bounced open and Jack rushed inside followed by Tipton as he carried a crying Lily. The little girl reached out to Thane and buried her face in his neck, clinging to him as if she'd never let go.

Thane rubbed a gentle hand along Lily's back and gave Tipton a questioning glance. "What happened?"

"They were helping Mr. Johnson give Rigsly another stroll around the deck when they spotted a whale. They watched it a few moments then suddenly Miss Lily burst into tears and wouldn't stop crying. No one knows what, exactly, is the matter, sir."

"Thank you, Tipton. We appreciate your assistance and care." Once the steward tipped his hat and departed, Jemma started to take Lily from Thane, but he maintained his hold on the child and sat down on a chair.

Jack stood nearby, looking frightened and alarmed.

"Do you know what made her cry, Jack?" Jemma asked, putting an arm around the boy and drawing him to her side.

Slowly shaking his head, Jack continued staring at his sister.

"Lily. You have to tell me what's wrong, honey. Why are you crying?" Thane gently pushed her back but she lunged forward, trying to keep her face buried against his neck. "What upset you?"

"The big fishie!" Lily shrieked. "The big fishie will eat us just like Jonah. I don't want to be in the fishie's tummy. Don't let it eat me!"

Chuckles threatened to rumble out of his mouth, so Thane let Lily grab him around the neck again while he rocked her back and forth and ran his hand soothingly along her back.

"It's okay, sweetheart. The whale won't eat you, or Jack, or anybody on the ship. I promise."

Lily's sobs calmed to whimpers then sniffles. Finally, she sat back and stared at her uncle. "You won't let the fishie get me?"

"No. I won't let it get you. You're safe with us. Your aunt and I will always, always take good care of you."

Lily leaned her head against his shoulder and sniffled, brushing her runny nose on his jacket before kissing his cheek and jumping down. "Love you, Uncle Thane."

"I love you, too."

After she skipped into her bedroom, they could hear her singing one of her made-up songs as she played with some of her toys.

Jack took the chair next to Thane's and sighed. "I'm sorry, Uncle Thane."

"For what, Jack?" Thane bent his elbows on his knees as he leaned forward, so his gaze met his nephew's.

"I'm the one who reminded her of Jonah's story while we were watching the whale."

"Not to worry, Jack. You didn't know she'd think it would swallow her. It's not your fault." Thane patted the boy on his knee and smiled at him. "Did you enjoy seeing the whale? Was it as all-fired enormous as they seem in the picture books?"

"Yes, Uncle Thane. It was huge! And it rose up out of the water and then..." Jack smacked the palms of his hands together. "Splash! He sent water everywhere. That's when Lily started to cry. Mr. Johnson didn't know what to do, so I asked if he could call Mr. Tipton."

"That was smart thinking on your part, son. You're a very clever boy."

Jack's chest puffed out at Thane's praise.

"I've never seen a whale myself. How about we go back out to the deck and try to spy another one?"

"Yes, sir!" Jack jumped to his feet and ran for the door. Thane hurried to remove his jacket. Jemma handed him a clean one, along with his Stetson before he and Jack went to watch for whales.

"Are you sure we didn't leave anything behind?" Jemma nervously glanced around her at their pile of luggage.

Thane insisted they be on the deck as they approached New York so she and the children could see the Statue of Liberty. She hurried to gather the last of their things and finish packing the trunks. Tipton made sure their belongings followed them up to the deck, ready to disembark at the White Star Line piers.

Due to her marriage to Thane, she was considered an American citizen so they could bypass the immigration lines at Castle Garden.

"As meticulous as you are, I'm certain nothing was left behind." Thane raised an eyebrow at her then turned his attention to the impressive gift France bestowed on America. The official dedication of the Statue of Liberty occurred just four years prior.

"She's breathtaking." Jemma's voice held a note of awe as she beheld Lady Liberty. "'Give me your tired, your poor...'" She went on to recite the remainder of the sonnet.

Thane looked at her in admiration and gave her a respectful nod.

Aware of his gaze, she smiled. "It's a beautiful poem, don't you think?"

"Yes, it is." The woman reciting the poem was quite beautiful, too, but Thane kept that thought to himself. Surprised by the knowledge contained in his wife's lovely head, he sometimes wondered if she didn't know more about his home country than he did.

Lily raised her hand above her head, mimicking the pose of the statue, making them laugh. "Look at me! Look at me!"

Thane kissed her cheek as he handed her to Jemma and picked up Jack, settling the boy on his shoulder so he could get a better view. The solemn child's face almost split with his broad grin.

"We'll be in port soon. I'll help you with the luggage and see to unloading your trunks from the hold," Tipton said as he walked up behind them.

Thane shook his hand and pulled an envelope from his coat pocket, handing it to their faithful room steward. "I appreciate your loyal service, Tipton. It's been a pleasure."

"Thank you, sir. Sailing isn't your favorite adventure, but I do hope if you have reason to cross the ocean again, you'll sail with us."

Jemma gave the steward a favorable smile when he turned to her. "You're most kind, Tipton, and much appreciated. As my husband stated, we value your generous and loyal service. Thank you."

Tipton bowed to them then went back to get Rigsly from his kennel.

When Thane had his new family on solid ground with their luggage around them, he looked around for a wagon or coach to take them to the train depot. "I'll see about securing a few wagons to take us to the depot. We should be able to catch a train heading west and get started on the last part of our journey."

He took only a step before Jemma grasped his arm, pulling him to a stop. "You don't mean to stick us on a train yet today?"

"I most certainly do. Time's wastin' and I need to get back to the ranch. Now, wait here with the children and I'll hire a couple of wagons."

"No, sir, I won't. I refuse to budge an inch unless it's to venture to a hotel and rest for a day or so before we take the train to Oregon." Defiantly, Jemma lifted her chin and glared at him with fire snapping in her eyes.

"This isn't the time for you to get stubborn on me, Lady Jemma. I've got to get back to the ranch." Thane watched as her lips compressed into a thin line and she glanced from Jack and Lily back to him.

Annoyed, he removed his hat and raked a hand through his hair then settled the Stetson back on his dark blond head. In an attempt to figure out her objection to going home, he narrowed his gaze and studied her. "What? Why won't you get on the train?"

Jemma set Lily down, maintaining a hold on her hand and motioned for Thane to bend down so she could whisper in his ear. The combination of her heady scent and the warm of her breath on his neck made heat zing through his veins, but he ignored it.

"The children, Thane. They've been so restless the last few days. They need a day or two to run and play, to relax where they aren't confined to the space of a stateroom or the deck of the ship. They won't have anywhere to exert their playful energy on the train. Please, for their sakes, can't we stay a day or two?"

Astounded by the rational sense of her words, Thane knew she was correct. It would make the journey west better for them all if they had a day or two before the long train trip. In his haste to get back to the ranch, he hadn't stopped to consider the needs of the children or Jemma. He knew she was tired from tending him and trying to keep the children entertained.

"Fine. We'll stay for a day, but then no arguments."

Jemma nodded in agreement.

Thane glanced down at the children then back at her. "You'll have to come with me to the depot because I'm not letting the horses or your precious treasures out of my sight until they're on a train headed west. After that, we'll find a hotel."

Overcome with relief at having a day of rest, Jemma threw her arms around Thane's neck and gave him a hug.

Of their own volition, his arms slipped around her and he held her close for a rapturous moment before stepping back and giving her a roguish wink. "If you can contain yourself, Lady Jemma, I'll see about getting those wagons." After tipping his hat to her, he walked off in the direction of the street where lines of wagons and buggies waited to provide transportation for a fee.

Tipton arrived with a cart bearing the first of their many trunks. Thane wanted to load them first then lead out the horses last. Rigsly barked at the foreign sights and sounds as Jack held tightly to his leash. Thane returned followed by three wagons and an open carriage. He assisted Jemma and the children into the carriage and made Rigsly sit at their feet before he went with Tipton to bring up the horses.

Jael and Shadow put on quite a show as they pranced down the gangplank to the pier. Jemma noted many people stopped to watch as Thane expertly handled the big stallion while three men led the other horses.

After locating the trunk containing tack, Thane hurried to saddle Shadow while the other horses were tied to the back of the waiting wagons. Jemma wished she could go to Jael and offer her a calming hand but she feared leaving the children alone for even a moment.

Their entourage of a carriage followed by three wagons, each trailing a high-strung horse, created quite a spectacle. Jemma's cheeks burned with heat as Lily bounced on her lap and Jack sat beside her. Rigsly sat on the floor beside the boy, anxiously watching the passing scenery. Thane rode beside them on Shadow. The horse wanted to stretch his legs and run, but Thane kept him under control as they made their way through the busy city traffic to the train station.

Once all their trunks and the horses were loaded, Thane made Jemma and the children say goodbye to Rigsly and stuck him in a kennel on the train as well.

Lily melted into an inconsolable tantrum. "I want my doggie! I want Rigsly! Don't send him away!" She cried until she fell asleep, but even in slumber the snuffling continued.

Thane disappeared inside the station for several long minutes, finally returning to their waiting carriage. Since there wasn't room for all of them on the seat, he settled Jack on his thigh and asked the driver to take them to the nearest respectable hotel.

The driver stopped the carriage several blocks away in front of an impressive brick building faced with white marble.

"Will this suffice, sir?" the driver asked as he turned around to look at Thane.

"This is fine. Thank you." Thane set Jack down and stepped out of the conveyance, walking around to take Lily from Jemma then offering his wife a hand. The driver motioned to the porter to take the luggage from the back of the carriage and he quickly loaded it onto a cart and rolled it in the door behind the tired travelers.

Jemma took Lily from Thane while he spoke with a bespectacled man at the front desk and accepted a room key from him. The porter led them down the hall to an elevator, something none of them had been on before, and escorted them up to a fifth floor suite.

The porter took the key from Thane, unlocked the door, and motioned them inside the luxurious space that put their elegant room aboard the ship to shame. Along with a fireplace and a large private bath, the room boasted a selection of seating as well as two bedrooms, one with two single beds and a second with a massive walnut bed.

Thane directed where the bags should go while Jemma walked to a window and looked down at the busy street below.

She felt Jack lean against her side and slipped an arm around him, giving him a hug, while Lily continued to sleep.

Worry creased the boy's forehead as he looked at her with concern. "Will Sir Rigsly be well, Auntie Jemma? He doesn't know anyone where we're going and he'll be scared without us there."

"He'll be fine, love. Your uncle wired his friend to meet the train and see to the care of Rigsly and the horses until we arrive. I'm sure he'll take grand care of our dog."

"I hope so." Jack didn't sound any more convinced than Jemma felt. She knew the dog was an unnecessary burden Thane had graciously accepted, but the way he abruptly loaded him on the train left her as upset as the children. The poor dog whined and cried as Thane led him away and it broke her heart to tell him goodbye, even if it was for only a few days.

"Do you want a rest, some food, or to go for a walk?" Thane asked after he tipped the porter and stood behind them as they stared out the window.

Jemma smiled at Jack as he gazed up at her. "Why don't you and your uncle go exploring while Lily and I rest? Upon your return, we can eat an early dinner, since you Americans don't have teatime."

Thane nodded his head. "Do you need help with Lily?"

"No. Go on and enjoy yourselves."

Thane and Jack took her words to heart, returning with tales of going to a big hardware and implement store where Thane ordered several things for the ranch.

The next morning, Thane directed them out to a waiting carriage that took them to Central Park.

As Lily and Jack ran around on the grassy expanse before them, laughing and enjoying the beautiful autumn day, Jemma strolled along with her hand looped around Thane's strong arm. "Thank you for giving them some fresh air and an opportunity to run to their heart's content."

"I'm sorry I didn't think about them needing a break from all the travel. Will they be ready to go in the morning?"

"Yes. We'll just have to wear them out today."

Thane took them to the Central Park Menagerie where they saw exotic animals like camels and lions, as well as bears and elephants. Swans, sheep and an assortment of other exhibits rounded out the collection. They rode the carousel, admired Belvedere Castle, and watched little boys send their sailboats across the lake.

As they took a carriage back to the hotel to change for dinner, Thane glanced at his wife and smirked as she brushed at a speck of dust on the rich navy fabric of her skirt.

"Is it a custom in England for a lady to change her dress multiple times in a day? You started out this morning in an elaborate pink gown then changed into this navy dress. You switched back to the pink when we ate lunch, then to the navy this afternoon. I've not yet figured out how you managed to pack an entire outfit into your reticule since we've not been back to the hotel when we left shortly after breakfast."

Jemma smiled at his teasing. "Indeed, Thane Jordan. I'm astonished you noticed what I was wearing. You can set your mind at ease, though. I've not changed my dress once today. It's called a surprise dress. Worn as I have it now, it serves as a perfectly respectable walking dress. If I unbutton the front placket and hook the skirt on the sides, it turns into a much more elaborate gown."

"Clever and practical." Thane reached down and lifted the hem to see the pink underskirt beneath the outer layer. Jemma batted at his hands so he lifted the hem higher before dropping it back into place with a wicked grin. "No matter how you wear it, you look quite lovely, although I think I'm partial to the pink."

Furiously blushing, Jemma nodded her head and turned her gaze to watch the passing scenery. Lily sat on Thane's lap, trying to doze, but he kept bouncing his legs to keep her awake. They wanted her so worn out, she'd sleep through the night and be ready for a few naps the following day.

Jack leaned against Jemma and fought to keep his eyes open.

"Did you have a fun day, Jack?"

"Yes, Auntie Jemma. It was wonderful." Jack turned to look at her with a contented smile.

"What was your favorite exhibit at the menagerie?"

Jack thought a moment before answering. "I think the camels. It would be fun to ride them, like they do in the desert. I liked the lion, too. What was your favorite?"

"The swans were most lovely," Jemma smiled at her nephew. "And I liked watching the bear. He appeared quite ferocious."

Thane glanced at Jemma then winked at Jack. "Bears can be ferocious, especially if you disturb them when they prefer to be left alone."

"Have you ever seen a bear up close, Uncle Thane?" Jack asked gazing at the man who was quickly becoming his hero.

"Just once, and that was enough." Thane growled then kissed Lily's cheek, making her giggle.

"Uncle Thane's a bear." Lily poked his chest and he growled again.

"Tell me about the bear you saw," Jack pleaded. He loved hearing Thane's stories from his life in the west.

"Some of us went into a mine shaft. We split up because there was a fork in the shaft. It's powerful dark down there, even with a light. My friend and I got down to work, not noticing a bear slept in the back of the tunnel. We woke him up and he chased us all the way outside. I learned two things that day."

Jack looked at him expectantly, as did Jemma. "What did you learn, Uncle Thane?"

"First, never enter anywhere dark without making sure there isn't already an occupant. Second, you only have to worry about a bear eating you if you're the slowest runner."

Jack laughed and Jemma smiled, amused by Thane's story. "Might I assume, then, that you were the faster runner of the two?"

"You assume correctly, ma'am." Thane tipped his head to her as the carriage stopped in front of the hotel.

After washing for dinner, they ate in the hotel's opulent dining room then went for a stroll, looking in shop windows as they meandered down the street.

"Is there anywhere you'd like to shop before we leave tomorrow?" Thane asked as Jemma looked in a dress shop window, admiring the American styles.

"I was hoping to find a particular type of store, but haven't happened across one yet." Jemma smiled at Thane as she turned back from the window and they continued on their way. Jack walked to her right, holding her hand, while Lily walked between her and Thane, holding onto both of their hands. The little girl alternated between quietly trudging along then chattering when she saw something that sparked her interest.

"What sort of store might that be?" Thane asked as they waited for traffic to pass so they could cross the street.

"A store that sells books informing one how to cook."

Thane's gaze snapped up and he looked at Jemma to see if she was teasing or not. Much to his dismay, she appeared quite serious.

"You don't know how to cook?" he asked, as they crossed the street and continued walking at Lily's pace.

"I do, but I assume American cooking differs from what I'm accustomed to. I've noticed just today that the food is different than our typical menu."

Thane absorbed that information and glanced around. Down the street, he saw what he was looking for. He picked up Lily and hurried them down the block and across another street to a dry goods store.

As he held the door open for Jemma and Jack to walk inside, the man behind the counter greeted them and asked if he might be of assistance.

"Do you have any cookbooks?" Thane asked, taking in tidy shelves filled with an assortment of merchandise.

"Indeed. We have several from which to choose. Right this way."

Thane motioned Jemma to follow the man while he kept the children occupied looking at a display of toys. Jack seemed quite taken with a train set while Lily couldn't keep her eyes off a beautiful baby doll.

Neither child asked for anything. Thane was once again impressed with their good manners.

When he noticed Jemma at the counter with the clerk, he herded the kids that direction and paid for the three cookbooks she selected, along with a licorice whip for each of them.

After picking up Lily in one arm, he took the books in his other hand and thanked the shopkeeper.

As they started down the walk, Thane looked around then set Lily down. "I forgot I wanted to ask if he knew how early we need to be at the train station. I'll be right back."

Thane ducked back inside the shop and returned a few minutes later. "We need to arrive about an hour before the train leaves. I've already secured our tickets, so we're all set."

Jemma gave him an odd glance, but didn't question his need to confirm details with the store clerk. While she held Jack's hand in hers, Thane carried Lily and they strolled back to the hotel for one more night of rest before the long trip across the country.

Chapter Eleven

"Might we expect to arrive in Baker City soon?" Jemma asked as she and Thane sat in the pre-dawn darkness on the train.

"It should be just a couple of hours. I can't wait to get off the train and go home." Thane raised his arms over his head and stretched as best he could in the close quarters.

The first leg of the trip, he'd managed to book a private car. It gave him room to stretch his long legs and the children a place to play. When they switched trains in Chicago, he was unable to secure anything private and they had no choice but to ride in one of the passenger cars. The children grew weary and irritable, sitting for hours on end.

Both he and Jemma had taken turns trying to entertain them, particularly Lily. She'd had a tantrum of monumental proportion before they tucked her into bed the previous night. Boredom and being forced to sit for hours and hours as the train chugged west caused much of her temper.

"They seem so angelic when they sleep," Jemma whispered, as they gazed at Jack and Lily in the muted light.

"It's hard to believe such a tiny little person could create so much chaos and work." Thane mulled over the constant attention Lily required. He dearly loved his niece, but he couldn't wait to set her down at the ranch and let her run off some of her bottled-up liveliness.

As though sensing his thoughts, Jemma leaned toward him with a teasing grin. "Just be grateful she's no longer in nappies. That would have made the trip quite miserable."

"Nappies?"

"Oh, what do you Americans call them?" She thought for a moment than glanced at Thane. "Diapers?"

Thane chuckled. "That definitely would have made for a miserable trip. Thanks for putting things in perspective."

"You are most welcome."

Thane could hear the smile in Jemma's voice although he kept his gaze on the children. When they weren't entertaining the youngsters during their days of travel, Jemma either gazed out the window at the passing scenery or studied the cookbooks she'd selected in New York. He wasn't worried about her cooking for him. There was a cook at the bunkhouse and, if needed, Thane could rustle up grub.

However, the thought of coming home after a hard day on the range to find a hot meal and a beautiful woman waiting for him held a certain amount of appeal.

While the children slept, Thane and Jemma talked about a variety of subjects. Amazed by her vast knowledge of many topics, she was well read and educated, putting his eight grades of schooling to shame. Most of his wisdom came from hard-earned experience.

Jemma shifted uncomfortably on her seat and Thane moved his arm so it rested around her shoulders. "Lean against me a while. It'll be more comfortable for you."

Stiff and rigid, she gingerly rested against his side, absorbing his warmth right along with his appealing scent.

When her hand brushed his leg she jerked it back, but not before feeling the rough fabric of the denim trousers covering his solid thigh.

"Why is it you wear those trousers? The construction is of denim, correct?" Jemma asked. Although she'd never admit it, she preferred seeing Thane in his western attire than the expensive suits he'd finally started wearing before they left England.

The Stetson on his dark blond hair, the chambray work shirts, denim pants and cowboy boots, as she'd learned they were called, fit the rugged personality of the man.

"They aren't denim trousers. They're called waist overalls, or even Levi's, made by Levi Strauss & Co. He came to California during the gold rush and ended up inventing durable overalls with a man named Jacob Davis. The reason I wear them is because they're strong, they don't rip easily, and the rivets help keep them together."

Jemma had noticed the rivets on the seams but had no idea what purpose they served other than decorative. Determined to change the subject from the pants that outlined Thane's form, she picked up on the mention of the gold rush. She'd read about the California rush and the madness that ensued as people fought over gold.

"You mentioned the other day that Baker City had a mining history. Was there a gold rush there, too?"

"As a matter of fact, there was in the 1860s and it's been picking back up again recently. There's also silver, coal, and quartz mines."

Jemma relaxed as Thane spoke, nestling against his side, enjoying the way his deep voice rumbled in his chest and vibrated against her back. "What made you choose to live there? I know Henry grew up in South Carolina, but he never mentioned his life there or any family."

"Henry and I grew up on a farm. Our mother taught school and our father raised cotton. That's how Henry got interested in creating inventions to improve the cotton industry. Henry was eleven and I was just a newborn when the war between the states broke out. Dad decided to go fight with the confederates and left my mother and Henry to care for the farm. She had no interest in the cotton and Henry was too young to have such responsibility on his shoulders. Our father returned from the war but my dad really never came home."

Thane tipped back his head as memories he'd long buried flooded over him. He didn't know why he shared them now, other than he was weary and it felt comforting and right to have Jemma pressed against his side.

"What happened?" she asked, hoping he'd continue his story.

"My parents fought all the time after the war. Dad left the better parts of himself, the gentle, kind parts along with an arm, on a battlefield in Georgia. He came home a hard, changed man and one day my mother just couldn't take it anymore. She left when I was ten and we never saw her again. Word came when I was thirteen that she'd been killed in a wagon wreck in Tennessee. My father died when I was fourteen. Henry had taken over raising me long before then, anyway. When I was sixteen, he came up with an invention he just knew would revolutionize the way mills processed cotton. He traveled around the south trying to find an investor while I worked the farm. Scraping together the last of our money, he decided to travel to England to see if he could generate interest."

"And he left you behind?" Jemma couldn't believe Henry would abandon his brother, especially at such a young, impressionable age.

"Not willingly. I didn't want to go and someone had to keep trying to make some money from our farm. The taxes were due and we were waiting to receive our payment from that year's cotton crop. I told Henry I'd keep things going until he got back. Since neither of us liked farming cotton, he told me if I had a chance to sell the farm, to do it. Henry left with a hopeful twinkle in his eye and a promise to be back in six months. As you know, I never saw him again."

"How did you end up leaving for Oregon, though? Did you sell the farm?"

"I did." Thane recalled the agony of making that decision on his own. Of selling something that had been in his family for three generations. "The money from the cotton crop barely paid the taxes. I started asking around town to see if anyone was interested in buying. There were always Yankees wanting to buy a piece of land at a good price. I happened to find one who gave me a fair deal so I sold the place, wrote Henry about what I'd done and bought a train ticket headed west."

Thane chuckled and moved his arm slightly, so he held Jemma a little closer. "I'd planned to go to Texas, since I'd heard all about the rough and rowdy men settling there, thinking I'd fit right in. On the train, though, I overhead some men discussing rich gold mines in Baker City, Oregon, so I decided to see if I could make my fortune. Not too many people are willing to let a sixteen-year-old kid prove himself, but I managed to work hard and save the money I earned. I bought my ranch and here we are."

Jemma thought about her husband, left completely alone at such a young age. At least she'd always had Jane. For the first time since she'd met her brother-in-law, she felt disappointed in Henry for not taking care of his younger brother. Admittedly, Thane was probably just as hardheaded and stubborn as a boy as he was now, though.

"Tell me about Baker City." Intuitively, Jemma realized Thane didn't want to discuss his past or his family further. "What's it like?"

"It's nothing like you're used to," Thane said, wondering how his wife would adjust to life in the rugged Eastern Oregon scrubland. "About three years ago, a big fire burned down a good portion of the buildings, so most of the businesses and homes are constructed of brick or volcanic tuff that's been quarried south of town past my ranch. There's a new hotel I reckon you'd find exceptionally nice. There are several restaurants, an orchestra, and an opera house. We have a variety of stores, even a dress shop, and a handful of churches. Some people refer to Baker City as the Denver of Oregon."

"I shall look forward to seeing it. How long will it take to get to your ranch from town?"

Thane tipped back his hat with the hand not wrapped around Jemma and rubbed his fingers across his forehead. "It's a good hour in the wagon, although not nearly that long horseback."

"I suppose with that distance, I shall need to continue Jack's lessons at home."

Thane turned to glance down at the top of her head and a plume from her hat tickled his nose. Wrinkling it, trying not to sneeze, he nodded his head. "I hadn't thought about it, but it's too far for him to go, especially with winter approaching. I can help with some of his lessons if need be."

"Thank you. I might call upon your expertise in certain areas beyond my abilities." Jemma noticed light beginning to streak across the morning sky.

"I can't believe there is anything beyond your ability, other than to find it in your cold, miserable heart to like your new husband."

Jemma jabbed his side with her elbow. "I might learn to like him if he wasn't so nasty and loathsome. There are some days, Mr. Jordan, when you are thoroughly unendurable."

As he chuckled, Thane ducked around the plume and lowered his head so his breath blew warm against her neck. "And what about those other days, my lady?"

His breath on her neck, combined with his scent and proximity made her heart beat faster while her stomach fluttered nervously. She had no idea how he unsettled her so, but he did.

"I won't dignify that with a response," she said, unwilling for him to know those other days found her intently watching his muscular form. On those days, she eagerly waited for the sound of his voice, listened for his laugh, watched him toss Lily in the air, making her giggle.

They sat in silence for a few moments then Thane's hand settled on her leg. The heat from his palm seared through the fabric of her skirt and petticoats, sizzling into her flesh. Too startled to move, she wished she'd never leaned against him. It was hard to keep her thoughts together when they lingered on how much she wished he'd kiss her again. He hadn't done more than peck her cheek since their wedding.

Forcibly willing away thoughts of his tempting lips, she considered the adjustments she'd need to make to life in the west. The biggest would be getting used to the idea of having a husband, albeit one who was maddening, bossy, opinionated, and incredibly handsome.

From her position, she could see Thane's chin out of the corner of her eye and noticed the blond stubble covering it. He'd informed her the second day they were on the train that he didn't fancy slitting his throat with his razor if the train hit a bump and wouldn't be shaving until they reached home, and only then if he was of a mind to.

Visions of the scraggly beard he'd worn up until their wedding day flew through her mind. She certainly hoped he had no plans to grow another. Inquiring about it would no doubt cause him to grow one down to his knees just to spite her.

Humored by the image in her mind's eye, she stifled a giggle, eliciting another tap from Thane's hand where it rested on her leg. Had they not been married, she would have shoved it away and slapped his face for his impudence, but she couldn't muster the will to do either.

"What's so funny?" he asked.

"Just a memory," she replied.

"If you're thinking about the past, would you tell me how you ended up caring for Lily and Jack?"

"I assumed Weston informed you."

Thane rubbed his hand along her leg, unaware of the unsettling effect he had on her. "No. Good ol' Weston told me I'd have to get the details from you. That man can be quite close-mouthed when he chooses."

"Remarkably so," Jemma agreed, thinking of all the times Weston could have told her about Thane before shocking her speechless when he read Henry's will. "I suppose I shall have to share the story, since you were kind enough to tell me yours."

"It's only fair, don't you think?"

The casual tone in his voice made her relax against him again. "My mother died when I was twelve. She took sick right after Easter that year and lost her health. It devastated my father. He was never the same after her death, like a part of him died right alongside her. Jane was seventeen then, courted by any number of handsome suitors. She and I clung to each other in our grief and found healing while Father fell deeper into his. In his distracted state, he made some rather poor investments. Within two years, we had to let most of our staff go, except for Cook and Greenfield, and move from our grand house to the cottage. Not long after we moved in, Father went for a walk and never returned. Greenfield found him in the meadow behind the stables, already gone. The doctor said his heart gave out on him, but I think it had completely broken."

Jemma took a deep breath before continuing. "Jane's suitors all turned to wealthier girls and we began selling the paintings, tapestries, and what-not in an effort to keep from losing everything. Then Jane met Henry. Handsome and charming, he claimed to have fallen for her the first time he saw her across the street in Bolton. After a brief courtship, Henry married her in the church where we wed and moved into the cottage. As his wealth increased, Henry began buying back the things we'd sold until all had been restored. Henry was a very kind, generous man and I miss both he and Jane greatly. By the time I was of an age to court, Jane was bedridden, expecting their first child. Unfortunately, that little one didn't make it. She recovered and went on to have Jack. She needed my constant help. After that, I didn't have time for anything besides caring for my family."

"But it wasn't your family, Jemma, or your responsibility." A wave of compassion swept over Thane for his wife. She'd relinquished the carefree days of her youth for his brother's family. "Henry should have hired a nanny or a nurse and let you have a life."

Jemma shook her head, unintentionally bobbing the plume in Thane's face. "I couldn't leave my sister when she needed me and I loved Jack from the first moment I held him in my arms, as I did Lily. I may not have given birth to them, but I've raised them, cared for them, and loved them as much as any mother could. I had a life, Thane. One full of laughter, joy, and happy moments, even after Jane died. It wasn't until Henry's death that life became uncertain."

"I'm sorry, Jemma. Henry should have left everything to you then you could have stayed at the cottage and raised the children as you saw fit. Although, I'm glad he didn't because I never would have met them." *Or you.*

"Poor Jack has grown so solemn, especially since Henry's death. You've helped him find joy in living again, Thane. He positively shines when he's with you, and for that I'd give up everything."

"Even the fourteen trunks of things that are waiting for us?"

"Even them." Jemma smiled at his teasing. Relaxed, her eyes grew heavy with sleep.

The next thing she knew, the porter walked through the car, letting everyone know they'd be arriving in Baker City within the hour.

As she pushed herself up, Jemma realized she'd fallen asleep against Thane and hurried to put a distance between the two of them. At least as much as the tight restrictions of the train would allow.

Lily yawned and stretched in her seat while Jack popped his eyes open and looked around. Spying his aunt and uncle smiling at him, he grinned and pressed his nose to the window, watching the passing scenery.

Thane leaned forward, placing a hand on Jack's back and motioning out the window. "See that smoke, Jack? That's from my ranch. I'll bet ol' Sam has stoked the fire in the bunkhouse and is frying up a pan of bacon for breakfast. Our place is just over that hill."

Jack turned to him with an excited look and pointed to the herd of red and white cattle grazing in the distance. "Are those your cattle, Uncle Thane?"

"Yep. That's part of the herd. We'll be rounding them up from the hills and keeping them closer to the cabin through the winter."

"Can I help bring them in?" Jack's gaze held a look of hope.

"You bet you can." Thane ruffled his hair then grabbed Lily before she rolled onto the floor. She whimpered and squeezed her eyes shut, burrowing against his chest before returning to sleep.

Carefully sliding back against his seat, Thane cradled the little girl and brushed her unruly curls away from her face. Her pink rosebud lips rested in a pout, tugging at his heart. He had no idea such a tiny person could command so much of his attention or stir such deep, fatherly emotions in him.

When his mother abandoned him, he vowed he'd never trust a woman. Resigned to spending his life alone, without children, he was glad he gave in to Weston's demands that he travel to England.

After meeting Jack and Lily, he couldn't imagine life without them in it, although it would be challenging in his small cabin in the coming months. If Jemma hadn't run screaming into the hills or back to England by spring, he'd purchase the necessary lumber to build a house. For the winter, though, they'd have to make do with the cabin. There wasn't time to get the lumber and build a house before the snow began to fly.

As the train chugged up the last rise and down into the valley where Baker City spread out on the relatively flat floor, Thane pointed out the mountains rising to the west. Snow already covered them nearly halfway down and Jemma wondered how long it would be before snow fell in the immediate region.

Still holding Lily, Thane reached out and slipped his arm in front of Jemma, bracing her in the seat as the train ground to a bone-jarring halt. She gasped at the feel of his arm across her middle and quickly pushed back against her seat.

Once the train stopped, Thane moved his arm, pulled his bag from beneath the seat then stood. Lily draped over his shoulder as he pulled their bags from overhead and handed the smallest one to Jack. With plans to take three of them, he left one for Jemma to carry.

He gave her his hand and helped her to her feet then watched with amusement as she poked at stray hairpins, adjusted her hat, and brushed at her dirt-streaked skirt. A spot of soot marred on one creamy cheek. Without thinking, he reached over and brushed at it with his thumb, causing her to still her movements and watch him with wary eyes.

"Smudge," he said, picking up the bags and motioning for Jemma to precede him down the aisle with Jack.

"Welcome to Baker City, ma'am. Enjoy your stay," the friendly porter said, smiling as Jemma stepped from the train onto the platform at the depot. Jack stayed close to her skirts as Thane stepped off the train, thanking the porter for his service.

Thane motioned Jemma toward a bench on the far end of the platform. They started that direction when a man nearly as handsome and tall as Thane shouted and waved, hurrying toward them.

"I must have spent too much time out in the sun because I can't believe what I'm seeing. Is that you, Thane Jordan?" The man stood with his hands fisted at his waist, legs spread apart with a big smile on his face. "You said you inherited two children, but you dang sure didn't mention a wife."

Chapter Twelve

Thane glared at his friend rather than answer. It only served to generate more commentary.

"What is a plug-ugly ol' coot like you doing with this beautiful woman and these two children?"

The man smiled at Jemma, giving her a flirtatious wink before grinning at Jack and hunkering down to his level. "Did he kidnap you?"

Jack shook his head, not sure what to make of the jovial stranger.

"Did he threaten to feed you to the bears? Make you walk the plank?"

Jack laughed, shaking his head again.

The stranger stood and addressed Jemma. "Did he take you against your will, ma'am? If he did, I'll haul this sorry excuse for a human down to the calaboose."

Jemma glanced uncertainly at her husband. A hint of a smile lifted the corners of his mouth. "Jemma, may I present my friend, Sheriff Tully Barrett. Tully, this is my wife, Lady Jemma Bryan Jordan."

Tully executed a bow worthy of a queen, sweeping his hat from his head and gallantly kissing the back of Jemma's hand.

She smiled at the man who seemed to be a good-natured tease, tipping her head to him. "It is certainly a pleasure to meet you, Mr. Barrett."

"Shucks, ma'am, just call me Tully. This cranky galoot is the closest thing I've got to family and I'm sure you'll see more of me than you can stand, so you might as well call me Tully."

"Very well, Tully. Please call me Jemma." She settled a hand on Jack's shoulder. "This is our nephew, Jack, and Thane is holding Lily."

"Jack, it's mighty fine to meet you. Say, do you own that big ol' dog I hauled out to the ranch day before yesterday? A note in his kennel said his name is Sir Rigsly. Is he a knight?"

Jack grinned and shook the hand Tully held out to him. "No, sir. He's just our dog."

"And a fine dog he is," Tully said, noticing Lily peeping at him as she hid her face against Thane's neck.

"Never thought I'd see the day when you'd roll into town with a wife and kids, Thane. Apparently, we're in for a long, deep, cold spell. If I remember right, you said the day you wed was the day that he..."

Thane took a step forward, bumping into Tully and cutting off his words. Jemma pressed her lips together to keep from laughing.

"Did everything arrive in good shape?" Thane asked as Lily raised her head and looked around at her surroundings. Overcome with the unfamiliar world around her, she reached out to her aunt. Jemma took her and began rocking the child from side to side.

"Sure did. Fourteen trunks, four horses, one dog, and a partridge in a pear tree." Tully slapped Thane on the back. "Your order from Chicago arrived last week and a few things arrived for you yesterday, too."

"Thanks, Tully. Want to help me with the rest of our baggage?"

"How can you have more after everything we hauled out to the ranch already?" Tully winked at Jemma as he and Thane wandered off in the direction of the baggage car further down the platform.

"I like Mr. Barrett, Auntie Jemma. He's funny." Jack looked up at her with a twinkle in his eyes.

"Yes, he is. We've just set foot off the train and already made a new friend. He said he's the sheriff. That is quite exciting, isn't it?"

Jack nodded his head. "Did you see his star and his gun? I wonder if Uncle Thane has a gun."

"Good heavens!" Jemma hadn't considered Thane swaggering around wearing a gun but when he returned to her side, he was in the process of buckling on a gun belt. She had no idea where he'd stored it, but he wore one just the same.

Startled by the sight of the weaponry hanging around his hip, she lifted her gaze. Once again, Thane looked fearsome and unapproachable, nothing like the man who'd spent the last two weeks trying to ease the burdens of travel for her and the children.

"Do you mind waiting here with Lily while we go get the horses? You can wait inside the depot. I'll take Jack with me." Thane pointed a hand toward the building behind her.

"That would be a satisfactory arrangement." She watched as he and Tully picked up all the bags they could carry but left behind the two trunks that had been in the baggage car.

Thane tipped his hat to her then walked off with Tully, answering Jack's questions about the town as they strode across the street.

As she opened the door to the depot and stepped inside, gratitude filled her to see a sign for a lavatory. After taking Lily, they returned to a bench near a window and waited. Fully awake, Lily wanted to explore her new surroundings.

"Where's Uncle Thane?" Lily asked as she swung back and forth, holding onto Jemma's hand.

"He went to get the horses."

"Why?"

"In order for us to travel to his ranch."

"Why?"

"So we can go home, Lily."

"To the cottage?" The little girl's voice sounded so hopeful, Jemma bit back the tears that pricked her eyes.

"No, poppet." Jemma picked her up and cuddled her close until Lily squirmed to get down again. "Your uncle's ranch is our new home."

Lily appeared thoughtful for a moment then began hopping on one foot, sending her wild curls into a frenzy of bouncing. "I'm hungry. Can we eat, please?"

"Yes, I suppose we should eat something before we venture into the wilds and leave civilization behind."

"I want bacon and toast. Please, Auntie Jemma. And marmalade. I want marmalade. Can Cook make marmalade for my toast?"

"No, love, but I'm sure we can find some jam. You like jam, Lily. Remember the lovely berry jam we had with our scones."

"Scones. I want scones with cream. Please? And crumpets!"

"We'll see, Lily. Shall we count your fingers? You didn't leave any on the train, did you?"

Lily's eyes dropped to her hands and she held them out in front of her.

"Oh, look." Jemma took Lily's tiny fingers in her own. "You've got them all. Let's count. One, two, three…"

Tired, in need of a bath, and every bit as hungry as Lily, Jemma wanted to crawl into a soft bed and sleep for a week. She'd settle for Thane coming and taking them to his ranch. He'd been gone what seemed like a very long time when she saw him walk in front of the depot windows and open the door.

Lily ran to him and held up her arms. He picked her up and tossed her in the air in their now familiar routine before stepping next to the bench were Jemma sat. Thane helped her to her feet, tipped his head to the ticket agent, and escorted her out the door.

"We're just around the corner," he said, cupping her elbow in his hand.

As they rounded the corner of the building, she observed a shiny new conveyance hitched to a large brown horse, waiting to carry them to the ranch. Jack sat on the front seat talking to Tully as he sat astraddle a buckskin horse.

The two trunks, along with their bags, sat in the back. The vehicle looked like a carriage or buggy but the body had straighter, more utilitarian lines like a wagon. Painted black, the gear gleamed in a shade of dark green with gold stripes, creating a striking appearance. She glanced at the padded backs and seats of leather in admiration.

"It's a buckboard. Had it shipped from back east since I didn't think you and the kids would enjoy bouncing along in my big farm wagon every time we need to come into town," Thane explained, walking her down a set of steps to where the wagon waited.

"How very thoughtful. Thank you." Jemma smiled at Tully and accepted the hand Thane gave her to step into the conveyance. Jack scrambled over the front seat to the back and Thane handed Lily to Jemma once she settled her skirts.

After climbing in, he picked up the reins but Jemma put a hand on his arm before he released the brake. "I know you are most eager to journey to the ranch, but could we please partake of some nourishment? The children need something in their tummies before we leave town."

Thane sighed, anxious to return to the ranch, but deferred to Jemma's wishes. He turned to Tully. "Want to join us?"

"Why not?" Tully grinned and rode beside the buckboard as Thane directed it down the broad dirt street and around a corner. A few blocks down Main Street, he pulled the horse to a stop in front of an impressive hotel.

Jemma craned her neck back and read the sign at the top of the three-story building. "Hotel Warshauer."

"Two brothers built this place last year. I think you'll like it," Thane said, taking Lily from her then assisting her out of the buckboard while Jack followed Tully down the sidewalk toward a set of double doors.

Warmth greeted her as they stepped inside. Jemma glanced around the hotel's lobby. While nothing like their luxurious accommodations in New York, this hotel had a certain elegance combined with a welcoming atmosphere. An ornate stained glass ceiling drew her interest as she admired the beauty of her surroundings.

Hurriedly eating their breakfast, they were soon back in the wagon, heading down Main Street for the far end of town.

Jemma took in a variety of businesses, from a clothing house and saddle shop to a grocer's store. Pleased by the assortment, she hoped one day soon Thane would bring her to town and let her explore.

Tully rode beside them as they left the town behind and began journeying over scrubby hills.

"What are those plants called, Uncle Thane?" Jack asked, leaning over the front seat between his uncle and aunt.

"Those pale greenish-gray bushes are sagebrush. There's nothing like the scent of sagebrush right after a rainstorm. Those other plants that are a brighter green are greasewood. We don't have many trees out here, although you might come across a random juniper or pine tree,"

Thane said, motioning toward a thick tree line on the distant hills. He and Tully offered names of plants, the mountains, and pointed to a small herd of deer.

Jemma noted the brown grass growing among the clumps of sagebrush and greasewood. When her husband said he lived in a climate vastly different from her home, she hadn't realized how true his words would be. Used to gentle rains, moist air, and green as far as she could see, the dry, brown landscape with billows of dust appeared ugly and uncivilized.

Despite it being mid-October, the day continued to warm to a level that left Jemma concerned she and the children would experience dreadful burns from the sun before they ever reached the ranch.

Overhead, a bright golden orb beat down on her, making her feel slightly lightheaded.

Thane pointed out a snake coiled by a rock. "Stay away from those snakes, Jack. They'll bite and their fangs are full of poison. I've known a few men who died from snakebite."

Shudders racked through Jemma. No one mentioned snakes. What had she done, bringing two precious children to a wild, arid country filled with venomous reptiles?

Queasy, she shifted Lily to sit next to Thane. She grabbed the edge of the seat to keep from falling off the buckboard as dizziness settled over her. The dust threatened to choke the air from her lungs and she couldn't get her breath.

Oblivious to her distress, the two men discussed what had happened at the ranch in the two months Thane had been gone. Lost in conversation, Thane remained unaware of Jemma's suffering until Lily yanked on his sleeve, capturing his attention.

"What is it, honey?" Thane asked, glancing down at the little girl.

"Auntie Jemma." Lily pointed to Jemma as she swayed on the seat, looking ill. In fact, her face appeared completely devoid of color except for two bright red spots riding high on each cheek.

Thane stretched his arm across the seat and placed the back of his hand to her forehead. It felt clammy to his touch.

"Jemma? Are you sick?"

She turned glassy eyes his direction and shook her head.

Thane handed Lily to Tully. The sheriff settled her in front of him on the saddle. The little girl laughed and kicked her tiny feet, wanting the horse to go faster.

"Head on to the ranch. We'll be right behind you," Thane said to Tully then turned to look at Jack, who continued leaning over the seat. "Sit back, son, and hang on. I don't want you to fall out."

Jack obeyed, scooting back on the seat and grabbing onto the side rail as Thane pulled Jemma closer to his side and wrapped an arm around her. "Just hold on, Jemma. We'll be home soon. You told me the first day we met you aren't a swooner and I'm holding you to it."

A firm slap of the reins across the horse's rump set him running at a fast pace, sending great clouds of dust churning in the air behind the buckboard.

Tully raced ahead with Lily while Thane urged the horse to go faster. Jemma looked as bad as he felt when he suffered from seasickness. His prayers winged heavenward that they'd arrive at the ranch before she fainted.

Another ten minutes passed before they topped a hill and the ranch came into view. Thane breathed a sigh of relief as he guided the horse along the familiar trail to the cabin. Ranch hands poured out of the barn, corral, and bunkhouse to greet them. Tully handed Lily to one of the men while he dismounted.

Thane stopped the horse by the cabin and hurried around to Jemma's side.

"Howdy, boss. We got your message and did as you asked," said Sam, the bunkhouse cook, as he approached, carrying Lily. "Congratulations on your kids. Is that the nanny?"

"Thank you, Sam. And no, she isn't the nanny. Just give me a minute to settle my wife and I'll be out to take a look over everything." Thane scooped Jemma into his arms as Sam stared at him, dumbfounded.

"Wife? You didn't mention a wife, just that you inherited two youngin's. I thought you said that snowballs would fall ten feet deep in the desert before you'd saddle yourself to a woman."

"Never mind what I said," Thane growled as he strode across the barren yard and up the steps to the cabin door. Tully beat him there and held it open while Thane crossed the threshold with Jemma. "Did you add the bedroom?" Thane looked back at Sam as he stepped inside and set Lily down next to her brother.

"There." Sam pointed to a door off the open kitchen area.

Thane stalked that direction and Tully opened the door for him. The large bed he'd asked Tully to order had been delivered and set up. Made of English oak, the headboard stood more than six-feet high with ornate carvings. A matching dresser sat against one wall while a washstand occupied the opposite wall. Although sparse, the room was well constructed and even had a plank floor.

Pleased with both the room and the new furnishings, Thane was grateful someone had made the bed with the linens he'd ordered.

"Wish she'd decided to get sick before we left town so I could have taken her to Doc's office," Thane complained as he laid Jemma on the bed. She fluttered a hand at him and muttered something he couldn't hear, so he turned to look at the men who crowded around the doorway.

"I appreciate all of you getting this room ready."

"Well, shoot, boss, we didn't know you ordered all that stuff for a new bride. Just thought maybe with the kids you'd gone and got civilized." A cheeky young cowboy named Ben gave Thane a broad smile while the men laughed. Lily shoved her way through their legs until she stood inside the door.

"Auntie Jemma?" she asked, scampering over to the bed. She started to climb up on Jemma, making the woman moan. Thane quickly picked her up and handed her to Tully.

As he caught Jack's eye, Thane bent over so he didn't tower over the boy. "How about you two go see if Rigsly needs some attention? I bet he'll be glad to see you both."

"Rigsly?" Lily squealed, making two of the hands grimace at her high-pitched excitement. "I want to see our doggie! See Rigsly right now!"

"Yes, ma'am." Tully took the two youngsters outside while the rest of the cowboys except Sam followed him.

"Do you need some help, Thane?"

Thane stared at the collapsed form of his wife on the bed. "I don't know. Give me a few minutes to see if I can figure out what's wrong. Go on outside and I'll holler if I need help."

"Might just be the change in climate and altitude, that sort of thing. Could be worn out from all the travel. Doubt it's anything serious." Sam nodded to Thane then pulled the door shut behind him, giving the couple some privacy.

Perplexed, Thane walked over to the bed and looked down at Jemma, unsure what to do. One thing was for certain, she needed to get out of her constrictive clothes so she could breathe and rest easier.

"Jemma, you need to get undressed. Can you do that?"

She didn't respond but weakly lifted a hand before dropping it back beside her.

Loudly sighing, Thane tossed his hat on top of the dresser and began unbuttoning the jacket of Jemma's traveling suit.

She pushed at him and whispered, "don't touch me," making him smile.

"Too late for that, Lady Jemma. I'm about to discover just how tightly you lace that corset you wear."

Thane heard her whisper an insult but chose to ignore it. Since his big hands weren't meant for such tiny closures, he fumbled with the buttons on her jacket. Doubtful her outfit would be the same after days of collecting soot and dust from the train, he took out his pocketknife and sliced down the front of the jacket.

"Stop!" she screamed, only it came out as a hoarse plea.

"I'll buy you a dozen new dresses to make up for it, but everything has to come off so you can breathe. Now hush and hold still." Thane slid his knife down the length of her skirt then carefully cut away her frilled white blouse. Jemma cried as he pulled off her petticoats and corset cover.

The corset proved to be a foreign item of clothing, drawing his intense scrutiny. It took him only a moment to decide to slice the stays on the back. As he rolled her onto her side, poising his knife at the ready, Jemma grasped the front of it with a strength he wouldn't have thought she could possess and began unhooking the busk.

He shoved her hands away and unhooked it then tossed her corset to the floor with the rest of her ruined attire.

She took in a deep breath, followed by another. A little color began to return to her face.

After removing her shoes, he pushed up the legs of her drawers and rolled down her stockings while she made idle threats, calling him a cad and bully. As he lifted her head and pulled out the pins in her hair, Thane had to close his mind to the number of times he'd envisioned doing that very thing, only with her looking at him with yearning instead of bordering on the edge of incoherency.

Mindful of her modesty, he left her attired in her chemise and drawers. He pulled back the coverings on the bed and settled her against the pillows.

Recalling how good it felt when she bathed his face and hands with a cool cloth while he was sick, he hurried to the kitchen and found a clean rag then held it beneath the pump. Rapidly working the handle until water splashed out, he soaked the rag, filled a glass with water, and returned to the bedroom.

He sat on the edge of the bed and lifted Jemma's head, making her take a long drink of the water. After setting the glass aside, he wiped her face, along her neck, across her chest, and down her arms and hands with the cool rag.

Heat spiraled through him followed by an incontestable longing for his wife. The unobstructed view of her exposed creamy, smooth skin, combined with the sensations created by touching her as he removed her clothes, made it perfectly clear what a desirable woman he'd married.

Before giving her another sip of water, he swallowed hard and squeezed his eyes shut to clear his thoughts.

"Better?" he asked, hoping she was only exceedingly tired or overheated. He hadn't counted on it being quite so warm this far into the autumn, but the area had been known to get a few scorching days in October followed by early snowstorms.

"Yes." Jemma reached out a hand to him and he took it, kissing her palm. "Thank you."

"Just rest for a while, my lady. I'll keep the kids outside with me."

He opened the window, allowing fresh air to blow in along with the sounds of Jack and Lily laughing and Rigsly barking.

After tucking a sheet over her shoulder, Thane left the room and closed the door behind him. He walked across the large open space that comprised his kitchen and sitting area. On the other side of it was his former bedroom. The men had cut a hole in the wall near his bedroom door and added a second bedroom, as he'd requested. A new small bed occupied the space. He planned for it to be Lily's room while Jack took over his old room.

He'd move out his clothes and belongings later into the bedroom he planned to share with his wife. Now that they were home, she'd just have to come around to the idea of sharing a bedroom with him because he wouldn't give her any other options.

Chapter Thirteen

Slowly awakening, Jemma lingered on the edge of consciousness where Thane held her close and told her how much he loved her. His masculine scent teased her nose while his warmth settled around her like a cozy blanket.

Unsettled and thinking herself silly for such romantic notions, she didn't know why visions of him shirtless and bronzed plagued her dreams and often interrupted her during the day.

She circled her thoughts back to the moment at hand and recalled feeling ill on the way to the ranch. Recollections of anything beyond Thane ordering her not to swoon seemed fuzzy.

Cool air blew above her although she felt content and safe. She could smell freshly cut wood and Thane's manly scent, along with something tangy bringing sage to mind.

The terrifying howl of a beast outside made her eyes pop open and she started to sit upright in bed. Something heavy held her down.

Tentatively reaching along her waist, her fingers brushed over an arm corded with muscles pinning her to the soft, warm bed.

A gasp of distress escaped her. She felt something stir behind her and concluded she'd been sleeping on her side.

"What's wrong, Jemma?" Thane's deep voice rumbled in his chest in a sleepy, altogether enthralling tone, while he tightened his hold around her. "Do you need something?"

"An explanation, sir, as to why you are in my bed and have taken liberties with my person." As she attempted to roll over to face the infuriating man, she found she couldn't move between his arm weighing her down and his body close behind her.

She reached back a hand to smack him and connected with the bare skin of his chest. Swiftly jerking her hand in front of her, she drew in another gulp of air. Memories of him carrying her inside the house and removing her clothes, despite her feeble protests, assaulted her.

Curious as to how long she'd slept, she worried about Jack and Lily.

Thane squeezed her waist. "Calm down. We're all worn out and in need of sleep. The kids are tucked into their beds. I guess I rolled over here in my sleep. That's all. We can argue about who sleeps where in the morning. For now, rest assured nothing happened. I've certainly not taken any liberties with your person or anything else, although I'd be happy to oblige if that's what you want."

"You are an insufferable rake!" Jemma shoved at his arm and rolled onto her back, realizing too late her mistake. It put her face next to Thane's and his mouth mere inches from her own. Still lying on his side, his body touched hers from shoulder to knee and she couldn't will away the delightful sensations his nearness produced. The ridiculous desire to roll into him, into his strength and ruggedness, made her head swim as she fought to bring her thoughts under control.

Thane smirked. "So you've mentioned before. If it makes you feel better, I'm only that way with you."

Subtle moonbeams slipping through the open window glided in a gentle caress on his wife, highlighting the fine curve of her cheek, the fullness of her bottom lip, and alabaster skin. Thane could plainly see concern on her face mixed with something he refused to identify.

He hadn't intentionally set out to hold her. When he fell asleep, he'd been on the far side of the bed. It wasn't his fault her enticing curves and the soft temptation she unknowingly offered drew him like a magnet to metal.

As he raised himself on one elbow, he noticed the strap of her chemise had slid off one shoulder. Auburn hair flowed all around her face and down her back in a tempting mass. He reached out one finger and gently traced it along the smooth skin of her collarbone then fingered a lock of hair where it rested above her heaving chest. Heat zinged through his veins as her decidedly feminine fragrance filled his nose.

Aware that any move on his part would push her further away, he unwillingly rolled onto his back.

"Do you need anything?" he asked, when Jemma continued to stare at him.

"I need to um… could I please… might I inquire as to the whereabouts of your lavatory." Need currently trumped prudence, although her cheeks flamed with embarrassment at asking the question.

Thane chuckled. "You might as well get used to calling it the outhouse or privy, because that's what we call it in these parts and no one will know what you're talking about if you ask for it by something different. There aren't many indoor bathrooms in Baker City, although I think one or two of the hotels offer them to their guests as well as the train depot. A few of the newer homes have added them, too. Come on. I'll show you where it's at."

Quickly sliding out of bed, he turned his back to her and yanked on the Levi's he'd left on the floor. After stuffing his feet into his boots, he lit a lamp he'd carried in earlier and set on the bedside table.

Jemma sat in the bed, unmoving.

"Are you coming? Are you still sick?" he asked, setting the lamp down on the dresser and holding a hand out to her, wondering if she felt dizzy.

"No, I feel much better. It must have been a combination of exhaustion and the heat. Perhaps the vile reptile added to my discomfort." She clutched the sheet to her chin as he wiggled his hand at her, indicating she should rise from the bed. "I don't have my dressing gown or slippers."

With a careworn sigh, he stepped to the far side of the room and opened the trunk she'd used both on the ship and in New York. He dug around until he found what he thought was her dressing gown. She had so many fancy, frilly clothes it was hard for him to decide what she considered undergarments and what served as outerwear.

When he held out the piece of lace-trimmed silk, she reluctantly climbed out of bed and hastened to stuff her arms in the sleeves then fasten the front. She rummaged through the trunk until she found her slippers and tugged them on her feet.

Quietly opening the bedroom door, Thane led the way through the kitchen to the front door then took her arm as he walked her down the porch steps and around the corner of the cabin to a small structure located away from the other buildings.

"Here you are, my lady." Thane bowed ceremoniously as he opened the door, checked to make sure no snakes lurked inside, then handed her the lamp.

Her scowl made him bite the inside of his cheek to keep from laughing as she stepped inside and slammed the door closed.

"Would you like me to wait for you?" he asked, entertained as gasps of disgust filtered through the cracks.

"That most certainly will not be necessary. Please return to the house."

"Yes, Lady Jemma." Thane strolled back to the cabin. Rigsly bumped into him and whined. Thane forgot he'd let the dog in the house before he went to bed. He stood on the porch, waiting for Jemma as he looked out over his ranch and scratched the dog behind his ears.

After a few days of settling in, he planned to leave Rigsly outside with the other ranch dogs. Until then, he didn't mind having the animal in the cabin. Apparently, Rigsly was so happy to see familiar faces, he no longer considered Thane a stranger but a friend.

The silvery glow from the moon enabled him to see the barn. The newly constructed addition at the back held the horses he'd brought from England along with all of Jemma's trunks.

His hired men did a good job on both the new bedrooms at the house as well as the added space to the barn. They'd kept things running just like he was there during his absence. Tully checked on them periodically, made sure they received their pay, and took care of buying supplies for them.

Blessed to have such good friends and loyal ranch hands, Thane smiled as he looked over the bunkhouse, the open shed where they kept equipment, the smokehouse, chicken coop, and springhouse.

Part of his remuda milled around in the corral next to the barn while fat cattle grazed on the pasture grass he'd planted on the surrounding hills. He'd built the ranch from the sweat of his brow and long, hard hours of labor, but he loved it. He prayed Jack and Lily would learn to love it too. In time, he hoped their prim and proper aunt would think of it as home.

Although he wouldn't admit it to anyone, especially her, Jemma somehow worked her way into his thoughts and his heart.

Despite his assumption that all women were like his mother, he knew to the very core of his being Jemma would never run off and leave him or the children. She'd given up everything familiar to her, everything she loved, to make sure they were cared for even though it took her thousands of miles from her home.

He trusted Jemma, admired her, and found himself completely infatuated with her.

Unless she returned his growing feelings in the foreseeable future, he needed to find a way to block her from his mind, build another bedroom, or get used to sleeping in the barn. He couldn't take too many nights of holding her close without making her his.

However, winters were too cold for sleeping in the barn, the men would tease him mercilessly if he slept in the bunkhouse, and he'd never live it down if he added another bedroom. He needed to learn to keep his longings in check and pretend Jemma was someone there to care for the children who happened to sleep on the other side of his bed.

The coyotes along the ridge continued their nocturnal serenade and Thane listened to them howl. He'd missed the sounds of his home during his absence and breathed in the sagebrush-scented air.

"Mercy!" Jemma's strained voice preceded her hurried footsteps as she ran around the corner of the house and jumped onto the porch. Wide, alarmed eyes gazed toward the hill where the coyotes yipped back and forth.

Frightened, she clutched Thane's arm in her free hand and took a step behind him, tugging him toward the door. "Will they try to eat us? Will they hurt the horses or cattle? What do you do to get rid of wolves?"

Thane chuckled and reached behind him, wrapping an arm around Jemma's shoulders. He could feel her trembling in fear. Soothingly, he rubbed his hand along her spine then glanced down at her and grinned. "It's just the coyotes welcoming us home. They like to talk at night. For the most part, they leave the stock alone, although they sometimes try to get at the chickens. You shouldn't encounter them during the day. Unless one is rabid, they'll leave you alone at night, too."

"Coyotes? Aren't they vicious carnivores? Don't they pose a dire threat to us?" Jemma asked, still not certain the terrible noises echoing around the house could come from a harmless animal. Rigsly brushed against her legs, making her jump. When she realized it was their dog, she let out a ragged breath of relief.

"No, they don't pose a threat. As long as they aren't starving, which they aren't this time of year, there's no need to worry about them. There's plenty of wildlife to keep them fed and happy."

Gently taking Jemma's arm, he turned her around and guided her inside the cabin. Once Rigsly strolled inside, he closed the door. Thane stepped over to the sink and pumped a glass full of water then handed it to his wife.

She set the lamp on the counter and accepted the glass. The cool liquid soothed her parched throat as she tipped her head back and drank deeply.

Thane watched with rapt fascination as she emptied the glass and set it on the counter. "Do you need something to eat? You missed supper."

"I'm fine, but thank you. I believe I shall return to bed. I appreciate you showing me the um... the place where... the..."

"Outhouse," Thane supplied, placing his hand on her shoulder and nudging her to the bedroom door. When they were both inside, he closed it. The click of the latch echoed through the tense atmosphere. He blew out the lamp and returned it to his bedside table. "It's okay, Jemma. It's what everyone calls it."

"It sounds so vulgar." Jemma wasn't convinced he didn't tease her with the name.

"How about privy? Does that sound better?"

"Marginally. I do believe I shall continue to refer to it as a lavatory, despite your suggestion otherwise." Jemma shook her head and watched in dismay as Thane worked off his boots then dropped his pants to the floor. Discomfiture burned her cheeks as she spun around, turning her back to him. "You are not planning to sleep here. I forbid it."

"Forbid all you want, but I'm beat and going to sleep. You can either crawl in here and stay on your side of the bed, or sit up at the kitchen table, because those are your two options." Thane lifted the sheet and slid beneath the covers, letting out a satisfied grunt as he sank into the comfortable mattress. He'd be sure to thank Tully for ordering the bedroom set for him. It was nicer than anything he'd expected.

"I'll go sleep with Lily." Jemma took a step before something grasped the back of her gown, jerking her to a stop.

Thane held a handful of her dressing gown in his hand and pulled her backward as he stretched across the bed. "She's got a single bed and needs to get used to sleeping alone. You're gonna spoil her if you keep sleeping in her room. Besides, you're my wife and this is where you belong. I won't have my hands thinking I can't control my household, and that includes you."

"If memory serves me correctly, you assured me not once but twice that you would share everything with me except a bed. Unless I've sustained a head injury and this is all a bad dream, I believe that is precisely what we're doing." Jemma glared at Thane as he gave another tug, making her fall back on the bed. "What, sir, are your intentions?"

"I'm intending…" Thane sat up and loosened the ties from Jemma's neck and waist. He grasped the top edges of her gown and gave it a jerk, sending buttons skittering across the floor. "To go to sleep, in bed, with my wife."

An incensed shriek escaped her lips when Thane yanked off her dressing gown and tossed it aside. He roughly grabbed her ankles and tugged off her slippers, throwing them on the floor. Before she could squirm away from him, he flipped the covers over her and pulled her against his chest.

"I don't intend to do anything other than sleep, Jemma. Just sleep. Understand? You're safe from my obviously unwanted attentions. When I said that about sharing a bed, I referred to, well... you know what I meant. Sleeping is all I have in mind."

She held her breath, feeling dizzy all over again as his warmth penetrated the thin cotton fabric of her chemise and drawers. Despite his assurance she was safe, he didn't seem to realize the war of temptation he set off inside her with his teasing words and welcome presence.

"Now, close your eyes and relax."

"I hardly think I can relax with you holding me captive against my will," she huffed indignantly.

Thane released his hold on her waist and settled his hand on the curve of her hip. "Is that better?" His voice came out in a husky whisper.

"Certainly not. You are the most intractable, incorrigible, imbecile I've had the displeasure of meeting." Aggravated, she shoved his hand off her hip.

"Fine, have it your way." Thane placed his hand on her backside and gently rubbed up and down, intentionally provoking her.

Shocked, she drew in a gulp of air and flipped onto her back, half-landing on Thane. "I ought to slap that smirk right off your face, you horrid..."

The bedroom door banged open and they both turned to look at Jack and Lily standing in the doorway, visibly frightened.

"What's wrong, my darlings?" Jemma sat up and held out her arms. Lily bolted across the room, clutching her favorite dolly to her chest. Jemma swooped her up while Jack ran over to the bed and climbed up beside his aunt.

"Are there wolves outside? Will they get into the cabin and kill us?" Jack asked. Lily screamed when the coyotes let out another series of howls.

"No, Jack. Those are just coyotes. They won't hurt you. They sometimes sing at night. I like to stretch out in bed with the window open and listen to their songs." Thane reached over Jemma and lifted Jack, setting the boy down beside him. He brushed Jack's bangs from his face and patted his back encouragingly. "Let's sit here a minute and listen to them sing. This time of year, the pups leave to find their own territories. I think the mamas are telling them to be careful and to mind their manners. What do you think?" Jack nodded his head and relaxed against Thane's side.

They listened to the coyotes howl for several moments. Rigsly wandered into the room and plopped down on the pile of Jemma's ruined clothes, letting out a contented sigh as he dropped his head to his paws.

Jack struggled to keep his eyes open while Lily fell asleep in Jemma's arms. Thane moved the boy so he rested beside him and motioned for Jemma to settle Lily next to her brother. As he slid down in the bed, Thane cast one more glance at his wife. "Good night, Jem. Welcome to the ranch."

Sunlight lazily stretched yellow ribbons across the morning sky, offering the promise of a beautiful autumn day.

The ranch hands stood outside the cabin, gazing at the door, wondering what to do. No smoke rose from the chimney, no sounds indicated anyone was awake inside.

Normally, Thane was the first up and the last to bed, working long, tiring hours. He never expected more of his hands than he was willing to do himself, and had long ago earned their respect.

This morning, though, they hadn't seen so much as a glimpse of him or his new family.

Thane taking a wife left them reeling in surprise. He swore up and down in front of them all on occasions too numerous to count that women were nothing but trouble and he'd never be mixed up with one.

However, one look at Mrs. Jordan and they could see why the auburn-haired beauty captured his interest.

Not only was she lovely, Tully told them she was a proper English lady. To the ranch hands, she may as well have been the queen.

"He's probably worn out from travel and getting the family settled in." Sam rocked back on his heels as he stared at the cabin. He'd already fixed breakfast for the hands and they'd done all the routine morning chores. They could proceed as they had been the last two months, but out of respect to Thane, they awaited his direction for the day.

"Ben, go knock on the door. Maybe we just didn't hear them. Or maybe something's wrong. See if that strange dog is in there, too. He wasn't in the barn this morning," Sam said, pointing from the young cowhand to the cabin.

"Why me?" Ben asked, glaring over his shoulder as one of the other cowpokes shoved him forward.

"Because you've got the most charming smile." Sam batted his eyelashes at the young man and held his hands beneath his chin, making the rest of them laugh.

"Fine, but someone else gets to do this next time." Ben settled his hat on his head and marched up to the door, briskly knocking.

When no one answered, he stuck his head inside and noticed the empty kitchen. "Halloo? Thane?"

Ben stepped into the room and walked across the floor, peeking into the smaller bedrooms, and finding them both empty. As he walked back across the kitchen, he looked inside the open door of the big bedroom and couldn't suppress the laugher that bubbled in his chest and spilled out his mouth.

Rigsly lifted his head from Jemma's pile of petticoats and woofed, joining in the hired hand's merriment.

Filled with hilarity, Ben backed out of the room to the cabin's door and looked outside. "They're alive but the boss will never live this down."

Upon hearing Ben's voice, Thane came instantly awake. Hastily attempting to sit upright in bed, he found he couldn't move. When he opened his eyes, a finger poked his left one and he blinked in pain. Further inspection revealed a tiny hand clutching his ear.

As he lifted the one arm he could move, he discovered Lily lying across his neck and part of his face while Jack sprawled across his chest and other arm.

Quickly working to free himself, he scooted Jack to his side and lifted Lily above his head, searching for a spot to place her. That's when he noticed his hands standing in the door, watching his every move.

"Mornin' boss," Sam lounged against the doorframe, grinning. "Looks like you've got your hands and bed full. If you want, we could bring in the other dogs, maybe a chicken or two. I can see now why you wanted such a big bed."

Thane glared at the men, making them shift uncomfortably while Lily flopped in his arms like a rag doll.

Jemma chose that moment to open her eyes and roll over, coming face to face with all of Thane's hired men. Grabbing the sheet that had fallen down around her knees, she jerked it up to her chin and screamed. "Good heavens! Thane? Thane!"

"You boys head out to the barn. I'll be there directly." Thane glared at them. "And shut the door!"

He heard Sam chuckling as he closed the bedroom door. Spurs jangled across the planks of the kitchen floor as the men trailed outside.

Lily and Jack startled at Jemma's scream, wiggling around. Thane scrambled out of bed and carefully settled Lily into the space he vacated. Jemma glared at him like a jezebel with her hair in a snarled mess, her chemise more off than on, and fury blazing in her copper eyes.

"To what sort of... of... perverted place have you brought us?" Jemma stabbed a finger in his direction. "What kind of men watch people sleep?" Incensed, she noticed her husband's smirk as he yanked on his denim overalls, pulled on a pair of clean socks, and put on his boots. With her fists clenched, she glowered at him. "What is so amusing?"

Thane lifted one of the shirts he'd moved to the dresser the previous evening and slipped it over his broad shoulders. Hurriedly grabbing his gun belt off the dresser along with his hat, he walked over to her side of the bed and bent down until his forehead almost touched hers. "You."

"Indeed, Mr. Jordan. I do not find a single tidbit of amusement in anything that has transpired since we set foot off the train into this detestable lair of debauchery."

"I'm right pleased you like the place." Thane gave her a wicked smile and leaned back. "If you need something, ask Sam. He'll be around the barn or the bunkhouse today. I'll be back in time for supper. I like to eat about six, but for today, we'll take our meals at the bunkhouse. Have a good day."

Thane swooped down and placed a hot, moist kiss to the exposed skin on her shoulder, making a wild tremor race through her. Before she could smack him, he stepped out of reach and looked back at her with a devilish wink. "Sleep in a while with the kids, Mrs. Jordan. You'll need all the energy you can muster for later and I'm giving you today to get caught up on your rest."

Rigsly, the traitor, hopped up and followed Thane.

As soon as the front door closed, Jemma jumped out of bed and shook with both anger and the incredible sensations created by Thane's lips on her skin.

Annoyed, she marched over to the dresser and glanced in the mirror, taking in her disheveled state. Appalled by her reflection, it was no wonder the hands stood gaping at her. She looked like she belonged in one of the houses of ill repute she'd read about in a dreadful book she'd found onboard the ship.

Determined to set herself and the cabin to rights, she took clothes out of her trunk and dressed while the children slept.

After combing her hair into a tidy chignon, she found the buttons to her dressing gown and set them on the dresser, planning to sew them on later. Folding the garment across the foot of the bed, she took the clothes Thane had cut and looked at them in dismay. The fabric had been all but ruined from the travel, but she'd planned to use what she could salvage to make something for Jack or Lily. Thane had only damaged a small part of the pieces, so she set them aside to tend to later.

Relieved, she lifted the petticoats and patted them, planning to move the money she'd tucked into special pockets sewn into the seams into her trunk, only to find it all gone.

Thane had taken her money and left her penniless.

Furious, she tossed down the petticoats and stalked out of the bedroom. Quietly shutting the door behind her, she yanked open the front door in time to see Thane ride off with two of the hands across one of the hills.

She fought the urge to slam the door, but managed to shut it softly then leaned against the wood of the doorjamb, staring at her surroundings. When Thane said his cabin was small and unfurnished, he hadn't spoken in jest. Jemma took in the large open room separating her bedroom from Jack and Lily's rooms.

One side had a sink with a pump, a long counter with cupboards, and a new stove. A table with two chairs provided a place to eat. On the far side of the room, one worn, overstuffed chair sat next to a square end table by a large rock fireplace. A trunk in the corner held extra blankets and a few pillows.

At least wooden planks covered the floors, instead of bare dirt. She'd read about homes in the prairies made of sod. Thoughts of living in a house of dirt, with all manner of insects and vermin burrowing inside made her close her eyes in revulsion.

Yes, she could be grateful for a solid, well-built cabin with windows and wooden floors, even if it didn't seem homey.

The two open doors on the far wall drew her interest. She examined the children's bedrooms. Jack's room must have been Thane's since it had a worn dresser and a bigger bed. A washstand with a mirror stood at the end of the room near a window.

Lily's room smelled of new wood and had no ornamentation at all, other than a white-enameled iron bed with a beautifully carved chiffonier.

Upon returning to her bedroom, Jemma noticed, for the first time, the beautiful bedroom set that appeared to be new. Thane must have ordered it after she accepted his proposal.

With no idea how he'd managed to have rooms added to the house and furnished, she decided to ask him later. As soon as she discovered the whereabouts of her money, she'd take him to task for finding such pleasure in her humiliation.

She opened her trunk and removed a small case, carrying it to the kitchen table. After settling her skirts around her on the rickety chair, she lifted the lid and removed several sheets of paper along with her inkwell and pen.

In need of a bracing cup of tea, a search of Thane's cupboard revealed little more than a tin of stale shortbread biscuits and a small sack of coffee beans. She removed the coffee from the cupboard and set it on the counter, looking for a coffee grinder and not finding one. She added it to her list.

Jemma pumped a glass of cool water and sat down at the table again.

Diligently compiling a list of everything necessary to them settling in, she would insist on going to town the following day to purchase supplies. If Thane wanted her to create a home for the children, he at least needed to provide her with the basics.

The money he inherited from Henry would easily provide Thane with funds to build a grand manor if he chose, so he could well afford to purchase rugs, material for curtains, food supplies, and the like.

If she could acquire her own money back from the arrogant man, she might even purchase one of those newfangled sewing machines she'd seen in a store window in New York.

As she made plans and wrote out more lists, she wondered what she'd feed the children when they awoke, then recalled Thane telling her to eat at the bunkhouse.

Bitterly swallowing her pride, she rose to her feet, opened the door, and marched down the steps then across the barren expanse of dirt and past the barn. The sound of horses whinnying caused her to change direction and enter the barn. Once her eyes adjusted to the dim light, she walked down a row of stalls and studied each animal. Thane owned an impressive collection of horses. In the end stall, she grinned as Jael poked her head through the open door.

"Hello, sweetheart. Did you miss me?" Jemma rubbed the horse's head and kissed her velvety nose. Jael nodded her head in response.

"You don't look any worse for wear. Perhaps tomorrow we can go for a ride, as soon as I find my saddle."

After giving the horse some attention and finding a bucket to give her a little extra feed, Jemma walked out of the barn and almost ran into Sam.

"Howdy, Mrs. Jordan, or should I call you Lady Jordan or is it..." Sam stumbled over what to say to Thane's wife. She looked every inch a proper lady in her fancy brocaded gown with her hair combed into a neat chignon at the back of her head.

Jemma forced herself to smile. "The proper title is Lady Jemma, but please, Mrs. Jordan or Jemma will suffice. You must be Sam. Thane said you'd be around the barn today and we're to dine with you."

"It's nice to meet you ma'am." Sam doffed his hat and managed an awkward bow. "Would you like some breakfast? I can whip up some griddlecakes or offer you biscuits and bacon."

"You eat biscuits for breakfast?" Jemma recalled Cook telling her something about American biscuits being different than those to which she was accustomed and that Thane liked them made with buttermilk.

"Sure do. We eat biscuits any time of the day — smothered in gravy, topped with jam, sweetened with honey." Sam walked beside her, holding open the bunkhouse door for her to enter. As she stepped inside, Jemma noted a large kitchen and long table with benches on either side at the front of the big space. A partial wall separated it from two rows of beds with a few dressers in the back.

"May I see a biscuit?" Jemma asked.

Sam gave her an odd look, but walked over to the table and lifted a round, fluffy circle and set it in her hand.

"This is an American biscuit?"

Sam nodded.

Fascinated, Jemma studied the quick bread she held in her hand, sniffed it then glanced at Sam again. "What do you call something sweet that you'd eat for a treat, perhaps dessert?"

"Cake? Pie?"

"No, something small, you can hold in your hand. It might have jam-filling or coconut, or even chocolate."

"A cookie?" Sam stepped over to the counter and removed the lid from a big jar. He took out a molasses cookie, handing it to Jemma.

"This is a cookie, not a biscuit?"

"Correct." Sam thought Thane's wife seemed slightly daft from her questions.

"I see." Jemma sank down on a bench and stared at the two baked goods in her hands. "I believe I have much to learn about American cooking, Sam. Would you mind sharing your knowledge?"

"I'd be happy to, ma'am. You just let me know when you're ready for a lesson."

"Thank you, sir. I appreciate your willingness to provide assistance." Jemma offered him a charming smile. "Do you perchance have a cup of coffee to spare to go along with my biscuit and cookie?"

Jemma visited with Sam while she ate, then returned to the house and started cleaning.

After the children awoke and ate breakfast, Jemma let Jack stay with Sam at the barn where he cleaned and repaired bridles and harnesses.

She tied a dishtowel over Lily's curls and gave the little girl a rag, asking her to help dust. While Lily flitted from room to room waving her rag in the air, Jemma began scrubbing the kitchen. She cleaned the stove, scoured the sink, and got down on her knees with a brush to clean the floor.

When she unearthed a nest of mice in the back of a cupboard, she screamed so loudly, Sam barreled into the house with his gun cocked, ready to kill whatever intruder threatened her life.

While Jemma gasped and pointed to the mice from her spot atop the table with Lily at her side, Sam nearly chewed a hole in his lip trying not to laugh.

He holstered the pistol and explained to Jack how to get rid of mice as the two of them took the nest outside.

Relieved and glad to be rid of the rodents, Jemma climbed down from atop the table and lifted Lily to the floor.

"Auntie Jemma?" Lily asked in a singsong voice while swinging back and forth as she stood with her arms wrapped around the table leg.

"Yes, poppet?" Jemma looked up from where she knelt, scrubbing out the cupboard, now devoid of its furry occupants.

"Can we go home?"

"Oh, lovey." Jemma rinsed her hands at the sink then picked up Lily and sank down on one of the two kitchen chairs.

Rocking the little girl in her arms, Jemma kissed her button nose and sighed. "This is our home, now. I know it's not like your wonderful, beautiful room at the cottage, but we'll make your new room special."

"Can we do it today?"

"No, Lily. Not today, but very soon. I promise."

"Okay." Lily hugged Jemma with one of her enthusiastically tight squeezes then jumped down and ran to her room with her dust rag.

Unable to hold back a sigh, Jemma attacked her cleaning with renewed enthusiasm.

Chapter Fourteen

Atop the crest of a hill on the back of Shadow, Thane breathed in the scents of sagebrush, dust, and the sweet fragrance of his wife. He held one of her lacy handkerchiefs to his nose, breathing deeply of her perfume.

During the last several weeks of staying at the cottage then traveling home to the ranch, he'd spent so much time in her presence, he missed her scent constantly around him. For a tough, take-no-mercy rancher, that woman was succeeding, albeit unknowingly, in grinding away his hard edges.

He stuffed the scented handkerchief he'd pilfered from her trunk back into his pocket then let his eyes rove over his land and the hundreds of cattle grazing contentedly below him.

Satisfied with his ranch, his hands, and the unexpected turns in his life, he bowed his head and sent up a prayer of thanks.

As he counted each of his blessings, he saved his wife for last.

Lifting his gaze to the snow-capped mountains in the distance, he recalled the way he'd tangled with Jemma before they fell asleep last night. He didn't know what it was about the woman, but it brought him an indescribable amount of enjoyment to do things that irked or unsettled her.

She'd lived in such an ordered world all her life, he thought it was good for her to have things out of balance once in a while, especially if he was the one to get her bloomers in a twist.

Thoughts of her bloomers and the feel of the light cotton beneath his hand when he'd been teasing her left him uncertain if he should have been grateful or mad the children barged into the room, interrupting whatever might have happened next.

In his current state, the only way he knew to keep his hands off his wife and fulfill his promise to her was to work so long and hard he had no energy left for anything else. After being gone for two months, he had plenty of work to do to keep him busy, at least until the snow started to fly.

He turned the horse around and urged him further down the fence line they rode to check for breaks.

When he arrived back at the barn a few minutes before six, Thane brushed down Shadow and led him into a small corral. After throwing in a forkful of hay and filling a bucket of water for the horse, Thane hurried to wash up with the rest of the hands.

Purposefully opening the bunkhouse door, he stepped inside and walked over to where Sam pulled a pan of cornbread from the oven.

The hint of spicy beans greeted Thane and he smiled as he watched the cook cut the cornbread into pieces. "How did things go today?"

"Other than a strange conversation about biscuits and cookies then having to rescue your wife from a nest of mice, it's been a quiet day." Sam grinned at Thane as he placed slices of cornbread on a platter. "Jack's a good boy. He helped me mend bridles this morning and I had him clean stalls this afternoon. The missus kept Lily with her in the house."

Thane nodded his head and thumped Sam on the back. "Thanks for keeping an eye on them for me."

"My pleasure." Sam set the cornbread on the table and took a seat.

Thane settled into a chair at one end of the table and looked up as the kidding and teasing conversations came to a halt and quiet descended across the room. The feminine figure in the doorway, flanked by Jack and Lily, drew the attention of all the men.

"I do hope we are not unforgivably tardy," Jemma said, offering the cowboys her brightest, most charming smile.

"No, ma'am." Sam rose to his feet with the rest of the hands following suit.

Appreciative of their efforts at upholding good manners, Jemma kept her tone friendly as she smiled at them. "Good evening, gentlemen."

If the ranch hands hadn't been half enamored with her from the brief moments they'd seen her earlier, they were in awe of the poised, elegant woman who stepped inside the bunkhouse.

The light floral fragrance floating around Jemma made every one of the cowboys take a deep whiff. Her melodic voice, with its proper British accent, washed over them like a soothing song.

Thane frowned at Jemma, noticing more than a few of his hands appeared smitten with his wife. Unfamiliar pangs of jealousy speared through him, making him irritable and out of sorts.

Enchanted by her beauty, he hurried over to her, taking in her perfectly coifed hair, expensive peach and gray silk gown, and the sparks dancing in her bright copper eyes.

Annoyed she looked so lovely, although he couldn't say why, he picked up Lily then took Jemma's elbow in his hand and walked her to the opposite end of the table from where he sat. He settled Lily on the end of the bench on a stack of books Sam left there after she ate her breakfast then turned to his men, keeping his face impassive.

"Gentlemen, I'd like to introduce my wife, Lady Jemma Bryan Jordan. Please address her as Mrs. Jordan. Jemma, these are the best ranch hands a man could have."

In a clockwise motion, Thane went around the table introducing each of his employees. Jemma caught a few of the names and would have to learn the rest. She remembered Ben, the teasing young man from that morning, along with Charlie, Ed, and Walt.

She tipped her head graciously to each one then settled into the seat Thane held for her at the end of the table. Before he moved from her side, he bent down and pressed his mouth close to her ear. "You don't need to dress for dinner. I'm sure whatever you had on would have been fine."

Her cheeks pinked at his comment and she felt the eyes of all the cowboys on her as they grinned, wondering what their boss said to make his wife blush.

Thane asked a blessing on their meal then a lively conversation ensued as the men began passing food around the table.

Jemma listened to them talk about ranch work and picked out several unfamiliar phrases. Ben seemed particularly excited in relaying a bit of news about someone the rest of the men apparently knew.

"You betcha, ol' Joe Lambery done loosened his hinges right there on Main Street in front of George's waterin' hole. He was on that crockhead bronc you told him wasn't worth beans, boss. That ol' cayuse set in to crowhoppin' to beat the band. Joe got him a face full of meadow muffins right in front of Pastor Eagan and commenced into a string of blasphemy that woulda peeled the hide off a lizard. Last I heard, he's barkin' at a knot over on some cocklebur outfit near Haines."

With no idea what the man had just said, other than relaying a tale about someone committing blasphemy in front of the pastor, she assumed Joe had done something humorous by the laughter of the men around her.

Thane furrowed his brow in thought. "Joe worked here for what, Sam? Two days?" Sam nodded his head. "He told us the working conditions weren't up to his standards."

Ben grinned. "I think what he meant was that the boss expected him to earn his keep and Joe doesn't like to work."

"I see," Jemma said, smiling politely and returning her attention to her meal. She'd never had cornbread and tried to decide if she liked the taste of it. After taking another dainty bite, she focused her attention on the aromatic bowl of beans called chili that Sam set before her. Spices tickled her nose as she lifted a spoon and took a bite.

Much to her dismay, it quickly became apparent the men didn't want a female on the ranch and had decided to hasten her demise. Flames of heat incinerated her tongue and she set the spoon down with a clatter.

The beans, seasoned with spices blended by Lucifer himself, set her mouth on fire and burned a trail down her throat all the way to her stomach. Afraid to swallow them, she certainly couldn't spit them out, and sat bug-eyed with the beans turning her tastebuds and tongue to ash.

"Get her some milk, Sam!" Thane barked as he jumped up and rushed down the length of the table to her side. Sweat beaded on Jemma's forehead and she whimpered in pain as he squatted beside her.

"Swallow, Jem. Just swallow it," Thane coaxed, taking the milk from Sam and holding it to her lips.

She shook her head, unwilling to trust any of the men, including her husband.

"Come on, Jemma. Open your mouth and take a sip. It'll make the burning go away."

Reluctantly, Jemma swallowed the bite of beans then took the glass from Thane, glugging it down in a few unrefined swallows.

Fire continued to burn in her stomach. She grabbed for her glass of water, but Thane moved it out of her reach.

"Pour her some more milk." Thane held the glass while Sam refilled it then tipped it to her lips. She drank half of it before pushing it away and leaning back in her chair, embarrassed but feeling slightly nauseous.

As her vision cleared, she glanced over in horror as Lily lifted a spoon of the beans to her little lips.

"No, Lily! Stop!" Jemma croaked, her voice not yet recovered from its introduction to Sam's chili.

Thane grabbed the spoon before Lily took a bite, making the little girl glare at him.

"Uncle Thane! I want my dinner! I do it myself!"

"Eat your cornbread, honey." Thane lifted Lily's bowl of chili away and pushed her cornbread toward her. "You can put jam on it. Sam has good jam."

"Don't want it. Want my dinner!" Tears pooled in Lily's eyes and she stuck out her bottom lip.

Thane set her bowl back down and Jemma grabbed his arm in dismay. He ignored her spluttering and picked up Lily's spoon. Scooping a tiny bite from the bowl, he gave it to Lily while Sam made sure her glass of milk was full. "Okay, honey. Try a bite and see if you like it."

Lily opened her mouth and took the bite, chewing and swallowing then wiping her mouth with her napkin, just like Jemma taught her.

Curls bounced as she cocked her head and smiled sweetly, holding out her hand for her spoon. "More, please."

Thane chuckled and gave Lily her spoon. "She must take after her father. He could eat anything." Thane glanced at Jack. "How about you, son? Do you like the chili?"

"Yes, sir!" Jack said, already halfway through his bowl.

"A couple of thoroughbreds," Thane teased, ruffling Lily's hair before returning to his seat.

Jemma rolled her eyes in disgust and nibbled at her cornbread between sips of milk. Her appetite was effectively scorched right out of her by the chili and Thane referring to the children as thoroughbreds. Evidently, she failed to meet whatever standard he'd set for that title. No doubt, he'd classify her as a nag or a mule.

As soon as Jack and Lily finished their dinner, she stood, causing the men to scramble to their feet, some with spoons still in their hands.

"Sam, thank you for another fine meal." Jemma smiled at the cook. "If you gentlemen will please excuse me, the children and I shall return to the house."

Although Jack started to protest, Jemma quelled him with a stern look and grabbed Lily's hand, herding them both out the bunkhouse door.

"I don't think she liked your Texas chili, Sam." The laughter of the men floated out the open door, taunting her as she marched back to the house.

She settled the children at the table with their lessons, neglected during the busy day. They studied until Jemma declared it time for Lily to go to bed.

The little girl fussed and whined, refusing to let Jemma tuck her in without Thane there, as had become their routine during the last few weeks.

Exhausted, she sent Jack out to find Thane. The boy finally returned with his uncle.

Bareheaded and shirtless as he stepped inside, Jemma wondered what Thane had been doing when Jack found him. His chest glistened with perspiration as he walked into the room. He swiped his forearm across his forehead, catching drips of sweat.

"What are you doing?" she glared at him as he wiped his hands on his thighs and knelt next to Lily's bed.

"Tucking Lily into bed," Thane muttered, turning to smile at the little girl. "Are you ready for sweet dreams, honey?"

"No."

"Why not? Would a story make you go to sleep?"

"Yes. Tell me a story! Please!" Lily wiggled around until she sat up in bed and gazed with adoration at her uncle. Primly folding her hands in her lap, she pursed her lips as she'd seen her aunt do many times and gave Thane a regal look. "You may begin."

Thane swallowed back a chuckle and nodded his head. He told her a story about a calf named Whitey and a barn cat named Blackie, creating an adventure of them chasing a bird. Most of what he said seemed like pure nonsense to him. He'd crawl in a hole and die if one of his hands caught him uttering such silliness, but Lily enjoyed it. She eventually leaned back against her pillows and her eyes slowly drifted shut.

Quietly rising to his feet, Thane kissed her cheek, careful not to drip any sweat on her, then moved out of the way so Jemma could pull up her covers and give her a kiss.

Jack, who lingered in the doorway, asked if he could play outside and Thane agreed, warning him to stay within sight of the cabin.

Returning to the kitchen, Thane used a dishtowel to mop the sweat away from his face then pumped a glass of water and chugged it down. Still thirsty, he worked the pump handle and refilled the glass.

Footsteps tapped behind him and he turned around. He leaned against the sink as Jemma stopped a few feet away, hands fisted on her hips as she glared at him.

Uncertain what he'd done to incur her wrath, he slowly finished his water, wiped his mouth on the back of his hand, and set the glass in the sink.

"You find some lemons to suck, Jem?" he asked, knowing it would infuriate her.

"Of course not. Don't be impudent." Nearly overcome with the urge to slap him, she clenched her hands at her sides. "Who gave you leave to call me Jem?"

"I didn't know I needed to ask permission, your highness. What's got you mad as a wet hen?"

She continued glowering at him.

"What's wrong with you? You've been in a snit since dinner. You're not still mad about the chili, are you?" Thane cocked a hip and crossed his arms over his chest, studying his wife.

When she was angry, her cheeks blossomed with color and her copper eyes glowed with fire. The fiery sparks in her eyes enticed him and he realized it was one of the reasons he constantly provoked her.

"No. I could care less about those beans Sam acquired from Satan himself. However, there is a matter that has left me quite distraught." Jemma folded her hands at her waist and once again settled her glare on Thane.

"Was it the mice? Sam told me about rescuing you from the nest." Thane took a step closer. "Did someone say something they shouldn't? If so, you just tell me who and I'll…"

Jemma reached out and placed her fingers over his mouth, silencing him. When he kissed her palm, she jerked her hand back and buried it in her skirt, hoping he wouldn't notice the way it shook.

Delightful tingles of excitement raced through her whenever he pressed his lips to her skin, leaving her addled.

Distracted, her eyes followed the lines of his suspenders as they created two vertical stripes down the broad plane of his chest and firm stomach. As he stood before her, slick with sweat, she wanted to reach out and touch one of his hard muscles in the worst way.

She forced herself to focus on her current reason for being angry with the man and blinked away her interest in her husband.

"Where is my money, Thane? I'd like it back, please." Jemma held a hand out to him, even though it trembled slightly.

"Money? What money?" he asked, puzzled.

"The money you pilfered from my unmentionables. The very ones you so uncouthly removed from my person yesterday."

Thane took another step toward her and bent down until she could see flecks of light and dark blue mingling in his eyes. He smelled of leather, horses, and something superbly masculine.

"You want me to check these petticoats, too? I'd be happy to do it right this minute." As he waggled his eyebrows at her, he reached down and grabbed the hem of her gown, lifting it nearly to her knees.

Maddened, she slapped at his hand. "You are the most infuriating, abhorrent man, Thane Jordan."

His cocky grin served only to stoke her temper.

"If you please, my money, sir!" Jemma tamped down the desire to stamp her foot — on top of his.

Gently taking her hand, he pulled her into the bedroom, opened the second drawer of the dresser, and moved aside a few of his shirts. He pointed to her money.

"I noticed it last night and didn't want anything to happen to it, so I stuck it in this drawer. I only need one drawer so the rest are yours." Thane motioned to her trunk. "Are you going to unpack your things?"

"I'll see to it later," Jemma said, glancing down at the money, relieved. Ashamed she accused him of stealing her money, she turned to him and placed a hand on his arm. "I'm sorry, Thane. I know you wouldn't steal my money, I just didn't think to look… My apologies."

Instead of accepting her apology or saying she was forgiven, he tipped up her chin so she had to look him in the face. "I don't want your money, Jem. I don't even want Henry's money. Besides, I thought Henry left you broke. You have almost six thousand dollars there. Where did you get it?"

"I sold some things before we left Bolton." Jemma turned away and studied the rough plank floor beneath her feet.

Thane's brow furrowed into twin vertical lines. "Sold some things? What things?"

Jemma walked over to her trunk and fiddled with a handful of handkerchiefs. She carried them to the drawer with her money and set them inside, avoiding his question.

"Jemma, what did you sell?"

"Paintings, tapestries, rugs, statuary, and the like. Things I couldn't pack into a trunk."

Thane sucked in a shocked breath, but she kept her back to him, even when he placed a hand on her shoulder. "What in the world did you do that for?"

"You told me I couldn't bring everything with me and it's not likely I'll return to England. I had nowhere to keep those things, anyway." Jemma moved away from him and stood in front of the window, watching Jack chase Rigsly in circles by the barn in the fading evening light. "Besides, I didn't know you well enough then to be assured you would provide for the children. I felt it necessary to acquire my own funding should the need arise to care for them without your assistance."

Thane growled as he stepped beside her and turned her to face him. "Let me make one thing perfectly clear to you. The moment I agreed to the terms of Henry's will, you and those children became my responsibility. I will always provide for you, shelter you, and take care of you. You can do what you like with your money, but if you plan to spend it on things for the house or the kids, get that thought out of your head. I'll pay for whatever is needed."

"That's unnecessary, sir." Jemma shook her head although she didn't pull away from Thane as he continued to stand with his hands on her arms, staring at her with a ruthless intensity.

"And it was unnecessary to sell your things. I know you couldn't bring everything with you, but if they meant that much to you, I would have…"

"Done nothing different." Jemma interrupted him, raising her eyes to his. "You have no room for anything here." She waved her hand around the room for emphasis. "I kept the things that meant the most to me, Thane. They are in the trunks in your barn. Perhaps someday I will use those things again. If not, at least I have them to pass along to Jack and Lily."

He reached out and tenderly brushed his thumb along her jaw. Her eyes fluttered closed, her thick lashes like delicate fans against her skin, making his heart race. "If you like, I'll go to the bank with you and you can open an account with your money."

"I appreciate your offer. Thank you." Jemma wondered how he could go from making her so angry she wanted to slap him to being so tender she could melt in his arms. Confused, she shoved aside her questions and gave him a sidelong glance.

While he seemed in an agreeable mood, she decided to bring up her next topic of concern. "May we please go to Baker City tomorrow? I have a long list of supplies."

"Can't it wait a few days? We were just there yesterday. I don't have time to cart you to town every time you get the whim to buy some frippery or nonsense. This isn't Bolton where you can walk into the village to shop whenever you like." Thane's voice sounded harsher than he intended. At the look of hurt in her eyes, he wished he hadn't spoken so quickly or curtly. He knew the house needed to be stocked for supplies, having noticed the previous evening the cupboards were empty.

Jemma's chin lifted defiantly, but he held up a hand to stop her from speaking. "Do you have a list?"

"Yes. It's on the table. The one with only two chairs, so even if I had any supplies to make a meal, only two of the four people inhabiting this cabin could sit to enjoy it." Jemma smiled the entire time she spoke but Thane felt her jabs with each word she said.

He followed her back to the kitchen where she took a list from the table and handed it to him. "This is what I would like to purchase."

Thane glanced through the list and didn't see anything ridiculous. During the course of the day, he'd thought of several things they would need to purchase. After sitting down at the table, he added them to Jemma's list.

"I'll take you into town tomorrow, but I want to be clear that you understand I can't make a habit of it. This is an exception."

Her fingers twitched with the urge to smack Thane upside the head. "I'll go alone, then. Show me how to hitch the horse to the wagon-thing we rode home in yesterday."

Thane's bark of laugher held a hint of disdain as he rose from the table. "I don't think so, my lady. It's called a buckboard. For one thing, you have no idea how to drive it even if you are good at handling horses. Due to the size of this list, you'll need my big wagon, anyway. Even if you could drive the wagon, you aren't going anywhere alone until you learn to shoot."

"Shoot? Are you insane? I'm not shooting a firearm."

Thane took a menacing stride forward, towering over her with a stubborn glint in his blue eyes. "Yes, you are. If you want to be able to do more than stay around this house, you'll carry a gun and know how to use it. Understood?"

Jemma meekly nodded her head.

"This isn't like Bolton, Jem. The sooner you accept that, the easier it will be on you."

He stepped back and glanced toward their open bedroom door as thoughts rolled through his head. "As you most likely observed, there isn't a lot of room here in the cabin. I'll add some pegs to the bedroom walls for your dresses, but you aren't going to be able to unpack much. If you need something out of the trunks in the barn, ask me or one of the hands and we'll get it for you."

"Thank you."

"I noticed you want to get a few pieces of furniture. Where do you think they'll fit?"

Jemma showed him how she wanted to rearrange the table and pointed out how she thought they could utilize the open area between the bedrooms for a small settee and a few chairs, a side table, and some lamps.

"Anything else?" he asked, agreeing to her requests. He assumed once he returned to the ranch, life would be much like it was before he received Weston's telegram advising him of Henry's death. Now that he was back with a wife and two children, he realized they all had some adjustments to make.

"You noted I had a sewing machine on my list?"

"Yes, I did. That's fine. It'll save you time, won't it?"

Surprised by Thane's response, Jemma offered him a small smile. "It shall indeed."

"We'll figure out somewhere to put it." The slow, deliberate perusal he gave her from head to toe sent his temperature soaring. Enthralled by how beautiful she looked in her silky dress, he remembered he wanted to discuss the matter of her attire.

"Look, Jemma, I know you're used to satin and silk, but life out here is hard and it'll ruin your pretty dresses in no time. You might want to get some calico or gingham at the store tomorrow to make you and Lily some plainer clothes. You can wear your nice things on Sundays or when we go to town, but around here, you definitely need something different. My friend Maggie has a dress shop in town. You might even find a few ready-made pieces there if you want to stop in tomorrow. Ask her about getting a riding skirt or two."

"I will take care of the matter tomorrow." Jemma had already surmised life on the ranch would destroy her wardrobe in short order and planned to acquire a few serviceable dresses.

Her attention lingered on Thane's mention of his friend owning the dress shop. She wondered if Maggie had been more than a friend to Thane. Perhaps he'd even been courting the woman before Weston beckoned him to England and he felt forced into marrying her for the sake of the children.

Concerned she'd come between Thane and the woman he loved, pain stabbed her heart at the thought of him holding affection for another woman. Out of habit, her fingers went to the cameo at her throat. She took a step toward the door, intent on calling Jack inside when Thane spun her around, drawing her closer to him.

His warm breath blowing across her cheek made her knees languid. She so desperately wanted to sink into his strength and rest in his comforting embrace, just for a moment or two, but that would never do.

As she raised her gaze to his, she noticed a humorous glint in his eyes. She braced for whatever insult he planned to deliver and stiffened against him.

"Why do you do that?"

"Do what?" Perplexed, she glared at him.

"Rub that cameo whenever something bothers you. You wear it more often than not, and if you've got it on when something kinks your rope, you go to rubbing it like an ol' codger with a nugget of gold."

"I do no such thing!"

"Yes, you do. You're doing it now." Thane stared at her fingers where they rested on the cameo. After taking her hand in his, he studied the piece of jewelry, noting the detailed craftsmanship.

Jemma released a sigh. "It belonged to my mother. Jane pinned it on my dress the day after mother's funeral and I found comfort in it. I suppose I rub it out of habit because it makes her seem closer. I know it's silly." Jemma dropped her gaze, embarrassed by her admission.

"It's not silly. I'm glad you have it."

Numbly nodding her head, Jemma raised her gaze to his and studied him before taking a step toward the door.

"There's one more thing we need to discuss." Thane smirked in the familiar way that both aggravated and excited her as she looked at him again.

"What might that be?"

"This…" Thane reached behind her, grabbing her bustle and giving it a gentle tug. She sucked in a gulp of air at his outlandish behavior. "Has got to go."

At her abhorrent glare, he let go of the bustle and took a step back, although his grin broadened. "You can't work on a ranch with that thing flopping around behind you. You can dress however you like when we go into town, but for life on the ranch, you need to put it away. While I'm on that subject, you can't go around with your corset laced so tight it makes you faint."

She glared at him. "I did not faint."

"You came darn close and I won't have you putting your health in danger just to make an already tiny waist smaller. You can wear it, if you insist, just don't lace it so tight. Since you're going to be getting new clothes, make sure you get them to fit with the corset loosened."

Jemma trembled with fury as she stood in front of him, about to combust with anger. She couldn't believe he would dare converse about such personal, sensitive topics as her bustle and corset. "You, sir, are a…"

"Save it, Jem. Unless you can invent some new words to call me, I've heard it before."

Thane gave her bustle another tug as he walked by, returning outside to where he'd been hammering horseshoes at the forge.

Chuckling to himself, he recalled the look on her face when he grabbed her bustle. He wondered if she'd heed his words or if he'd get to oversee its removal. Either way, he was bound to be entertained.

Chapter Fifteen

From her position on the hard wagon seat next to her husband, Jemma glanced around at the miles of sagebrush-dotted hills surrounding her. As she breathed in the autumn air, she caught a whiff of the pungent plant along with Thane's scent.

She wanted to slide closer to him and take another deep breath. Instead, she folded her hands primly on her lap and sat with a stiff posture until the wagon hit another bump and she grasped the wagon seat to keep her balance.

"You doing okay, Jem?" Thane gave her a concerned glance, but kept both hands on the reins instead of reaching out to her like he wanted to do.

"I'm very well, thank you. It's quite a lovely morning, isn't it?"

"Lovely," Thane muttered. His wife put the gorgeous fall day to shame with her creamy complexion, rich auburn hair, twinkling copper eyes, and attractive ensemble. When she stepped out of the cabin that morning wearing an outfit he'd not yet seen in a vibrant shade of cobalt blue, he had to catch his breath.

A high-necked blouse topped by a jacket embellished with ornate braiding along the edge highlighted a brocade overskirt floating on top of a velvet underskirt. The striking shades of blue made roses bloom in each of Jemma's cheeks and her lips look invitingly kissable. A deeper blue hat adorned with cobalt plumes and plump silk roses perched at a sassy angle atop her head.

No doubt, her appearance would set tongues wagging throughout town about his elegant, beautiful bride. Determined to force his attention away from Jemma, he glanced over his shoulder at the children and smiled at them.

"Are you two okay?"

"Yes, Uncle Thane. We're great," Jack enthusiastically replied from his spot on the bench in the wagon bed. Thane had Ben help him fasten the bench in the back of the wagon so Jack and Lily had somewhere safe to sit on the long ride into town. He was afraid Lily would topple off the tall wagon seat where he and Jemma sat, and, in truth, he wanted an excuse to have his wife sit with him without one or both children between them.

"Aren't you gonna ask about me?" Sam asked with a sly grin as he drove a wagon beside Thane's.

"No, I'm not, you ol' buzzard." Thane looked at the older man and grinned. Sam agreed to accompany them to town in a second wagon to help haul home supplies. The bunkhouse cupboards needed to be stocked and Thane decided if they were making a trip to town, they might as well make it count.

"Look how he treats his elders." Sam smiled at Jemma and waggled a bushy eyebrow. "I don't care if you're the one who pays my wages, you should show more respect to those older and wiser than you, boss."

"When I meet someone who fits both categories, I'll keep that in mind."

Sam snorted and Jemma hid a smile behind her gloved hand. She listened as Thane and Sam discussed the ranch and some of the neighboring ranches as they rolled into town.

Their first stop was the bank. Sam waited outside with the children as Thane introduced the bank president to his wife. He added her name to his accounts then waited as the man opened an account for her, in her name only.

Although the banker obviously found the arrangement odd, he refrained from saying anything, especially considering the amount of money Thane recently transferred into the bank.

While Sam went to the feed store, Thane drove toward Main Street. Jemma and the children stared as the sprinkler wagon rolled by, sprinkling water on the broad street.

Shaped like a big wooden barrel, the wagon featured a seat atop on end where old Mr. Bentley sat, driving his lumbering horse up and down the streets in an effort to keep the dust to a minimum. Water dripped out of the wagon, settling the dust.

"What's that, Uncle Thane," Jack asked, standing up and holding onto the back of the wagon seat.

"It's a sprinkler wagon, son. It keeps the dust down and gives Mr. Bentley something to do."

"What a novel idea," Jemma said.

They continued down the street until Thane stopped in front of a large furniture store. He jumped down from the wagon then held up his arms and caught Jemma around the waist, swinging her to the ground. Jack scrambled down while Thane lifted Lily into his arms.

She squirmed to get down, but Thane held onto her. "Lily, honey, I need to carry you in this store because there's lots of big pieces of furniture and I don't want you to get lost behind them. This way, you'll be able to see things better and can help your aunt pick out something new for us. How does that sound?"

"I get to help pick?" Lily turned wide coppery eyes, so like Jemma's, to him.

"Yes, you do." Thane held open the door while Jemma and Jack preceded him inside.

"Thane Jordan! I haven't seen you in a coon's age, maybe longer. I heard you just got back from your trip." A short, rotund man walked up to Thane and balanced his girth from his toes to his heels as he smiled at Jemma. "I also hear congratulations are in order."

"Mr. Patterson." Thane switched Lily from his right arm to his left so he could shake the man's hand. "I'm pleased to introduce my wife, Jemma, our nephew, Jack, and our niece, Lily. Jemma, this is Irvin Patterson, owner of this fine establishment."

Mr. Patterson bent in a grand bow, making Jemma bite back a laugh at his efforts as the hair he'd combed over a bald spot on his head flopped forward, hanging like some kind of vermin over his brow.

Lily started to point and giggle, but Thane quickly shook his head at her and she quieted, although laughter sparkled in her eyes.

As he returned to an upright position, Mr. Patterson swept his hand over his head, smoothing his hair into place.

"It's a pleasure to meet you, sir." Jemma smiled at the funny little man as he kissed the back of Lily's hand and winked at Jack.

"The pleasure is all mine, fair lady. How may I be of assistance to you today?"

Jemma told him what she was looking for and he led her around the store, showing her the options he had available.

While Jemma perused the various sofas, Thane wandered around the store with the children. Lily wrapped one hand around his neck, glancing this way and that, intently studying the various displays as she looked for something specific.

"That one, Uncle Thane! Please, can I pick that one?" Lily pointed to a sleigh rocking chair with tapestry upholstery and gleaming mahogany wood.

Thane walked over to the chair and set Lily down on the seat. She wiggled back and forth until the chair started rocking and let out a contented sigh. He remembered the rocking chair in her bedroom at the cottage. Jemma also often sat by the fire and rocked her in the drawing room.

No wonder the child liked the chair so much. It must remind her of home.

Although the chair would look ridiculous in his rough cabin, he knew it would go home with them.

He turned and caught Mr. Patterson's attention, motioning him over.

"Miss Lily would very much like this chair," Thane said, raising an eyebrow at Jemma as she approached and studied the chair with her head tipped slightly to the left.

She bent down and smiled at Lily while running a hand over the green, cream, and peach floral upholstery. "Do you like this chair, poppet?"

"Oh, yes, Auntie Jemma. It's like the one at home. I love it!" Lily rocked with more enthusiasm. Thane slid his foot forward to keep the rocker from gaining any more momentum.

"In that case, Mr. Patterson, please show me the sofas available that will match Lily's chair." Jemma stood and gave Thane a look that made heat spiral from his head to his toes. Uncertain what he'd done to deserve it, he enjoyed it all the same.

Before she followed the storeowner back to the selection of sofas, Jemma gently grasped Jack's chin with her fingers and smiled at him. "Since Lily got to choose a chair, would you like to select one, too? We'll need a side chair. Perhaps you could choose chairs for the dining table. Or maybe you'd like to select a set of lamps?"

Jack grinned and nodded his head. "I'll pick the lamps, Auntie Jemma." She watched as he hurried over to where a large selection of lamps glistened in the light streaming in the store windows.

Thane watched her walk over to where Mr. Patterson waited, pleased at the way she included Jack. Most women wouldn't let two children pick out their furniture but Jemma seemed more interested in making the children feel involved than if the furniture matched.

Once they finished choosing their selections, Thane helped the delivery boy load the purchases into his wagon then drove down the street to a dress shop. Jack decided to wait in the wagon while Thane escorted Jemma and Lily inside.

Thane held the door and waited for Jemma to walk in with Lily skipping along behind her before entering and removing his hat.

As the bell jingled above the door, an attractive woman with a head full of dark brown curls strode into the room, wearing a beautiful gown and a welcoming smile.

When she saw who stood inside her shop's door, the woman's smile broadened and she rushed over to Thane, throwing her arms around him in a warm hug.

"Thane Jordan! How could you go and break my heart?" The woman slapped his arm and gave him a pouty look before squeezing his hand with a familiarity that made Jemma work to keep from losing her temper. "Tully told me you brought home the most beautiful girl in England for a bride, but I thought he was teasing. For once, it appears he was telling the truth."

"Yes, ma'am." Thane smiled at the woman then at Jemma. "Jemma, this is my friend, Maggie Dalton. Maggie, this is my wife, Lady Jemma Bryan Jordan. And this is Lily, our niece."

"It's such a pleasure to meet you, Lady Jemma." Maggie offered a curtsy before looking hopefully at Jemma. "Is that right? I'm hopeless when it comes to remembering proper titles. Please forgive me if I botched it, but I hope we can be friends."

Enchanted by the woman's friendly manner and her mirthful eyes, Jemma relaxed. "Please, call me Jemma and it would give me great joy to have a friend here in Baker City."

Maggie nodded then winked at Lily and tweaked her nose, making the little girl laugh as she leaned against Thane's leg.

He smiled and looked at Jemma. "Maggie and her husband, Daniel, traveled west with Tully and me. We all worked a claim together until Daniel died, then Maggie opened up this shop. She keeps Tully and I walking on the straight and narrow and from running around naked."

Maggie shook her head. "What he means is that I won't let them wear their clothes until they look like tattered rags. Someone has to keep these men in line, but I'm glad I can turn Thane over to you." The woman studied Jemma, gasping when she recognized her gown. "That's a Madame Beauchene original, isn't it?"

"Yes, it is. She made my wedding gown and trousseau." Jemma was nearly shocked speechless the dressmaker recognized Madame Beauchene's designs.

Thane had no idea where Jemma's wedding gown came from but he recalled how beautiful she looked wearing it. How much he enjoyed kissing her that day.

Desperately wanting to kiss her again, he brought his attention back to the present then found himself distracted by how lovely his wife looked in the bright blue outfit. He wondered who paid for her wardrobe and decided Weston probably had something to do with it.

"Aren't you a lucky girl, then?" Maggie reached out to touch the sleeve of Jemma's jacket, where beads formed an intricate floral pattern above her wrist. Suddenly, she snatched her hand back. "I seem to have completely forgotten my manners today. My apologies."

Jemma laughed, putting everyone at ease. "Not at all, Maggie. Would you like to try on the jacket?"

"Goodness sakes! I'd love to, but I don't want…"

Jemma already had the jacket off and held it for Maggie to try on over her own deep green gown. Hurrying over to a full-length mirror in the far corner, Maggie looked into the glass, smiling at her reflection as her finger caressed the fine fabric of the jacket.

"It's exquisite!" Maggie carefully removed the jacket and started to hold it for Jemma, but Thane took it in his hand before his wife could slip it on. She glared at him, but held her tongue.

"Other than to introduce you to my girls, I'd like you to outfit Jemma with clothes more appropriate for the ranch. As you can see, her things are far too nice to wear out there. She needs some every day dresses and a couple of riding skirts. Can you set her up?"

"I've got several things I think will fit, unless you want to special order the pieces." Maggie glanced at Jemma with a critical eye, guessing measurements and deciding what colors would best match her peaches-and-cream complexion.

"No special orders. What you've got in stock will be fine." Thane interrupted Jemma when she started to speak. "While I'm being a bossy, boorish man, I'll also state that I want those dresses to fit with a looser corset. She can't get anything done with that thing laced so tight."

Jemma started to splutter a protest, but Thane took a step back and opened the shop door, draping her jacket over the end of a display case. "I'll leave you ladies to your shopping. Jemma, when you're finished, meet us around the corner at the restaurant and we'll have lunch before purchasing the rest of the supplies."

He started out the door, but glanced back to see his wife glaring at him with sparks shooting from her eyes, as he knew they would be. "Don't forget what I said about that bustle either."

Echoes of his chuckles floated around them after he shut the door. As Thane approached the wagon, he motioned for Jack to climb down.

"What's funny, Uncle Thane?" Jack asked, hurrying to keep up with his long strides.

"Your aunt. She makes me laugh." The truth of his words hit him with a sudden surprise that almost made him trip as he walked down the block.

Since he'd met Jemma, the emotions he liked to keep on an even keel exploded into a flurry of confusing feelings. He'd never laughed as much, been as angry, or felt such tenderness flood through him as he had in the past six weeks.

"Do you like Auntie Jemma?" Jack glanced up at his hero.

"Of course I like her. I married her, didn't I?" While they waited for a wagon to pass, he put a warm hand against Jack's back and smiled at the boy.

"Yes, but I heard Cook telling Greenfield that you married her so you could bring us to America. I'm glad we're here, Uncle Thane, but I want Auntie Jemma to be happy, too."

Struck by the boy's words, Thane hunkered down so they were closer to eye level. "I want her to be happy, Jack. Do you think she's unhappy? Did she say something that upset you?"

"No. It's just…" Jack studied the toe of his shoe instead of looking at his uncle.

"Go on, son. You can tell me anything."

Jack lifted his head and Thane took in the solemn, sad look the boy so often wore when he first arrived at the cottage. In the last few weeks, it had nearly disappeared, but occasionally he caught glimpses of it.

"It's okay, Jack. Tell me what's on your mind." Thane patiently waited for the boy to continue.

"Sometimes Auntie Jemma seems very happy. She smiles more than she ever used to and I even heard her humming the other day. She never did that at home, I mean our old home." Jack looked at Thane for reassurance. When his uncle nodded his head and smiled, Jack continued. "But sometimes after the two of you talk all quiet and you leave, she gets quite angry and mutters things I can't hear. Twice, when she thought I was asleep, I heard her crying. I don't like Auntie Jemma to cry. It makes me sad."

"It makes me sad, too, Jack. I appreciate you telling me all this and I promise I'll do my best to make your aunt happy."

The boy impulsively hugged Thane then stepped back and looked around to make sure no one was watching. Relieved they were alone on the street, he grinned at his uncle. "Where are we going?"

"Just around the corner." Thane put his hand to Jack's back again and guided him inside one of his favorite stores in town, the Saddle and Harness Shop.

Jack's eyes widened as they entered the long, narrow store, inhaling the marvelous scent of leather. The center aisle featured a double row of hand-made saddles on display while bridles, reins, soft leather gloves, harnesses, collars, and coils of rope hung from the high ceiling. Shelves held tins of oil and harness soap, saddle blankets, spurs, bits, cinches, currycombs, brushes, cowboy boots and hats.

One corner, oddly enough, boasted a line of sewing machines. Thane headed toward it and held out his hand in greeting when one of the storeowners greeted him.

"Mr. Palmer, this is my nephew, Jack." Thane nudged his nephew forward and the boy shook the storeowner's outstretched hand. "Jack, this is Mr. Palmer. He has some of the best saddles in Eastern Oregon right here in his shop."

"I bet you might like this one." Mr. Palmer picked up Jack and set him on one of the display saddles. The boy grinned from ear to ear as he settled onto the seat and stretched his legs down, trying to reach the stirrups. "Why don't you try a few of them on for size while I help your uncle?"

Jack nodded his head and began climbing from saddle to saddle while Thane and Mr. Palmer walked toward the sewing machine display.

"You pick up some new skills while you were gone?" Palmer teased as Thane looked over the machines.

"Nope, but my wife plans on doing some sewing and I figured one of these machines would make it go faster."

Palmer took a step back, staring at Thane. "The rumors are true? You came home with a wife? I thought you said…"

Thane held up a hand before he could finish. "I know what I said, but it doesn't change the fact that I have a wife and she needs a sewing machine. I want one that's easy for her to use, yet does a good job. Which one do you recommend?"

Palmer went over the selling points of his two favorite models and nodded approvingly when Thane made his selection.

"Anything else you need today?" Palmer asked as he wrote out a receipt for the sewing machine.

"As a matter of fact, there is." Thane tipped his head toward Jack. "I've got a boy in need of a saddle and a pair of boots."

When Sam strolled into the shop a few minutes later, Jack ran up to him, excitedly showing off his new boots while Thane looked at the saddles.

"Did you leave your wagon out front?" Thane asked as Sam walked up to him.

"Sure did, boss, just like you asked." Sam winked at Jack as the boy clomped around the store, thrilled with his boots.

"Good. I didn't fancy packing that sewing machine back to the dress shop where I left the wagon."

Sam raised his eyebrow but didn't say anything as he and Thane loaded the sewing machine, two saddles, and a box of assorted supplies.

Once everything was loaded, Thane slapped Sam on the back and they drove the wagon to the restaurant where they planned to meet Jemma and Lily for lunch. The girls hadn't yet arrived, so Thane told Sam and Jack to go in and save them a table while he went to fetch the girls.

As he opened the door to the dress shop, his gaze settled on Jemma leaning against the counter, laughing at something Maggie said. When the women noticed him, they looked at each other and laughed even harder.

"If I'm the source of your amusement, you better fess up." Thane almost stepped on Lily as she sat on the floor at Jemma's feet playing with a ball made from fabric scraps.

"I'm not confessing anything, Thane. You should know by now you can't intimidate me." Maggie narrowed her gaze, although a smile played around her mouth.

Thane turned to Jemma but she shook her head. "I am not saying a word. Before you attempt to pry information from a baby, Lily has been so occupied playing with the ball Maggie kindly gave her, she hasn't paid a speck of attention to what we discussed."

Thane frowned at Jemma, uncertain he liked the way she and Maggie appeared to become fast friends. He, Maggie, and Tully had a long history together, having stuck by each other when they had no one else, and a childish part of him wasn't sure he wanted to share his friends with his wife.

Convicted by the absurdity of his thoughts, he took a deep breath and glanced down at the wrapped parcels on the counter. "Did you find a few things that fit?"

"Yes, I did. Maggie has a wonderful selection and we even found a dress for Lily."

"That's great. Are you ready to go?" Thane paid the bill and accepted the packages Maggie handed him, smiling at Lily as she got to her feet clutching her ball.

Jemma nodded at him then gave Maggie a friendly hug. "Thank you for your wonderful assistance, Maggie. I do hope you'll keep your promise to visit soon."

"I will." Maggie bent down and brushed a hand over Lily's curls before tickling the little girl beneath her chin. "You keep your Uncle Thane out of trouble. Okay, Lily?"

Lily nodded her head then gave Maggie a curtsy. "Thank you for my ball."

"You're welcome, sweetheart. Have fun playing with it."

Thane held the door as Jemma and Lily walked outside. Glancing back at his friend, he smiled. "Can you join us for lunch, Maggie?"

"Not today, but perhaps another time." Two steps brought her close enough to Thane she could speak without Jemma overhearing. "You have a lovely bride, Thane. I think she's the girl you've been waiting for all these years."

Thane grinned and tipped his hat to her before hurrying out the door.

Quickly stowing the packages under the seat in the wagon, he picked up Lily in one arm then held out the other to Jemma, escorting her to the restaurant where Sam and Jack waited.

The lunch conversation was lively as Jack talked about everything he saw at the saddle shop. Lily proudly showed off her colorful ball, sewn with pieces of velvet and stuffed with soft cotton.

After lunch, Sam and Thane drove the wagons to the mercantile where Sam filled a list of supplies for the ranch while Thane found pants and shirts in Jack's size, along with a pair of sturdy boots for Lily.

Jemma purchased lengths of cloth and the necessary trims to make a few dresses, along with fabric for curtains and toweling.

A display of quilts, made by a local woman, drew Jemma's attention and she fingered the intricately stitched bed coverings.

"Do you want one?" Thane asked, stepping behind her, making her hand fly up to the cameo pinned at her throat as she spun around.

"Oh, I... they're quite lovely." Jemma returned her attention to the assortment of quilts. "I should think they would provide a warm covering for a bed this winter."

"I suppose," Thane said. The word bed made him think of Jemma sharing his, so he cleared his throat and focused on the stack of quilts. "If you want one, get it."

"Actually, if you have no objection, I'd like two. I'd like to purchase one for Lily's bed and one for... ours." Her cheeks filled with color at the reference to their shared bed.

Thane coughed to hide his chuckle. "That's fine. Choose whatever you like."

Jemma nodded and looked through the colorful quilts again, making her selection. Picking up Lily, she let the little girl choose the one she liked best for her bed. Excited that she picked her own quilt, Lily ran to Thane and tugged on his hand, eager for him to see her selection.

Thane met Jemma on her way to the front counter where the clerk tallied up their purchases and took the quilts from her.

"Add this to the total, would you, Frank?" Thane asked.

"Sure thing." The man folded the quilts and set them in a box.

"Do the quilt patterns have names?" Jemma asked, looking at Thane. She was unfamiliar with American quilts, but found herself thoroughly intrigued by the idea of making one. Perhaps after she'd acquired some fabric scraps she could spend time learning to quilt during the winter months.

Thane shrugged his shoulders and glanced at the clerk.

The man nodded to Jemma and placed his hand on Lily's pink, white, and green quilt. "This one is a rose wreath pattern. See how the pieces look like rose wreaths?"

"Yes, I did notice that. Thank you, sir, for pointing out that distinctive feature." Jemma smiled at the man and the tips of his ears reddened. "What about the other one? Does it have a pattern name as well?"

"Well, sure, ma'am. That's a wedding ring quilt. Seems fitting since you and Thane are recently wed."

"Yes, fitting." Jemma snapped her mouth shut as Thane took her fingers in his, lifting them to his mouth and pressing a kiss to the back of her gloved hand. When she stared at him, he gave her a roguish wink.

Aware of his teasing, Jemma glowered at him before pasting on a smile for the clerk. "It was a pleasure to meet you, sir. I shall look forward to frequenting your establishment in the future."

"Thank you, ma'am." The clerk nodded to her as she took Lily's hand and escorted her and Jack outside the store.

As he watched her walk outside, the clerk grinned at Thane. "That's quite a wife you got there, Thane, and two nice kids. You're a lucky man."

In agreement, Thane nodded his head as he picked up their purchases and headed toward the door.

After a stop at the grocer's store, they started home. Jemma flapped her handkerchief in front of her face to chase away the dust and stir a breeze. Although the nights were cool, the past few days had been as warm as many summer days at home in Bolton.

Catching herself, Jemma knew she had to stop thinking of Bolton as home. Baker City was her new home. If the nice people she'd met today were an indication of what it would be like to be a part of the community, she decided it might not be all bad, even if she had to put up with Thane to live there.

Never quite certain if she should love him or loathe him, she wavered between the warring emotions. One minute he could charm her like no man she'd ever encountered. The next he could infuriate her beyond the point of reason. She struggled to maintain a balance between the two.

Despite how angry he could make her, a glimpse back at the wagon bed full of purchases made gratitude swell in her for Thane. He never questioned anything she wanted to purchase, encouraged her to buy more than she thought they needed, and made the day into a grand adventure for the children. Right now, they sat on the new sofa licking lollipops Thane handed them once they returned to the wagon.

"I do believe, Mr. Jordan, the children and I are in peril of being spoiled." The smile she gave Thane warmed him more than the afternoon sun beating down overhead.

"What makes you say that?" He grinned as Jemma tried to hold a handkerchief in one hand, a parasol in the other, and maintain her balance on the wagon seat as they bumped along the road toward home.

"You were quite openhanded with the purchases today. This is far beyond what we need and I thank you sincerely for your generosity." Jemma glanced over her shoulder at Jack and Lily, lowering her voice before she spoke again. "It was truly a wonderful day for the children. It takes so little to make them happy and you've far exceeded their expectations."

"You're welcome, Jem. I enjoyed the day, too." Thane leaned over until his mouth was close to her ear. "I'm looking forward to seeing the clothes you found at Maggie's. If you got a new corset, maybe you'd be of a mind to model it for me."

The smile dripped off Jemma's face as she raised her chin and offered Thane an irritated glare. "You're impossible!"

Slapping a hand to his chest, Thane slumped against the seat, acting as though he was greatly relieved. "Whew! I'm so glad to hear that. Here I thought I'd been entirely possible all day and it might ruin me yet. I'm glad to know I'm as cantankerous as ever."

Sam roared with laughter as he drove beside them, making Jack and Lily giggle.

Jemma inched her spine upward, sitting so straight Thane had no idea how she could even breathe. Evidently, she had enough air in her lungs to mutter while shooting him exasperated scowls.

"Preposterous, outrageous man."

Chapter Sixteen

A mountain of trunks in the back of the barn drew Jemma's scrutiny as she tried to decide how best to reach the one she wanted.

She'd asked the men to bring in one trunk or another while she set the house to rights, but hated to bother them with another request, especially when all she wanted was her riding boots.

In the last week, she arranged the furniture, sewed curtains for the windows and dresses for Lily, hung paintings on the cabin's bare walls and turned the rough structure into a cozy home. With the house in order, she wanted to ride Jael while the nice weather continued. Just that morning, Sam and Thane discussed the possibility of snow.

Jemma dreaded the thought of the cold winter ahead. She wanted to savor every moment she could outdoors while she had the opportunity.

After leaving the children at the bunkhouse with Sam, Jemma returned to the house and dressed in one of the three split skirts Maggie insisted she needed.

She tucked a peach-colored cotton blouse into the waist of the dark brown skirt, slipped on a jacket, grabbed a broad-brimmed straw hat and a pair of leather gloves then hurried out the door before she changed her mind.

As she rushed out to the barn, she decided she could quickly become accustomed to the ease of movement provided by the skirt that left her legs free of the confining layers of petticoats and heavy skirts.

With no one else around to help her, she grabbed the handles of one of the heavy trunks and scooted it over, dragging it from one stack to another, trying to work her way down to a trunk near the bottom of the pile.

A grunt escaped her as she attempted to lift a heavy trunk. When strong arms bracketed her and lifted the trunk effortlessly, she swallowed down a shriek.

Once the trunk rested on the ground directly in front of her, gloved hands spun her around and she looked into Thane's blazing blue eyes.

"What did I tell you about not lifting these trunks?" Thane towered over her as his hands held her arms, keeping her from moving.

In her efforts to get to the trunk containing her boots, she hadn't heard him approach. "Mercy! Did you have to sneak up on me?"

"Sneak up on you? I stomped in here with my spurs jingling. If you can't hear that, then maybe we better talk to the Doc about getting your ears checked the next time we're in town." He continued staring at her as she glared at him. "What did you need so bad it couldn't wait until one of the boys could get it for you?"

"My riding boots." She pulled out of Thane's grasp and pointed to the trunk she wanted. "I need my boots and saddle. They're in that trunk right there."

Thane moved two more trunks piled on the one in question and hefted it where Jemma could open the lid and dig inside. The scent of leather drifted up from the trunk when she opened it and she pulled out a pair of tall brown riding boots. After setting them down, she lifted out her sidesaddle and Jael's bridle.

Pleased to have what she wanted, she started to close the lid of the trunk, only to have Thane push it open and grab her sidesaddle away from her. "You don't need that."

She jerked it back and frowned. "I do if I want to ride Jael. We've both been cooped up too long."

Thane pried the saddle from her fingers, stuck it in the trunk, closed the lid, and sat on it. Before Jemma could storm off angry, he snaked out a hand and grabbed her arm, pulling her against him. He spread his legs apart and tugged until she sat on his thigh then trapped her legs by draping his calf over them, effectively caging her.

"You're an inexcusable bully."

"Probably, but I want you to listen to what I'm trying to say." Thane waited until she looked at him to continue. "It's too dangerous for you to ride the sidesaddle, Jem. There are holes, snakes, scraggly brush, varmints of all shapes and sizes out there. A sidesaddle isn't safe here on the ranch. I don't care if you ride, but you'll do it on a western saddle, astride."

"I'll do no such thing!" Jemma stiffened and unsuccessfully tried to wiggle free of his hold. It would be one thing if they were truly married, but since they weren't, she found his behavior scandalous. His inappropriate familiarity both irked and enticed her. Perched as she was on Thane's solid thigh, she considered the impropriety of the situation. His body heat warmed her everywhere they connected. "It would be indecent."

"No, it wouldn't. Hundreds of women ride astride every single day. If you want to go for a ride, it's my way or not at all." Thane set his jaw and leveled his steely blue stare to her snapping copper gaze.

"You do not possess even the most rudimentary knowledge of the notion of compromise." A beleaguered sigh rose from her chest and floated out her lips. She debated what she wanted more — to ride Jael or annoy Thane by marching back inside the house and slamming the door. The desire to ride trumped salvaging her pride, so she nodded in agreement. "Fine. I shall ride as you suggest, but if any one accuses you of having a loose woman for a wife, it is through no fault of my own."

Thane smirked and released his hold as he stood and set her back on her feet. "Put the bridle on Jael while I get your saddle."

Jemma walked to her mare's stall and rubbed the horse's neck and along the slope of her face before slipping on the bridle.

As she led the horse out of the stall toward the door of the barn, she watched Thane step out of the tack room with a saddle blanket and a beautiful new saddle.

Detailed floral tooling made it clear the saddle was intended for a woman to use. Jemma's eyes lit with surprise and delight as she took the blanket from Thane, settling it on Jael's back.

"That is a lovely saddle," she said quietly, observing as Thane set it on the horse's back and adjusted it.

"It's yours. I got both you and Jack saddles the other day. I hope this one is the right size for you. Once you're seated, I'll adjust the stirrups." Thane motioned for her to stand beside him and explained how a western saddle was different from an English saddle, and any other pertinent details he felt essential to share.

He finished tightening the cinch, then started to give her a hand up when she remembered her riding boots. She ran to the back of the barn, sat on top of the trunk, and removed her shoes then yanked on her boots. When she rushed back to Thane, he fashioned a step from his intertwined fingers. She grinned at him and lifted her foot, stepping on his hand as she grasped the saddle horn and pulled herself up.

When he settled his hand on her knee, checking the length of the stirrup, tingles raced from her leg to her head and back down again.

"It looks about right," he said, adjusting her foot in the stirrup. "How does it feel?"

"Fine, I think."

He walked around the horse and checked the other side then looked up at Jemma. "Where's your gun?"

"In the house."

Thane had purchased a small revolver for her to carry. A few evenings, he made her practice out behind the barn where she could shoot into a hillside and not injure anything. Ordered to carry it if she went beyond the ranch yard, she left it in her dresser drawer since she hadn't ventured anywhere. In her excitement at going for a ride on Jael, she'd forgotten to slip it into her pocket.

Resigned to carrying it, she started to dismount to get it, but Thane waved a hand at her. "Never mind about it today, but next time I better not have to remind you. Is that understood?"

"Understood? Yes. Appreciated? No."

Thane's frown made her squirm in her seat as she watched him take long strides over to where he'd left his horse, Ghost, tied to a hitching post. The irony of the two brothers living thousands of miles apart yet having nearly identical horses and naming them Ghost and Shadow wasn't lost on her. Despite an ocean and more than a decade of years separating them, they seemed to have shared many similar thoughts.

However, she couldn't picture Henry ever living such a rough, demanding life as Thane. The man was up long before anyone else and rarely came to bed before late at night. It was long after she retired for the evening.

Thoughts of their current sleeping arrangements made another rush of heat fill her cheeks. Thane insisted they share a bed to save face with his hands. He couldn't sleep in the barn or the bunkhouse and there wasn't anywhere in the house for him to sleep since the sofa was far too small for his big frame.

Plans to bring Lily into the big bed, move Jack to her room, and let Thane resume sleeping in his old room quickly fizzled when he convinced Jemma the children would mention the arrangement. Assured he'd lose his credibility with the men if they thought his wife ruled the house, she relented.

The argument he offered held some measure of validity, but she couldn't quite bring herself to fully embrace the situation. A barrier down the middle of the bed, made with extra pillows and blankets, gave her a small sense of security. Although they slept in the same bed, Thane stayed on his side and she huddled on the far edge of hers.

It would be a long, long winter with them pretending the other wasn't sleeping in the same room and bed. With no other solution presenting itself, she didn't know what else to do.

"Come on, I'll show you around the ranch." Thane tipped his head toward the hills and motioned for her to follow.

They rode out of the ranch yard in silence and up over a ridge. Thane slowed Ghost to keep step with Jael as they walked along. He pointed out the nearby river that ran through their property and provided an important source of water for the cattle.

He showed her his cattle and the pastures he'd planted, wrestling the ground away from the brush. As they circled around one of the pastures, he pointed to the railroad tracks. Although they didn't come near the house, they did run along his property line on the eastern border of the ranch.

At the crest of his favorite hill, he stopped and watched a herd of cattle grazing in the stubbly pasture grass. "What do you think of the ranch, Jemma?"

"In spite of its rustic setting, it appears to be quite well run. You obviously take good care of that which belongs to you."

Thane turned and gave her a long, inquisitive look. "What makes you say that?"

Jemma adjusted her seat on the saddle. The unfamiliar riding position left her a little sore. Although she'd never admit it to Thane, she thoroughly enjoyed the stability and freedom the western saddle provided.

"Your cattle are fat and content, your horses are well trained and gentle, the land you've wrested from the brush is pleasing to the eye and the buildings around the cabin are well tended and orderly. It speaks well of a man that he gives such care to those things."

"What else speaks well of a man?" Thane kept his gaze on the cattle, wondering if she'd make any other observations.

"The way he treats children and dogs. The excitable beasts you claim are cowdogs are obviously happy and loved." Jemma gave him a sidelong grin. His two dogs, Salt and Pepper, frightened Jemma the first time she met them due to their exuberance. She'd quickly learned they meant no harm, but had high-strung personalities. "Somehow, you've convinced Rigsly that you're a friend. I've taken it as a personal insult he prefers your company to mine."

Thane nudged Ghost toward Jael until he could reach out and take Jemma's hand. Mesmerized by the warm fire in his eyes, she didn't resist when he pulled off her glove and pressed a heated kiss to the palm of her hand.

"I'm sorry, my lady, but Rigsly has discerning taste, you know. Only the best for him."

Jemma laughed, too entertained by Thane's attempt at affecting a British accent to be annoyed by his words.

"I am compelled to tell you, good sir, you've misused a phrase any number of times calling me 'my lady.' The appropriate term is 'milady,' should you need to address any other noblewoman."

Thane kissed her hand again then moved on to her wrist before raising his head with the smirk she had come to love. "I know the difference, Jem. I wasn't referring to you as a woman of noble birth. I refer to you as mine. My lady."

Flustered by his words and his amorous attention to her hand, Jemma didn't know what to say. In fact, so befuddled by the man, she sat with her eyes locked to his, wondering what it would be like if he kissed her again.

At night, she curled on her side and inhaled Thane's masculine scent, reliving in her dreams the kiss from their wedding, the few times he'd kissed her cheek, and the touch of his lips on her bare shoulder the first morning they awoke at the ranch.

If she cared to admit it, which she most certainly did not, she'd even entertained the notion of taking Thane's fine-looking face in her hands and kissing him with all the longing he stirred in her heart. A lady would never do such a brazen thing.

However, wearing her split skirt and riding astride a western saddle out in the arid country of Eastern Oregon with her handsome husband, she felt her inhibitions starting to slip. Before they fell completely away, she pulled her hand from Thane's grasp, took her glove from him and slipped it back on, then turned to look out over the landscape.

"I heard you and Sam discussing the weather this morning. Do you truly think it will snow soon?" Weather seemed like a safe topic that wouldn't cause her thoughts to rattle around in her head like rocks in a tin can.

Good heavens! She was starting to think like a westerner!

"Why? Are you in a hurry to have me trapped in the house with you for the winter? I can think of a few enjoyable ways we could pass the long, dark evenings."

Suggestively, he waggled an eyebrow at her. Accustomed to his teasing, she shook her head and smiled. "I shall not even bother to respond to that statement, sir."

When she nudged Jael into a trot, Thane rode beside her on Ghost. "Why not? I think I deserve to hear your thoughts on the matter."

Thoroughly disappointed she didn't splutter at him in feigned disgust, he wondered if he was losing his touch or she had decided not to let him annoy her. Either way, he missed seeing her eyes spark at his implication.

She glared at him. "What if I responded that I thought it was a brilliant idea?" The confounded look on his face made her laugh. Before he recovered his composure, she urged the horse to run.

Thane pulled his hat down and gave Ghost his head, letting him chase after Jael down a well-worn path.

As they raced back to the ranch yard, the two horses seemed to enjoy the fast-paced ride as much as their owners. Reining to a stop outside the barn, Thane grinned as Jemma jumped down and patted Jael on the neck.

She looked breathtaking with wind-whipped cheeks, her eyes shining brightly from the excitement of their race, and her hair falling around her face in silky tendrils. The speed of the ride left her hat dangling by a ribbon around her neck while her hair threatened to fall out of the confines of her hairpins. Full of graceful movements, she removed Jael's saddle and led her around to cool her down.

He walked Ghost along behind her, enjoying the view provided by her split skirt. Eventually, they took the horses into the barn, brushed them down, and fed them. Jemma started to shove the trunk they'd left sitting in the aisle of the barn back toward the stack. Thane stepped in front of her, lifting it and setting it aside before stacking the remainder of the trunks. He set it on top, in case she wanted something from it later.

She picked up her discarded shoes and began meandering toward the house but Thane pulled her to a stop before she left the barn.

"Jemma, I um…" Tongue-tied and uncharacteristically nervous, he struggled to express himself. "It was… I meant to say… I enjoyed riding with you today. I hope we can do it again soon."

"Thank you, Thane. I enjoyed it as well. The ranch is truly beautiful. Thank you for showing it to me."

"I'm sorry it took so long. I meant to take you out last week, but things have been so busy."

Jemma placed her hand on his arm and looked into his face. "I understand. I know you have many responsibilities to see to and you can't spend all your time with the children."

Although he loved Jack and Lily, he didn't feel a desperate need to be close to them. Rather, it was the beguiling woman standing beside him with her hand burning a hole through his shirtsleeve who constantly captured his attention.

"I better relieve Sam of the children. I'm sure he has grown tired of Lily asking 'why' and Jack wanting to find you or play with the dogs or ride his horse. Thank you for giving him his own horse, by the way. He hasn't stopped talking about it since the moment you put the reins in his hands."

"Every rancher needs a good horse. Jack will grow into Nick."

As she recalled Jack's excitement at having his own horse, she smiled at Thane. "It meant so much to him for you to entrust an animal to his care."

He nodded as she turned back toward the barn door. One of Lily's doll dresses on the ground caught her eye. When she bent over to pick it up, Thane reached out and brushed his hand over the curve of her rear.

She shot upright as if she'd been branded. Fire blasted from her eyes as she spun around and glared at him. "Mr. Jordan, that is completely and absolutely unacceptable. Do I make myself clear?"

"Yes, ma'am."

"And wipe that smirk off your face!"

"That, I can't do." Thane's wicked smile did little to calm her pounding heart or the breath she drew in with tight, short gasps. He touched his fingers to his hat, strolled out of the barn then looked back at her with a wink.

Frustrated, she stamped her booted feet then marched to the bunkhouse. She wanted to chase after Thane, spin him around, and slap his face — or kiss him until she lost what little sense she had left. The thrilling sensations created by his hand on her posterior made her wonder what it would be like to truly be Thane's wife.

Heat seared her cheeks and she took a moment to gather her composure before entering the bunkhouse. As she opened the door and stepped inside, Lily sat at one end of the table drawing a picture with a pencil while Jack and Sam worked on oiling bridles at the other end.

With a calming breath, she forced a smile to her face and held out her hands. "Did you have fun with Sam, my darlings?"

"Auntie Jemma!" Lily hopped down from the bench and ran over to her, eager to be cuddled and showered with kisses.

Jemma gave her an extra squeeze before setting her down and walking over to where Jack and Sam worked. As she placed her hand on Jack's shoulder, she looked at Sam.

"Your afternoon went well?"

"Yes, ma'am. We had us a good time and even made some cookies that ain't half bad."

"Is that so?"

"Yes, Auntie Jemma. Try one of our cookies. Please?" Lily tugged on her hand until she sat down at the table and accepted a cookie from the plate Sam held out to her.

Lily climbed on her lap and Jemma handed her the doll dress. "I thought I told you not to play in the barn, Lily."

"I didn't. Pepper took my dolly's dress." Lily's lip inched out in a pout.

Jemma looked to Jack and Sam. The cook nodded his head. "She was playing on the porch and Pepper grabbed the doll. Jack got it away from the dog, but the dress came off in the process."

"I see. We'll have to get your dolly a clean dress when we return to the cabin." Jemma patted Lily's back and smiled. The little girl leaned against her, wiggling her feet as she hummed a tune known only to her.

"Did you enjoy your ride?" Sam asked, pouring two cups of coffee and setting one down in front of Jemma.

She gave him a grateful nod and took a sip, although she would have much preferred tea. "Thane accompanied me. I enjoyed his tour of the ranch. It's quite a large place, isn't it?"

Sam grinned. "Yep, boss has a big spread with more than ten thousand acres. Not too many places are that big, but that includes the mountain property."

Jemma choked on her sip of coffee. Thane hadn't showed her thousands of acres on their ride. "What do you mean ten thousand acres?"

"The ranch. I thought you said Thane gave you a tour?" Sam gave her an odd look.

Jemma described where they went and Sam shook his head. "That's just the acreage around the home place." He lumbered to his feet and motioned for her to follow him outside.

Sam pointed toward the mountains in the distance as they stepped away from the bunkhouse. "You see the tree line at the base of the snow on the mountains?"

Jemma nodded.

"Thane's holdings go from the trees to the west of us to just past where the railroad cuts through on the east. He owns all the ground south of us for about five miles and north for about two miles."

Shocked, Jemma sank down on a porch chair and stared at Sam. "How did Thane acquire all this property?"

Sam laughed and took a chair close to hers. As he leaned back, he stuck out his legs and crossed his boot-clad feet at the ankle. "Gold, mostly. He still owns three... no, four mines around these parts. The railroad paid him a pretty penny to lay track out there, too. Thane's got more money than he could spend in ten lifetimes. Sounds like his brother did well, too."

Stunned by this revelation, she tried to embrace the notion that her husband was a wealthy man long before he set foot in England. From his manners, his work-grade clothing — everything about him, she assumed he didn't have much money of his own. Shortly after meeting him, she realized he didn't want Henry's money, although it would have been an enticement for most men, especially considering the circumstances.

Determined to understand her husband, she turned to Sam. "If he has an abundance of funds, why does he live in such a small cabin? Why doesn't he hire someone to manage his ranch and enterprises? Why does he work so hard?"

Sam studied her for a long moment. "That's just Thane. He don't put on airs, try to be someone or something he ain't. He's just a hard working man doing something he loves. He wouldn't hire someone to do what he can do himself. As for the cabin and such, Thane is of the opinion money shouldn't be wasted on things that ain't necessary. He had somewhere to sit at a table and sleep in a bed that kept the cold, rain, and varmints off him. That took care of the necessary."

"I see." In truth, Jemma didn't see anything clearly. Thane was cut from a different cloth than any other man she knew, Henry included. He'd been generous with her and the children, but part of her resented the fact Henry left everything to a brother he hadn't seen in fourteen years.

She recalled all the things Thane purchased for them, for her. Jemma held a new respect for the man. Most likely, all the money he'd spent on her and the children was his own, not what he inherited from Henry.

Admittedly, her husband was a solid, good, caring man, even if he teased her mercilessly and made her think things no lady should.

Chapter Seventeen

"Mercy!" Jemma grabbed the skillet off the stove, yelping in pain as the hot handle seared her palm. Clanging the cast-iron pan back down, she snatched a dishtowel off the counter and picked it up again before setting it on the table with a thud.

Jack and Lily stared at the steaks in the pan. No longer thick and juicy, the meat more closely resembled the jerky they'd seen the men eating one day as they rode in from the range.

"That isn't the way Sam makes it." Jack poked at the steak with his finger. The shriveled, blackened meat appeared anything but appetizing.

Near tears, with her hand throbbing from her burn, Jemma tried to think of something else she could fix for dinner, now that she'd ruined the steaks. It would be only a few moments before Thane walked through the door, expecting a hot meal. Fretful, she wondered if he'd complain about fried eggs and ham again. She'd been trying to learn to make American foods he seemed to enjoy, but some things she had yet to master. Like steak.

"Auntie Jemma?" Jack's voice sounded troubled, drawing her from her thoughts.

"What is it, lovey?" Jemma smiled at the boy. He appeared to have grown two inches in the weeks they'd been at the ranch.

"There's smoke coming from the oven." Jack pointed to the stove where puffs of smoke began to fill the room with a burnt odor.

"No! Not the biscuits!" Jemma grabbed the towel again, yanked open the oven door and choked as a billow of smoke wafted into her face.

Frantically flapping the towel, she grabbed the pan of hard, blackened orbs and dumped it into the sink, pumping water over the mess.

Jack ran to the door to let in fresh air but before he could reach it, Thane swung it open and rushed inside.

"Is everyone okay? I saw smoke." Concerned, he glanced around but his panic gave way to mirth as he took in the soggy biscuits in the sink and smoke drifting away from the open oven door. He bent down and winked at Jack. "Guess we better eat at the bunkhouse tonight, huh?

"Yes, sir!" Jack grabbed his coat and tugged it on, starting out the door, but Thane called him back. "Take Lily with you." Thane helped her on with her coat, kissed her cheek, and shooed her out the door with her brother.

Thane fanned the door a few moments until the worst of the smoke cleared. Quietly closing it, he strode over to where Jemma stood at the sink, unmoving. After pushing open the window, he watched her shiver in the chilly air that blew around them, pulling out the last of the smoke.

"Jem?"

Unusually quiet, her gaze lingered on the ruined biscuits, ignoring his presence behind her.

A big, warm hand touched her arm. "What's wrong? This isn't the first pan of biscuits you've ruined."

Instead of glaring at him or offering a barbed retort, she sniffled and stepped away.

"Jemma?" Thane put a hand on her shoulder, turning her around. Tears dripped down her cheeks, through a streak of flour by her nose. "What's wrong?"

"I burned your steak and the biscuits. It's impossible to cook your blasted American food properly and I think my hand may require medical attention." The words burst out of her followed by a sob as she turned her head away from Thane.

He lifted both her hands and examined them, noticing the raw, red blister on the palm of her left hand.

"Here, run some water on it." Thane held her hand beneath the faucet while he pumped water on the burn. She bit her lip as water cooled the spot. After letting the water run over it for a minute, Thane dried her hand then took a box from the top shelf of a cupboard and removed a tin of salve and a roll of gauze. Carefully rubbing the medicine onto her palm, he wrapped it with a length of the gauze then kissed her fingers.

When he held her hand to his lips with heat flaming in his eyes, Jemma forgot about the burn, their ruined dinner, and everything except Thane.

"Thank you," she whispered, gazing at his face. He hadn't shaved the past few mornings, and golden stubble covered his cheeks and jaw.

Her focus centered on his mouth. His full bottom lip intrigued her, as it had so many times in the past and she wondered what it would be like to kiss it again. To kiss it as a woman who loved Thane, not just the wife he felt compelled to marry.

Before she surrendered to her longings, she backed away from him and walked over to the table, glaring at the ruined steaks.

"It's a pity to ruin such lovely cuts of beef," she said, starting to pick up the skillet in her right hand, holding her bandaged hand at her waist. Thane took the pan from her and opened the cabin door. Whistling for the dogs, he gave each one a piece of tough, overcooked beef and warned Rigsly to share before shutting the door. He set the skillet in the sink and filled it with water to let it soak. Since the room had sufficiently aired, he closed the window before turning back to Jemma.

"I admit I'm a little disappointed I won't be having steak and buttermilk biscuits for supper, but it isn't worth crying over, Jem. You're doing fine and I don't mind eating the um… interesting dishes you've cooked."

"You don't like my cooking?"

The accusing glare she sent him made him uneasy. "You're a good cook, Jemma, it's just that English food in general seems kind of bland compared to what I'm used to. I noticed that when I was in England. If I didn't know better, I'd think you all horde spices like precious jewels."

The starch left her spine as she slumped into a chair. She crossed her arms in front of her on the table, and buried her head, bursting into another round of sobs.

Thane pulled out the chair beside her, sat down and started rubbing gentle circles on her back, letting her cry. He hadn't seen her have a good cry since the night they stayed at the Weston's and he figured she was about due. From what he knew about women, which was precious little, they sometimes needed to cry.

"I'm a terrible cook!" Jemma snuffled, fishing a handkerchief from her apron pocket and dabbing at her tears. "I'm an awful wife, a horrid mother, and I don't belong on this ranch. I won't ever grow accustomed to mice in my cupboards, barnyard filth on my floors, or having to use that rickety, vile outhouse!"

Thane grinned to hear her finally use the word outhouse rather than lavatory. In her distraught state, she didn't notice his amusement at her expense.

"Everything is so hard, and exhausting, and covered in dirt, Thane. There's a never-ending supply of dirt."

Jemma did her best to keep the cabin spotless, but it was a futile battle at best. If the wind blew at all, which it did most days, dirt sifted in around the door and windowsills, coating everything in a fine powder. Once it snowed, she wouldn't have to deal with the dust, but the winters were cold, dark, and long.

Personally, he was glad the weather continued to be mild. It made it easier for him to work until it was too dark to see and Jemma and the kids slept. Waiting until his wife slumbered was the only way he could go to bed, sleeping so close to the object of his desire yet adhering to his promise not to scale the wall she set around herself.

Unsure if Jemma would ever welcome him to her side of the bed, he thought they worked well together in all other aspects of their marriage.

Jemma had turned the cabin into a cozy, inviting haven with the furniture he hauled home from Baker City as well as some of her paintings, a handful of small rugs, and a few pieces of frippery.

She kept everything from the socks in his drawer to the stack of plates in the cupboard neat and orderly. He always had a filling, hot meal to eat for breakfast and supper, since he often didn't come in off the range for lunch or took that meal with the hands at the bunkhouse. Even if he didn't always appreciate the food she cooked, she put in the effort.

Energized when they matched wits, he'd begun to think she enjoyed their sparring matches as much as he did. She'd stopped looking wounded or affronted by his words weeks ago.

Jemma wouldn't have been his choice for a wife because he never intended to marry in the first place. However, since he had to take one, he figured she suited him about as well as anyone could have. She didn't chatter all the time or make unreasonable demands. She asked intelligent questions, could converse on almost any topic, and went about her work with diligence and efficiency.

Even with eyes red from crying and flour on her face, his wife's outward beauty made his gut tighten and longing wash over him in overpowering waves.

When she started dressing in the plainer cotton dresses she purchased from Maggie, he hoped it would alter her appeal. If anything, he found her even more attractive without the preposterous bustle blocking the view of her skirts swishing across her backside.

Mindful of how right she felt in his arms, how much he enjoyed hearing her laugh, seeing her smile, watching her eyes spark with fire, he considered what a good mother she was to Jack and Lily. The children were disciplined when they needed it, yet she never raised her voice in anger.

She poured out her love to them in so many little ways — a touch, a word of encouragement, a kind smile. Despite their losses, being uprooted from their home, and forced to live in a place vastly different from what they were accustomed, the children adjusted smoothly. That was thanks to Jemma.

Although he had dreaded making room in his life for the children and Jemma, Thane wondered how he ever existed before them. His life felt so much fuller and complete now that they'd joined him on the ranch.

Scrupulously studying the woman who continued to sniffle and wipe away tears, he leaned back in his chair with a cocky grin, hoping to either tease her out of her sorrows or make her mad enough she forgot about them.

"You certainly are a poor excuse for a wife and mother. Constantly harping and nagging. I've never seen such a bad cook, either. And did I catch you yelling at Rigsly this morning? Animal abuse, too? I don't know about you, Jem. Maybe I should haul you into town and let you fend for yourself. If you can't learn to make American biscuits and cook my steak without burning it, I think the deal is off."

Startled by his words, Jemma stared at him, trying to decide if he was sincere or teasing. When she noticed his grin, the corners of her mouth lifted in response. "If you'd be so kind as to bring in one of my trunks from the barn, I'll pack and leave posthaste."

Thane reached out and grabbed her around her waist, pulling her onto his lap. "Nah. I think you'd better stay. I'm just starting to get you trained."

Lost in the look in his eyes, Jemma couldn't form a response. She could barely think at all.

Thane dropped his head until their lips were just a few inches apart. Not moving any closer, he gave her a long, tender glance and waited.

In agony, she wanted his kiss so badly her mouth watered and lips tingled. Emboldened by the wanting in his eyes, she wrapped her arms around his neck and pulled his head down the remainder of the distance. Engulfed by the charged currents sparking between them, she closed her eyes. His lips brushed hers as the door banged open and Jack ran inside.

Thane jerked his head up and looked at the boy.

"Is Lily here?" Jack asked, out of breath as he stood in the open door.

"No. Isn't she at the bunkhouse with you?" Thane jumped to his feet, still holding Jemma by her waist. She popped his shoulder with her hand and he set her down then ran out the door with Jack as she followed close behind him.

"Where did you last see her?"

"We were all sitting down to eat supper and Lily said she had to use the outhouse. Sam told her to go ahead then hurry right back. She ran out, but was gone an awful long time, even for Lily. I went to check on her, but the outhouse door was open. I looked in the barn. Lily likes to play with the barn cat's kittens even though you told her to leave them alone, Auntie Jemma."

Thane ran to the outhouse, to make sure Lily wasn't there. As he turned around, Jemma peered over his shoulder.

"She couldn't fall in, down the... in the hole could she?"

Thane took her hand in his and tugged her away from the privy. "No. Come on, we'll find her. She's probably playing with the kittens or something."

Jack, accompanied by Salt and Pepper, followed them as they rushed across the ranch yard, calling Lily's name.

Thane glanced at the boy. "Son, run into the bunkhouse and ask them all to help us look."

Jack took off and Thane hurried inside the barn. "Check all the stalls while I climb up to the loft to see if she somehow got up there."

A quick look around the barn showed Lily wasn't there.

Fear unlike any Jemma had known slithered up her spine, threatening to choke the air right out of her. Panic or hysterics wouldn't help find her beloved girl, so she ran outside, continuing to call Lily's name.

Thane joined her as they looked through the shed where he kept his wagons and equipment. The hands joined them, searching every building, every place they could think of for a child to hide.

As the evening shadows lengthened with the approaching night, Jemma grabbed Thane's arm, desperate to find Lily. "Where could she be? What if some wild animal grabbed her or a snake bit her or..."

Gently shaking her, Thane took her in his arms. "Stop it, Jem. She's fine. She just wandered a little farther away from the house than she should have. We'll find her."

Blindly nodding her head and blinking back tears, she followed Thane as he ran out toward a recently constructed pen where he'd pastured a few of his bulls. Rigsly barked out a warning, causing them to run faster. They both came to a halt as they topped the rise.

In the midst of the pen, Lily stood with a quirt in her hand, flicking it at the bulls and yelling, "get up there!"

just like she'd seen the ranch hands do. Rigsly sat at the fence, barking fiercely, as if he was trying to tell the child she was in danger.

Thane clapped a hand over her mouth before Jemma could scream at Lily to run out of the pen. "Stay quiet. We don't need the bulls any more worked up than they already are. Go get Sam and the boys."

Jemma picked up her skirts and spun around, sprinting back toward the bunkhouse while Thane eased over the fence. Concerned about the dog getting in the middle of things, he motioned for the canine to sit down.

"Hush up, Rigs. You're a good dog, but you need to be quiet now."

Rigsly stopped barking and anxiously sat by the fence, moving his front paws like he wanted to jump in and help.

Slowly walking into the pen, Thane kept one eye on the milling animals and the other on his tiny niece.

Details he normally wouldn't notice stood out to him with vibrant clarity: the ripe smell of fresh manure, the aroma of the sagebrush on the evening breeze, the scent of Jemma's fragrance clinging to his clothes from holding her earlier.

Fear, sharp and bitter, lingered on his tongue as he inched his way toward Lily. Strawberry-blonde curls encircled her head like a fiery halo as the setting sun glowed around her. Her voice carried to him, a sound of pure childish delight, as she giggled and snapped the quirt again.

Particles of dust floated in the air in the golden orange beams of light filtering into the pen. Thane took in the dusty red hides of the beasts, intermixed with once-white splotches on their faces. Individual blades of grass bent beneath his booted feet as he worked his way across the pen.

With her back to him, Lily wasn't aware of his approach until he stood right behind her.

"Lily, honey," Thane bent down and whispered in her ear. "We're going to play a game. We're going to see if we can run faster than the bulls to the fence. When I pick you up, you put your arms around my neck and hang on as tight as you can, okay?"

"Okay!" Lily spun around and encircled his neck with her little arms, still holding the quirt. Thane held her against his chest with one solid arm. He rose and turned, then started running for all he was worth. The bulls grunted and gave chase. Pounding hooves vibrated behind him along with the snorting sounds the animals made as they raced to catch him.

"They're getting closer, Uncle Thane." Lily laughed, thinking it a grand game.

With a final burst of speed, Thane clutched Lily tightly as he leaped up and cleared the pole fence seconds before one of the bulls plowed into it, making him glad the hands reinforced the fence like he asked. As he hit the ground on the other side, he rolled, using his body to cushion Lily before sitting up, placing the child on her feet.

Carefully rubbing his hands over her head, along her arms and over her back, he couldn't feel anything broken. She wiggled and grinned, bouncing on her toes in excitement. "That was fun. Let's do it again!"

She grabbed his hand and tugged in the direction of the fence. Before she could take another step, Jemma swept her into her arms and rained kisses along her cheeks and neck, holding her so tightly Lily squirmed against her.

Overwrought, Jemma dropped to her knees in the dust and held Lily's little face in her hands, unable to think about how close her niece and husband had come to being trampled by the bulls.

"Lillian Jane Jordan. Don't you ever, ever do something like that again."

Lily's lip puckered and tears glistened in her eyes. "What did I do bad, Auntie Jemma?"

"You mustn't ever climb in with the animals, poppet. They could trample you to death. Do you understand, Lily? It's dangerous and you could have been gravely injured."

"I don't want to be dead!" Lily wailed, burying her face against Jemma. "I don't want hurted!"

The hands gathered around them, looking from Thane to Jemma. Thane got to his feet and rolled his shoulders to make sure he hadn't loosened too many of his bolts and hinges when he landed. Everything seemed to be in working order.

"I'm sorry, Uncle Thane. It's my fault," Jack said, looking up at him with sorrowful eyes.

"It's not your fault, son." Thane hunkered down by the boy, keeping a grunt of pain from escaping by clenching his jaw. Apparently, he landed on his hip harder than he thought.

"It is my fault. I should have gone with her and made sure she came back."

"You didn't do anything wrong, Jack. I would have done the same thing if we'd been there. You can't take the blame for something your sister did. She knew she was supposed to come right back to the table, not wander around outside."

Relieved, Jack hugged his uncle, upset by the whole ordeal. He and the hands arrived in time to watch Thane clear the fence with Lily held tightly in his arms.

Thane straightened and gave Jack's back a reassuring pat then walked over to where Jemma and Lily sat crying in the dirt.

"Lily, honey, your aunt is correct. You shouldn't have been out here. I want you to promise me you'll never, ever climb in a pen with animals again." Thane tipped up the little chin and looked into his niece's eyes. "Do you promise?"

Lily nodded her head, still snuffling. "I promise."

"Good girl." Thane picked her up and hugged her close. His knees wobbled at thoughts of what could have happened to the little girl. She and her brother had become so precious to him, he couldn't bear for anything to happen to either of them.

"Am I still in trouble?" Lily's lip stuck out and tears threatened to again spill from her eyes.

"Yes, you're in trouble for not minding Sam when he told you to come back. You won't get any dessert tonight and you can't play with your dolly before bed."

Lily's lip curled into a full-fledged pout, although she didn't cry. "Can I finish my supper?"

"Yes, honey. You go on with Jack and you both finish your supper."

Undaunted, she grabbed Jack's hand and started skipping back toward the bunkhouse. "Come on, Jack. I'm hungry."

Thane drew Jemma to her feet and shook his head, watching the children run down the path toward the ranch yard with the hands.

"'And though she be but little, she is fierce.' That quote has a whole new meaning for me now."

Dazed, Jemma couldn't believe Thane stood beside her quoting Shakespeare. Too distressed by Lily's actions to think clearly, she struggled to imagine how Thane knew Shakespeare's works, forgetting his mother had been a schoolteacher.

The depths of her husband's intellect and heart constantly surprised her. Because of his rough appearance at their initial meeting, she'd judged everything from Thane's level of intelligence to his emotional capacity based on that first impression.

The process of knowing Thane Jordan was akin to peeling back the layers of a never-ending surprise. It made her think of a gift she received as a child — a ball of tissue that held numerous gifts. As she unrolled the tissue, each new layer revealed something more wondrous than the previous layer, with a promise of something else exciting awaiting discovery.

Much like she experienced with her husband.

Suddenly, the full force of what transpired in the past few moments hit her. Unable to breathe, Jemma swayed on her feet.

"Don't you dare faint, Jem. For a woman who promised she wasn't a swooner, you've sure put that theory to the test." Thane wrapped his arms around her and held her upright as she leaned into his chest. "No one got hurt and everything is fine. What's eatin' at you now?"

A shaky gulp of air filled her lungs as Jemma tipped her head back so she could look at Thane, take in every nuance of his beloved face. Vertical worry lines etched between his brows, while time spent in the sun and laughing created crinkles at the corners at his eyes. She observed the mole on his cheek, the scruffy stubble on his chin, the outline of his lips, and the light glowing in his normally cool blue eyes.

Shaken, she placed a hand on his cheek. If something had happened to Lily or Thane, she would have been inconsolable because she owned a ferocious love for them both.

"I'm just so glad you and Lily are fine. What if we hadn't found her when we did? What if Rigsly hadn't been barking? What if you hadn't made it out of the pen? What if…"

Thane lifted her off the ground and pressed his lips to hers, effectively silencing her fears. Driven, demanding kisses poured out his passion along with a soothing balm to her soul. She slipped her arms around his neck and held on, returning his ardor.

If he didn't stop, he'd carry her to the house, bolt the door, and break the promise he'd stupidly made that day at the cottage.

Slowly lifting his head, he kissed her temple then slid her down to her feet.

"What if you don't worry about the what ifs and be happy that all is well?" Thane gave her a gentle smile then looped her hand around his arm. "Let's go see if Sam made enough supper to feed us, since you burned mine beyond recognition. I think I saw Pepper burying his steak. It's pretty bad when the dogs won't eat it."

His teasing brought out her smile since Jemma knew it was his way of putting her at ease.

After that kiss, though, she didn't think anything would ever be fine again, especially not when Thane refused to break his vow of remaining her husband in name only.

As they walked back to the bunkhouse, she studied him out of the corner of her eye. There was no doubt her husband was strong and capable, but watching him run across the pasture and leap over the fence created an entirely new level of admiration in her for his physical abilities.

"I can't believe you jumped over the fence." The look she gave him carried a sense of awe.

"To tell you the truth, I can't believe it, either." Thane grinned at her as he held open the bunkhouse door. "Evidently, desperation can give your feet wings."

Chapter Eighteen

The sound of riders approaching drew Jemma's excited gaze out the kitchen window as Maggie and Tully dismounted in front of the cabin. Tully took the reins of the horses and strolled toward the barn while Maggie hurried down the walk.

With a final glance at the tea she'd prepared, Jemma smoothed her hands down her skirt, patted her hair, then rushed to open the door.

Maggie smiled as she stepped across the porch and inside the warmth of the cabin.

"I am so very pleased you were able to visit today, Maggie," Jemma said, taking the woman's coat and hanging it on a peg by the door. Maggie unwound a scarf from around her head and neck, hanging it on her coat then removing her gloves and stuffing them into her coat pockets. Dressed in a riding skirt with a frilly lace-trimmed blouse, she glanced at Jemma's striped silk gown and sighed.

Although it was too late to worry about it now, she wished she'd dressed in something nicer and brought the buckboard Tully had offered to drive.

"Thank you for inviting me to tea. I've never attended a real English tea before, so you'll have to excuse my ignorance if I pick up the wrong spoon or something." Maggie gave Jemma's hand a squeeze as they walked into the sitting area in front of the fireplace.

"It's just tea, not dinner with the queen." Jemma grinned at her friend, thrilled to have a female visitor. Tully had been out to the ranch numerous times, but this was the first time Maggie had visited. The woman was busy with her dress shop and Jemma felt honored she'd take an afternoon off to visit.

As she warmed her hands by the cozy fire, Maggie glanced at the lace-covered table where a silver tray held an assortment of treats and steam rose from a delicate china teapot.

"This is lovely, Jemma. Do you have tea every day?" Maggie turned her back to the heat and held her hands behind her as Jemma stood by the sofa. Admiring the lovely furniture and the artful way Jemma arranged it, she had no idea a little loving care could turn Thane's rough cabin into a welcoming home.

"No, although we did before we left England. I do pop on the kettle and make myself a cup of tea most afternoons. There is something about the ritual of heating the water, brewing the tea, and sitting quietly to sip it from one of my mother's teacups that brings me a measure of comfort and peace."

"It sounds wonderful." Maggie took a seat in Lily's rocking chair. A sigh escaped her as she settled against the thickly padded seat and back. She closed her eyes and rocked the chair a few times before returning her gaze to her friend. "This is the most comfortable chair I've ever sat in."

"Lily picked it out at Mr. Patterson's furniture store." Jemma smiled as she handed Maggie a cup of tea on a saucer. "She spied it and begged to have it, and neither Thane nor I could tell her no. I think it reminds her of the rocking chair we had in the nursery at the cottage."

"Have the children missed being in England? Have they settled in here?" Maggie laughed when Jemma told her about finding Lily with the bulls a few weeks ago. "I do believe your little Lily is going to be quite a handful."

"Yes, she is, but I'd rather have her that way than not be interested or engaged in the world around her." Jemma placed a few treats on a plate, handing it to Maggie.

Maggie sampled a dainty sandwich, took a bite of something Jemma called a crumpet, and tasted an egg custard tart. Everything was delicious and she asked Jemma for a recipe for the tart, liking the hint of nutmeg with the rich, creamy filling.

"No wonder Thane seems so happy these days," Maggie observed, helping herself to another bite of the tart. "You've created an inviting home, feed him delicious food, and are everything a man could ask for in a wife."

Jemma clanged her cup against her saucer and set both down on a side table, staring at her friend. "You think Thane is happy? With me?" Jemma waved her hand around the room. "With this?"

"Of course! He'd have to be blind and stupid not to be and I know for a fact he isn't either of those things." Maggie grinned as she took a sip of her tea. "I wouldn't believe it if I couldn't see it firsthand, but you've done the thing Thane vowed would never happen."

"What might that be?" Jemma asked, curious and somewhat befuddled by Maggie's words.

"You've made him fall in love."

Jemma sat back against the sofa, opened her mouth to speak, then found words failed her. It couldn't be. Thane didn't love her.

He tolerated her. Teased her. Frustrated her as much as she annoyed him.

Somewhere in the past few months, they'd become good friends.

But love?

No, it was impossible to think of the man falling in love with her.

"He didn't have to marry you, Jemma. He wanted to." Maggie observed as she took another sip of her tea.

"He married me for the children, so they wouldn't be uprooted from everyone they knew and because he needed someone to care for them. I was the logical choice." Jemma stared at Maggie, wanting to believe her but afraid to hope Thane could hold feelings for her.

Maggie smiled knowingly and set down her tea. "If that's all he needed you for, he would have hired you as his nanny or found one. After swearing he'd never wed, he didn't seem to have any trouble taking you as his bride. He might not admit it to himself, but he's in love with you. As sure as I'm sitting here enjoying this lovely tea, Thane Jordan loves you. You can see it in his eyes, hear it in his voice, and feel it in the air when you get close to each other. Sparks fairly fly off the two of you."

"But he... we... no, it can't be true." Jemma forgot about maintaining a proper posture and slumped against the soft cushions of the sofa. "I dare not hope such a thing."

"Why not? It's obvious you love him, and you are married, after all. One thing I learned is not to waste a single day you have together because they can end all too quickly. I think you should not only dare to hope he loves you, but also acknowledge the truth of the matter. I've known Thane for a long time and I can tell you right now, he's never been as happy and content as he's been since you and the children moved to the ranch."

Instinctively, Jemma knew she could trust Maggie to keep her secrets and offer good advice. "How can I know for certain he loves me? He won't even... he refuses to...he hasn't yet..."

"I'd bet you my whole store that Thane loves you, if I were a betting woman. What does he refuse? What won't he do?"

"To um... to... well, we haven't exactly... he promised he wouldn't...he vowed we..." Jemma struggled to find a delicate way to say she and Thane had yet to consummate their marriage.

Maggie grinned and rocked back in the chair. "You mean to tell me that Thane Jordan married one of the most beautiful women he's ever seen and vowed he wouldn't make her his true wife?"

Jemma's cheeks flamed with hot embarrassment, but she nodded her head. "He promised I'd share everything but his bed when he proposed this arrangement. Technically, we share a bed, but he stays on his side and I stay on mine."

Eyes wide with disbelief, Maggie stopped rocking and stared at Jemma. "That right there should tell you how much he loves you. Any man but Thane, and maybe Tully, would have broken that promise within a few days. They certainly wouldn't have lasted this long. You've been married what, about two months or so?"

Jemma glanced at the clock. "Eight weeks, three days and twenty-three hours."

Humored by the situation, Maggie resumed her rocking. "Oh, you sweet, naive girl, he definitely loves you. Now, we need to figure out a way to force him to realize it. Did you like the bedroom set? When Thane wired Tully to order one, he asked me to help pick it out."

"No wonder it's so lovely. Thank you." Jemma rose to her feet and motioned Maggie to follow. "Would you like to see it?"

After admiring the bedroom set and the quilt Jemma purchased for the bed, they returned to the sitting area and Jemma refreshed their tea.

Time passed quickly as they sat visiting. They both looked up as Thane and Tully walked inside followed by Jack.

"Tea time, is it?" Thane asked, smiling at his wife and Maggie. "Hope you saved me some."

"There is gracious plenty." Jemma retrieved more plates and cups, carrying them to the low table in front of the sofa. Jack took a seat in the side chair closest to the fire while Tully sank onto Thane's old overstuffed chair close to the rocking chair where Maggie sipped her tea.

Thane leaned down and kissed Maggie's cheek before taking a seat next to his wife on the sofa. She handed him a cup of tea and a plate of treats. Spying the custard tarts he favored, he bit into one then drank his tea.

Tully slathered a warm crumpet with butter and jam, taking a big bite before slurping his tea. As he glanced around the room, his eyes rested on his hostess. Despite their obvious differences, the woman domesticated his friend and put a warm light in his eyes that had never been there.

Jemma looked like she belonged in some fancy drawing room with her creamy complexion, perfectly styled hair, and expensive gown. Back ramrod straight, holding a delicate cup and saucer in her hands, she was the epitome of a grand lady.

Thane, on the other hand, sported a pair of worn denims, splotched with mud and manure from working around the cattle earlier that day. The faded flannel shirt he wore with the sleeves rolled up to the elbows appeared out of place next to Jemma's finery. Judging by the stubble on his face, Thane had been in too big of a hurry to shave for a few days or had misplaced his razor again.

In the past weeks, Tully witnessed the two of them butting heads over one thing or another. Thane liked to goad Jemma just to see how she'd react most of the time, not because he needed to prove his point.

As he stared from the woman of noble birth to the man who worked hard every day to wrest his ranch from the Eastern Oregon scrubland, Tully couldn't help the snort of laughter that escaped.

Thane glanced at him as he took a bite of a jam-filled cookie. "Care to share your joke with the rest of us?"

"The two of you go together like crumpets and cowpies."

Jemma choked on her tea and set down her cup while Thane gently thumped her on the back and handed her his napkin. Maggie shot Tully a cool glare, letting him know he'd crossed over a line.

"I just meant that Jemma is such a fine lady and Thane is about as rough and tumble as they come. By the way, these crumpets are tasty, especially with jam sinking into all the little holes. Mmm, mmm. I could get used to your English tea parties, even if Thane prefers biscuits to crumpets."

Mad at his friend, Thane narrowed his glare and wished he could punch Tully in the nose. Not only had his words been insulting, they were true.

When he walked in and found Jemma sitting at tea with Maggie, looking every bit as proper and pretty as she had the first day he met her, he couldn't help but think how out of place she was in his chink-walled cabin.

She needed to be somewhere like the cottage, surrounded by warmth, comfort, and beautiful things she treasured. Not on some scrubby ranch in the middle of nowhere with a bunch of ill-mannered men.

Disturbed, he removed his hand from her back and slid over on the sofa, leaving more space between the two of them. Maggie raised a questioning eyebrow, but it went unnoticed. Thane seemed too lost in his thoughts to pay her any mind.

Tully and Jemma carried the conversation until Maggie declared it time to head back to town. Although Jemma asked them both to stay for dinner, Maggie insisted she wanted to get home before dark.

Tully and Thane went out to get the horses while Jemma helped Maggie on with her coat. Generously placing bread and sweets into a basket, Jemma tucked a cloth around the top and handed it to Maggie.

"Something for you to enjoy later."

"Thank you, Jemma. You think about what I said and don't let that obstinate cowboy fool you into thinking otherwise." Maggie gave her an encouraging pat on the back. "I can't leave without seeing Lily. Is she still napping?"

"Yes. However, if I don't wake her soon, she won't want to go to bed tonight. She had a busy morning chasing after the dogs and one of the hands let her ride with him out to check on the cows." Jemma opened Lily's bedroom door and smiled at the little girl who gazed at her with sleepy eyes.

Lily grinned when she saw Maggie in the doorway and held out her arms to her.

"Hello, Lily. How are you?" Maggie asked, picking her up and kissing her cheek.

"I'm great! How are you?"

"I'm great, too." Maggie carried her out to the front room and held her a minute until Thane and Tully returned with the horses.

Quickly wrapping a shawl around her shoulders, Jemma took Lily from Maggie and folded the material around her as well before stepping outside. Maggie grabbed the basket of treats then hurried over to where Thane and Tully waited. She hugged Thane and whispered something in his ear then patted his cheek with a fond look before swinging into the saddle.

The woman's familiarity with Thane made jealous pangs stab at Jemma even though she knew it was ridiculous. Maggie was a good friend, nothing more.

With a wave at Tully as he mounted his horse, Jemma started down the steps with Lily as her two guests rode out of the ranch yard.

"Where you headed?" Thane asked, falling into step beside her.

"Lily needs to use the, um… privy." Jemma glanced at him and noticed his grin at her use of the word.

"I'll take her. It's getting cold out here and you'll freeze in that outfit."

Lily hugged Thane around the neck as he carried her toward the outhouse while Jemma huffed in annoyance and marched back inside the cabin.

Jack sat curled up in a chair by the fire with a book in his hand, reading a story while eating the last sandwich on the tea tray.

"Do you want some tea, Jack? Would you prefer a glass of milk?"

"No, thank you." Jack didn't even look up as he answered, turning the next page in the book.

Pleased that Jack found a book he couldn't put down, Jemma stepped into her bedroom. She changed out of her gown into a dark blue calico dress sprigged with yellow flowers. After tying on a fresh apron, she returned to the kitchen and began cleaning up the dishes from the tea service.

Jack set down his book and helped carry teacups and plates to the sink.

"Auntie Jemma?" He asked as he leaned against the counter and watched her pour a kettle of hot water into a dishpan and shave in a few curls of soap.

"Yes, lovey?" Jemma motioned for him to pick up a dishtowel so he could dry. He accepted the plate she handed him and began wiping away the drops of water clinging to the surface.

"May I ask you a question?"

Glancing over her shoulder at him, she smiled. "You may ask me anything you like, Jack."

"Do you think my mum and papa would be terribly disappointed that we moved here?"

Jemma stopped washing the dishes and wiped her hands on her apron. She took the plate and towel from Jack's hands then walked him over to the table and sat down on a chair.

Despite his usual protests that he was too old for cuddles, she pulled him onto her lap and wrapped him in a comforting hug. Tenderly brushing his bangs away from his forehead, she placed a kiss there and rocked him back and forth.

"Oh, sweetheart, I think your mum and papa would be very happy to see you living with your Uncle Thane. I know I'm glad we left England and came here."

"You are?" Jack sat up and gave her a look of surprise. "I didn't think you liked living here."

"Why would you say that?"

Jack scrunched up his nose and rubbed it with his index finger before looking at his aunt again. "You hate all the dirt and you're terrified of the snakes and coyotes. You call the outhouse an abomination, and you and Uncle Thane quarrel all the time. I don't think you like him very much."

Jemma took a moment to collect her thoughts before answering. "You are quite correct that I am not fond of dirt or snakes or coyotes. I do hate that thing your uncle calls an outhouse. It's utterly uncivilized. As for Thane, though, I like him very much. Although I admire and respect him, he and I enjoy saying things to annoy the other much like you enjoy stealing Lily's dolly or pulling on Rigsly's tail to get them to play with you. It's all in fun. I'm terribly sorry, Jack, if you were under the impression I don't like your uncle. I care for him a great deal."

"Then you don't wish we could go home, back to the cottage?"

"No, lovey. I don't wish to return to England. I miss Catherine and Charles, Cook and Greenfield, and the Westons, along with some of our other friends. Sometimes I miss all of the nice things we had at the cottage, like a bathroom. Occasionally, I even miss the gentle afternoon rains, but I don't want to live there. My life is here with you, Lily, your uncle, the ranch hands, and the new friends we're making, like Maggie and Tully."

"I'm glad, Auntie Jemma. I love it here, much more than I did at the cottage, although the bathrooms were nice."

"Yes, they were. Now, let's finish these dishes and you can get back to your book while I begin preparations for dinner."

As they stood, Thane opened the door and set Lily inside the house then hurried off before Jemma could say a word to him. Alarmed by what called him away with such urgency, she watched him eat up the ground to the barn with long strides. A few moments later, he rode out on Shadow and headed off toward one of the pastures to the west.

While Jack read his book, Lily played with her doll by the fire. When she grew tired of that, she talked Jack into rolling the ball Maggie had made for her back and forth, which the boy did while continuing to read his story. Lily finally grew upset with his halfhearted efforts and stomped over to where Jemma worked at preparing dinner.

To keep the child occupied, she gave Lily the job of setting cutlery and napkins on the table. As Lily skipped around the table singing, Jemma used leftover potatoes and vegetables from the roast dinner she served the previous day to make bubble and squeak, a traditional English dish both children loved.

At the pleasant dinner the day before, Thane had heaped praises on her for the tender beef roast, crispy roasted potatoes, delicious vegetables, and Yorkshire pudding. As she learned to incorporate more of the spices Thane liked into her cooking, she enjoyed experimenting with them.

Even though the ranch was remote with infrequent trips to town, the hands kept her supplied with an abundance of fresh milk and eggs, as well as beef, pork, and chicken. Although the men didn't raise a garden, Thane purchased a variety of canned goods along with boxes of apples, and big burlap sacks of potatoes, carrots, and onions that went into a cellar by the springhouse to ensure they had plenty to eat during the winter.

Jack closed his book and set the table while Jemma fried slices of the leftover roast and warmed the leftover Yorkshire pudding.

Thane ambled inside and removed his outerwear as she set the meat on the table. "Looks like it might snow soon. It's getting cold outside. Glad we've got everything ready for the winter."

While he washed his hands at the sink, Thane grinned down at Lily when she fastened her arms around his leg and stood on his foot. "Walk me to the table, Uncle Thane!"

The precocious child rode on his foot to the table. Thane picked her up and playfully blew on her neck, making her squeal with delight.

He set her down on the chair where they kept a stack of books so she could reach the table, then held Jemma's chair for her and waited for her to take a seat.

Although she'd changed her dress, he thought she still looked lovely. Too lovely, especially for an uncouth, scrabbling man like him.

Swiftly shutting down those thoughts, he asked a blessing on the meal and glanced over the table. Jemma's cooking had steadily improved. The roast she made the previous day had been so tender it fell apart at the touch of his fork. Fully anticipating more of it and the Yorkshire pudding, which seemed like an eggy biscuit to him, he stared at a platter that held something she hadn't served before. As she passed it to him, he tried to decide what it was and took a serving.

"It's bubble and squeak," Jack said as Thane passed the platter to him.

"Come again?" Thane stared at his plate. Golden brown on the outside, he cut into the mystery food. The inside looked like it contained vegetables and he couldn't decipher what else.

"Just take a bite. You'll like it." Jemma grinned at him while cutting Lily's meat into small pieces.

Hesitantly forking a bite, Thane stuck it in his mouth, prepared for some strange texture or flavor but found he enjoyed the savory bite. After taking another, he smiled at his wife. "That's good. What's in it?"

"Leftover potatoes and vegetables from dinner yesterday, and a few drippings from the bacon we had this morning." Jemma let out a sigh of relief, inordinately pleased Thane liked something that was such a reminder of her home and brought her comfort to both prepare and eat.

"Definitely make it again." Thane helped himself to more and ate his dinner with enthusiasm.

He helped clear the table then shrugged back into his coat, promising to return to tuck Lily and Jack into bed. Even though he often stayed out late, he always came in for a few minutes to tuck in the children and wish them sweet dreams. Jemma often wished he'd do the same for her.

After washing the dishes, she sat on the sofa in front of the fire, sewing buttons onto a new shirt she made for Jack while Lily wiggled beside her, pretending to read a story. Jack sat at the table working over some math problems she wrote out on a piece of paper.

Right on time, Thane appeared to help tuck the children into bed then disappeared outside again. A draft of cold air blew in as he shut the door, making her chilled.

In need of something to soothe her weary body and confused thoughts, Jemma heated several kettles of water on the stove, preparing to take a hot bath.

She dragged in a galvanized tub they used for bathing from where it hung on the side of the cabin. Briefly, she debated whether she should set it in the bedroom for more privacy or in front of the crackling fire. The sound of the wind howling outside tipped her decision in favor of the fire. She pushed back the table by the sofa to make more room for the tub and filled it with the steaming water. After adding a pitcher of cool water, she hurried into the bedroom and returned wrapped in a towel with a bar of fragrant soap she'd brought from England.

To test the temperature, she lifted her foot and stuck one toe in the water. Finding it to her liking, she sank into the tub, lathered herself with the soap, then let the hot water ease her tense muscles and tired mind.

Relaxed, she tipped her head back, closed her eyes, and let her thoughts drift as she dozed in front of the fire.

A sound woke her from her slumber and her eyes snapped open. Uncertain how long she'd been asleep, Jemma stood and wrapped the towel around herself then stepped out of the tub. When she turned around, she bit back a scream. Thane stood just inside the door, gaping at her

Mortified, she ran into the bedroom and shut the door.

Thane watched her go, rooted to the spot.

He had stayed outside after tucking in the kids until he couldn't stand the cold any longer, hoping Jemma was asleep. Quietly entering the cabin, he shut the door and turned around, gawking at her still form in the tub in front of the fire. All he could make out from his position by the door was her shoulders and the arm she had draped along the edge of the tub.

Then she awoke and stood.

The vision of Jemma rising from the tub, sleek and wet, embraced in the glow of the fire, danced through his mind, tempting and teasing him. The sight of what hid beneath all her proper clothes set his blood boiling at such a high heat, he thought he might combust.

If he went to her now, if he opened the bedroom door and stepped inside, he wouldn't be able to keep his hands to himself. He'd break his promise and her trust, and he couldn't do that no matter how much he wanted her.

Hurriedly grabbing two buckets from beneath the sink, he emptied the water from the tub outside. He had to breathe through his mouth to keep from inhaling the luscious scent of the soap.

Finished with the chore, he stood in front of the bedroom door with his hand lingering on the knob. Everything in him told him to open the door, take his wife in his arms, and confess the deep love he held for her.

Before he could make that move, Tully's words echoed in his head about crumpets and cowpies.

Convicted by the truth, he strode across the floor, opened the door, and went back out into the cold night.

Chapter Nineteen

"Have you seen Thane?" Jemma caught Sam as he walked out of the bunkhouse on the way to the barn.

"He stopped by real early this morning, had me rustle him up some grub. Said he was gonna ride out to check on the mines then spend a few days at one of the line shacks to make sure the cattle in the southwest section are doing fine." Sam patted the pocket of his coat and pulled out a folded sheet of paper. "He asked me to give you this. Almost forgot."

Sam handed her the missive and tipped his hat before continuing on to the barn.

Jemma stood in the middle of the ranch yard, staring at the paper in her hand, dreading what it would say. Fortified with a deep breath, she unfolded the sheet and read Thane's words.

Jemma,

My apologies for what happened last night. I assure you, it was not intentional.

It's past time for me to check on work at the mines. On my way back, I reckon I'll spend a few days at one of the line shacks before returning to the ranch. I'll be home for Thanksgiving.

After giving our arrangement consideration, I realize it's unfair to burden you with such a rough existence. Although I can't give up Jack and Lily completely, if you'd like to move into Baker City, I could visit them frequently and make sure you have a comfortable home in which to raise them. Of course, I would see to an annulment of our marriage so you would be free to find a husband much more to your liking.

Please tell Jack and Lily how much I love them and give them a hug from me.

With admiration,

Thane

"Oh, that stupid, stupid man!" Jemma wadded the paper into a ball and tossed it on the ground, giving it a vicious stomp before picking it back up and marching into the cabin. She slammed the door for good measure, cringing as she heard Lily cry out in startled surprise from her room.

Forgetting the children slept, she hurried to comfort Lily, hoping she'd go back to sleep.

When she did, Jemma tossed the note into the stove and took pleasure in watching it burn.

If Thane thought he could get rid of her that easily, he had much to learn about women in general and her in particular.

"Burden me with such a rough existence, my foot." Jemma worked the pump handle at the sink with such force, it squeaked and rattled in protest of the rude treatment.

After filling the teakettle, she placed it on the stovetop and stoked the fire.

She'd been horrified beyond words when she turned around last night and saw Thane watching her with a dazed look on his face. Frantically rushing to the bedroom, she dried off and slipped on her nightgown, expecting him to walk through the door and say something to make her blush even more.

The sounds of his footsteps and the front door opening and closing let her know he emptied the tub and carried it outside.

As she continued waiting for him to enter the room, her conversation with Maggie filled her thoughts.

Jemma was tired of skirting around her feelings for Thane.

She loved him, had fallen in love with him, and wanted him to be her husband in every sense of the word. Ready to take that step, she anxiously waited for him to walk in so she could tell him what was in her heart.

From the look on his face and the fire in his eyes in the brief moment her gaze met his before she hurried into the bedroom, she admitted Maggie spoke the truth. Thane cared for her, longed for her, too.

That's why she turned back the covers on the bed and removed the barrier she'd placed there with pillows and blankets. It was time to remove the wall that separated their bed as well as the one that kept him out of her heart.

When his footsteps approached the door, she held her breath in anticipation then let it out in a disappointed whoosh when the front door opened and all grew quiet.

Quickly opening the bedroom door, it was obvious by the empty room that Thane had gone.

Annoyed with herself and him, she climbed into bed and fumed until sleep eventually claimed her.

In hopes of waking to find him beside her, she opened her eyes that morning to discover he hadn't come to bed at all.

Angry, she hurried to dress and went outside to search for him. Ghost was missing from the barn so she knew Thane was gone even before Sam confirmed her suspicions.

If the numskull thought leaving her a ridiculous note was a proper way to say goodbye, she'd certainly educate him on the matter when he returned.

The whistle of teakettle caught Jemma's attention. She pulled it from the heat and made herself a bracing cup of tea then sat at the table, trying to decide what drove Thane away.

Since only he could answer the question, she forced herself to calm down as she sipped her tea. When he finally hauled himself home, she intended to ask him.

Until then, she had children to care for, holiday surprises to plan, and recipes to practice. Maggie assured her the upcoming Thanksgiving holiday was a celebration Americans took seriously. Even if it killed her, Jemma intended to master the basics of a traditional Thanksgiving dinner.

Jemma forced a smile to her face as she glanced first at Jack then Lily. The two of them played with their food, rather than ate it, and their gazes continued to drift to the door of the cabin, as though their wishes could make their uncle magically appear.

After laboring for days to prepare the elaborate meal on the table, Jemma hoped Thane would return from wherever it was he went to hide to enjoy Thanksgiving with her and the children.

As the day wound to an end, it became unmistakably clear her wishes and work at making the meal had been in vain.

That morning, she drove the buckboard into town so she and the children could attend the Thanksgiving service at church. Maggie invited them to spend the day with her, since she was cooking a meal for several people who had no other family, like Tully, but Jemma wanted to hurry back to the ranch in case Thane put in an appearance.

The afternoon sped by as she cooked. She hurried to change into one of her best dresses, styled her hair in a loose chignon, then dressed Lily and combed her hair while Jack changed into one of his suits.

Disheartened, she waited as long as she could before she made the children join her at the table for the meal. She'd cooked turkey with stuffing, baked yams smothered in butter, mashed potatoes to serve with creamy gravy. The meal also included green beans and corn, as well as fluffy yeast rolls with berry jam, and pumpkin pie for dessert. The feast, made for her absent husband, settled like a rock in her stomach.

Anger gnawed at her as she thought about him missing such an important day with the children.

It was one thing if he chose to ignore her, but he didn't seem to realize how much his absence hurt Jack and Lily. Since he left so unexpectedly, Jack reverted to his quiet, solemn ways and Lily constantly asked if he was dead like her papa.

Disappointment drew out her sigh. Sam told her Thane would probably be gone for at least two weeks by the time he rode to each of the mines then spent a few days on the range. They'd already passed that mark and neared three weeks.

No amount of encouragement from Sam or Maggie made her feel better about him leaving without even saying goodbye to her or the children. They deserved better than that. She deserved better than that.

Tired of poking at her food, she finally gave up and set her fork on the edge of her plate. "You two may be excused if you're finished with your meal."

Jack nodded and carried his plate to the sink, scraping his uneaten supper into a bucket. Lily did the same before shuffling across the floor and climbing into the rocking chair by the fire. As she set it into motion, the child hummed a song to herself, one Thane had sat in that very spot and sang to her many times.

With her heart aching for the children, Jemma determined she'd give Thane Jordan a piece of her mind when he came home. She might even forget she was a lady and pop him in the nose, although it would be a pity to break one quite so handsome.

Furious with herself for the direction her thoughts headed, she pulled on a wide apron to keep from soiling her dress and stored the leftover food in the icebox Thane purchased on his last trip to town. As she washed and dried the dishes, she kept an eye on the children. Both stared listlessly into the fire and she didn't know what to do to bring them a bit of cheer.

After wiping off the table and blowing out the candles she'd lit, she returned her grandmother's crystal candlesticks to the mantle above the fireplace, removed her apron, and fetched her coat.

"Come along, children," she said, motioning for them to join her at the door.

"Where are we going, Auntie Jemma?" Jack asked as he and Lily walked over to where she waited. She handed him his coat then helped Lily slip into hers. When they both had their coats buttoned with knit caps and mittens in place, she lit a lantern, wrapped a scarf around her head and neck, then slid on a pair of warm gloves.

Lifting the lantern in one hand, she opened the door then took Lily's hand in the other.

"I think some fresh air would do us all a world of good."

"But it's dark out and cold," Jack said, pointing out the obvious as he closed the door behind him.

"I know, but let's think of this as an adventure." Jemma smiled brightly, walking down the porch steps and across the ranch yard toward the trail that went past the bunkhouse and out toward the north pasture. Rigsly, Salt, and Pepper followed along, chasing each other and barking at the fun they created.

The snow that fell earlier in the week crunched beneath their boots as she led the children on a walk, pointing out the shapes of rocks and brush in the shadows of the evening. The moon did little to provide light, so they depended on the lantern to illuminate the darkness.

Not wanting to get too far away from the ranch yard or help, should they need it, Jemma realized she forgot to bring a pistol with her. Although the snakes were no threat in the cold temperatures, there were still concerns of coyotes and the occasional cougar in the area.

One of the ranchers several miles to the north related a tale after church one Sunday of killing a bear on his property. Thane assured her the man's ranch was in the mountains and bears preferred that area to the scrubby sagebrush of his place.

The coyotes howled in the distance and Jemma stopped, listening to their cries. Accustomed to their racket, she bent down, grinning at Lily and Jack. "Can you hear the coyotes tonight? What do you suppose they're singing? A love song? Telling a story?"

"A story," Lily said, regaining a little of her enthusiasm. "It's a story about a papa who gets lost and forgets to come home and his babies are very, very sad."

Jemma lifted her eyes heavenward, sending up a prayer for Thane and for the children they both loved. She handed Jack the lantern and picked up Lily, kissing her cool cheek and giving her a warm hug.

"I think that's enough adventure for tonight. Let's go home."

Although she tucked Lily into bed when they returned, Jemma waited a while to check on Jack. He sat in his bed with a book open on his lap, but he wasn't reading. His brow furrowed in twin vertical lines, looking so like his uncle when something concerned him. It made her heart catch to see him.

"Auntie Jemma?"

She sat on the edge of his bed and ran a gentle hand along his forehead, pushing his bangs away from his face. "Yes, lovey?"

"Is Uncle Thane ever coming back?"

"Yes, Jack. He'll come home soon, I'm sure. Sam said his mines are spread all over the valley and it takes time to ride to each one."

"I know, but I miss him being here. If Uncle Thane isn't here, I want to go home."

"Oh, sweetheart." Jemma pulled Jack into her embrace and kissed the top of his head. "I miss your uncle and wish he'd come home very soon. Until he does, though, I think we should make some plans for Christmas. Tomorrow, let's make a list of all the fun things you'd like to do, decorations we can make, and treats you'd like to have. How does that sound?"

"Good." Jack gave her a smile, but it was more for her benefit than because he held any excitement for the upcoming holiday season.

"Get some rest, Jack. Don't worry about your uncle. He can take care of himself."

"I love you, Auntie Jemma." The boy hugged her again then snuggled into his pillow.

Jemma pulled the covers up around him, kissing his cheek. "I love you, my darling boy. Now, go to sleep."

A few more days passed with no sight of Thane. Sick with worry, Jemma took her concerns to Sam.

"I'm getting a might unsettled myself. I'll send a couple of the boys out to check the line shacks. If they don't find him there, I'll have them ride on out to the mines. If the boss says he'll be back at a certain time, he's usually here or sends word he'll be late. It ain't like him to disappear, and it sure ain't like him to miss Thanksgiving, especially with you and the youngin's here."

"Thank you, Sam. Please let me know when you hear anything."

Sam tipped his hat to her and smiled reassuringly. "I will, ma'am. Don't you worry about a thing."

Chapter Twenty

Thane turned up his coat collar, hoping the sheepskin would block some of the wind trying to blow icy snow down his neck. If he hadn't left the ranch like a whipped dog, sneaking off in the early morning hours so he wouldn't have to face Jemma, he would have packed warmer clothes and made sure he'd grabbed a scarf.

He only had a few more miles to go to reach the last of his four mines. He'd checked in at the silver mine, and two of the gold mines, finding everything in good order, although it had taken a week longer than he planned to go over all the books and inspect each mine.

Tired and cold, he planned to speak with the foreman at the last mine, review the ledgers, and make sure they had all the supplies they needed before he left. He'd still check the fences on his way back to the ranch, but he missed home. He missed Jack dogging his every step as well as Lily's giggling and singing silly songs. He especially missed their beguiling aunt.

Every time Thane closed his eyes, he pictured Jemma rising out of the tub in the firelight. Heat speared through him.

It was wrong to think such lustful thoughts of a woman he'd just offered to give an annulment, but the last thing he wanted was for her to move to town and take the children.

Afraid to tell her the truth, tell her how much she'd come to mean to him, he fully expected her to toss his feelings back in his face.

Although, as he recalled the few kisses they shared, she'd eagerly returned his passion and hunger. Maybe she wouldn't be completely opposed to being his wife in every sense of the word.

However, if she stayed at the ranch and became his true wife, she'd sentence herself to a life of hard work. There'd be snakes and dust to contend with in the summer, freezing temperatures and months of snow in the winter, and critters of all sorts throughout the year.

Granted, she appeared to be settling in and adjusting to life on the ranch, he just didn't want her to feel like she had an obligation to stay. He wouldn't mind at all, though, if she chose to make it her permanent home, especially if she would release him from his promise and let him love her like he dreamed of doing.

As his thoughts warred between holding Jemma tight or letting her go, an unearthly boom shook the ground beneath him. Thane lifted his gaze as a great puff rose into the wintery sky.

Only a mile from his mine, he had a bad feeling it came from there. Uncertain if the dark cloud was smoke or dust, he kicked Ghost into a gallop and raced toward the mine.

After leaving the horse at the bottom of the hill, away from the mine, Thane scrambled up toward the opening when another boom shook the earth and the sound of timbers cracking echoed above him.

Shielding his head with his arm from the rocks and debris that blew out the mine opening, Thane hurried forward.

When he reached the mine entrance, he impatiently waited for his eyes to adjust to the darkness. In the inky blackness, he felt along the wall inside the entry until his hand connected with a box and he lifted a candle. Hurriedly striking a match, he hoped it didn't set off an explosion of escaped gas. He glanced into the tunnel and noticed two men amid the rocks and chunks of wood that had been support beams before the explosion. Rock and broken timbers filled the tunnel behind them.

Recognizing one of the men as a miner who'd worked for him for several years, Thane established he was unconscious, not dead. The way the man's leg bent awkwardly to the side, it had to be broken. He also had several gashes on his face. Until he got the blood cleaned away, Thane wouldn't be able to assess the damage.

The other miner, a young man barely old enough to shave, groaned and opened his eyes. He started to stand, but Thane put a restraining hand on his shoulder, holding him down.

"It's okay, son. Just take a minute to get your bearings. What's your name?"

The young man blinked and coughed before speaking. "Dale Darcey."

"Well, Dale Darcey, I'm Mr. Jordan. I own this mine. Where's the rest of the crew?"

"In the hole, sir. John and I were pushing a cart of ore out when Mr. Gaffney started yelling for us to run for the opening. John and I made it this far before it caved in."

"How many others are with Mr. Gaffney?" Thane hoped his foreman and the other men were fine. He hated cave-ins, hated the thought of the mine taking the life of one of his men.

"There's three others, sir."

Thane nodded his head and reached down a hand to Dale. "Can you stand? Do you hurt anywhere?"

The young man got to his feet. He worked his arms and legs, twisted his neck, and decided other than bumps and bruises, he was uninjured. "I'm right as rain."

"Help me get John to the cabin. I've got something I need you to do."

Carefully moving the injured man to the cabin where the workers bunked, they removed his filthy, torn clothing and settled him on his bed. Thane put water on to boil and asked Dale to stay with John while he returned to the mine.

Lighting two lanterns, he carried them inside the mine to where the cave-in sealed the tunnel. The pile of rock and debris wouldn't be easy to move, especially with huge timbers in the way. It would take more muscle than just he and Dale to move the solid beams.

"Gaffney? Can you hear me? It's Thane."

He listened and thought he heard something. Encouraged, he pushed and shoved some of the smaller rocks. The pile shifted slightly and he jumped back, waiting to see if anything else happened. When it didn't, he continued moving rocks until he made a small hole. Even by holding the lantern up to the spot, it was impossible to make out anything in the penetrating darkness.

"Gaffney? Are you there?"

"Thane? Is that you?" The response of a weak voice made Thane release a sigh of relief.

"It's me. Are you hurt? Are the others okay?"

"We're all alive, thank the good Lord. I don't think any of us have anything broken. How about Dale and John?"

Thane tried to peer into the hole he made, but couldn't glimpse anything beyond swirling darkness. "Dale's fine. John needs some tending. If you're okay, I'm gonna take care of him. Do you have enough air? Can you sit tight for a while?"

"Yeah, we're okay. Can you leave a lantern by the hole? It helps to have a little light shining down here."

"Sure, Gaff. I'll be back as soon as I can."

Thane set the lantern on a shelf of rocks by the hole he'd made and hurried out of the tunnel. Quickly returning to the cabin, he found a piece of paper and wrote a hasty note then scribbled out a list of supplies.

"Dale, I want you to take this letter to Sheriff Barrett, pick up these supplies, and tell Milt at the livery I said to give you a team and wagon. If he has questions, have him talk to the sheriff. Then you hustle back here as fast as you can. Do you understand?"

"Yes, sir." Dale pulled on his coat and wrapped a scarf around his neck. Thane handed him the pieces of paper along with a handful of money to cover the expenses.

"Remember, hurry back, son. The lives of those men in the mine depend on it."

Dale nodded his head and raced out the door. Thane heard the sound of horses' hooves beating against the frozen ground as Dale rode toward town.

Grateful he'd thought to put water on to heat, Thane filled a pan with warm water from the stove and sponged John's face followed by his arms and torso. He had a few cuts and bruising, but nothing that looked to be particularly damaging. John groaned when Thane touched his side and added cracked ribs to the list of injuries.

Intently studying the man's broken leg, Thane knew it needed to be set before they could move him to town. He wasn't a doctor, but he'd set plenty of broken bones, including a few of his own.

A search through the cabin turned up the necessary supplies. He prayed John would remain unconscious as he pulled the bone back into place. Once it slid into alignment, he secured two sturdy sticks around the break and wrapped it tightly. He dribbled water into John's mouth, then covered him with a thick blanket.

After stoking the fire in both the stove and fireplace, Thane filled jars with water, found a tin of crackers, and loaded a box with supplies before returning to the mine.

Determined to make the hole at least big enough to get some supplies to the men, Thane knew he wouldn't be able to get them out until Dale returned with the supplies and some help.

With the pile of rocks and timbers covering the tunnel, the easiest way to clear it would be with a blast. Nonetheless, the safety of those trapped inside ensured blasting wasn't a viable option.

Instead, they'd have to shore up the weakened tunnel then dig out the men using pry bars and muscle.

Carefully setting down the box of supplies he carried, Thane worked at moving some of the smaller rocks until he had a hole big enough to stick his hand through.

"Gaffney? Can you see my hand?"

"Yep." Gaffney grabbed Thane's wrist and gave it a shake.

Relieved, Thane released his breath. "Good. I'm going to get some supplies in to you, starting with some candles."

Slowly, Thane passed a handful of candles and a few holders, the crackers, jars of water, and a box of matches through the hole.

Gaffney lit the candles and set them around. Thane put his face to the hole and peered inside. The men looked tired and bruised, but not injured. Thankful for that, he tried to determine how far back they could move, but couldn't tell in the dim light.

"Can you get very far back in the tunnel?"

"About forty feet, so we've got a little wiggle room," Gaffney said, then took a drink from one of the jars.

"At least this far into the mine, it's somewhat insulated."

Gaffney snorted. "Always looking on the bright side, aren't you boss."

"It could have been so much worse, Gaff. I'm glad you're all alive."

"I know, Thane. Me, too. How long do you think it will be before you can get us out of here?"

"I sent Dale to town to bring back supplies and help. We're going to have to shore up the tunnel before we can try to dig you out. If I move to many more rocks, it might bring the whole thing down on you."

"I reckon we can sit tight for a while. Do you think you can get some blankets stuffed through the hole so we can sleep tonight? I doubt Dale will get to town and back before sometime tomorrow."

Thane nodded his head, although he doubted Gaffney could see him. "That's what I thought, too. I'll bring some blankets back with me in a little while. I'm going to check on John again. If you hand me back those empty jars of water, I'll fill them up."

Gaffney passed him the jars and Thane set them back in the box, promising to return soon with more supplies.

He spent the next several hours going between the cabin and the mine, caring for John and his men trapped beyond the rock and timber wall.

"Boss, you better get some rest. We'll be fine for the night. It's not like anything can get to us and you'll know if the mine collapses again. See to John and get yourself some shut-eye."

Thane pressed his face to the hole and glared at Gaffney. "Who's in charge around here?"

"Me. You made me the foreman for a reason. Now get out of here."

Thane chuckled as he turned and walked out of the mine, praying for the safety of his men through the night.

As he sponged off John's feverish brow, Thane worried the man suffered from an internal injury. He'd awakened a few times and groaned in pain before falling back asleep. Thane had no idea what to do to help him, other than to try and make him comfortable and keep pouring water down him.

Aware that he needed rest if he planned to continue caring for his men, Thane flopped down on one of the beds and closed his eyes.

"I hate to say it, Gaff, but I don't think Dale is coming back." Thane stood outside the hole in the tunnel and looked at his foreman in the light from the lantern he held in his hand. "It's been four days since I sent him to town and he should have been back long before now."

"He probably took the money you gave him and ran. He's young and stupid. I wouldn't put it past him."

"He either better be dead or prepared to become that way if I ever lay eyes on him again."

Thane's words made Gaffney chuckle.

"He's probably halfway to California by now. If I was going to steal money from my boss, I'd at least head someplace warm to hide out."

"California sounds pretty good right now," Thane said, not pleased by the amount of snow that had fallen the last few days. It was going to make it harder to ride for help. "John needs to see the doctor and I need to get you all out of here, but I hate the thought of leaving long enough to ride into town. I'll wait until noon and if Dale hasn't showed by then, I'll ride out for the ranch and send someone to town to get what we need. I'm so sorry to leave you boys in there for so long. If Dale had done what I asked, you'd be curled up by a warm fire with a hot drink in your hands, spinning tales about all this."

"Did you have to go and mention a warm fire and hot drink?" Gaffney glared through the hole at Thane. "As much as we appreciate your efforts to bring us hot coffee, the pot's half-frozen by the time you get it here from the cabin."

"I know, but I don't want to chance building a fire here in the tunnel. I'm truly sorry, Gaff."

"It ain't your fault, boss. You're doing the best you can. If you decide you need to ride out, the boys and I might just see if we can move some of these rocks regardless of the consequences. We can't take too many more days down in this dark hole."

Thane nodded his head and turned away, leaving the lantern burning outside the hole to provide added light in the men's unending darkness.

Stamping the snow from his boots, he entered the cabin and checked on John. His fever wasn't better or worse, at least that Thane could tell. He spent most of his time sleeping and the few times he did awaken, he muttered nonsense.

Thane put together a pot of stew with canned beef and vegetables. The smell of it filled the cabin with a savory aroma that made him look forward to eating a bowl. As soon as he fed the men in the mine, he'd saddle Ghost and ride to the ranch.

Gone more than a week longer than he planned, he hoped Jemma missed him, at least a little. Thoughts of seeing her again, breathing in her alluring fragrance, holding her in his arms, made even his cold toes warm as he whipped up a batch of biscuits and placed them in the oven.

Movement outside the window caught his attention as he filled extra jars with water and made another pot of coffee. He checked the gun holster on his hip then grabbed his coat and rushed outside. Unable to believe his eyes, he grinned as Ben and Walt dismounted from their horses and hurried his direction.

"Man alive, boss. You've got half the county in a fuzz trying to find you," Ben said, grasping his hand and giving it a hearty shake. "I'm pert near teary-eyed to see you alive."

"You two are a sight for sore eyes. What are you doing here?" Thane asked as they tied their mounts to the hitching post outside the cabin.

"Your wife must miss you something awful. Miz Jordan asked Sam if he could send someone to find you, since you missed Thanksgiving and all. According to Jack, she put out quite a feast with turkey and all the trimmings. He said she even made pumpkin pie. Course we had our own dinner at the bunkhouse."

Thane's mouth watered thinking of the meal he missed, as well as his delectable wife missing him.

"Anyhow, Sam decided you'd been gone longer than he expected so he asked us to ride out to all the line shacks to see if you were holed up in one. When we didn't find you at any of the line shacks on the ranch, Sam asked us to check each of the mines. This was the last on our list. Guess we shoulda started here first, but since it's the furthest ride, we kinda hoped to catch up to you sooner."

"I'm powerful glad you boys made it. I've got four men trapped in the mine and an injured miner in need of a doctor. I sent the one idiot on the payroll to town for help and I think he skipped out with the money I gave him to buy supplies."

"What can we do, boss?" Walt asked, following Ben into the cabin. The two cowboys made note of the injured man on the bed, giving each other a concerned glance.

"Warm up and get some food in your bellies. I'll take this stew up to the men and be back in a few minutes. Walt, I'd like you to ride into town and get Tully to round up some help along with the supplies I need."

Walt nodded his head as he took the bowl of stew Thane held out to him.

"Ben, I'd appreciate it if you'd ride back to the ranch and let them know I'm okay. Maybe bring a wagon back with some blankets and padding so we can get John into town to Doc. I hate to move him, but he can't stay here."

"Sure, thing, boss. Soon as my toes no longer feel like they'll chip off in my boots, I'll hightail it for home." Ben grinned at Thane as he sat down at the table with his bowl of stew and two hot biscuits.

Thane hurried out to the mine, letting the men know two of his hired hands arrived and they'd have help soon.

"Thanks, Thane," Gaffney said, sticking his hand through the hole to shake his hand. "We'll be fine a while longer, now that we know help is coming."

"I'm sorry it took so long. I should have left Dale here and gone myself."

"Who's to say that ignoramus wouldn't have stolen what money and gold is here and left us all to die." Gaffney gave him a pointed glare. "No, you did what was best."

"Glad you think so, Gaff. Just hang in there a little while longer."

Thane returned to the cabin, glad to see Ben and Walt ready to ride. He gave Walt a list of supplies and sent him on his way. Relieved the ordeal was nearly over, he sat at the table and wrote a note to Jemma then one to Sam, handing them both to Ben.

"Be careful out there and tell my wife I apologize for being gone so long."

"She'll understand, boss. If it were me with such a pretty filly at home, I wouldn't have wandered off in the first place. Isn't that what you've got all of us for?"

Thane slapped Ben on the back then watched as the dependable young man got on his horse and rode away.

Late the following morning, the sound of jingling harnesses greeted Thane like a welcome chorus.

He grabbed his coat and rushed out of the cabin to greet Tully and Walt as they approached with two wagons of supplies. Ben and a few of the ranch hands followed with another wagon full of blankets and food.

"With all this help, we'll have the men out of there in no time," Thane said, thumping Tully on the back after he jumped down from the wagon.

His friend gave him a broad smile. "Way I hear it, there's a lonely woman back at the ranch who can't wait for your return, or so the story goes."

"Let's get John in the wagon and headed to town to the doctor before we do anything else." Thane's hired hands packed the food inside the cabin then hurried to the mine to begin the hard work of freeing the trapped men. Thane and Tully carried the injured man out and settled him in the nest of blankets Jemma had no doubt sent. Ben drank a cup of hot coffee before climbing back on the wagon seat to take John into town.

Thane glanced up at him as he gathered the reins in his hands. "Did you give my wife the note I sent?"

"Sure did, boss."

"Did she read it? Say anything?"

Ben grinned. "I believe her exact words were, 'That infuriating lunkhead! Just wait until he gets home! I'll show him a thing or two...' Then she shoved the note in her apron pocket and stormed off toward the house. Don't know what you wrote, boss, but it sure made her face turn red."

"Good. If you beat me home, tell her I intend to do exactly what I said in the letter."

Ben chuckled as he released the brake and clucked to the horses. "Will do, boss, but if you head straight home, you'll most likely get there before I do."

"We'll see. Thanks for your help, Ben, and be careful out there."

Thane rushed to help the men unload the timbers and long metal rods they'd use to hold the beams in place and move the heavy rocks.

Within two hours, the men who had spent almost five days trapped in the dark mine tunnel sat in the cabin in front of a roaring fire, drinking their fill of hot coffee.

Assured his men were fine, Thane thanked everyone for their help and watched as the wagons headed back to town.

Anxious to return to the ranch and his family, Thane gathered his few belongings and rushed out the door. If he rode hard, he could make it home by the time dark settled for the night.

He ignored the cold biting at his exposed cheeks and turning his fingers into ice inside his gloves. Instead, he focused his thoughts on seeing Lily, Jack, and Jemma.

A grin lifted the corners of his mouth as he thought about Jemma's reaction to his letter. He looked forward to discovering just what she had in mind to show him. Maybe it was wishful thinking on his part, but he certainly hoped it involved several welcoming kisses that led to something more.

Chapter Twenty-One

Jemma sighed with relief when Ben rode in after dark, half-frozen and exhausted, explaining there had been a collapse at Thane's mine and he needed help.

She spent hours helping Sam prepare food to send in the wagon as well as gathering blankets and other needed supplies.

Before he climbed onto the wagon seat to head back to the mine in the pre-dawn hours the following morning, Ben patted his pocket and pulled out a piece of paper in an envelope, handing it to Jemma.

"Thane asked me to give that to you. I plumb forgot about it last night." Ben watched as she scanned Thane's note.

Uncertain whether to laugh or cry at the message written in her husband's bold hand, she read it a second time.

My Darling Wife,

Rather than your leathery steak and burned biscuits, I heard you made quite a feast for Thanksgiving. I'm sorry to have missed it.

Would you make me a pumpkin pie? I'd share a bite or two with you. Maybe even three.

I'm definitely willing to share that big ol' bed in our room. It's been absolute misery trying to sleep without your snores ringing in my ears at night, although I'm purely tired of your pillow barricade. Do you think you might be willing to tear it down and toss it aside?

If you aren't so inclined to remove the wall between us and share yourself along with the bed, I'll take you and the kids into town and set you up in a house as soon as I return. The choice is yours.

Your devoted husband,
Thane

"That infuriating lunkhead! Just wait until he gets home! I'll show him a thing or two…" She marched to the cabin with Ben's chuckles following her across the ranch yard.

Angry, yet oddly energized by Thane's note, she looked forward to his return.

Early that afternoon, she put a roast in the oven then baked two pumpkin pies.

While Lily napped and Jack stayed with Sam at the bunkhouse, Jemma took a bath and changed into one of her best dresses then carefully styled her hair.

In need of something to calm her nerves, she made herself a comforting cup of tea, glancing out the window as Maggie rode into the ranch yard. Jemma hurried to the door and motioned her friend inside while one of the hands took the horse to the barn.

"What are you doing out on a cold day like this?" Jemma asked as Maggie breezed inside, carrying a basket on her arm.

"Tully told me he heard from Thane. He's taking some men and supplies up to the mine to help. I just wanted to make sure you knew he was fine and see how you're holding up."

"I'm well and I appreciate your thoughtfulness." Jemma took the basket Maggie held out to her and lifted the cloth covering.

"Those are muffins I made this morning with some huckleberry preserves. I think you and the children will enjoy them. I like them for breakfast, warmed with butter."

"They smell delicious." Jemma poured a cup of tea for Maggie and led the way to the sofa by the fire.

Maggie sat in the chair closest to the crackling flames and stretched out her feet, absorbing the warmth. "My, but that feels good. I didn't realize how chilly it was until I was halfway here."

"I'm glad you came, but I hate for you to have to ride back in that cold."

"I'll be fine. Are you excited for Thane to come home?" Maggie sipped her tea and studied her friend.

"Yes... No... I'm not sure." Jemma blushed and set down her teacup. "If he walked through that door right now, I'm not sure if I'd kiss him first or take him to task for disappearing like he did."

Maggie laughed. "Kiss him first. There's always time to argue later, but don't ever miss the opportunity for kisses. Love him all you can while you can. You'll never look back and wish you'd had more harsh words instead of kisses."

"Oh, Maggie, this must be terribly trying for you." Jemma leaned forward and placed a hand on her friend's arm. "I hope it doesn't bring difficult memories to mind."

"I'd be lying if I said it didn't, but it helps knowing everyone will be fine. My poor Daniel died in a gas explosion, along with two other men. Thane would have, too, if he hadn't been the one who pushed out a cart of ore." Maggie dabbed at her eyes with a handkerchief she pulled from her pocket. "Tears won't bring him back or change anything, though. Now, have you decided how you're going to woo your husband?"

Jemma's cheeks felt hot with embarrassment as she glanced at Maggie. When the woman wiggled her eyebrows at her, Jemma giggled.

"I'm beginning to think he might be more interested in forgetting about his ridiculous vow than I first anticipated."

"What makes you say that?"

Quickly removing Thane's note from her pocket, Jemma gave it to Maggie. "This."

Maggie read the note, wearing a big smile as she handed it back to Jemma. "I think that should clear up any questions you might have. Did you bake him a pie?"

"Two." Jemma looked at Maggie and they burst into giggles.

As the afternoon progressed, Jemma became more distracted, continuing to glance out the window as she walked from the sofa to the kitchen table and back again.

"You'll wear a hole in the rug with your pacing, and it's much too lovely for that." Maggie smiled at Jemma over the cup of tea she held in front of her mouth.

Jemma walked to the kitchen window to stare outside again then glanced over her shoulder at her friend, wondering if Thane would ever come home. "I know, but I can't seem to help myself."

She felt Maggie's hand on her shoulder and welcomed the woman's comforting embrace.

"He'll be home before you know it, but I better head back to town before dark."

"I'm so glad you came today, Maggie. Thank you for keeping me company." Jemma held Maggie's coat for her while she slipped it on. "I'll return the favor one of these days."

Maggie grinned at her as she wrapped a scarf around her head and tugged on her gloves. "I doubt it will be anytime soon. As soon as Thane gets home, he won't be willing to let you out of his sight for a good while to come."

Lily wandered out of her room before Maggie opened the door to leave, so she spent a moment visiting with the little girl. Jemma hurried to the barn to have one of the hands bring Maggie's horse to the end of the walk then rushed back inside the warmth of the cabin.

"It is so cold out there, Maggie. Are you sure you don't want to stay the night? You could have Jack's room and he could stay in the bunkhouse for tonight." Jemma hated to think of Maggie traveling alone on the trail to town, especially in the cold.

"I'll be fine. I've got on plenty of layers to keep me warm and it doesn't take nearly as long to get there on horseback as it does in the buckboard."

Jemma hugged her friend and walked her outside. "Be careful and we'll see you at church Sunday."

Maggie mounted her horse and turned to grin at Jemma. "Make sure you give Thane a welcome home he won't soon forget!" Amused by Jemma's flushed cheeks, Maggie turned her horse toward the trail and waved one last time.

After stepping inside the cabin and shutting out the winter air, Jemma combed Lily's hair and helped the little girl into one of her favorite dresses. She draped one of her mother's linen tablecloths over the table, set out her best china, and tried to steady her nerves.

Preoccupied, she listened to Lily sing a silly made-up song as she rocked her doll in the chair by the fire. Jemma glanced down from her vigil at the window when Lily yanked on her skirt.

"I'm hungry, Auntie Jemma. Can we eat soon?"

"Yes, poppet. We'll eat soon." Jemma lifted the child in her arms and kissed her pert little nose. "We're going to have a wonderful dinner, aren't we?"

"I hope so. My tummy's talking to me." Lily glanced down at her stomach.

Jemma smiled and playfully poked Lily's tummy. "What is it saying?"

"Feed me! Feed me!"

Laughing, Jemma swung Lily around in her arms and stopped mid-swing when Jack burst into the room, eyes glowing with happiness.

"He's back, Auntie Jemma! Uncle Thane's back! He said to tell you he'll be in soon." Jack yanked on her hand in his excitement.

"Uncle Thane!" Lily squealed, wanting down so she could run out to see him.

"No, lovey, you stay in the house with me. Jack, you may go back out to the barn and come in with your uncle."

"Thank you, Auntie Jemma!" Jack turned and ran out the door, forgetting to close it behind him. Jemma shut it then set Lily down. The little girl's lip protruded in a pout as she scuffed her toes across the floor to her chair at the table.

"Are you excited Uncle Thane is home, Lily?"

The little girl nodded her head.

"You don't want to greet him with a pout, do you?"

Another nod.

"I'm sure Uncle Thane would appreciate a big smile and a hug or two. Do you suppose he'd like to hear one of your new songs? Can you sing one for him?"

Lily's eyes brightened as she bounced up and down on her toes. "Yep!"

"Wonderful! Why don't you practice the one about the princess?" Jemma grinned as the little girl began flitting around the room singing about a beautiful princess and a magic pony.

Jemma stood at the stove stirring a pan of gravy when cold air blew behind her from the open cabin door. Spurs jingled as Thane stepped inside with Jack. Lily screamed and ran across the room, flinging herself into her uncle's arms.

He lifted her up, tossing her in the air twice, before cuddling her close and kissing her cheeks and forehead.

"How's my Lily? You just get prettier every time I see you, honey. Did you miss your ol' uncle?"

"Yes, Uncle Thane. I missed you whole bunches." Lily squeezed his neck and pressed her little cheek against his, making a lump catch in his throat.

He couldn't and wouldn't leave them again for an extended period. He missed both the children more than he would have dreamed possible.

Nearly as much as he missed Jemma.

While Lily wiggled in his arms, telling him all about the things she'd done that day, his gaze lingered on his wife.

Thane stared at Jemma, taking in the sight of her from the rich, auburn hair pulled into a neat chignon and the fire radiating from her coppery eyes to the deep blue of her gown and the cameo pinned at her throat.

"You seem well," he finally said, unable to stop gawking at her. Although he'd been gone less than a month, he'd nearly forgotten the breath-stealing beauty of his wife.

"Thank you." Jemma tipped her head demurely, but not before she gave Thane a thorough once-over. Flakes of snow covered his hat, his hair brushed the top of his coat collar, and a scruffy beard covered his cheeks and firm jaw.

At that moment, she didn't care if his beard reached his knees and housed a flock of pigeons. She was grateful to have him home, where he belonged.

"I'm glad you've returned. Is all well at the mine?" She wanted to diffuse the tension that flowed between them, threatening to pull her into the current and drag her under.

"It is now. Thank you for the food and blankets you sent with Ben." Thane kissed Lily's cheek again and set her in her chair before removing his outerwear.

While Jemma dished up their supper, he stood beside her, washing his hands and breathing deeply of her fragrance. He'd missed it nearly as much as the sight of her. The handkerchief he'd pilfered had lost much of her scent, although he continued to carry it in his pocket as a reminder of what awaited him at home.

As he dried his hands on a dishtowel, he noticed two pumpkin pies sitting on the counter. Quickly tossing aside the towel, he leaned around Jemma and blocked her in at the stove. "I see you made pies. Is one of them for me?"

Engulfed by Thane's warm presence, Jemma could barely think much less form a response. She'd missed this so much — his teasing, the way he managed to press close to her while pretending innocence, the fiery longing in his eyes.

Ensnared by those two glowing orbs as she gazed over her shoulder at him, he lowered his face closer to hers.

Numbly nodding her head, she hurriedly spooned green beans into a bowl and handed it to Thane, needing some space between her and his strong body. Before he stepped away from her, she felt his breath blow across her ear.

"Did you miss me? Even a little?"

"Yes, Thane. I did." Her voice sounded breathy and strange to her own ears.

He grinned and set the bowl on the table. If the pies and the look in Jemma's eyes were any indication, he might not have to work as hard as he thought to get her to remove the barrier from the middle of their bed and release him from his promise.

"I'm so hungry I think I could eat just about anything, even some of your burned biscuits." Thane smirked at Jemma as she set a platter of meat on the table then turned to lift a basket full of hot biscuits.

As she set it on the table, she raised her eyebrow at him, challenging him to offer more insults about her cooking.

"Did you make them yourself?" Thane eyed the biscuits, his mouth watering as he thought of eating a fluffy biscuit slathered with butter.

"I did. I believe you will find them to your liking." Jemma sat in the chair Thane held out for her and draped a napkin across her lap. She glanced at him, waiting for him to offer thanks for the meal, smiling when his deep voice filled the cabin.

While she placed food on Lily's plate and cut the little girl's meat, Thane told them about some of the interesting things he saw while he was visiting the mines. Jack asked several questions about the mining process and Thane promised to take him to see one of the mines when the weather warmed.

He drew the children into a lively conversation about the approaching holidays. Mindful of Jemma's eyes on him, he lifted his gaze to hers and sent her a flirtatious wink that left her flustered yet anxious for the children to be in bed.

"Would you care for a slice of pie now?" Jemma asked as Thane leaned back in his chair and rubbed his flat but full belly.

"No thanks. But I plan to sample one later. You outdid yourself, Jemma. That was a fine, fine meal and the biscuits were as good as any I've eaten. You've been practicing." Thane's smile held admiration and a touch of softness when he glanced her way.

"Thank you." She hurried to carry dirty dishes to the sink so Thane couldn't see how much his words pleased her.

"I'm tired of biscuits. Auntie Jemma's baked them every day for weeks and weeks, trying to get them just right." Jack tattled on his aunt. She gave him a reproving stare he either didn't notice or ignored. "I hope she got them right so we can eat something else now."

Thane chuckled and reached out to ruffle Jack's hair. "She got them just right, son. Maybe she'll make some Yorkshire pudding tomorrow or a few crumpets. I wouldn't mind some myself."

"You wouldn't?" Jemma asked as she continued clearing the table. She slipped a voluminous apron over her head to keep from ruining her dress and began washing dishes.

"I've grown to like some of your strange English concoctions and ways, wife. Some, I even missed."

"Did you miss me, Uncle Thane?" Lily climbed onto his lap and placed her small hands on his cheeks, then pulled his head around until he looked directly at her.

"Yes, honey. I missed you and your brother very much." Thane held her close and kissed the top of her head when she settled down against him.

"Did you miss Auntie Jemma, too?" Jack gave Thane a hopeful glance. "She missed you, didn't you, auntie?"

Annoyed the boy put her on the spot, Jemma turned to look over her shoulder with a smile. "I did miss your uncle, Jack. It was lonesome without my sparring partner constantly bandying about insults and barbs."

Jemma's impish grin made Thane smile in return. "I'll try to make up for lost time."

He rose to his feet and carried Lily over to her favorite chair by the fire. With a contented sigh, he sank into the comfortable rocker. He shifted Lily over and motioned for Jack to join his sister on his lap.

The boy hesitated only a moment before he leaned against Thane's broad chest, happy to share in his uncle's attention.

When Thane's chin brushed against Lily's face, she scrubbed a fist at her cheek and glared at him. "You're scratchy and itchy, Uncle Thane. I like your face better smooth. And you're stinky." Lily crinkled up her little nose.

"Lillian Jane!" Jemma admonished the child. "It is not acceptable for you to speak to your uncle, or anyone in such a manner. You know it is impolite to tell someone they are stinky, even if they smell as though they've wallowed in a pile of filth and the wiry growth on their face could be used as a scrub brush."

Thane took Jemma's comments as agreement that he needed a bath and shave. If it hadn't been so cold outside, he would have stopped by the river and bathed before he returned home, but the notion of jumping into the freezing water held no appeal.

"I promise I'll smell better tomorrow, Lily, and my cheeks will be much smoother."

"Okay." Lily jumped off his lap and ran off to her room to retrieve a book she wanted him to read. He read and rocked her until her eyes could no longer stay open and Jack fought to keep awake as well.

Jemma smiled at the children. "Jack, you get ready for bed while I help Lily, then we'll tuck you both in."

She bent down and lifted Lily, kissing her forehead. "Come along, poppet. It's time for bed."

Lily mumbled something about Thane helping her. Jemma rolled her eyes at him. "I'll pop her into her nightdress and you can tuck her in."

Thane nodded his head, watching Jemma tenderly carry their niece across the room. He'd missed observing her graceful moments, hearing the melodic lilt to her voice, resting in the comfort of her presence.

He'd closed his eyes for just a moment or two when he felt something bump against his leg and glanced down at Lily's upturned face.

"Tuck me in, Uncle Thane. Please?"

Thane picked her up in his arms and carried her to her bed. Carefully tucking the covers around her, he kissed her cheek and promised to be there to have breakfast with her in the morning.

"Sleep well, honey. I love you."

"Love you, Uncle Thane. Don't be deaded anymore."

Thane shot Jemma an inquisitive look, but she shook her head, indicating she'd explain later as she lifted the lamp and they walked out of Lily's bedroom.

"What does she mean dead?" Thane asked as they stepped over to Jack's bedroom door.

"She thinks if you leave for more than a day, you've died, like her mummy and papa. She was convinced you were dead and wouldn't return."

His steps came to a stop and he turned to Jemma with a sorrowful look on his face. "I'm so sorry, Jem. I didn't realize it would upset the kids to have me leave like that. I promise I won't ever disappear without saying a proper goodbye. I'll even try not to be gone that long again. I fully intended to return before Thanksgiving, but there were unexpected delays and then the mine collapsed."

"I understand, Thane. Just please try to be more considerate of the children in the future." *And me*, she wanted to add. She'd been every bit as distraught as Jack and Lily to find him gone. Now that he was home, she didn't quite know how to act around him.

Together, they tucked in Jack and wished him sweet dreams before returning to the kitchen.

Thane asked for a piece of pie and Jemma cut a generous slice, putting it on a plate with a dollop of whipped cream.

"Would you like me to make a fresh pot of coffee?" she asked as she set the plate in front of him at the table.

"No. What I'd really like is a cup of your tea and if you tell anyone I requested it, I'll deny it to my dying day."

"Tea it is, then." Jemma smiled as she slid the teakettle onto a hot part of the stove and prepared two cups of tea. A short while later, she set a steaming cup in front of Thane, noticing he'd devoured his pie. "Would you like another slice?"

"Yes, please. It's very good, Jemma. I appreciate the fact I married a good cook."

She glanced at him to see if his words were sincere and determined they were before she cut him another slice. She set the plate back in front of him and started to return to her seat, but Thane grabbed her hand and pulled her down onto his lap.

Wrapping an arm around her waist, he smirked at her.

"Ben said you read the note I sent."

Entranced by the light in his eyes, she held still. "Yes."

Thane waited for her to elaborate but when she remained close-mouthed he took a bite of pie and studied her a moment.

"What did you decide?"

"About which particular topic?" Jemma attempted to sound cool and aloof, but it proved challenging when she wanted so badly to sink into Thane's strength and never leave the safety of his arms.

"Sharing."

"I made you not one but two pies. I hoped that with your gluttonous tendencies toward sweets, you would satisfy yourself and leave a piece or two for the children." Jemma kept her face impassive but her tone carried a hint of mirth.

Thane raised an eyebrow at her and cut off another bite of pie. Holding it to her mouth, he waited for her to take the bite. When she did, he watched her tongue come out and lick a crumb off her lip. He fought the urge to do the same.

"I'm more than happy to share, my lady. In fact, there are untold wonders I can hardly wait to share with you, if you're of a mind to let me."

Jemma stared at him when he held another bite of pie to her lips. She chewed thoughtfully while he wolfed down the remaining bites on his plate. The tea grew cold as their gazes locked and held, exchanging promises and dreams.

Slowly rising to her feet, she took his hand and pulled upward, motioning for him to stand. She meshed their fingers together and tugged him to the door of their bedroom. As she pushed it open, Thane noticed the bed lacked the barricade of pillows and blankets marching down the center that had resided there since the second day they were at the ranch.

"I do believe, Thane Jordan, I'm ready to share more than just your pie." Jemma's smile held an invitation that warmed Thane more than the fire or the hot meal he'd just eaten.

"Are you sure, Jem? Are you ready to release me from my promise?" He took her arms in his hands and studied her face.

She blushed but held his gaze as she nodded her head. "I'm sure, Thane. I formally and completely release you from an idiotic promise you should never have made in the first place. Although, in all honesty, I wouldn't have married you if you hadn't."

A chuckle rumbled in his chest and he started to pull her into his embrace, but she pushed against him, turning her face to the side.

"However, Lily is correct. You smell quite malodorous. If I didn't know better, I would be given to thoughts that you rolled in something dead, like your despicable mutts have taught Rigsly to do."

Thane chuckled again and took a step back from Jemma. He planned to take a bath regardless of whether she removed the barricade or not. Now that he knew she'd welcome his affections, he'd even take time to shave. He had all the time in the world to seduce his wife and he planned to make it a night she'd never forget.

He turned his thoughts back to her comment. "I'll have you know Salt and Pepper are two of the finest cowdogs you'll find in Eastern Oregon. A friend of mine breeds the dogs to be intelligent, agile, and good with cattle. He'd take it as the worst kind of insult to know you called those two mutts. Besides, Rigsly likes being here on the ranch where he can chase birds to his heart's content."

"I've noticed. He brought home some bedraggled looking bird just yesterday with the most beautiful feathers. Sam said it was a grouse."

"Yep, the males, like most species, have the beautiful coloring."

Jemma put her hands on her hips and stared at him. "I do believe you could turn into a peacock strutting about with little to no trouble."

"Maybe, but this is one peacock who truly would like a bath. It's too cold to take one at the barn and I'm not going to the bunkhouse, so you'll have to make do with me setting the tub in front of the fire."

Thane waited for her to argue about the impropriety of him doing such a thing, but she nodded her head in agreement. He noticed she'd already set several pans of water on top of the stove to heat. She must have planned for him to take a bath all along.

Fully anticipating a hot bath as well as the evening ahead, Thane hurried outside, brushed the snow off the tub, and set it by the fire to warm. He filled a bowl with warm water and took it into the bedroom where he whipped up a creamy lather, brushed it across his cheeks and chin, and shaved in front of the mirror above the dresser.

When he finished removing his beard, he decided he appeared much more presentable. After turning the wick of the lamp on the dresser so it burned soft and low, he took the bowl of suds back to the kitchen. He dumped it out then glanced at the tub where steaming water rose in feathery plumes.

"That looks like a little bit of heaven, Jem. Thank you." Thane walked to where she poured in one last kettle of water into the tub.

"If it's too hot, let me know and I can add some cooler water."

"I'm sure it's fine." Thane gave Jemma a long glance as she stood unmoving, staring at his face. As he leaned toward her, he smirked. "Want to help me shuck out of these clothes?"

"No, you... you..." Jemma spluttered, although the idea held considerable appeal.

"Insufferable beast? Incorrigible brute? Unendurable dolt?" Thane supplied, using terms she'd called him numerous times since they first met in September.

"Yes, to all the above." Jemma grinned as she took her coat from a peg by the door and slipped it on.

"Where are you going?" Thane stopped in the process of removing his boots as she wrapped a scarf around her neck.

"I should very much like to visit the horses. Ghost needs a treat for taking such good care of his master." Jemma wound a scarf around her neck and ears then yanked on her mittens.

"I don't want you out there in the cold, Jem. Stay in here. Stay with me."

"I shan't stay here while you strip down to..." Jemma's cheeks flushed bright red as she pictured Thane naked in the firelight. Shaking her head to clear her thoughts she jerked open the door, welcoming the cool air on her hot cheeks. "I'll only be gone a few minutes, I assure you." She sailed outside, quietly shutting the door behind her.

Thane grinned at her flustered state as he removed his clothes and sank into the tub of hot water. Thoroughly soaping himself, he used the washcloth Jemma left on the edge of the tub to scrub away what felt like a month's worth of grime, then spent a moment letting the heat from the water sooth his tired muscles.

He closed his eyes and let his thoughts drift to Jemma. She stole the breath right out of him when he walked in the door before supper. His wife was beautiful, charming, graceful, frustrating, exasperating — and all his.

Cool air circled through the room when Jemma returned. Excited and curious, he kept his eyes closed, waiting to see what she would do.

He could tell from the noise behind him she removed her outerwear and hung it by the door. Her quiet footsteps moved across the floor, accented by the rustling of her skirts. He opened one eye and saw her peering at him from near the kitchen table.

"I won't bite," he said in a deep, husky voice, turning his head and smirking at her.

"Oh, I thought you were asleep." Caught ogling him from afar, heat seared her cheeks.

"No, ma'am. I'm just enjoying the water and the fire, thinking of you." Thane started to rise from the tub but Jemma spun around. He stepped from the tub, grabbed a towel she left on the hearth, and dried.

In no hurry, he wrapped the damp towel around his waist and studied Jemma. Although her back was turned, he grinned as she peeped through her fingers over her shoulder.

"Why don't you come over here, my lady?" Thane held out a hand to her.

Awed by the sight of the firelight playing across his muscles, turning his skin to bronze, she swallowed hard. Hesitantly, she took a step forward and stopped.

Fear and anticipation warred within her.

Thane was her husband. The man she loved. The man she wanted to spend the rest of her forever loving.

She had nothing to fear.

Thane smirked, that familiar lifting of the corners of his lips that she adored, creating twin brackets around his alluring mouth. He crooked his finger, motioning her to approach him. "Come over here, Jemma."

She took a few more steps until she stood an arm's length away from him.

He shook his head as a fiery flame danced in his eyes. "That's not good enough, sweetheart. Come a little closer."

She took another step.

"Closer." Thane reeled her in with the look in his eye and the love in his heart.

Her next step brought her toe-to-toe with him, although she still wore her boots and he stood barefooted. She glanced up at him, lost to everything except her love for the rugged, teasing, astoundingly handsome man in front of her. "Is this close enough?"

"Nope. I need you closer." He wrapped his arms around her and pulled her so close nothing but her clothing separated them.

Lowering his head to hers, he teased and tasted of her lips, reveled in the sweet richness of them. Rapidly working her into a state of longing so intense, she moaned as she wrapped her arms around his neck, trying to get closer to him.

As they kissed, Thane maneuvered her backward until they stood inside their bedroom.

Absently pushing the door closed with his foot, he continued working a mesmerizing spell with his lips as they traveled from her ear along her neck and back to her mouth.

One by one, he removed the pins from her hair, carelessly letting them fall to the floor. In the amber glow from the lantern, he untwisted the long, silky rope of her hair and watched it fall around her shoulders and down her back.

After running his hands through it, he buried his face in the glorious tresses and inhaled the intoxicating scent.

"Jemma, do you have any idea how much I want you? How long I've wanted you?" Thane looked into her copper eyes, blazing from the inner fire he continued to stoke.

"Almost as long as I've wanted you," Jemma whispered, returning his gaze with a shy boldness that made heat pour through Thane with an almost painful force. "I love you so much, Thane. I think I've loved you from the first day you set foot in the cottage."

"I loved you from the moment you stood framed by sunlight in the cottage door, looking at me like I was something you needed to scrape off your boot." Thane ran his thumb across her cheek and along her lower lip. A lip he intended to kiss many, many more times before the night was through. "You were, and are, the most beautiful woman I've ever seen. I'm sorry I ran away, Jem. I just couldn't stay here any longer and not have you."

"If you'd opened the door that night, Thane, you wouldn't have needed to leave. I moved the pillows while you emptied the water from my bath." Jemma removed her cameo and set it on the dresser.

Thane groaned. "You mean I spent the last miserable weeks thinking you were gonna leave me for no reason?"

"Yes, you have. And you made me suffer in the process. I fully expect you to make up for it." The saucy look she gave him made him reach out and begin unfastening the buttons on the front of her dress. "Just so you understand what's going to happen, Jem, the only thing I'm not taking off you are my eyes."

"Then by all means, sir, make haste with those buttons." Jemma tipped her head and grinned while Thane smirked again.

"Yes, my lady."

Epilogue

"Morning, Jem. Merry Christmas."

Jemma stretched lazily in the haven of Thane's arms and rolled onto her back as she opened her eyes. While blinking away the last vestiges of sleep clouding her thoughts, she smiled into his beloved face.

She reached up a hand and ran it over his firm jaw, already rough with stubble although he shaved the previous morning. His hair stuck out around his head in messy spikes and the fiery light in his cool blue eyes made warmth spiral from her heart to her toes and back up to her head. Breathing deeply of his scent, absorbing his comforting presence, she snuggled closer against him.

"Good morning, Thane. A happy Christmas to you."

In the past two weeks, since they opened their hearts to each other and admitted their love, Thane spent every day falling more and more in love with the enchanting, teasing, tempting woman he currently held in his arms.

"Are you ready to do this?" He gazed into her copper eyes and knew they had only a few moments before Jack and Lily would pound on their door, anxious to discover what Saint Nicholas left in their stockings as well as rip into the packages beneath the tree.

Jemma released a sigh and wrapped her arms around his neck. She inched closer to him and kissed his chin, followed by a spot on his neck that made him groan and tighten his hold on her.

"I shall most likely sound like an ungrateful, uncaring wretched excuse of a person, but my preference would be to stay right here with you all day. Unfortunately..." she kissed her way down one side of his chest and up the other, igniting tendrils of fire every place her lips touched. "The children will be most excited to see what gifts await them and I need to begin preparations for dinner as soon as we finish breakfast. Before our day erupts into a busy whirl of activity, I want you to know how much I love you, Thane Jordan. I'm so grateful to be a part of your life and be loved by you."

"I love you, too, Jemma. So, so much." Thane nibbled her ear as he pulled her closer against him. "You're the only, and the very best, gift I could ever want."

"Oh, Thane, my love, when you aren't teasing me without mercy, you say the nicest things." Jemma kissed him again, trailing her fingers across his chest and down his sides.

As he nuzzled her neck, pounding on the door drew their attention. Jemma grabbed her dressing gown off the end of the bed and hastily pulled it on while Thane rolled off the other side of the bed and yanked on a clean pair of Levi's then slipped on a shirt.

He opened the bedroom door and grinned down at Jack and Lily who both stood wide-eyed, waiting for him and Jemma to join them.

"Merry Christmas to you both! It looks like Santa found the cabin even though you were worried he'd fly right by."

Jack had made it perfectly clear to Thane he no longer believed in Santa, but went along with the stories for Lily's benefit. As he stood gazing at the packages beneath the tree and bulging stockings hanging on the mantle,

Thane thought maybe the boy might still believe in a little Christmas magic.

Thane knew he certainly believed in the magic of the season as he gazed at his pink-cheeked wife. Or maybe it was the wonder of being in love.

Either way, he was a very happy man as he gazed around their cozy cabin, trimmed with fragrant pine boughs, satiny red ribbons, and a beautiful Christmas tree they'd spent one day riding all the way out to the tree line to chop down together and bring home.

As he swung Lily into his arms, the little girl giggled excitedly. Thane carried her over to the fireplace and handed her a stocking filled with nuts, an orange, a handful of wrapped chocolates, and a whistle she promptly blew with sharp, shrill bursts until Jemma distracted her with a piece of candy.

A smile stretched across Jack's face as he emptied his stocking. He stuffed a chocolate in his mouth then unwrapped a pocketknife. Reverently holding it in his hands, he glanced at his uncle.

"I think Santa knew a boy like you could use a good knife. I know you'll take good care of it, just like I showed you." Thane squeezed the boy's shoulder with a gentle hand and felt his heart soften at the look on his nephew's face. He recalled the day Henry gave him the knife. It was a Christmas morning when Thane was Jack's age.

His brother's words of "keep it sharp and dry, and it should last you a lifetime," echoed in his ears.

"If you'd rather have a new knife, you can pick one out next time we're in town, but I thought you might like to have this one, since your dad gave it to me when I was your age."

Jack nodded and threw his arms around Thane's waist, giving him a tight hug. "Thank you so much, Uncle Thane."

"You're welcome, son." Thane bent and kissed the top of the boy's head, swallowing down the emotion in his throat. "I think we should open the rest of these presents."

Jemma had been nearly as bad as the children when Tully brought a huge crate out to the ranch in the back of his wagon a few days earlier. She noticed it shipped from a store in New York, but her many questions to Thane went unanswered.

He'd simply told her, 'It's Christmas, the season of secrets and surprises."

After the children were in bed the previous night, Thane brought in brightly wrapped packages and tucked them under the tree. When Jemma tried to peek, he playfully smacked her bottom and assured her good little girls minded their own business if they wanted to get any presents.

Now, they both sat on the sofa, watching as Jack and Lily gleefully opened their gifts.

"When did you order the toys for them, Thane?" Jemma leaned against his side, smiling as Lily showed her a beautiful baby doll. Thane not only purchased the doll, but a little bed for the doll to sleep in. Jack carefully removed a train set he'd admired in New York from a box. Thane scooted down on the floor to help him set up the track.

"The day we stopped in New York at that store where you bought the cookbooks, I saw the kids admiring some of the toys. I went back and purchased a few things then asked the owner to ship them just before Christmas."

Surprised he had thought that far ahead, Jemma stared at her husband, amazed by his thoughtfulness for two children he barely knew at the time he bought the gifts.

Lost in her thoughts, she startled when Thane handed her a large package wrapped in plain brown paper. "I think you'll like this one."

"What is it, Thane?" Jemma felt the package, convinced it held a picture frame.

"Open it and see." He grinned at her and put a hand on her knee. The warmth from his fingers made heat flow through her extremities, so she forced herself to focus on opening the package. Jack and Lily stood beside her, waiting to see her gift.

When the paper fell away, Jemma gasped as she gazed at a painting of her beloved cottage. She had no idea where or how Thane found it, but she loved it.

"This is wonderful, Thane." Her voice broke and tears clouded her vision as she looked from the painting to her husband. "Thank you."

"You're welcome, sweetheart." Thane kissed her cheek then took the painting and hung it on a hook he'd already installed above the mantle of the fireplace. "Now you can visit the cottage any time you like, at least in your memories."

"It's a perfect gift. Wherever did you acquire it?" Jemma rose from the sofa so she could study the painting.

Thane wrapped an arm around her waist as she stepped beside him and kissed her temple. "When you agreed to marry me, I asked Weston about having it painted. I knew you'd miss your home and I appreciated the sacrifice you were willing to make to marry a stranger you didn't much like and move to a remote ranch in America. He commissioned the artist and sent the painting to Tully when it was finished. I couldn't have you finding it before Christmas, could I?"

"I love it, Thane, and you."

"I love you, too, Jem. More than anything."

"I'm so glad." Jemma lifted her face for a kiss, but Lily shoved against her legs.

"Are you going to get all smoochy again?"

Thane laughed and picked up the little girl, placing noisy kisses on her cheeks, making her giggle. "You better get used to us being smoochy, Lily. I love your aunt very much and can't keep from ravishing her with kisses."

Jemma's heated glance made Thane wish the children hadn't gotten up quite so early that morning.

In need of a distraction, he pointed to the painting. "I think it will look wonderful above our new fireplace."

His wife gave him a befuddled glance. "What new fireplace?"

"The one in the new house we're going to build in the spring as soon as the snow thaws. I plan to build you a proper house with a big, sunny kitchen, a parlor for you and Maggie to sit in and drink tea, and an office for me. You just tell me how many bedrooms you want and we'll have one of my friends in town draw up the plans."

"I don't care how many bedrooms, but can it please, please have a bathroom?"

"You can have three, if you want. I know you hate the outhouse." Thane smirked at her as joy filled her face.

Jemma squealed and wrapped her arms around both him and Lily. "This is marvelous, Thane! I can hardly wait!"

"Spring will be here before you know it and I for one will be glad to have a little more room and privacy." He winked at his wife then tweaked Lily's nose. "Weston sent a letter addressed to us both. I thought we could read it together." He plucked an envelope from the branches of the tree and handed it to Jemma.

"Let's sit down on the sofa." Jemma took a seat while Thane sat next to her and settled Lily on his lap. The little girl clutched her new baby doll in her arms while she sucked on a peppermint stick. Jack sat on the floor beside Jemma and looked at her with an expectant gaze.

She used her fingernail to break the seal on the envelope and removed a thick piece of parchment with another envelope. Quickly scanning Weston's letter, she gasped in surprise.

"Oh, Thane. There's a letter from Henry!" Jemma set aside Weston's missive and picked up the envelope with Thane's name on the front, written in Henry's hand. "Here, you read it."

Taking the envelope from her, Thane tore it open and removed a sheet of paper. Holding it above Lily's head, he began reading aloud…

My beloved brother, Thane,

If you are reading this then the unthinkable has happened and I have departed this life long before I would choose to leave.

Undoubtedly, you will find the terms of my will to be unacceptable, crazy, and obscure. There is a method to the madness, little brother. Although I haven't laid eyes on you in more than a dozen years and, as I write this, have just recently discovered you reside in the wilds of Oregon, I know you are a good man. It's who you were raised to be. A good, honest, caring man.

I was able to discover you have no need for the money I plan to leave you upon my death. I congratulate you on your successful enterprises. I always knew you could take care of yourself, and quite well, I might add.

The reason I have left Jemma without a penny isn't out of cruelty or because I don't value what she sacrificed for my family. On the contrary, I am forever in her debt. She dedicated her life to my children, to giving them a mother's love even before we lost my dear, sweet Jane. She is witty, intelligent, charming, beautiful, stubborn, and infuriatingly independent. My fondest wish, one I had hoped to somehow bring about while I lived, was to introduce Jemma (one of the very finest women I've known) to the finest man she could meet, my own brother.

Had I left her with means of support, she would have no reason to wed. If I'd not made it clear to Weston he would need to insist you travel to England to settle my estate, you'd remain a lonely, crusty ol' bachelor on that sagebrush-covered ranch of yours.

I certainly hope as you read this, you have made Jemma your wife. I imagine with the two of you holding such strong opinions on nearly every topic, it makes for some interesting moments. How I wish I could witness the sparring that no doubt takes place. You both possess a passionate zest for life as well as tender hearts.

Cherish each moment you have together, because the days flee so fast.

Please raise Jack and Lily as your own. Tell them how much their mother and I loved them and will miss them. Please love them as though they belong to you, because they now do.

Above all, love each other and know you are held in the deepest regard with the truest affection.

With all my love,

Henry

Jemma opened her arms to Jack while tears rolled down her cheeks. The boy climbed onto her lap and sniffled, brushing away his tears. Thane clenched his jaw and cleared his throat, staring into the fire until he could control his emotions.

"It seems Henry got his wish," Thane said, lifting his gaze to the solid beams of the ceiling, scrambling to regain his composure.

"I'm glad he left me without a penny and at your mercy," Jemma whispered, gazing at her husband, grateful for Henry's plotting.

"Me, too, sweetheart. I've never known a finer Christmas than this one spent with all of you." Thane moved his arm so she could lean against his side.

The rest of the Christmas gifts sat forgotten as they quietly lingered in the tender moment, content to be together, wrapped in the gift of love.

When Weston summoned him to England, Thane never dreamed he'd return home a man rich beyond his ability to fathom. It wasn't the money he inherited, but the children and beautiful woman who gave him immeasurable wealth.

"Is Henry my papa?" Lily asked, breaking the silence.

"Yes, poppet. The letter is from your papa." Jemma dabbed at her tears and gave Lily a watery smile.

The child stared at her. "Is he coming back?"

"No, honey. Your papa isn't coming back, but he'll always be with you. You carry a little piece of him right here." Thane tapped Lily's chest with his index finger.

"Does Jack got Papa in him, too?" Lily stared at her brother's chest.

"He certainly does." Thane smiled at the boy who looked so like Henry.

"And you're my papa now?"

Thane looked at Jack before he answered. The boy nodded his head. "Yes, honey. I'm your daddy now and Jemma is your mama. We'll do our very best to take good care of you and your brother."

"May we call you Mama and Dad?" Jack asked, looking from Jemma to Thane. "Do you think Mummy and Papa would mind?"

"Oh, lovey, I think they'd be quite pleased." Jemma kissed Jack's forehead and gave him a hug.

"We'd be proud to have you call us Mama and Dad." Thane spoke the words around the lump in his throat.

He bent over and placed a kiss on Jemma's cheek, watching the light of the fire reflected in the coppery depths of her eyes. "It seems Henry knew what he was doing all along."

"He most certainly did." Jemma offered Thane a sassy smile. "Even if he sentenced me to a life of outhouses, cowpies, and howling coyotes."

Thane chuckled and kissed her again. "Don't forget sagebrush, snakes, and dirt, my lady. Or the man who loves you more than anything else in this world."

Jemma's heart shone from her eyes as she fastened her gaze to Thane's. "No. I'd never forget him. Not for a single moment."

Crumpets

Prior to writing this story, I'd never tasted a crumpet. Since they aren't readily available to purchase in my little corner of the world, I decided to make a batch. After searching for an authentic recipe, I reached out to a wonderful friend in England and she shared one that was easy enough even I could follow the directions.

The key component of crumpets, from my limited understanding, is to have plenty of holes in the surface to hold the melted butter. Crumpets were quite popular for teatime in the 1800s and many British families continue to enjoy them today, particularly for breakfast. You can top them with jam, eat them plain – but most definitely serve them with a spot of tea.

Crumpets

2 cups flour
1 package instant yeast
1 tsp. granulated sugar
1 1/2 cups warm milk
2/3-1 cup warm water
1/2 tsp. baking soda
1 tsp. salt
oil for cooking

Mix flour and yeast in a bowl. Set aside.

Warm milk until it no longer feels cool to the touch, but isn't hot. (Think baby bottle temperature.) Add sugar and stir until dissolved then stir into flour mixture with a wooden spoon.

Continue stirring 3-4 minutes until batter is smooth. Cover and set aside for at least 20 minutes, up to an hour. It should rise up in the bowl and have holes on the surface.

Fill a measuring cup almost full of warm water. Stir in the baking soda and salt until dissolved, then slowly add to the batter. You want the consistency to be like heavy cream. If it still seems too thick, add a little more water. Cover and set aside for 20 minutes.

Heat a griddle or cast-iron skillet over medium heat. Pour a little oil in the bottom. You will need rings for cooking the crumpets. I used pancake rings, but you could use a round cookie cutter, a jar ring, etc. Make sure your rings are well-greased inside. (You can also purchase special crumpet rings if you are so inclined.)

Spoon the batter into the rings until they are about three-fourths full. Cook a couple of minutes until bubbles appear and the surface looks set. Remove rings, turn over and cook another two to three minutes. Serve immediately with plenty of butter or toast before eating.

Author's Note

Research is something I enjoy entirely more than I probably should. With a love of history, it truly is fun for me to dig into old facts, photographs, and details to find little golden nuggets to include in my stories.

Crumpets and Cowpies is the first book in the Baker City Brides series. Originally, I intended this to be a stand-alone Christmas book. After I met the characters and began writing the story, I quickly changed my mind and made it into the first book in a brand-new series.

I began research for this story by selecting a town. I wanted somewhere with train service. Somewhere in Oregon. Somewhere close to the mountains with miles of sagebrush and a lack of close neighbors.

Baker City, Oregon, is located in the Northeastern section of the state. While I-84 runs right past the town today, back in the 1800s, it was a stop along the Oregon Trail.

In the 1860s, a gold rush brought travelers to the area. Another surge in the gold industry began in the early 1890s, which is when this series takes place.

Known as the "Denver of the Blue Mountains," Baker City offered many of the conveniences found in larger cities during its boom era.

Today, many old buildings remain and visitors in town can stay at the Geiser Grand Hotel, a National Historic Landmark. The hotel opened in 1889 as the Hotel Warshauer. The Geiser family later purchased and renamed the hotel, but if you're ever in Baker City, be sure to pay it a visit.

Once I decided on Baker City as the setting, I began filling in the rest of the details.

It is difficult to put into words how much I enjoyed researching the ship for the story. The *Teutonic* really did exist. As part of the White Star Line, it was built for speed while offering grandeur. The *Teutonic* and its sister ship, *Majestic,* were known as the first modern liners because they offered three classes of accommodations: first class, cabin class, and third class. Take a look at the photos available of the ship and you might see how it could be called a forerunner to the *Titanic*.

Liverpool made a logical choice for the beginning of the story, based on Thane and Henry's history with cotton. For more than a hundred years, most of the world's raw cotton traveled through Liverpool, on its way to textile mills. The finished goods were sent back to Liverpool to be shipped all over the world.

The fashions of the day make my heart pitter-patter with joy. I could spend hours and hours studying the beautiful gowns, hats, and hairstyles of this era. My favorite outfit associated with the story is Jemma's "Surprise Dress." There really was such a thing and the entire idea behind it fascinates me so.

For those of you curious why any sane person would include the word "cowpies" in a book title, I did it for three reasons. First, I liked the way it sounded in the title. "Crumpets and Cowpies" just rolls right off the tongue. Second, it illustrates the vast differences in the backgrounds of the two main characters. Third, it's just fun!

If you enjoyed ***Crumpets and Cowpies***, I hope you'll come along for the next Baker City Brides adventure in ***Thimbles and Thistles***!

Thank you for reading ***Crumpets and Cowpies***.
Now that you've finished Thane and Jemma's story,
won't you please consider writing a review?
I would truly appreciate it.
Reviews are the best way readers discover great new
books.

Never miss out on a new book release!
Sign up for my newsletter today!

http://tinyurl.com/shannanewsletter

It's fast, easy, and only comes out when new books
are released or extremely exciting news happens.

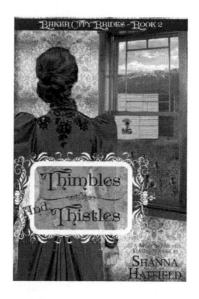

Thimbles and Thistles *(Baker City Brides, Book 2)* — Maggie Dalton has no need for a man in her life. Widowed more than ten years, she's built a successful business and managed quite well on her own in the bustling town of Baker City, Oregon. Aggravated by her inability to block thoughts of the handsome lumber mill owner from her mind, she renews her determination to resist his attempts at friendship.

Full of Scottish charm and mischief, Ian MacGregor could claim any single woman in Baker City as his own, except the enchanting dress shop owner who continues to ignore him. Not one to give up on what he wants, Ian vows to win Maggie's heart or leave the town he's come to love.

Turn the page for a preview...

by SHANNA HATFIELD

Chapter One

Eastern Oregon, 1891

The pungent scent of sagebrush filled her nose and burned her eyes as Maggie Dalton struggled out of the bush that bore the brunt of her fall.

Dark brown eyes sparked with anger as she glared at the flighty horse that panicked at the sight of a rabbit and unceremoniously dumped her to the ground.

Before she could grab the reins, the horse snorted and took off at a dead run in the direction of town.

"You stupid, stupid beast!" Maggie stamped her boot-clad foot in frustration. "Next time Tully threatens to shoot you, I'll load the gun myself!"

Pride thoroughly stung, she brushed at the dirt coating the back of her riding skirt and glanced around. Somewhere between town and her destination, she decided she might as well walk to Thane and Jemma Jordan's ranch rather than return home in defeat.

If Sheriff Tully Barrett, owner of the lunkheaded gelding, caught her walking back to Baker City, he'd never let her live down the fact Loco bucked her off.

Despite his warnings and dire threats to stay away from the crazy horse, she'd snuck over to his barn that morning. She waited in the shadows until Tully left for work, saddled the horse, and rode him around the corral a few times. Just to prove the arrogant man wrong, she decided to take the lunatic equine for a ride out to the Jordan Ranch.

Generally regarded as a good hand with a horse, this one unseated her with so little effort, she agreed with Tully — Loco lived up to his name.

A cloud of dust billowed in his wake as the animal raced toward Baker City. No doubt, he'd return to the barn on the outskirts of town and be waiting there when Tully arrived home.

Maggie had known Tully since she was sixteen. In the twelve years since they'd met, the sheriff had been a good friend, especially when her beloved Daniel died.

Memories of her husband made her heart ache, so she shook off her melancholy and walked down the dirt road.

At least the day was pleasant. Although it started out cool, by mid-morning, the April sunshine spread welcome warmth across her back and shoulders as she walked. She'd gone a few hundred yards when the jingling sound of a harness announced the approach of a wagon.

Embarrassed by her situation, Maggie straightened her shoulders and waited for the wagon to pass, prepared to put on a good face.

The day rapidly deteriorated from bad to worse. The sight of the wagon driver forced her to release a long-suffering sigh while her smile melted into a frown.

Maggie tended to like everyone, but something about the owner of the lumberyard in town made her cross and jumpy. Unable to pinpoint what it was about the man that invoked her ire, she went to great lengths to avoid speaking to him.

With his wagon bearing down on her, she couldn't exactly run into the brush and hide. Fisting her hands at her hips, she struck a defiant pose and braced herself for whatever he might say to irritate her.

In the bright spring morning light, Maggie took note of the sunlight glinting off his hatless blond head. He wore his hair longer than she deemed proper and more often than not, it appeared tousled and wild, rather like the man himself.

Broad shoulders looked like they could carry the weight of the world. Forearms corded with muscles drew her attention as he stopped the wagon beside her.

Brilliant blue eyes twinkled with humor as he leaned forward and rested an arm on his upraised knee. "Weel, lass, what on earth are ye doin' traipsin' around on foot out here in the middle of nowhere on such a bonny day?"

The man's Scottish brogue unsettled her, in particular when the letter "R" rolled off his tongue with a delightful burr. The hair on the back of her neck stood at attention, as if eagerly awaiting the sound of his voice, while her knees wobbled. His effect on her only infuriated her further.

"Not that it is any of your concern, Mr. MacGregor, but I'm on my way to the Jordan Ranch." Determined to ignore the way the corners of his sculpted mouth lifted into a smile, she narrowed her gaze and offered him a cool glare.

She wondered what his face would look like without the abominable growth of scruff he sported. The fuzz on his face was just long enough to give him a rakish appearance and set all the twitterpated girls in town into a frenzy of whispers whenever he passed by.

Fortunately, Maggie was long past the age of having her head turned by the considerable charms of a man like Ian McGregor.

"On foot? Come, now, Mistress Dalton. Yer known for yer fine thimble work as well as yer talent with horses, but the crazy beast gallopin' past me wouldna have been yer mount, would he? Surely ye didn't let the sheriff's horse get the best of ye?"

Indignant, Maggie huffed and started walking again. "As I already stated, Mr. MacGregor, it isn't any of your concern."

"Och, lass, but it is." Ian MacGregor set the brake on the wagon, wrapped the reins around the handle, and jumped down. A puff of dust covered his boots when he landed, but he failed to notice as he hastened to catch Maggie before she marched too far away from him.

"Please, Mistress Dalton, allow me the pleasure of yer company to Thane and Jemma's place. 'Tis their ranch where I'm headed at this verra moment. It would be a great honor to have ye accompany me." Ian hurried in front of her then executed a gallant bow before winking at Maggie.

Another sigh escaped her throat. Begrudgingly, she nodded her head. "Fine. I'll ride with you, Mr. MacGregor, but please cease in your flirtatious behavior."

Ian slapped a hand to his chest and grinned, dropping most of his accent. "I would never behave in such a manner, lass. It's not flirtatious if you mean it."

Maggie rolled her eyes and ignored the hand Ian held out to help her climb onto the high seat of his big lumber wagon.

"While you're still speaking to me, would it be too much to ask, again, for you to call me Ian?"

She glanced over her shoulder at him as she pulled herself up onto the seat and scooted over to the far side. "As I've told you before, Mr. MacGregor, calling you Ian is entirely too personal. To do so would hint at a familiarity that simply is not acceptable."

"But you call the sheriff Tully and refer to Thane and Jemma by their Christian names." Ian's gaze was both imploring and teasing when he settled it on her. "What must I do to earn such a privilege?"

Flustered by the intensity of his sapphire eyes, Maggie cleared her throat and smoothed a hand down her skirt. "Nothing, Mr. MacGregor. Despite your petitions otherwise, I shan't call you by your first name. However, should you persist in nagging at me like a fussy old woman, I will most certainly bestow a few other names upon you."

Ian chuckled as he climbed onto the seat. The deep sound of his laughter echoed in her ears.

Aware of his stare as he took a seat beside her, Maggie forced herself to keep her attention fixed on the horses standing patiently in their traces. The urge to squirm nearly overtook her as she waited for Ian to pick up the reins and continue on his way.

"And why, by all that is right and good, didn't you say you were injured in the first place?" Ian reached out and grasped Maggie's upper arm with gentle fingers. "How did this happen?"

Upset by the horse for running off and the arrival of the lumberyard owner, she hadn't paid any mind to the sting of a cut. Ian's big, warm hand on her arm made her skittish. She tried to shake it off, but he held fast.

"Calm yerself, lass." Ian's brogue thickened as he peeled back the torn, blood-soaked fabric of her blouse and examined the wound on her arm. Although deep, the cut didn't appear serious and had already stopped bleeding. He pulled a clean handkerchief from his pocket and pressed it against the spot.

When he lifted his gaze to Maggie's, her face hovered just inches away from his. Time ground to an abrupt halt as he studied the dark, almost black ring around the iris of her eye while the circle closest to the pupil glowed in a beguiling shade of topaz.

Slowly inhaling a deep breath, the scent of sage mingled with her sweet perfume, further ensnaring his already entangled senses.

His eyes trailed over her face, taking in her determined chin, stubborn jaw, and creamy cheeks along with rosy lips just begging for a kiss. Bereft of the ability to stop himself, he leaned toward her.

She gasped and jerked away from him.

"Mr. MacGregor!" Maggie shoved him back and yanked the handkerchief from his hand, slapping it over her cut. "I'll thank you to mind your manners and stay on your own side of the seat."

A lazy smile he'd used to charm plenty of women did nothing but cause the pretty female glaring daggers at him to stiffen. "If you want to split hairs, Maggie, the entire seat is mine, but I'm more than happy to share with you." Ian picked up the reins, released the brake, and clucked to the horses. The well-trained team immediately leaned into the harness and started down the road, easily pulling their heavy load. "As a matter of fact, I'm happy to share anything at all. You only need to request it."

Maggie scooted over until she pressed against the far side of the high seat, leaving plenty of space between the two of them. "I do believe, Mr. MacGregor, you're nothing more than a scandalous tease."

"Och, lass, you wound me with your words." Ian switched the reins to one hand so he could slap the other to his chest in feigned insult.

He smiled as he reached over and plucked a bit of sagebrush from Maggie's hair. She ran her hand up to her thick braid and dislodged another piece, tossing it aside with a huff.

Errant curls escaped their confines and danced along her temples and neck. Ian fought down the urge to reach out and finger one.

"I always did like the smell of sagebrush." He leaned closer to her and sniffed, inhaling her enticing scent. "Yep, I certainly do love that perfume."

Red suffused her cheeks and she glared at him, refusing to dignify his comment with a reply.

Ian chuckled again and turned his attention to the team, although he watched Maggie Dalton out of the corner of his eye. He'd noticed the striking widow the very day he arrived in Baker City two years ago.

When he discovered a lumberyard for sale in the growing town, he purchased it sight unseen. The previous owner greatly embellished both the state of the yard and his detailed attention to running the business.

Everything seemed in shambles when Ian arrived, but he was too excited at owning a business with such potential for the man's deception to deter him.

The first evening he was in Baker City, he strolled down the main street, glancing in shop windows and studying the town he'd rashly made his new home. He'd stopped to admire a saddle in a window display and turned as a lovely, dark-haired woman breezed out of a dress shop across the street. He watched as she locked the door then looked his direction.

She offered him an interested glance before ducking her head and hurrying down the boardwalk. He'd remained unmoving, watching silken curls bounce around the fashionable hat perched at a saucy angle on her head. In that moment, Ian's heart flew out of his chest and followed her down the street.

It didn't take long for him to learn she was a widow of several years, a talented dressmaker, a skilled horsewoman, and a close friend of the sheriff's.

He'd often seen her in the company of Tully Barrett, and Thane Jordan, for that matter. Then Thane rushed off to England to settle his deceased brother's estate and returned home with a niece and nephew, along with a beautiful bride.

Not for the first time, Ian wondered what Maggie's feelings were for the sheriff. She was right in that it wasn't any of his concern, except for the fact she'd captivated him for two long years.

Instead of returning his interest, she often looked at him as if he was barnyard muck clinging to her boots.

Ian wasn't one to give up easily, though. Only a fool would give up on winning the attentions of one such as Maggie Dalton.

Or maybe it was a fool who'd pursue her.

Amused at himself, Ian laughed and glanced at Maggie, silenced by her frosty glare. Mindful not to stoke her simmering anger, he turned the conversation to the safe topic of their mutual friends.

"Have you been out to see Thane and Jemma's house recently?" Ian kept his gaze on the horses, hoping Maggie would at least respond to his question. He held back a grin when her husky voice tantalized his ears.

"Not for a few weeks. I've been busy completing orders for Easter. Now that the holiday is behind us, I thought I'd take advantage of this sunny day and ride out to see for myself how things are progressing."

Maggie always closed her shop on Sundays and Mondays. However, during the hectic Easter and Christmas seasons, she worked every minute she could spare to complete the deluge of orders she received for new dresses. Occasionally, she made men's shirts and suits, but the majority of her business came from the women in and around Baker City.

"I saw you burning the midnight oil many an evening leading up to Easter. Do you not have anyone who can help you?" Ian couldn't count the times he'd started to knock on her door, just to make sure she was fine, but always stopped himself. Intuitively, he sensed his concern would only make Maggie more distant and cool toward him.

"A few women in town help when they can, but most of the time I can handle everything on my own."

"I'm sure you can, lass." Ian raised a hand over his head and waved as they approached the Jordan's yard. An impressive two-story house took shape set back from the rest of the outbuildings.

Ian and Maggie both grinned as Jemma Jordan ran out of the small cabin where the family currently lived. She caught three-year-old Lily before the child ran too close to the hulking wagon.

"Good morning!" Jemma called with a happy smile as Ian stopped the wagon and tipped his head toward her. "How wonderful to see you both. Can you pop in for a spot of tea?"

"I thank you for the invitation, Jemma, but I'll take the lumber over to the house and help unload it straight-away. I know Thane is impatient to finish your new home." Ian jumped down and jogged around the wagon. Not waiting for Maggie to climb down, he reached up and spanned her waist with his hands, lifting her to the ground.

Angry sparks shot from her eyes and she stepped away from him as soon as her feet touched the ground. She couldn't have acted any more insulted or offended if he'd called her a hurtful name or offered some tart remark.

Ian swallowed a chuckle and followed her back around to where Jemma held a squirming Lily.

"Ian!" The little girl shouted his name and held her arms out to him.

"How's my wee bonny lass today?" Ian asked as he took her then tickled her sides, making Lily giggle and wiggle.

"I'm wonderful. How are you?" The impish child stared at him with coppery eyes and tilted her head. Unruly curls sprang out every direction.

"Much better now that I'm holding you." Ian kissed the little girl's cheek. She gave him a tight hug then turned to hold her arms out to Maggie.

Maggie took her and gave her a tender hug. "Hello, sweetheart."

"Hi, Aunt Maggie! Did you come to spend the day with me?"

"Part of the day." Maggie looked over Lily's head at Jemma. "If you'll have me."

"Of course we'd love your company." Jemma smiled at Maggie and looped their arms together as they started toward the cabin. She turned back to Ian. "You'll stay for lunch, won't you, Ian?"

"I wouldn't miss it." Ian swung back onto the wagon and guided the team toward the house while the women watched him drive away.

Lily wiggled down and skipped into the cabin, leaving Jemma and Maggie alone.

Jemma raised an eyebrow at her friend. "While I get a bandage for that cut on your arm, you can tell me how you came to be in the company of that 'detestable Scotsman,' as you so often refer to Mr. MacGregor."

Maggie glared at Jemma but found the woman's enthusiastic smile too hard to resist. A grin lifted the corners of her mouth upward. "I'm blaming it on Tully."

Jemma laughed. "That explains everything."

Pendleton Petticoats Series

Set in the western town of Pendleton, Oregon, at the turn of the 20th century, each book in this series bears the name of the heroine, all brave yet very different.

Dacey *(American Mail Order Brides Book 12)* — A conniving mother, a reluctant groom and a desperate bride make for a lively adventure full of sweet romance in this prelude to the beginning of the series.

Aundy *(Book 1)* — Aundy Thorsen, a stubborn mail-order bride, finds the courage to carry on when she's widowed before ever truly becoming a wife, but opening her heart to love again may be more than she can bear.

Caterina *(Book 2)* — Running from a man intent on marrying her, Caterina Campanelli starts a new life in Pendleton, completely unprepared for the passionate feelings stirred in her by the town's incredibly handsome deputy sheriff.

__*Ilsa*__ *(Book 3)* — Desperate to escape her wicked aunt and an unthinkable future, Ilsa Thorsen finds herself on her sister's ranch in Pendleton. Not only are the dust and smells more than she can bear, but Tony Campanelli seems bent on making her his special project.

__*Marnie*__ *(Book 4)* — Beyond all hope for a happy future, Marnie Jones struggles to deal with her roiling emotions when U.S. Marshal Lars Thorsen rides into town, tearing down the walls she's erected around her heart.

__*Lacy*__ (Book 5) — Bound by tradition and responsibilities, Lacy has to choose between the ties that bind her to the past and the unexpected love that will carry her into the future.

__**Bertie**__ *(Book 6)* — Haunted by the trauma of her past, Bertie Hawkins must open her heart to love if she has any hope for the future.

Hardman Holidays Series
set in the historic Eastern Oregon town of Hardman

The Christmas Bargain *(Hardman Holidays, Book 1)* — As owner and manager of the Hardman bank, Luke Granger is a man of responsibility and integrity in the small 1890s Eastern Oregon town. Calling in a long overdue loan, Luke finds himself reluctantly accepting a bride in lieu of payment from the shiftless farmer who barters his daughter to settle his debt.

The Christmas Token *(Hardman Holidays, Book 2)* — Desperate to escape an unwelcome suitor, Ginny Granger flees to her brother's home in the Eastern Oregon community where she spent her childhood years. Not expecting to encounter the boy she once loved, her exile is proving to be anything but restful.

The Christmas Calamity *(Hardman Holidays Book 3)* — Arlan Guthry relishes his orderly life as a banker's assistant in Hardman, Oregon. His uncluttered world spins off kilter when the beautiful and enigmatic prestidigitator Alexandra Janowski arrives in town, spinning magic and trouble in her wake as the holiday season approaches.

The Christmas Vow *(Hardman Holidays Book 4)* — Columbia River Pilot Adam Guthry reluctantly returns to his hometown of Hardman, Oregon, to pay his last respects after the sudden death of his life-long best friend. Emotions he can't contain bubble to the surface the moment he sees the girl who shattered his heart eleven years ago.

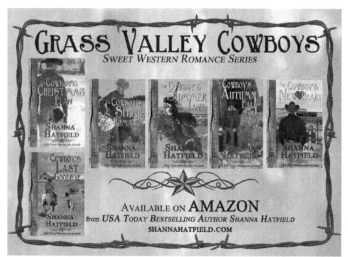

Grass Valley Cowboys Series

Meet the Thompson family of the Triple T Ranch in Grass Valley, Oregon.

Three handsome brothers, their rowdy friends, and the women who fall for them are at the heart of this contemporary western romance series.

Book 1 – *The Cowboy's Christmas Plan*
Book 2 – *The Cowboy's Spring Romance*
Book 3 – *The Cowboy's Summer Love*
Book 4 – *The Cowboy's Autumn Fall*
Book 5 – *The Cowboy's New Heart*
Book 6 - *The Cowboy's Last Goodbye*

Love at the 20-Yard Line — Brody Jackson lives and breathes football. As a wide receiver for a popular arena team, he's determined to make it back to the NFL. Cocky and confident, he doesn't have the time or energy to be bothered with a serious relationship. Brody is blindsided by the girl who captures his attention during the first game of the season and breaks through his defenses. He has to decide if he'll let go of his dreams or fumble his chance to win Haven's heart.

Haven Haggarty is woefully inept when it comes to men and matters of the heart. Successful in her job as an image consultant with an up-and-coming company, Haven wishes she could enjoy as much triumph in her dating efforts. Falling for the local arena team's handsome wide receiver, Haven realizes she needs to tackle her fears or miss the opportunity to experience once-in-a-lifetime love.

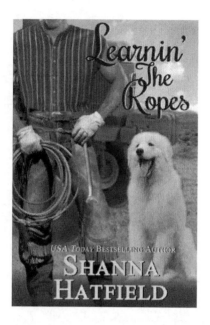

Learnin' The Ropes — Out of work mechanic Ty Lewis is out of options. Homeless and desperate to find work he accepts a job in the tiny community of Riley, Oregon. Leaving everything he's ever known behind in Portland, he resolves himself to this new adventure with an elusive boss, Lex Ryan, someone he has yet to speak with or meet.

Lexi Ryan, known to her ranch hands and neighbors as Lex Jr., leaves a successful corporate career to keep the Rockin' R Ranch running smoothly after the untimely death of her father. It doesn't take long to discover her father did a lot of crazy things during the last few months before he died, like hiding half a million dollars that Lexi can't find.

Ty and Lexi are both in for a few surprises as he arrives at the ranch and begins learnin' the ropes.

The Coffee Girl - Former barista Brenna Smith dreams of opening a bistro where she can bake her specialty pastries and serve delicious coffee. Envisioning a rich, aromatic life full of savory moments, she instead lives at home with her parents, making a long commute each day to work for a boss who doesn't know beans about his job. If it wasn't for the hunky guy she sees each morning at the coffee shop, her bland existence would be unbearable.

Charming, smart, and good-looking, Brock McCrae is a man comfortable in his own skin. Owner of a successful construction company, he decides to move to the small town where his business is located and immerse himself in the community. Brock doesn't count on his new client being the cute and quirky woman he knows only as the Coffee Girl from his daily stop for coffee.

The QR Code Killer —— Murder. Mayhem. Suspense. Romance.

Zeus is a crazed killer who uses QR Codes to taunt the cop hot on his trail.

Mad Dog Weber, a tough-as-nails member of the Seattle police force, is willing to do whatever it takes to bring Zeus down. Despite her best intentions, Maddie (Mad Dog) falls in love with her dad's hired hand, putting them both in danger.

Erik Moore is running from his past and trying to avoid the future when he finds himself falling in love with his employer's daughter. Unknowingly, he puts himself right in the path of the QR Code Killer as he struggles to keep Maddie safe.

From the waterfront of Seattle to the rolling hills of wheat and vineyards of the Walla Walla Valley, suspense and romance fly around every twist and turn.

The Christmas Cowboy - (Rodeo Romance, Book 1) Flying from city to city in her job as a busy corporate trainer for a successful direct sales company, Kenzie Beckett doesn't have time for a man. And most certainly not for the handsome cowboy she keeps running into at the airport. Burned twice, she doesn't trust anyone wearing boots and Wranglers, especially someone as charming and handsome as Tate Morgan.

Among the top saddle bronc riders in the rodeo circuit, easy-going Tate Morgan can handle the toughest horse out there, but dealing with the beautiful Kenzie Beckett is a completely different story. As the holiday season approaches, this Christmas Cowboy is going to need to pull out all the stops to win her heart.

Wrestlin' Christmas *(Rodeo Romance, Book 2)* — Sidelined with a major injury, steer wrestler Cort McGraw struggles to come to terms with the end of his career. Shanghaied by his sister and best friend, he finds himself on a run-down ranch with a worrisome, albeit gorgeous widow, and her silent, solemn son.

Five minutes after Cort McGraw lands on her doorstep, K.C. Peters fights to keep a promise she made to herself to stay away from single, eligible men. When her neighbor said he knew just the person to help work her ranch for the winter, she never expected the handsome, brawny former rodeo star to fill the position.

Ready to send him packing, her little boy has other plans...

The Women of Tenacity Series

Welcome to Tenacity!

Tenacious, sassy women tangle with the wild, rugged men who love them in this contemporary romance series.

The paperback version includes a short story introduction, *A Prelude*, followed by the three full-length novels set in the fictional town of Tenacity, Oregon.

Book 1 – *Heart of Clay*

Book 2 – *Country Boy vs. City Girl*

Book 3 – *Not His Type*

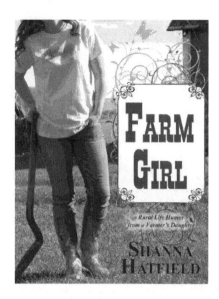

Farm Girl — What happens when a farmer who's been wishing for a boy ends up with a girlie-girl?

Come along on the humorous and sometimes agonizing adventures from a childhood spent on a farm in the Eastern Oregon desert where one family raised hay, wheat, cattle… and a farm girl.

Fifty Dates with Captain Cavedweller — Waking up one day to discover they'd gone from perpetual honeymooners to a boring, predictable couple, author Shanna Hatfield and her beloved husband, Captain Cavedweller, set out on a year-long adventure to add a little zing to their relationship.

This G-rated journey through fifty of their dates provides an insightful, humorous look at the effort they made to infuse their marriage with laughter, love, and gratitude while reconnecting on a new, heart-felt level.

ABOUT THE AUTHOR

SHANNA HATFIELD spent ten years as a newspaper journalist before moving into the field of marketing and public relations. Self-publishing the romantic stories she dreams up in her head is a perfect outlet for her lifelong love of writing, reading, and creativity. She and her husband, lovingly referred to as Captain Cavedweller, reside in the Pacific Northwest.

Shanna loves to hear from readers.
Connect with her online:

Blog: shannahatfield.com
Facebook: Shanna Hatfield
Pinterest: Shanna Hatfield
Email: shanna@shannahatfield.com

If you'd like to know more about the characters in any of her books, visit the Book Characters page on her website or check out her Book Boards on Pinterest.

32992892R10198

Made in the USA
Middletown, DE
26 June 2016